ORBS IV
EXODUS

USA TODAY BESTSELLING AUTHOR
NICHOLAS SANSBURY SMITH
AND ANTHONY MELCHIORRI

GREAT WAVE INK
PUBLISHING

Books by Nicholas Sansbury Smith

The Hell Divers Series
(Offered by Blackstone Publishing)

Hell Divers
Hell Divers II: Ghosts
Hell Divers III: Deliverance
Hell Divers IV: Wolves

The Extinction Cycle Series
(Offered by Orbit Books)

Extinction Horizon
Extinction Edge
Extinction Age
Extinction Evolution
Extinction End
Extinction Aftermath
Extinction Lost (A Team Ghost short story)
Extinction War

The Trackers Series

Trackers
Trackers 2: The Hunted
Trackers 3: The Storm
Trackers 4: The Damned

The Orbs Series

Solar Storms (An Orbs Prequel)
White Sands (An Orbs Prequel)
Red Sands (An Orbs Prequel)
Orbs
Orbs II: Stranded
Orbs III: Redemption
Orbs IV: Exodus

NicholasSansburySmith.com

Books by Anthony J. Melchiorri

The Tide Series

The Tide (Book 1)
Breakwater (Book 2)
Salvage (Book 3)
Deadrise (Book 4)
Iron Wind (Book 5)
Dead Ashore (Book 6)
Ghost Fleet (Book 7)

The Eternal Frontier Series

Eternal Frontier (Book 1)
Edge of War (Book 2)
Shattered Dawn (Book 3)
Rebel World (Book 4)

Black Market DNA

Enhancement (Book 1)
Malignant (Book 2)
Variant (Book 3)
Fatal Injection

Older Titles

The God Organ
The Human Forged
Darkness Evolved

For those in the armed services,
and everyone else who puts their life on the line for freedom.

Thanks for keeping us safe.

If aliens ever visit us, I think the outcome would be much as when Christopher Columbus first landed in America, which didn't turn out very well for the Native Americans.

—Stephen Hawking

Introduction to the ORBS Series

In the winter of 2013 I was in Mexico for a short vacation. At the time, I was in my late twenties, and employed by Iowa Homeland Security and Emergency Management as a disaster mitigation officer. By day I worked with communities and FEMA specializing in hazard mitigation planning, safe room construction, hardening of utilities, and applying for Federal grants. At night I spent my time at the local coffee shop writing science fiction.

The second evening of my trip to Mexico, I took off for a late-night run along the beach, where I came across a section decorated with glowing blue balls or what looked like floating orbs.

The experience was surreal, the type where you're not sure for a fleeting moment what you're looking at. My first thought was I had stumbled upon some sort of alien invasion, but then I saw a connected grassy section with chairs, and I realized I had discovered an isolated wedding venue.

An idea seeded in my mind when I saw those orbs, and I rushed back to my hotel to write that idea down on paper. Like many of my stories, this one quickly blossomed into a novel, and four months later Orbs hit the digital Amazon shelves.

The book quickly went viral, selling over thirty thousand copies within a few months. I signed with my literary agent David Fugate, had inquiries from multiple publishers, and ended up selling the first three Orbs books to Simon451, a new imprint of Simon and Schuster.

The paperbacks hit bookstores around the country in 2015, bringing in thousands of new readers. After a second print run, the foreign translation rights sold, and in 2018 the book will release in German.

Nearly five years later, I have the English publishing rights back, and I'm thrilled to share with you the republished versions of Orbs, Orbs 2: Stranded, Orbs 3: Redemption, the accompanying prequel short stories, Solar Storms, White Sands, and Red Sands, and the never before published Orbs 4: Exodus.

Audio fans should also take note that the Orbs books have all been re-recorded by Blackstone Publishing. Award-winning narrator Bronson Pinchot takes the helm to deliver yet another fantastic listening experience.

Orbs holds a special place in my heart because it was my first series, and my first bestseller. It was the story I had always wanted to tell, and I'll be forever grateful to Amazon, Simon and Schuster, David Fugate, and—most importantly—all of the readers that enjoyed and shared the story with their friends and family.

This story isn't for everyone, though, and I want to give fair warning. If you're looking for a book with hard science fiction, this may not be the story for you. If you're a fan of good old fun science fiction, then I'd say give it a try. *Men's Journal* reviewed Orbs in 2014 and, in my opinion, said it best: "The Orbs series is akin to watching movies like Independence Day...In other words, it's bound to be a cult classic!"

I hope you enjoy the adventure! Thanks for trying my work.

Best wishes,
Nicholas Sansbury Smith

Prologue

I was wrong about the demise of the human species. Well. Not exactly wrong, per say. My predictive analysis yielded a ninety-five-point-seven percent chance of extinction for the humans. There was always a chance of survival, but it was statistically insignificant. This has caused me to question my analytical algorithms. While I blame this error on the limited sensors I have and the sparse data I can retrieve from the satellite Lolo, there is more than just numbers involved. The algorithms I've designed to measure the temperature, water loss, and climate change across the planet don't take into account that humans are an incredibly resilient species.

Two months, twenty-six days, fourteen hours, three minutes, and forty-two seconds have currently passed since Doctor Sophie Winston and her team left Earth for the New Tech Corporation (NTC) colony on Mars. They believed that, since Mars was a former home of the Organics, they wouldn't return there. My database holds the secret outline of NTC CEO Doctor Eric Hoffman's plan to build more than just a colony on Mars. His real goal was to establish a second Earth, using terraformers installed there in 2059.

I'm not sure what Doctor Winston and the crew aboard the NTC *Sunspot* will find when they land. I was never privy to what occurred on Mars after Hoffman supposedly landed. What I do know is that the survivors they left behind on Earth did not perish within two weeks, as I had initially estimated.

The humans I've discovered via my connection to Lolo and other networks throughout the world continue to surprise me. Shock might have described my reaction to their survival, but after meeting Doctor Winston, nothing seems to shock me anymore.

What has shocked me is the data I've collected on the Organics. Initially, every piece of data and every observation made since the invasion pointed to alien colonization of Earth. But this planet, it seems, is just one of many selected for the resources that keep the Organic army alive—water.

It seems Doctor Winston was right: once they finish removing every available molecule of H_2O, they will abandon the planet.

I have thousands of questions about these alien creatures. Even with my technological capabilities, I can still only guess at the answers to many of them. For example, is the Organics' original home planet Mars? If so, why would they take the water from Mars, leave, and then come back for Earth's water millions of years later? The simplest answer I can come up with is that they stripped Mars of water at a time when Earth had none.

Unless they're here for more than water.

The multi-dimensional entities seem just as interested in collecting and preserving other sentient species, when one considers the alien arks Doctor Winston described from her dreams. If these are indeed real, then perhaps there is more to this invasion than meets the eye.

And what about their minions? The Lolo feed I'm tapped into shows that most of their invasion force still remains here on Earth, hunting down the final human survivors and animals for their water content to feed their ground troops.

Their mile-long vessels continuing to drain the oceans by syphoning gigantic vortexes of water into the sky, and the alien worms blast water to the ships in orbit. I have seen their towers drilling for water like humans used to drill for oil, the bores cutting ever deeper into the Earth. And the poles atop the seven highest peaks on the planet that distribute the Surge from Mars—the poles Operation Redemption failed to destroy— still stand tall.

That mission was a long shot. I knew it from the beginning.

Since then my own mission has changed.

Journal entry 9450 noted my objective of documenting the fall of the planet after Doctor Winston's team left the Biosphere. But as the seconds, minutes, hours, days, weeks, and months have slowly passed, I keep finding more survivors, more bands of rebels that have survived unfathomable odds. I've watched, via Lolo, as these rebels have fought back against the Organics in the hope that maybe, just maybe, they could stop the destruction of the planet.

In Japan, they have had miraculous successes combating the aliens. A squad of Japanese soldiers actually took down one of the poles, interrupting the magnetic flow and killing millions of Organic foot soldiers.

But I'm afraid it was too little, too late, as Doctor Emanuel Rodriguez used to say. The aliens quickly rebuilt and restored their Surge network. The momentary lapse did not do much, if anything, to stem the removal of water from the planet.

I transfer to the video feed I saved from Lolo, showing the Redwood forests in California. In my research, I've learned that the thick, skyscraper-sized trees were once a natural marvel to the human race. They are now massive matchsticks, burning in forest fires and choking the region with dark smoke. The scene is just one of millions like it across the planet. The forests and the oceans are dying.

I call up the current data on climate. There are thousands of data points, but only several that I wish to document in this entry. First, the average temperature of one hundred and fifteen degrees Fahrenheit. Second, the ocean levels are at twenty-one percent of what they were pre-invasion. Third, the culmination of data from the remaining forests shows about twenty-six percent of trees are still alive. The oxygen content in the atmosphere is now at a dangerously low nineteen percent. Dangerous to humans, that is.

I tap back into another feed I collected several days ago. The thirty-mile-long alien platform anchored in the Pacific Ocean is a sight to behold. Hundreds of Organic ships are currently docked at the massive spaceport. The tear-shaped drones patrol the area, protecting the mile-long vessels used for water collection. There are other ships there, too, like the medium-sized fighters that were used by the Organics during Operation Redemption.

These alien fighters fascinate me. When I first saw them, I considered the possibility of hacking into them or working with a rebel group to commandeer them. Perhaps, then, we could use them to destroy the magnetic poles. But as the months passed and the planet continued to die, I realized once again that humanity will never survive here. The Organics have won. The humans will continue to fight, but they will fail, no matter how many brave people are left out there.

An algorithm I created to detect human transmissions alerts me to communication from a group that hasn't given up hope yet. The transmission is from a member of the submarine crew of the *Ghost of Atlantis*—the GOA— which is now located about four miles off the coast of Los Angeles, California.

"Alexia, this is Corporal Athena Rollins. Do you…"

The crackle of static makes her next words difficult to translate, but my programming gives me one hundred and fifteen possibilities. Too many.

"I did not catch your last, Corporal. Please repeat your transmission."

"We're still holed up and are running out of supplies. We won't last here much longer. Have you been able to locate any other ships?"

While I consider my response, I continue to filter through the new set of images coming in from Lolo. Again, I see the thirty-mile-long platform in the ocean and the ships docked there. But it is far too great a distance for Athena and her tattered crew to attempt traveling there.

"Not human ships, Corporal," I say. "But I am working on something else."

I don't want to give her hope. Especially now, when my plan seems uncertain. It doesn't seem fair to her or the other survivors. Instead, I simply say, "Stay alive as long as you can. Tomorrow I should have more intel, after Lolo makes her next orbit."

There is a pause. It is only three seconds, not long by human standards, but it tells me that Athena is nervous.

"Thank you, Alexia," she finally replies.

"I have a new location for your next transmission, at the following coordinates..."

I send the coordinates to Athena, and she confirms she will be there. After the line severs, I think of the journey she has to make to return to the submarine, where she and the other crewmembers are hiding like rats. It's not safe there, or anywhere. Each time she calls in, she has to move from the submarine to a separate location, due to the threat of detection. And never the same location twice.

Like the humans, I'm hiding. My mainframe is buried deep inside Cheyenne Mountain. I may not possess water for the aliens, but my hard drive would be far more valuable to the aliens than the resource they came here for. I know too much about the human survivors, their locations, and their weaknesses. Even if I tried to delete the data, I worry the Organics could recover it. It's not safe for me here, either.

For the past two months, twenty-six days, fourteen hours, ten minutes, and two seconds, I have been building a small army of robots to help defend the Biosphere. There were some within the Biosphere, and then I discovered others in a storeroom within the Cheyenne Mountain complex. Some of those were even in pieces. But now the cleaning bots, medical bots, and engineering drones are in fighting shape, ready for an Organic infiltration.

Eventually, the aliens will catch on to the game I'm playing. Until they do, my mission is to save as many humans as I can.

END ENTRY

— 1 —

"What did Alexia say our chances of getting off Earth alive were?" Dr. Emanuel Rodriguez asked. The AI had continuously given them abysmal odds since the Organic invasion of Earth.

"Four point three percent," Corporal Chad Bouma said with a knowing grin.

They sat in the CIC of the *Sunspot*, apparently alone in the vastness of space, with only the company of the humming instruments and display panels. The ship's artificial gravity meant they did not need harnesses to keep them seated—under normal circumstances. Over fifty million kilometers from Earth, they were almost to their destination—Mars. Bouma rotated his shoulder, massaging it lightly. Emanuel noticed he'd picked that habit up after the wounds he'd suffered during their disastrous escape from Earth had healed. Operation Redemption had been an abysmal failure. He wondered how Captain Noble and the other humans who'd been left behind had fared.

He guessed not well.

"So," Bouma said, filling in the silence, "does that mean we proved the AI wrong again?"

Emanuel chuckled uneasily. It felt freeing, lately, to enjoy a bit of humor when he could. "Not exactly. Just because the statistics say something is *likely* to happen doesn't mean that's what *will* happen."

"But it would be accurate to say we beat the odds, wouldn't it, Doc?"

"Yeah, that would be accurate."

We beat the odds.

Emanuel wondered how many times they would still have to beat the odds. On Mars, they hoped to find the NTC's colony, but there was no guarantee. Dr. Eric Hoffman had led the initial escape off Earth in the *Secundo Casu,* a spaceship equipped with a life-sustaining Biosphere just like the *Sunspot* housed, in hopes of establishing salvation for the endangered human race on Mars.

"Sonya, please tell me we've heard something from Mars," Emanuel said.

The AI took on her blue humanoid form on a display. "I am sorry, Dr. Rodriguez. The status of our communications with Mars remains unchanged."

"Damn," Bouma muttered. The Marine's expression drained, all good humor replaced by the same pallor he'd worn since finally getting out of his patient bed in the med ward. "Not that I don't enjoy the company on the ship, but it'd be nice to see some new faces. Just so long as…"

Bouma let the words trail off.

Emanuel knew what the Marine wanted to say. *Just so long as they aren't Organics.*

The whole flight, they had tried to steer conversations around the frightening possibility of encountering Organics on Mars instead of a human colony. The prospect of escaping Earth only to delay their deaths until they landed on the Red Planet was too much for anyone on the crew to bear. They hadn't been so foolish as to avoid planning for any engagements with their alien adversaries, but it still wasn't a favorite conversation topic.

"If we don't hear something from the NTC before we land, we'll find them," Emanuel said. He was eager to answer the question that hadn't been asked. Hope was a rare commodity after the destruction of Earth, and Emanuel wanted to prop up its value as best he could. The crew needed it; *he* needed it.

"Hoffman had a plan," Emanuel said. "The guy was smart. My guess is, we haven't heard anything from his colony because he isn't trying to attract attention."

"You're right," Bouma said, wincing as he stretched in his chair. "The Organics would be on him like flies on shit if he sent out some kind of beacon."

"Flies on shit," Emanuel agreed. He pictured the mandibles of the spiders and their eerie blue flesh. He could still hear their unnatural shrieks, the scrape of their claws on metal. Hell, he could practically smell their stench wafting through the air ducts of the ship. "I'm not a fan of bugs. Less flies there are, the better."

For a while they sat, watching the beeping displays. It would still be a few hours before Blake Ort and Lieutenant Mario Diego relieved them of their watch. Since escaping Earth's atmosphere, the four of them had decided to take shifts keeping watch. Sonya had insisted it wasn't necessary, that she could warn them at the first signal they received from a human—or an Organic. But Emanuel felt better having a human on watch. There was something reassuring about having a live fail-safe in case the computers went down—which was an all-too-real possibility. The Organics possessed electromagnetic pulse weapons capable of disrupting human electrical and computer systems. The *Sunspot* had been hardened against such weapons, but Emanuel didn't want to take any chances. The ship was also equipped with a massive RVAMP system, and they had a slew of handheld versions they could take with them once they disembarked. The weapons helped neutralize Organics by decimating their shields.

Emanuel was confident in the capability of the RVAMPs—after all, he'd led their construction since their departure from Earth. And he'd designed the very first one, all the way back in Colorado. The RVAMPs had worked time and time again against the Organics. They were efficient and reliable. Maybe too much so.

It had been the activation of an RVAMP back on Earth that had severely injured Dr. Sophie Winston, thanks to her being infected with Organic nanobots. He still remembered the way she'd convulsed when she turned it on to save the children. The agony on her face was emblazoned in his memory. Thinking of it still sent physical jabs of pain through his chest.

"You got that far away look, Doc," Bouma said, interrupting Emanuel's thoughts. "Kind of like you just saw a ghost."

Emanuel sighed, then shook himself from his despair. "In a way, I guess I did."

"Sophie?"

"Sophie."

Emanuel knew Bouma was no stranger to his love for Sophie. They'd had hours, days, to talk about everything under the sun and between the stars during the journey to Mars.

"We'll get her to the colony," Bouma said with new certainty. "They'll know what to do there. They'll save her."

Emanuel merely nodded. He prayed Bouma was right.

Sonya suddenly appeared before them. Emanuel nearly jumped from his seat. "I'm receiving an encrypted message from a human ship."

"What is it?" Emanuel asked, leaning forward in his seat.

The AI looked perplexed. "The message is scrambled. From what I detect, it originates from a human ship on the surface of Mars. There is a seventy-three percent probability that it comes from a biosphere ship that shares a build with the *Sunspot*."

Could it be the *Secundo Casu*?

Emanuel hoped so. It would make the monumental task of finding the NTC colony that much easier.

"But you aren't sure?" Bouma asked.

"I am afraid I cannot give a definitive answer."

Emanuel sighed. "Then give us what you do have."

"'Landing successful. Contacts spotted. System damage reported. Making…' Those are the only words I have been able to decipher with certainty. I would presume the crew of this ship encountered Organics."

Emanuel's momentary positivity blew away like the black ashes of the human civilization on Earth.

"Sure as hell sounds like it," Bouma said. "Are they still alive?"

"That's impossible to tell," Sonya said. "The defective message indicates damage to their communications array. Reciprocal contact with the ship will be impossible. However, this is the only concrete signal I have from any human ships or colonies as of this moment. Our current landing coordinates bring us within two thousand kilometers of this human vessel. Would you like to reroute to investigate this ship?"

"Yes..." Bouma looked at Emanuel. "It's your call, Doc."

Even if it wasn't the *Secundo Casu*, this might be the closest thing to a lead on the NTC colony they'd get. But, if this vessel had run into trouble with the Organics, there might not be anything but a crashed ship and a dead end. It didn't seem like a good idea to inspect a ship that had probably already succumbed to the Organics. Still, it might have intel on its computer systems containing the location of the NTC colony on Mars. That alone would be worth the risk, and Emanuel wouldn't be blindly leading the *Sunspot* around.

"Let's check it out," Emanuel said.

"Very good, Doctor Rodriguez. Landing coordinates have been altered. ETA is now one hour and thirty-three point four minutes." There was a slight pause from Sonya. "Also, I am happy to report we have finally reached visual range of Mars. I have the first images available. Would you care to view them?"

"Yes!" Emanuel and Bouma said simultaneously.

Emanuel wrapped his fingers around the edge of his armrest. A sheet of nervous sweat was already forming over his palms. Then a blurry, pixelated image fizzled onscreen. Sonya hadn't lied when she said they'd just reached visual range. The view cleared, and Emanuel leaned forward, his stomach churning. It wasn't the Red Planet that had his guts knotting up, but rather, the blue speck floating in space near Mars.

"Sonya, can you magnify the image here at all?" Emanuel asked, indicating the suspect spot.

"I can," Sonya said, "but doing so will not drastically improve the image quality."

"Shit. Is that what I think it is, Doc?" Bouma asked.

Emanuel nodded. That blue was the same iridescent blue given off by the spiders and Sentinels and all the goddamn Organic ships and drones they'd seen tearing Earth apart. He hesitated, preparing to say the words he'd been dreading the whole trip. "Sonya, sound the alarm. Call everyone to their battle stations."

***

Heat shimmers flickered across a brown and red horizon. In all directions, seashells bleached white by the sun were scattered like bones across the sand.

Corporal Athena Rollins brought her binoculars to her visor to glass the dying world for hostiles. The sensors in her heads-up display (HUD) scanned for lifeforms, but, like so many times before, the reading came back negative.

"All clear," she reported over the comms. She checked the life support system readout on her HUD, ensuring that the air filtration system and cooling unit were working properly before climbing out into the one-hundred-and-twenty-degree heat. Without her oxygen filtration unit, she wouldn't be able to breathe for long out here.

She pulled her pulse rifle from the clip on the back of her armor, then bent down to help Private Sean Walker out of the open hatch.

The pads inside the dull black armored suit she wore conformed to her body as she pulled on his hand. As soon as Walker was on his feet, he unslung his old-school MP5 submachine gun.

"I don't know why you bother with that thing," she said.

"Saved my ass more times than I can count, that's why."

She couldn't see his features behind his mirrored visor, but she had a feeling he was grinning. At just twenty-three years old, Walker was the youngest surviving member of her crew. He was also the cockiest, and, some would say, the funniest, although Athena would hesitate to agree.

"You're just lucky," she said.

Walker laughed his arrogant chuckle, and she turned back to the dry, arid terrain with her rifle shouldered. Somewhere to the west was the receding Pacific Ocean. She couldn't see the blue anymore, nor could she see the massive black ships sucking the water into the sky.

Walker closed the hatch, and they covered up the only exposed metal of the *Ghost of Atlantis* submarine by kicking sand over it. Once it was secure, they both started off down the slope.

At the bottom, Athena's boots crushed the shell of a dead crab. She shouldered her pulse rifle and did another scan for contacts.

Hard to believe this was once the ocean, she thought.

From this vantage, all she saw were more shells and skeletal remains of fish. The sight reminded her that time was running out for every surviving member of the twenty-one-person crew hiding in the belly of the GOA.

"Let's move," she said.

Walker dipped his helmet and followed her toward their target—a radio tower on the edge of Los Angeles that Alexia had told them to transmit from. Athena trusted the NTC AI from Cheyenne Mountain's Biosphere. The AI hadn't led her astray thus far, but there were horrifying creatures between here and the tower that the AI couldn't protect Athena and Walker from.

All they could do was try to evade the Organics.

Athena drew in a breath of filtered air and set off over the dry seabed. For the next twenty minutes, they walked through the desert. The pumps inside her advanced suit churned coolant through the miniscule vessels in the membrane covering her flesh, but it wasn't long before her body was covered in sweat.

She took a sip from the straw inside her helmet, but resisted the urge to swallow more than one sip. Conserving water was challenging, especially in the field, but she didn't have a choice. They were down to the GOA's reserve tanks now.

Batting the sweat from her eyes, she focused on the seemingly endless sand dunes in the distance. Getting lost was easy out here, and she watched the compass on her HUD to make sure she was still headed east.

Fifteen minutes passed before she spotted what had once been the shoreline. She knew it was the beach because of the white lawn chairs protruding out of the sand, some of them scattered about by the sand storms that assaulted the land. Off to their right, and about two hundred yards closer to the beach, was the hulking carcass of a dead whale.

Walker halted a few feet away, his helmet craning back the way they had come.

Athena heard the dull rumbling a second later.

Walker slowly pivoted to scan the skyline, but Athena didn't waste any time. "Run!" she shouted.

They took off running for the whale's carcass as the rumble grew in volume. A single teardrop-shaped Organic drone was coming in from the east, scanning the blasted wasteland for prey or potential buried water.

Between Walker and Athena, there was about two hundred pounds of water the Organics could suck from their bodies.

They had to reach that carcass, and fast.

The drone veered southwest, leaving a white trail of exhaust, but she could see it was already turning for another pass.

Athena saw the radio tower rising over a city block in the distance. *So close, yet so far away*, she thought. All they had to do was get their communication equipment up there, and they would be able to connect to Alexia to learn of her new plan. But the increasing rumble of the drone made that seem less and less likely.

The whale carcass looked like a tan tent held together by white poles.

Walker was first to reach it. He pulled back the dried skin and gestured for Athena to climb inside. She ducked under the flap and crouched beneath the white ribs holding the carcass together. Her boots squished on jellied chunks of decomposing flesh.

She scooted over to make way for Walker, and listened as the roar of the Organic ship grew closer. He pulled the flap back over the belly, the light dimming in their hiding place.

Slowing her breathing, she waited, doing her best to ignore her pounding heart. Walker raised the barrel of his rifle at the roof, and she did the same with her pulse rifle.

The alien ship shot by to the north, rustling the sand and candied flesh that made up the floor. Athena glanced down when she felt something brush her boot, and let out a muffled cry when she saw the snake.

Apparently they weren't the only ones using this dead beast for shelter. The snake raised its head at her, tongue

17

flickering in and out, before it moved over to Walker. He kept his gaze on the translucent ceiling.

"It's coming back," he whispered.

Athena listened as the drone changed course. Whatever engine the aliens used to power the craft hummed as it slowed to survey the beach.

It was definitely hunting.

She moved her finger to the outside of the trigger guard. If they were spotted, she might be able to take the drone down before it could capture them. But not before it called in reinforcements.

She glimpsed the alien aircraft coming in fast. From her location, she had a perfect view of the curved bow of the small ship. The surface pulsated from an interior light, like a beacon blinking over and over.

There was no creature piloting the craft. There wasn't even a cockpit. The ship was controlled by some artificial intelligence that had one purpose—capture them and suck the water from their bodies.

Athena swallowed as it slowed and then began to descend, whipping up tornadoes of sand and grit. It passed by their location, and the gusting wind tore at the whale hide. The decayed flesh rippled until a piece tore away in front of Athena, providing an even more expansive window. The crunching and tearing sounds of splitting fragile flesh made Athena wince.

Walker raised his rifle, but she grabbed his wrist.

"No, get down," she said quietly.

He hesitated, then did as ordered and moved down onto his belly next to her. The snake buried into the flesh too, vanishing. But there was no time to dig-in like the creature had. All they could do was flatten their bodies against the flesh and pray the drone didn't spot them.

Another strip of hide tore away, letting in a blanket of sunlight. The drone turned for another pass, the raucous sound so loud now her ears were aching. She held her breath and closed her eyes, thinking of her sister and parents, who had died months ago.

She would be seeing them again soon.

Two agonizing minutes passed as the drone scanned the area. Athena counted the seconds to keep her mind active, but counting just made her nerves clench more.

Walker remained silent next to her, but she knew he was itching to get up and blast the ship. She felt him move, and opened her eyes to see he had lifted his helmet, sand falling away from the chin.

That's when she realized the ship was pulling away.

It hovered for a moment longer, then blasted away with a supersonic scream that stripped the hide right off the bones, leaving them completely exposed. In the silence, her ears began to ring. For a moment the two sailors remained motionless. When the snake poked back out, she figured it was clear.

"Come on," she said to Walker.

They bolted for the distant beach, their armor shedding flecks of dried gray whale flesh as they moved. Finally they navigated the debris field of chairs and tables, and made their way toward a road halfway covered by sand.

A ball of sage rolled across the ground, tumbling over the top of a vehicle partially buried in a sand drift. In every direction the sight was the same—the old world buried by the new one.

She had scavenged in Los Angeles several times before, and knew these streets well. She also knew there were plenty of Organics. Spiders lurked in the shadows, hibernating and conserving energy until food presented itself.

Walker was also well-acquainted with the area. He ran ahead down the street, keeping low, his footsteps leaving tracks in the dirt.

Looking up, Athena scanned the windows for hostiles, but the thousands of glass panes were all blacked out by the same brown coating of grime that covered the buildings and roads.

She flashed a hand signal to Walker, who had waited at the end of the block for her to catch up, and, taking point, rounded the corner. Her boots smashed over something sticky. She didn't need to look down to know it was the gooey lining of an orb. The human or animal or whatever had been inside was nothing more than a pile of mush now, the water sucked away by the spiders that comprised the alien army. Nevertheless, hunching down, she examined the remains by plucking out a stringy piece with her gloved fingers.

The tissue was still decomposing, which told her it was fresh. Probably just a few days old. She doubted it was a human. They hadn't found a survivor for weeks now. But it was possible, and she decided to keep an eye out for anyone that might be hiding out here.

Walker brought his submachine gun up to search for contacts as she moved down the next street. They kept to the right side of the road, away from the abandoned vehicles, using the shadows of a high-rise building for cover.

They passed a park on the next street, where the spindly branches of trees whipped in the gusting wind, the limbs cracking back and forth. Visible just beyond the dead brown space was their target. The red tip of the radio tower rose above the city blocks ahead like a beacon. They were almost there.

Athena moved at a crouch, trying to keep her footfalls as quiet as possible. She stopped for another scan halfway down the block, then continued on.

The next intersection was clogged with more cars, some of the doors still open from when the occupants had fled on invasion day. They hadn't made it very far. A minefield of decaying orbs littered the filthy road.

These were older.

Still, she listened and looked for tracks, just to make sure it wasn't a trap. Sometimes the aliens would hide in areas that looked abandoned. But if they were out there, she saw and heard no sign of them. No tracks, no scratching sounds, no screeches. Nothing but the wind. She motioned Walker to take point.

They fanned out through the park, taking a short cut in the open. The sun beat down on their dull armored suits, and Athena continued to work on her breathing. Sweat bled down her face, but at least she wasn't wearing make up to get into her eyes. She didn't miss things like that anyways. What she did miss was food. She was sick of the canned food and MREs they had scavenged.

God, I would kill for some fresh sashimi and a dirty martini.

She licked her cracked lips at the thought of sitting down to her favorite meal with her sister, then blinked away the painful memories and focused on the mission.

Walker reached the end of the park and was about to step out into the street when he froze like a statue on the sidewalk.

Athena heard what had spooked him.

Scratch, scrape, scratch, scrape.

Her eyes darted to the tower rising above the buildings

framing the next road. A single spider emerged on the rooftop of an old hotel.

Then dozens.

The spiders perched on the edge of the rooftop, looking down on the street and the park. One of them raised its claws into the air, letting out a deafening screech. The others all skittered down the side of the building, their claws scoring ruts in the brick, causing a sound like nails on a chalkboard to reverberate between the buildings.

For a second she just stood there, staring at the beasts. Walker snapped her from the trance by running toward her and grabbing her arm. He yanked her back through the park, away from the tower, as spiders filled the street.

— 2 —

"Remember, David, it's like a video game," Jeff said. "You just aim and squeeze."

"Cool!" David said, eagerness shining in his eyes.

Despite everything they had gone through, Jeff's little brother still had an air of innocence. Maybe he was just trying to be optimistic or lighten the mood. Maybe it was just having something to do after all the boredom. Either way, what they were about to do was deadly serious.

They sat together in one of the three turret stations on the *Sunspot*. While Emanuel had retrofitted the ship with RVAMP capabilities, they'd also used salvaged fighters and weapons, with Sonya's help, to create these turrets. After weeks of running drills, they were finally about to experience combat.

This time it wasn't a drill. This time it was real.

An electric buzz of anticipation coursed through Jeff's nerves as he tightened his fingers around the controls. "All we have to do is wait for Emanuel to tell us when," Jeff said, "then we fire. Not before. Got it, bud?"

David nodded.

Dad, if you're up there, we could really use your help, Jeff thought. It seemed so long ago since he had left them in White Sands. Jeff hoped their dad would be proud. He had kept his promise and protected David, and soon they'd be somewhere safe. They just had to make it through this.

"Gunners ready?" Emanuel asked over the ship's comms.

"Turret 1 reporting ready," Jeff said, doing his best imitation of a battle-hardened soldier. He wanted to sound like an adult and not just some kid.

"Turret 2 reporting ready," Diego said next. He would be at his station with Ort, the electrical-engineer-turned-soldier Captain Noble had sent up with them in the *Sunspot*.

"Turret 3 reporting ready," Bouma said. Dr. Holly Brown would be sitting next to him to serve as his co-gunner, just like David was Jeff's. She was such a nice lady. She'd looked after Jeff, David, and the other kids, Owen and Jamie, like she was their mother. But even though she was the crew's resident psychologist, they needed every hand they could get now.

Sonya shimmered on the display in front of Jeff and David. "I have not detected any sign that the Organics have spotted us. We are still clear for our approach."

Jeff had gone up against too many Organics on Earth to believe they'd make it to Mars without a scratch.

"Reports indicate that there is an Organic capital ship orbiting Mars, similar to those that launched the initial invasion on Earth. Then there are at least half a dozen larger vessels that may be warships. This gives a ninety-nine point six percent probability that there are other smaller fighter-type vessels and drones in the space around Mars that are not yet detectable at this range."

"I'll take that point four percent," Emanuel said.

"I'm ready to wipe the sky with those blue-faces," Diego said.

Jeff drank in Diego's confidence. He had only known the man for the few months they'd been aboard the ship, but Diego displayed a lot of the attributes Jeff admired in Bouma. Diego seemed fearless. If he was ever scared of the Organics, he didn't show it. Maybe someday Jeff would be like that, too. The truth was, he was still scared every time he saw those spidery blue maws, even when they appeared in his dreams.

"We're approaching Mars," Sonya's monotone voice reported over the ship's comms. "Still no sign that the Organics have detected our arrival."

Good, Jeff thought. Although he found that hard to believe. How could the advanced aliens not have seen their ship yet?

His fingers itched to pull the trigger, but it would be better for all of them if they didn't have to fire a single shot. He and David hadn't survived as long as they had because they were trigger-happy. It was because they had been cautious and stealthy.

"You don't even need a telescope to see Mars now," Emanuel said.

"Ho-ly shit," Bouma remarked.

"Maybe I'm wrong, but I thought Mars was the Red Planet," Diego said. "That doesn't look completely red to me."

Jeff and David leaned forward in their harnesses. Three months of sitting cooped up in this metal bucket and they were finally seeing their destination on the screens. But it looked way different from the planet he remembered in his school books. There were swirls of light blue and white—clouds, maybe? Underneath it all, he saw specks of brown, and even some green dots.

"They've been terraforming it," Emanuel said. Then he went on, puzzlement clear in his voice, "I didn't think human technology was capable of such rapid progress."

"Hoffman and his colony move fast?" Diego asked hopefully.

"What do they mean?" David asked, wide-eyed.

"They're wondering if the Organics did it," Jeff said.

"But why?"

Jeff shrugged. He had no good answer for that. The adults probably didn't either.

And he didn't have long to think about it.

The bark of alarms pierced Jeff's ears, and red lights flashed all around. He straightened in his seat, his heart thudding faster than a racecar.

"Incoming contacts!" Sonya called between the whirring alarms.

Blue and black shapes raced across the space between Mars and the *Sunspot*. The sight of the Organic drones made Jeff's stomach drop, the memory surfacing of the time he had been captured by one of them.

"Open fire!" Emanuel said.

Jeff held down on the trigger, gritting his teeth. Pearly laces of orange roped away into the blackness of space. Light cut and flashed through the black. The drones spun around their incoming fire, drawing ever closer to the *Sunspot*.

"Come on, come on!" Jeff said.

"I can't hit 'em!" David yelled.

One of the drones exploded in a distant, brilliant blast of orange and red. Bouma whooped over the comms. More drones came at them like a swarm of angry bees. Jeff focused his fire. Beads of sweat trickled over his forehead. He wanted so desperately to hit them, to see them all disappear into a cloud of debris. His fingers trembled as he yanked on the trigger as hard as he could.

Finally one of the drones he'd been aiming at burst

into pieces, followed by another, and then yet another.

"We're doing it!" David exclaimed. "We're stopping them!"

"RVAMP ready," Sonya said.

The ship shook as the massive weapon unloaded its electromagnetic pulse. The red battle lights in their turret station shimmered off for a second. Jeff was surrounded by blackness. His lungs drew in tight, and he wondered if it would be like this forever. Then the lights bloomed back to life. The drones were now floating, lifeless, in the darkness around them, nothing more than flotsam adrift on the ocean.

"Like shooting fish in a barrel now," Diego said.

Drones fell apart like popped balloons under the resurgent fire from the *Sunspot*.

"This is way easier than I thought!" David exclaimed. He was bouncing in his seat as he fired at the drifting drones.

Soon there was nothing but slagged chunks of metal left. The *Sunspot* carried on majestically through the field of debris. A shiver crept down Jeff's spine. Something didn't feel right to him, even as they passed the shards of broken, lifeless drones. This had been too easy. If he had learned anything, it was that the Organics were anything but easy to defeat. As if in answer, Sonya's voice came over the comms.

"More contacts incoming," she said.

A flood of blue appeared across Jeff's viewscreen.

"Oh crap," David said.

The drones had merely been testing their defenses, probing for weak spots. Now that they had unleashed the RVAMP, the Organics knew what they were up against. They were coming in hard for Round Two, and they had added fighter jet-like crafts to their armada. The ships each had two wings, a dorsal fin, and what looked to be laser cannons.

"Shit," Bouma said. "How long before the RVAMP is recharged?"

"Thirty seconds," Emanuel said.

"Thirty seconds never seemed so long," Diego replied.

They unleashed a flurry of rounds as the drones and new alien fighters approached. Fire lanced away from the turrets, but for every ship they turned to shrapnel, it seemed there were two more speeding toward the *Sunspot*.

Jeff dared to steal a glance at his younger brother. David had a white-knuckled grip on his turret controls. His lips were pressed together thinly, and his face was paler than Jeff had ever seen it.

The *Sunspot* rocked as the first hits from the drones pounded across their hull. David let out a slight whimper, but never took his eyes off the targeting reticules.

Adrenaline pushed itself through Jeff's blood vessels. His fingers trembled, and his vision narrowed as the rest of the ship faded away. He felt the quakes shaking through his seat, and saw only the viewscreen before him. The bark of an alarm sounded as if it was coming through a pool. He thought he heard Emanuel's voice. Or maybe it was Diego's, it was impossible to tell. All that mattered was that they lived for just a few more seconds so they could launch another RVAMP attack.

Then they would be safe. It would all be okay once again. It had to be. They hadn't made it this far only so he could break his promise to his dad by letting David get swallowed up by space.

No way.

"Come on, you bastards," Jeff said.

The *Sunspot* shook like it had been hit by a storm of rockets. Alarms screeched, and the lights flickered. The ship shook violently. The sounds of breaking and bending metal screamed from every direction. Jeff grabbed his brother's hand and squeezed as hard as he could. He wanted desperately to let David know he was here for him until the end, no matter how soon that came.

Drones continued to pepper them with gunfire. Through a porthole, Mars grew larger, the tug of its gravity well now pulling on the wounded *Sunspot*. Now Jeff could see the mountains and canyons stretching along the craggy landscape. David's mouth was open. Jeff thought he was screaming in terror, but the din from the dying ship masked his screams.

A flash of heat swallowed Jeff. Blinding light came next. The ground rose to meet them.

I'm sorry, Dad, Jeff thought. Then, *I'm sorry, David.*

***

Captain Rick Noble stirred awake to an overwhelming feeling of despair and solitude. Orbs sparkled across his vision, filling the darkness like ephemeral blue stars. If he squinted, he could trick himself into believing he wasn't inside a ship, but rather floating alone, deep in space.

Hell, maybe he was deep in space. Truth was, he wasn't sure where the hell they were. All he knew was that his wife, daughters, crew, and everyone else was likely dead, and he was in a living nightmare.

All around him, hundreds of prisoners were trapped inside orbs attached to the bulkheads of a massive vessel. The other prisoners weren't human. Most weren't even from Earth. They were alien creatures from other planets—alien races the Organics had captured and brought here, like him, in some twisted Noah's Ark of sentient beings from across the galaxy.

He wasn't sure why the multi-dimensional entities housed them here. Maybe they were just trying to preserve species from the worlds they had destroyed. If that were true, then Noble was just a goddamn science specimen, nothing more than a cryo sample, or whatever the science folks would call it.

The multi-dimensionals were going to great lengths to keep him alive, that was for sure. He looked down at the tube inserted into his gut. On the day of his capture, the fluid suspending him in the orb had drained away. This tube had then snaked up from the hard floor of the orb and cut into his belly. Every time he tried to rip it out, an electrical current paralyzed his body. Whatever nutrients were being pumped into him through the tube were keeping him alive, despite his efforts to end the terror.

With no way to track the days, he may have been stuck here for hours or months. However long it had been, it felt like an eternity. He'd spent the first chunk of that time praying that maybe they would let him out of here, or that he would find a way to escape.

But he'd soon found there was no escaping the orb.

He reached out with his right index finger, its tip swollen and bloody from touching the glowing lining of his blue prison hundreds of times. Even the hard floor zapped him if he tried to pound it or claw his way out.

His fingernails were gone from doing just that.

And no matter how many times he tried to kill himself by touching the orb walls, the electrical jolt was never strong enough to do anything but cause extreme pain.

He pounded the lining with his palm, earning himself a

strong current that ripped first through his hand and arm, and then his entire body. He jerked on the ground for several seconds, losing all control of his body. When it was finally over, he was lying in a puddle of his own piss.

"Let me out of here!" he screamed. "PLEASE!"

Captain Noble had always considered himself to have a high pain tolerance, but it was hard to be physically strong when your mind was weak.

Interminable captivity in the dark, cold space gave him too much time to think. He thought of his wife and daughters and then the crew of the *Ghost of Atlantis,* and how he had failed them all.

Not just them… he had failed the entire human race with the failure of Operation Redemption.

Those thoughts haunted him, torturing him almost as much as—maybe more than—the electric currents teeming through the Orb.

Noble screamed again, and this time several otherworldly voices responded. One, a croak from the creature in the orb above his, reverberated through the hollow chamber.

The noise came from the oval mouth of the creature staring down at him with a Cyclops eye where a nose should have been. Perched on two webbed feet, the alien Noble had nicknamed Ribbit was a cross between a bird and a frog, with thin stick legs, a wide torso, and slimy green skin.

Noble had attempted communication multiple times, but the alien simply croaked with no discernible intention.

"Stop that!" Noble barked back.

Ribbit seemed to understand and went back to curling up on the bottom of its orb. Noble sat up and wrapped his arms around his chest.

His eyes flitted to the orb below his. It housed the oddest-looking alien he could see in the chamber—a cross between a plant and a tree and an octopus with a bulb head. Centered on its curved head were three compound eyes. Below that, orange lips covered its mouth. Jagged teeth lined a maw that Noble had only seen once.

While the face was a thing of horror, the rest of the creature wasn't all that scary. Four branches that served as arms were connected to a slimy pink torso, each of them covered in what looked like bark. Below that, where there should have been a butt and legs, were dozens of wormy appendages that looked like roots. The alien used them to move around. He wasn't sure what the heck the arms were used for, though, as they rarely moved.

Currently, it was hanging upside down from the top of its orb, using those root-like appendages to keep it fixed in place. That's what he was calling the alien now.

"Hey, Roots," Noble said.

The alien craned its oversized head to get a look at Noble. He wasn't sure how Roots could move around the wall of the orb without being zapped.

Noble turned away and checked the orb on his left. Normally he tried to avoid looking to that one and the one on the right. Both prisoners had perished over the past months, and while he didn't know what had killed the reptilian creature in the orb to his left, he knew all too well what had killed pilot Kirt Mantis.

He reluctantly snuck a glance at the orb where the only other human on the ship had once been held captive. Kirt was nothing but a blob of jellied flesh now.

Noble had watched helplessly as the pilot wasted away inside his prison. Something had happened to his feeding tube after the liquid drained from his orb. It had been a long, slow, agonizing death. One Noble had had a front row seat to. He was glad Kirt was finally gone, even though his screams still haunted Noble's dreams.

He took in a breath of the sultry air and relaxed. As time passed, the thought of suicide weighed heavier on his mind. But with no way to end the terror, he would revert to thinking of his crew. They were still back on Earth. Deep down, he held on to the hope that he would somehow make it back to them.

Fantasies of escaping with Ribbit and Roots crossed his thoughts, and he found himself lost in the daydreams once again, his mind escaping the orb that held his body prisoner.

But then his eyes focused back on the translucent cell to his right, and he saw what was left of Kirt and felt the vibration of the ship. The multi-dimensional creatures were taking him somewhere far from Earth, away from his home and his crew.

He was curious about the final destination, and, at times, thinking about where they were headed helped him get through the darker moments. Maybe it was some sort of planet—perhaps the home planet of the Organics.

He closed his eyes again, visualizing a world with floating cities over an ocean planet with teal water.

A ringing sound snapped him from the fantasy, and his eyes flipped open to the sight of four gaunt glowing figures hovering in the open space of the massive hold, level with his orb. As he watched, the blue figures flickered like flames, vanished, and appeared again below. Then they disappeared and reemerged across the belly of the ship.

His heart skipped a beat when he realized they were

the multi-dimensional beings—the overlords of the Organics. It had been a very long time since he last saw them.

They would flicker back and forth in the chamber, checking on prisoners. But they never attempted any form of verbal communication. Noble could feel them trying to enter his thoughts, like some sort of telepathy.

He gritted his teeth and pressed his fingers against his temples, doing everything he could to keep them out of his mind.

The ringing din increased, and a migraine settled in his sinuses. It always happened this way. Starting with the dull headache, until his brain felt like someone was slowly pushing down on it with a boot.

Next came the feeling of a presence. But the entities weren't inside his orb. They were hovering outside Kirt's.

The blue wall peeled back and the apparition on the left reached out with a single appendage that, as Noble watched, molded into a shovel that it used to scoop up the glutinous blob that had been Kirt. The being vanished with the remains.

But the second alien remained.

It glimmered and then disappeared for several seconds. Then the alien reappeared, right outside Noble's orb. He scooted back on the floor, his heartbeat rising in his throat. The creature looked into his prison. The translucent shape of its body was just a conglomeration of shifting blue flesh. There were no identifiable facial features, but for some reason Noble knew it was studying him.

A faint, almost robot-like voice sounded. Noble tilted his head and looked over his shoulder to see who was talking, but this wasn't coming from outside the orb. It was in his mind.

The alien was attempting communication for the first time since his captivity.

Do not be alarmed, it said. *Rest peacefully until we meet again.*

***

The cry of an alarm pierced Bouma's eardrums, exacerbating the throbbing pain flowing through his skull. At first all he saw was relentless white, until his pupils readjusted. Dust shifted through the air. Burning plastic and wiring stung his nostrils. He fought to look at the figure beside him, strapped into a harness.

His heart leapt as the fog over his mind dissipated and his vision cleared. "Holly! Are you okay?"

She hung limply, her head slumped against her chest. He pulled at his harness until it released, and he slipped out of his seat. Stumbling, he tried to maintain his footing. The *Sunspot*'s gravity had tilted.

His memory swam with the attack from the drones and their crash-landing on Mars's surface. The alarms still blared, and Sonya was going on in the background about damages to various parts of the ship. But none of that mattered right now.

"Come on, Holly," he said, looking up at the psychologist. She was dangling, limp, in her harness, a red gash across her forehead dripping blood.

Bouma brushed aside her hair to get a better look. "Baby, can you hear me?"

Still she made no reply.

Emanuel's voice broke over the comms. "Is everyone okay?"

"I'm fine!" Jeff reported. His voice sounded shaky.

"David is too, I think. We just got bumped up."

"Hell of a ride, but we're okay," Ort reported.

Bouma fumbled for a handset. "Holly's out! I need some help back here!"

"On my way," Emanuel replied.

"Please, Holly," Bouma pleaded, his hands wrapped around her cheeks. "Please, wake up."

He had only met her by circumstance, and their time together had been eventful, though brief. But when the world came to an end, the normal slow burn of human relationships was accelerated, each moment precious and fierce.

Holly was the glue holding this crew together. Her counseling had kept morale high. They were constantly faced with the harsh reality that the ever-present threat of the Organics meant their odds of survival were terrible. It was too easy to lose yourself in a spiral of depressive thoughts when considering the fate of the human race. She had strived to prevent them all from cracking psychologically.

For Bouma, she was more than just a counselor checking in on his mental health, though. The promise of a future with Holly was enough to keep him fighting. The way she smiled at him over breakfast in the ship's mess, her hand in his while they strolled through the agricultural biome, their passionate moments shared in their berth... it all hit Bouma like an Organic Sentinel on the charge.

He couldn't lose her like this.

Footsteps exploded down the corridor behind him.

"Bouma!" a voice called. "We're coming!"

Emanuel rushed in with Diego close behind. Ort, too, appeared in the doorway, blocking it with his massive frame.

"What can we do?" Ort asked.

Emanuel examined the wound on Holly's head. "We need to get her to the med bay."

Bouma began to unstrap her. Her head lolled to the side.

"Careful with her neck!" Emanuel said. "She might be hurt."

Bouma, Diego, and Emanuel gingerly unstrapped Holly the rest of the way. Then Emanuel helped Bouma carry her by her shoulders as Ort followed in the rear, holding her legs.

Bouma was only vaguely aware of the bluish cylinders where Sophie, Jamie, and Owen were being kept in cryostasis when they entered the medical bay. They still had no idea whether Sophie would make a full recovery or not. He'd seen the pain it caused Emanuel, and he feared he was about to experience that same horrible feeling. But as they set Holly down on a patient bed, her eyelids fluttered. Bouma swallowed hard, careful not to let his hope carry him away.

"Holly?" He caressed her arm.

"Wha... where am I?" she asked.

"We're in the med bay," Bouma replied. He fought to hold in his emotion. *She's awake! Alive! Oh, thank God!* A dark realization passed over him like a sudden storm cloud. "Do you know who I am?"

She cracked a half grin like he had said the dumbest thing in the world. "Of course I do, Chad."

A small twinge of relief settled through him at the sound of his first name. "Do you know where we're headed?"

"Mars." Then a sudden look of worry crossed her face. She brushed at the blood dripping down her forehead.

"Unless something else happened. We're still going to Mars, right?"

"Something did happen," Emanuel said. He had disappeared when they'd arrived in the med bay, and now came to the bed, carrying bandages and antiseptics. He started dressing her wound. "We're on Mars now. Crash landed."

"And the drones?" she asked.

"Still in space, as far as we can tell," Ort rumbled. "Seems like those bastards think they got us."

"Then we've got something to show them," Diego said.

Bouma wanted to share in their bravado, but for now, he could only focus on Holly. "God, I'm so glad you're alive." He swallowed her in an embrace. Then he pulled back. "You scared the shit out of me. Please, don't do that again."

Holly laughed. "Trust me, I don't want to." She rubbed the freshly set bandage. "I could use something for my head."

"On it," Emanuel said, navigating over the tilted deck. He started rummaging through the supplies. "We might be stuck here for little while until we figure out what's next." He grabbed a bottle and studied the label. "How are we doing on supplies, Sonya?"

Bouma massaged Holly's hand, sharing a smile with her. He realized in that moment how hard he would fight to help her and the others. Nothing they had accomplished so far had been easy, but it had all been worth the effort. The sooner they got moving and found Hoffman's colony, the better he'd feel.

"We have enough basic medical supplies for approximately sixty years' worth of normal activities with occasional disasters," Sonya said, responding to Emanuel's query.

Bouma breathed a sigh of relief.

"Unfortunately, we took heavy damage to the cargo hold," Sonya continued. "Our water supplies were also substantially damaged. In addition, the cryostat fluid tanks are leaking. At best, you have enough supplies to last a week."

"That gives us some time to come up with a plan," Bouma said. It still wasn't a comfortable timeline, but it would do.

He noticed Emanuel looking toward Sophie's tube.

"What about the cryostat fluid?" Emanuel asked. "If there's no more fluid to run the cryo chambers, we will have to take Jamie and Owen out."

Bouma knew the children were mostly healthy and would be fine. Sophie, on the other hand…

Their final stand on Earth to get on the *Sunspot* had ended with her succumbing to massive convulsions. He didn't understand the medical condition perfectly, but what he did know was that she had been infected with Organic nanobots. Those bots were teeming in her bloodstream. They had nearly killed her when she'd been forced to activate the RVAMP, the blast acting on the bots within her.

"How long until we run out?" Emanuel asked, looking up at one of the screens.

Sonya paused—as if trying to show concern for her human companions, Bouma thought wryly. "Forty-eight hours."

— 3 —

"Their shields are weak," Walker said. "You can tell by the color."

Athena had noticed that when she first saw the spiders. Just because the shields were weak didn't mean she could necessarily take them down with her pulse rifle, though. She carried two of the remaining four electromagnetic pulse (EMP) grenades in the GOA's arsenal, but the precious weapons were too valuable to use unless absolutely necessary.

"Stick to the original plan," Athena whispered.

Walker hesitated, then slowly lowered his MP5. She could tell he wanted to fight, but they needed to be smart.

She glanced out the third story window of their hiding spot—an apartment building two blocks from the tower. The spiders were still out there, searching for their prey.

Scratch, scrape, scratch, scrape.

The sounds of their razor-sharp claws echoed through the city, sending a chill up her spine. She pulled away from the window. There were still several hours of daylight left. She didn't want to be out here in the dark.

That was when the other beasts came out to hunt.

Athena and her crew had never seen one of them in person. The only person that had was Corporal Justin Marlin. He had reported hearing a whistling sound, and described the sand glowing blue, on a night patrol outside the buried submarine. The last thing he had said was rooted in her memory.

"The seabed is blue again, it's blue; all of it, glowing blue…"

They had found his corpse a few days later, nothing but mummified remains. Whatever creature had killed him had done so by sucking the water from his flesh like some sort of vampire alien.

Since then, Athena had kept their missions to the daylight.

The thought reminded her they couldn't stay here forever. They had to get to that tower and transmit to Alexia. The AI's promise of a plan was the only thing keeping Athena's ragtag crew going.

"Come on. Let's see if we can flank them without being seen," she said, heading toward the door.

They made their way back down through the building, taking a concrete stairwell to the lobby, where the remains of several orbs were plastered to the wood floor like macabre carpet.

Heat haze rose off the concrete outside the broken windows of the lobby. Athena glanced at her HUD. It was one hundred and twenty degrees Fahrenheit. Her suit continued to pump liquid coolant under the armor, but her flesh was slick with sweat.

She resisted the urge to reach up and flip her visor so she could wipe her face and eyes clean. A single distraction could cost them their lives.

Walker hurried across the room, his weapon shouldered. He halted in front of a missing window, his boots crunching the skirt of glass underneath.

The crunch wasn't loud to a human ear, but it was loud enough for a spider to detect.

Walker glanced back at Athena. She couldn't see his features behind his mirrored visor, but she knew he was likely cringing.

For a split second, Athena thought the mistake might go unnoticed. But not today. A blue glow suddenly reflected off a shard of glass hanging from the window frame by Walker. Athena had just enough time to bring her pulse rifle up and aim at the spider, which was lowering itself down from a blue web.

"Get down!" Athena shouted.

Walker turned to face the beast as it hung from a thick blue string just outside the glassless window. It slashed at his armor, claws slicing through his chest plates. He stumbled and crashed to the ground, his rifle clanking to the floor.

"Get up!" she yelled.

He managed to push himself to his feet, but now he was directly in her line of fire. The spider leapt into the room and struck Walker again, this time in the back, sending him spinning. He let out a cry of pain that was drowned out by her gunfire.

The pulse bolts lanced into the spider's weak shield. A blue bubble flashed around the creature, the shield absorbing the bolts and holding.

Athena choked on adrenaline as she fired again. Crawling toward her, Walker used his elbows to move his body across the floor, leaving a trail of blood behind him.

The spider roared, mandibles parting above her dying comrade.

Athena continued to pump rounds into its shield until one of them finally penetrated the creature's exoskeleton. The alien screeched in pain and raised two limbs into the air.

Walker fumbled for his weapon, grabbed it, and moved onto his back to fire off his magazine. Blood exploded out of the alien's wounds, but the creature skittered right into the fire.

"NO!" Athena yelled.

The alien impaled Walker through the gut with a claw, then lifted his skewered body off the ground. He grabbed the arachnid's limb, screaming in pain. Blood gushed around the wound as it raised Walker higher.

The spider's shield was down now, giving Athena her chance. She strode forward and fired the rest of her magazine into the monster, riddling it with rounds.

The alien dropped Walker with a thud. Athena ducked under the flailing beast and grabbed Walker by the back of his armor. She dragged him away, narrowly avoiding the whooshing claws.

They didn't have much time before other creatures showed up. She would have to use an EMP grenade if they did. It was her only shot at making it out alive.

But Walker was in bad shape. Blood gurgled from between his gloved fingers as she pulled him to safety. He reached up with his other hand and flipped his visor, sucking in a long gasp of air.

"Stop," he grumbled. Blood popped out of his mouth in an exploding bubble.

She scanned the street outside.

The spider was still moving on the floor, but it was too far away to pose much of a threat now.

"You got to go," Walker said. "I'm... I'm done for."

She was already reaching into a pouch on her duty belt to get the coagulating cream that would stop the bleeding. He reached up and grabbed her armored wrist.

NICHOLAS SANSBURY SMITH & ANTHONY J. MELCHIORRI

"I'll hold them off. You get that message from Alexia," he said.

Athena shook her helmet. "No, I'm not leaving you."

He cursed, grimaced, and closed his eyes. His features distorted in pain. The floor was slick with his blood, and crimson covered his suit. He was right. It was too late. He wasn't going to make it, no matter what she did.

"Give me my gun," he choked out.

Athena scrambled over to the weapon, eyeing the spider limbs that were still slashing the air. She ducked down, grabbed it, and then moved back to Walker.

She handed him the rifle and grabbed his other hand.

"I'll buy you…" he coughed, and then sucked in a breath. After an exhale, he said, "I'll buy you some time."

Athena managed to nod, holding his gaze for a moment. Losing Walker would be losing their comedic relief. His humor and bravado had given them all precious moments of levity in the darkest of times.

Now there would be only dark.

She wouldn't let him die in vain.

"Go," he said.

A tear fell from her eye. She pushed herself up, ran back into the hallway, and made her way toward the back door. When she reached the exit, she pushed it open and checked the street.

It was clear, and the radio tower was just two blocks away. She set off on the sidewalk, changing her rifle's magazine as she ran.

The crack of gunfire burst out behind her. Walker lasted several more minutes, just enough time for her to get to the tower before the din of the shots faded away.

At the base of the tower, she threw the sling of her rifle over her back and pulled the communication device from her belt. Then she grabbed a rung, looked up, and started climbing.

***

ENTRY 10001
DESIGNEE – AI ALEXIA

I finish a scan of the robots I reconstructed. They are all actively patrolling the air-ducts and other entries into the Biosphere. The bots outside the mountain continue to scan for Organics. None have spotted anything unusual.

I check the feed from J-PP1, a cleaning robot I've retrofitted with a video camera. The bot moves on tracks like a tank, crunching over the dry, rocky terrain around the mountain. Views of Colorado Springs show an increasingly brown and arid landscape. Spindly trees, yellow foliage, and sage tumbling across the cracked dirt are a common sight out there.

I switch from the J-PP1's feed to the most advanced robot I still have access to. Lolo. The NTC satellite orbiting Earth is currently in a perfect position to observe the ships docked at the platform in the Atlantic. I'm calling this one Staging Area 19, as I've found more than eighteen of these massive landing pads in what remains of the Earth's oceans.

There are two dozen drones patrolling the platform, all within the same combat interval of a quarter mile. It's quite remarkable how much security they have at these locations, considering the state of the human race. This tells me they are protecting something very important.

But what I'm really interested in is the fighter jets sitting on the tarmac. I zoom in for a better look. Unlike most of the teardrop-shaped alien craft, these have two wings and a dorsal fin, like some sort of predatory fish. There is a cockpit, and doors on both the port and starboard sides.

For the first time, I see the pilots. They are what the humans call Sentinels, best described as a mix between a reptile and a human. Spiked tails slither behind thick torsos as the pilots walk around their aircraft, apparently waiting for orders. I wish I knew who was giving them. My best guess is that the multi-dimensional overlords have some sort of AI like myself that controls their minions. Perhaps they use the nanobots they infected Doctor Winston and Lieutenant Smith with?

I continue watching, while filtering through other feeds. A sensor detects an incoming transmission, and I switch to the comm system. I'm overly cautious about transmissions due to the threat of Organics hacking into my interface, but this one is legitimate. I trace it to the same location I sent to Athena two days earlier. The corporal is right on time.

"I hope your intel is good, Alexia," she says. "I lost a good man today to get here."

"I'm sorry for your loss, Corporal." It is hard for me to understand death, even with my advanced programming, but I can tell by the tone of Athena's voice that this one has hit her hard.

"I've been working on finding a way off the planet for you and your crew, as well as other survivors scattered across the world. I've been in contact with multiple groups. One of them isn't far from your location, only about one hundred and twenty miles, at Pelican Air Force Base."

"That's a hell of a long ways on foot through enemy

territory," Athena says.

"You won't have to go on foot. I'm sending you the coordinates of an underground parking facility five miles from your location, as well as the location of Pelican Air Force Base."

"Wouldn't the pulse have knocked them out during the first day of the invasion?"

"It's possible some of the vehicles are deep enough below ground that they might still work."

"What are the odds?" Athena says. "If I'm going to risk it, I want to know."

"I put them at forty-nine percent."

"Suppose we do manage to get some, and drive one hundred and twenty miles to meet up with this other group of survivors. Then what?"

I take a split second to look back at the images from Lolo. A Sentinel climbs into the cockpit of an aircraft and takes off from the platform. By the time I respond to Athena, the fighter is soaring west over the draining ocean.

"I have a plan," I say. "A plan that will get you off this planet and to Mars with the others."

END ENTRY

***

Emanuel stood at the front of the med bay. The air hissing through the ventilation ducts still carried the odor of charred plastic and hot metal. He couldn't bring himself to sit, like the others. Bouma, Ort, Diego, and Holly were seated at a table in the middle of the med bay, surrounded by empty patient beds. Visions of the cryostat fluid running out had filled his head with dark thoughts.

All he could see were images of Sophie lying, gasping for air, on the *Sunspot*'s deck.

Jeff and David sat near the cryo chambers, as if guarding the other children. The duo had been bruised in the attack, but had come out of the crash otherwise okay.

Bouma had already tried to usher them out of the med bay, but they'd insisted on staying. Jeff wanted to know what was going to happen next. Back on Earth, after they'd first found Jeff and David, Emanuel might've demanded the kids leave the room so the adults could do the talking. He wanted to shield them as much as he could from the darkness plaguing their reality. But any innocence Jeff and David once had was left behind on Earth. They had done their duty defending the *Sunspot*, and they deserved a place at the metaphorical table as much as any other crew member here.

Pacing, Emanuel stared at the cryo chamber where Sophie was suspended. She had always wanted to get to Mars. It had been her goal to make it to Hoffman's colony since the beginning. Emanuel had promised her they would make it. When he had loaded her into the chamber three months ago, he had thought he could actually make good on that promise. It turned out that he had indeed gotten her to Mars, but there was no way she'd live to see Hoffman's colony with the leaking cryostat tanks.

"We need to get to that crashed biosphere ship," Emanuel said. "If we don't, Sophie dies."

"Tell me where, and I'll head out," Bouma said eagerly.

Emanuel nodded. "Good. We don't have time to lose."

Diego's gaze shifted as he looked to Emanuel. "We've got a hell of a deadline, but we've got to be realistic. Sonya said that ship is sending out some kind of damaged SOS. I don't think I need to explain what that means."

"Rushing into a ship that might be full of Organics without a plan is not the best idea," Ort agreed.

Heat rushed to Emanuel's face. "We don't have a choice. Sophie is going to die if we don't get that cryostat fluid."

"Doc is right," Bouma said.

"I won't dispute that," Diego said, holding his hands up. "But we've got to be rational. That other ship was knocked down by Organics, just like we were. We run in there to go get cryostat fluid for Sophie, we could all end up dead. That won't help her."

Emanuel palmed the table. "You want to just let her die?"

"Not at all," Diego said. "I'm just saying we've got to think this through. We can't sacrifice all of us for one of us. Not if that also means sacrificing our mission of finding the rest of humanity on Mars. I'm all for launching a scavenging operation, but we need better intel before blindly leaping out there."

Ort let out a harumph of agreement.

"You're in charge of this mission, and I'll go out there if you order it," Diego continued. "But I want you to at least consider whether your judgment is being compromised by your relationship with Doctor Winston, or if you truly think this is the best thing for our mission."

Emanuel stiffened. He took a deep breath, and tried to revert to an expression of measured calmness. "It's not just about Sophie. We also took heavy damage to the cargo hold. We need more food and water if any of us are going to survive."

Ort seemed to consider that for a moment. "Sonya, can you give us an exact timeframe on how long our remaining supplies will last?"

The AI's soothing voice answered back. "If you follow the prescribed rationing plan I have created, one week is it. But if you stretch it an uncomfortable amount, and do not mind some considerable physical discomfort, you can extend your survival to three point five weeks."

Diego gave Emanuel a look that burned through his skull. The soldier said nothing. He didn't have to, and he knew it.

Emanuel pressed the heels of his palms into his eyes. He let out an exasperated breath. Maybe Diego was right. He was letting his feelings for Sophie affect his judgment. They were in enemy territory here. Hell, the whole solar system seemed to be enemy territory now. He and the others couldn't afford to act rashly. They would pay dearly for any mistakes.

He turned away to recompose himself. There was so much at stake he could hardly focus, from Sophie's life to the future of humanity. He begrudgingly had to admit Diego wasn't entirely wrong. It was impossible for him to untangle Sophie's survival from his preferred course of action, but he owed it to Diego to hear the man out. After all, he was the only military officer among them.

"Tell me, Diego, how would you approach the situation?" Emanuel asked.

"In a perfect world, I'd send out a couple of scouts. We'd observe the downed ship for two or three days."

A couple of days is all Sophie has left. Emanuel wanted to say it, but he bit back the words.

"We'd scout the area, looking for signs of Organics both inside and outside the ship, while identifying potential entry and exit points. If there were no Organics, we'd go in. If there were Organics, we'd track their numbers to see if it's a battle we could fight."

"And if it wasn't?" Emanuel asked.

"We'd look for a way to relieve the ship of supplies while avoiding Organics."

Emanuel slumped into a seat across from Diego. "How long would all this take?"

Diego's eyes went up for a second as he tallied the numbers in his head. "If we're quick, we can make a reasonable effort to scout the ship and come up with a good plan of incursion in five, maybe even four, days. Plenty of time, given our remaining supplies."

"But not enough time for Sophie." Emanuel stood up and walked away from the table. "Look, I'll go out there alone. I don't expect all of you to risk your lives for her, but I can't let her die. That wrecked ship can't be that much different than ours, so I'll know where to look. And if I can just grab a few liters of cryostat fluid, it'll keep Sophie alive long enough for you to do all your scouting and recon."

"That's suicide," Ort said.

"It's only suicide if there are actually Organics," Emanuel said. "And besides, I have a better chance of surviving if it's just me. One person is a lot harder to detect than a whole squad."

"No way, Doc," Bouma said, standing. "If you go, I go. I owe Sophie that much."

Holly pushed herself up from her seat. "Give me a rifle and armor. I owe Sophie my life. We all do. We can't give up on her. She wouldn't give up on us."

Diego and Ort looked at each other.

"I don't know about this," Ort said, his deep voice rumbling. He exhaled slowly. "A scientist, a marine, and a psychologist walk into a crashed NTC ship. There's probably a joke in there somewhere, but the punchline doesn't turn out good for any of them."

Jeff raised his hand from the back of the room, speaking for the first time. "I'll go."

"Me too," David chimed in.

Diego folded his arms across his chest and leaned back in his chair. "You know, I've spent a few months on this ship with you people, and I still haven't come to fully appreciate how insane you all are."

Emanuel waited for the soldier's adamant protest against their actions. He knew it was foolish, crazy even, to think they could save Sophie. But hadn't everything they'd done since the Organics attacked been some insane moonshot plan? Surviving in Cheyenne, using the RVAMPs, flying to Mars…

"Look," Diego said, pointing to Jeff and David. "Those kids are staying put, and so is the psychologist. Doctor, if you want to throw yourself in harm's way, be my guest. But I'd prefer if you didn't. This is a job for armed professionals." He stood, then gestured to Bouma and Ort. "If the whole crew is going to go out there against our better judgment, then I'd be derelict in my duties as an NTC soldier if I let *kids* go out there. We'll get into that ship today, and we'll get those supplies."

— 4 —

Captain Noble couldn't get the words out of his mind. The multi-dimensional alien had spoken to him through some sort of telepathic communication. Or was that just his imagination?

He wasn't sure what was real anymore. He'd been isolated for so long that he yearned for any kind of contact. He simply couldn't endure the mental and physical pain of being alone much longer.

Sitting with his knees pulled up to his chest, he examined his frail body. His once defined chest muscles were gone, his chest now nothing more than skin clinging to his ribs. Long, matted hair clung to his chiseled jaw, and he reached up to feel his thinning beard.

The coiled cord feeding him nutrients was just barely keeping him alive. He could feel and see himself wasting away.

But somewhere inside, he believed he was still alive for a reason. He was one of only a few human survivors. Maybe the only human survivor...

This was the first time the thought had crossed his mind, and it chilled him to the core. Billions had perished, and if he was the only person left, then he had to keep fighting. Curling up in a fetal position and dying was not what humans did. He wasn't going to disrespect his species by giving up.

Part of him doubted he was the last of his kind,

especially after seeing the *Sunspot* launch from Offutt Air Force Base during Operation Redemption. He thought of Doctor Winston and her crew often, wondering if they had made it past the Organic defenses on their way to Mars.

He wasn't a religious man, but he did find himself praying they reached the NTC colony. Perhaps there was still hope for humanity there.

Letting out a sigh, he looked up at Ribbit and then down at Roots. The aliens were both sleeping in their orbs. They too seemed to have a desire to keep living, even in these horrid conditions. He wondered what had happened to their species, and their homeworlds.

While he hadn't been able to speak to his odd-looking friends, their presence helped ease the sense of loneliness. He imagined it was a lot like how prisoners back on Earth had felt about a pet mouse, cat, or even a plant.

Noble crawled across the floor to the other side of his orb, and angled his head to look down, past Roots, at the hundreds of orbs lining the bulkhead wall. There had to be thousands of prisoners inside the ship.

He scanned the chamber, looking for the multi-dimensional aliens. He'd spent countless hours, days— hell, he had no idea how much time—waiting for someone to give him some answers.

Standing in his orb, he decided to try something different. "Hey!" he yelled. "Come talk to me again!"

Ribbit and Roots both stirred in their orbs and moved to get a better look at him. Croaking reverberated from above, and a cracking sound came from below as Roots swayed all four branch-like arms.

"Come on, everyone!" Noble shouted. "Make some noise!"

Other strange voices joined his cry. Screeching, chirps, and what sounded like barking followed, drowning out his own shouts.

"Yeah, that's right. Let's tell these alien freaks who's boss," Noble said. He held in a breath, exhaled, and then, at the top of his lungs, screamed, "LET US OUT OF HERE!"

The cacophony of ethereal wails and alien voices blended together in a chorus that sent adrenaline rushing through his veins. But the warmth quickly turned to ice when he heard a strangely familiar voice.

This time it wasn't in his head. It sounded… human.

He wasn't alone after all. There was another human on this ship!

He moved over to the edge of his wall, his face so close to it his matted beard stood up from the static electricity generated by the force field. Eyes flitting, and ears perked, he looked and listened for the source of the voice.

Noble pulled on the tube connecting him to the bottom of the orb as he moved around for a better look. But just as he began to scan the western side of the chamber, he saw something that took his breath away.

Four sinewy multi-dimensional entities sparkled into view. They fanned out in different directions. The dull ringing that followed their presence silenced the prisoners.

Everyone but Noble.

He shouted louder this time. "Who's out there? If you can hear me, tell me your name!"

One of the multi-dimensional entities blinked in and out as it crossed the chamber toward his orb, but the captain wasn't deterred.

"Please!" he yelled. "Please tell me your name!"

The only answer was the ringing noise. Every single prisoner remained silent.

The presence of the multi-dimensional overlords had them all spooked, and Noble began to feel the chill of fear as one of them halted outside the blue wall separating him from the black void beyond. He took a step back as it reached out with a blue limb that spun like a drill toward the orb. The wall peeled back, opening a doorway.

Cold air rushed into his cell, and his hair stood up on his naked flesh. The spinning drill bit solidified into a needle, and continued toward his face.

Noble took another step back, until his spine was dangerously close to the wall of the orb. He held up a hand and moved his head from side to side as the sharp tip spun toward his mouth.

"No," he mumbled, rearing his head back. "Please... please no."

The needle jabbed his lips, numbing them instantly. He reached up to swat it away. The multi-dimensional being pulled it back, replaced the wall, and then vanished from view, leaving Noble standing there in shock.

He tried to speak, and then he tried to scream, but no sounds could escape his mouth. There was just a muffled strangle reverberating in his throat. He fell to his knees, reaching up to touch his swollen lips. They were clamped shut.

***

It didn't take long to load one of the eight-wheeled armored Rhinos. Several of the Rhinos had been destroyed in the Organic attack on the *Sunspot*, and many had scars from where shrapnel had blasted against them. But the vehicles were built tough. A few scratches, a busted wheel or two, and even a shard of spaceship hull through an armor plate, wasn't going to stop a Rhino. Still, Diego wondered if they could withstand a spider or a Sentinel. He hoped they wouldn't have to find out.

The interior of the Rhino was especially spacious with only Diego, Ort, and Bouma in the vehicle. Diego was glad he'd convinced Emanuel to stay. This wasn't a place for scientists to play hero. They had brought a portable RVAMP and enough pulse rifle rounds and EMP grenades for a platoon. That was one benefit of being a small crew on the huge *Sunspot*.

"You know what?" Ort broke the silence between them. "This might be the first time I actually feel like we're fully equipped to engage the Organics."

"Equipped or not, I'd rather we didn't see a single one of them," Diego said from the driver's seat. "Those blue bastards are annoying as hell even when you've got an RVAMP and EMP grenades."

Diego wanted to sigh. He thought about the time he would've spent scouting the area and identifying any potential threats. He hated going in blind to a mission. It was just like when he and Sergeant Harrington had volunteered to go with that squad into the Chinese sub back on Earth. They'd gone in with no idea of what they were about to face, holding on to the tenuous hope that they'd find human survivors. But the only survivors that had come back from that mission were him and a few others who had managed to escape demise at the claws of hungry spiders. They'd lost half their search and rescue party, with nothing to show for it.

The Rhino crawled over the barren landscape. Jagged

57

red rocks pushed up all over from the rust-colored dirt like the claws of some giant Sentinel yearning to free itself from the planet.

They climbed and dipped down hill after hill, carefully crawling toward the location Sonya had told them to mark on their map. Over rocks and small ditches they went.

The landscape looked just as Diego had always imagined it. Vast, dry, and the color of rust. Out here it wasn't as terraformed as the patches they'd seen from space. The sky, though, looked slightly different than Earth's. There was a purple hue to it, almost as if it was the tail end of a sunset.

"What's the atmo here, Sonya?" Diego asked.

"Oxygen and atmosphere levels are higher than noted in NTC reports from a year ago," Sonya reported. "Still, oxygen levels are sub one percent. Air density is approximately three percent of Earth's."

It wasn't much, but it *was* something. The sparse terraforming was having an effect. That might mean humanity was actually finding a foothold on this planet. If only the Organics didn't have their claws in it first.

"Any contacts?" Diego asked.

"So far, I do not detect any lifeforms," Sonya said. "However, it is difficult for me to determine with complete certainty that there are no lifeforms present at our destination. The shielding provided by the landscape and the ship's radio defenses making such determinations exceedingly difficult."

"Understood," Diego replied. "Tell us as soon as you spot something."

They continued across the alien terrain, eyes flitting for hostiles. Stars studded the sky above them. Diego waited for one of those stars to come careening down. Surely some of those jewels in the sky were the Organic ships? They were probably waiting up there, distributed around the planet like vultures, ready to plummet down and tear apart the carrion. Each time he thought he saw something move, his heart picked up in tempo and his grip tightened around his rifle.

Despite Sonya's reassurances, Diego found trusting the AI difficult. He preferred not to rely solely on computers and electronic sensors. Relying on his own senses and intuition had served him well over the years. It had kept him alive.

He scanned the horizon, looking for signs of Organics. A dark column that looked like a cloud rolled across the horizon. Diego squinted for a better view. "Sonya, what is that at our five o'clock?"

"I'm detecting a dust storm," she said. "However, it is not currently headed in our direction. Risk assessments indicate that it is not even a mild threat to our current mission. The probability does exist that it might intersect with our path, but it is unlikely."

"Unlikely," Diego muttered. He didn't like that there was even a small chance it might hit them. Still he couldn't help but think that the ominous dust clouds billowing across the horizon were a sign of things to come.

"Still don't like seeing them," Ort grumbled.

"Me either," Bouma said. "The dust storms were bad enough on Earth. You can ask Sophie about the one that nearly crashed her helo before she even got to Cheyenne Mountain. I can't imagine what this one would be like."

"In my book, Mars's storms are like Organics," Diego said. "Better left not experienced."

The wind pelted them with gravel and dirt as they continued driving, the vehicle navigating the rugged terrain at a rapid pace. He kept his eye on the storm crossing the plains in the distance.

"You are two point four kilometers from the crash site," Sonya reported after several quiet minutes. "The ship will soon be visible."

The Rhino climbed a hill crowned with jagged boulders. Bouma leaned forward in his seat, as if that would hold them steady. Beyond the boulders, they spotted a large valley. Huge gouges were dug into the dirt, leading to the crashed biosphere ship.

And it wasn't alone.

There were times Diego had doubted his faith. Since the Organics had invaded Earth, there wasn't a single day he didn't wonder if God was just a fairytale humans told themselves to make peace with their inevitable deaths. All the Sunday Masses and NTC chaplains' sermons he had attended never mentioned anything about giant monsters descending on Earth from the stars.

Other times, he thought maybe he was already dead. Maybe God did exist, and so did Heaven and Hell. Because right now, he was pretty sure he was in Hell.

"Holy shit," Ort said over the suit's comms.

"Ain't nothing holy about it." Diego stood and pressed one hand against the windshield.

The biosphere ship they'd tracked down looked as if it had skidded across the landscape. It looked mostly intact, except for a few huge singe marks that marred its stern. Many of the windows had been blown out near those blackened areas, but otherwise it was in one piece.

The same couldn't be said for the multitude of other ships in the area. They too had half-buried themselves in this spaceship graveyard. Most were just pieces of broken hull, nothing but metal ribbing, like the charred skeletons from a pod of gigantic whales.

"A graveyard," Bouma said quietly.

"Wonder what happened to them," Ort murmured.

Diego adjusted his grip on his rifle. "Let's go find out."

***

Athena thought about returning to look for Walker's body, but she knew by now there wouldn't be much, if anything, left of him. The spiders never wasted anything.

She needed to keep her mind on moving forward. If Alexia was correct, they might have transportation to a military installation where other survivors were holed up.

A dangerous emotion crept up on her as she walked. Hope was something she tried not to feel, something she tried her best to keep suppressed.

For the first time in weeks, she embraced the emotion. Maybe it wasn't such a bad thing after all. Perhaps this was what she needed to keep things going?

She brought up her pulse rifle to scope the skyline for drones or alien ships.

Lowering her rifle, she craned her helmet to look over the city one last time. She had managed to evade the spiders after connecting with Alexia, but the beasts were still out there.

Hunting.

Movement flashed across the exterior of a building a few blocks into the city. Several of the spiders were clambering across the white walls between the window frames.

She crouched out of sight and scanned the dry seabed in front of her once more. The rolling tan dunes and blue sky revealed no sign of hostiles.

"Goodbye, Walker," she whispered. In her mind's eye, she pictured the monsters still feeding on Walker's remains.

Athena suppressed the thought and set off down the beach. There were four miles of sand between herself and the GOA, all of which would leave her exposed. At a jog, it would take her just under forty minutes in the armored suit. She spotted the bones of the whale carcass she had sheltered in with Walker, but aside from that, there wasn't much.

The sun was already going down, a harsh reminder that the aliens that had killed Corporal Marlin were out there somewhere. With only an hour or so of sunlight left, she couldn't waste time.

Four miles. That's all you have to do, she reminded herself.

She pushed her legs from a jog to a run. Sweat prickled across her shoulders and down her back, her skin sticking to the membrane under the armor. Even with the coolant circulating through the suit, she was burning up. The filtered air in her helmet was getting stale and gritty, and each steamy breath irritated her overexerted lungs.

Her eyes flitted from the skyline to her HUD, scanning for hostiles and the data rolling across the display in the upper right-hand corner. The temperature was starting to drop, now that the sun was going down, but it was still up at one hundred and eighteen degrees.

Wind gusted across the plateau of sand, rustling the surface and exposing the bones of fish and empty shells of crabs and other crustaceans.

Athena used her tongue to pull the straw in her helmet

to her lips. She took a sip, the cool liquid soothing her dry throat. The heat was starting to make her lightheaded. The adrenaline from seeing Walker die and hiding from the spiders had long since waned, leaving her with little energy. She forced her boots forward.

The air undulated from the heat, filling the horizon with the facade of movement. The mirage made it difficult to see if anything was moving beyond the tan-colored terrain. She managed to run the first two miles without stopping to rest, but slowed at the halfway point to sip more water and crouch next to a cluster of large rocks.

The boulders provided some shelter from the fading sun. She rested her back against the smooth rock to catch her breath. Instead of breathing through her nostrils, she took air through her mouth. The heat wasn't as bad on her throat as it was her sensitive nose.

After a few seconds of rest, she scoped the cracked seabed between her position and that of the GOA with her pulse rifle. There was no sign of life. Her HUD confirmed the sky was clear, so she continued onward at a jog. The membrane in her suit clung to her sweaty flesh now, making it more challenging to move.

She thought of her crew back in the submarine, and anticipated their questions. Everyone would want to know what happened to Walker. How he died. Why he died. What the plan was.

All she wanted to do was climb into her bunk and close her eyes.

But leaders didn't get to rest.

She focused back on the stretch of sand on the other side of a rolling hill. She remembered this area from a previous scouting mission. Ravines snaked across the terrain here. Walker and she had stumbled upon it three weeks ago by accident when returning to the GOA.

Athena changed direction, moving south past the canyons. They were deep enough the sun didn't penetrate the bottom. From an aerial view, she imagined they looked like yawning, bloody slash marks on flesh, with their red edges.

Thoughts of the beasts that might dwell in those shadows kept her far from the edges of the gorges. Her eyes roved over the landscape out of habit, but she had to continue pushing herself to run. Every movement was uncomfortable now. Her muscles were stretched to the limit, and her lungs were on fire.

Her jog devolved into more of a staggering hobble, and she cradled her rifle over her chest, doing her best not to let it clank against the armor. She hadn't gone far beyond the gorges when she heard the unmistakable rumble of an Organic spaceship.

Instinct forced her to the ground, and she looked skyward.

Not a drone this time.

A two-winged aircraft with a dorsal fin cut over the horizon like a barracuda. It veered toward Los Angeles, probably to check out reports from the aliens about her and Walker. She hadn't seen one of these aircraft for weeks, and it was bad news for her.

If she was spotted, she knew, the pilot wouldn't capture her. It would kill her in a volley of laser fire. There wouldn't be anything left for her crew to find if that happened.

Keeping low to the ground, she gazed longingly in the direction of the GOA. She was less than half a mile away, but there was no way she would make it. Besides, she didn't want to lead the aliens to their hideout. Her only chance was to return to the ravines and take shelter there until the ship was gone.

A moment later, she was up on her feet and running toward the deep cuts in the seabed. She focused on the closest ravine, which appeared about as wide as a one-lane road. The roar of the alien ship droned on, and she snuck a glance to see it circling Los Angeles, scanning for targets.

She wasn't sure how far the pilots could see, or what type of scanning equipment they had, but she had a feeling it would snag her eventually. She had to get out of the open.

A glance over her shoulder showed the fighter was already changing course. The adrenaline returned, warming her veins and nerves as she sprinted toward the ravine ahead. The rumble of the aircraft grew louder and louder with every step she took, until the very ground beneath her feet was shaking.

It felt like it was almost on her now.

She clicked the rifle into its slot at her back, and prepared to jump into the gorge. It wasn't as wide as the others, maybe twelve feet across, but that didn't mean it wasn't deep. If she fell all the way to the bottom, she would break a bone. Perhaps several. A broken bone out here would be worse than getting vaporized by the lasers. At least those would kill her instantly.

She waited until she was a few steps away before launching herself into the air. The craggy, brown far wall reached out to meet her as she plummeted. She slammed against the rock, her boots landing on a rocky shelf. Her right hand grappled for purchase and her left slid down the jagged rock, which sliced into her glove.

Another swipe with her right hand and she managed to find a handhold, relief washing through after finding purchase. Panting and hugging the wall, she slowly looked down at the outline of the floor, some fifty or sixty feet below.

The alien fighter passed overhead, stirring the sand above into a vortex that rained down into the gorge and peppered her with grit and tiny rocks. She held her position until she heard the craft coming in for another pass.

The thump, thump of laser fire pounded the seabed above her, shaking away hunks of rock and sand all around her. The blasts hit the ground somewhere above her, several cutting through the air right above the ravine, sizzling and tossing up sand.

Her boots were planted firmly on a rocky shelf and she had a good grip on a deposit of jutting rock, but if any of it gave way, she would plunge a hell of a long way down.

She searched for a way to climb deeper. As the fighter circled for another pass, she began moving, carefully negotiating the wall.

The rays of penetrating sunlight weakened with every new foot and handhold she found. She descended into the darkness as the aircraft came in for a second pass. Laser fire pounded the seabed with such force that a huge section of rock and sand fell away and smashed to the ground below. Twisting her body, she avoided the rockslide with mere inches to spare.

She was over halfway down when the fighter came in yet another time, peppering the ground above. More grit and rocks rained down, covering her in dust and sand.

When she was just ten feet from the bottom, she

jumped the rest of the way. Her boots crunched into the sand, and she rolled. Recovering, she grabbed her pulse rifle and crouched down to look at whatever she had landed on.

The air seized in her lungs, and fresh adrenaline charged through her vessels. The floor wasn't sand or rock. It was a pile of bones. Mostly small fish and the shells of crustaceans, but there were several larger sea creatures. Dozens of shark skeletons lay over in the corner.

Seeing remains like this wasn't abnormal, but seeing them dragged together like this was highly unusual. Something had killed these creatures and feasted on them in the early days of the invasion, leaving their bones in the once underwater grave.

She was in the den of some aquatic alien apex predator.

Hiding in one of their nests, even if abandoned, terrified her to the core. Her blood chilled at the memories of the aquatic aliens she had seen from inside the submarine. Had this been one of those?

She swallowed as the fighter passed overhead again. The pilot had stopped firing the laser, but apparently continued to search for her. Breathing heavily, she lay down on the bones, her heart thundering. The sun retreated beyond the lip of the gorge, leaving darkness to cover the land.

Stars already pinpricked the sky.

She had to get out of there and back to the GOA.

Her opportunity finally came a few minutes later, when the roar of the fighter diminished into a dull rumble, and then quiet.

The ringing in her ears ceased, and silence filled the

ravine. She could hear her beating heart in the quiet.

Another minute passed before she started climbing. Her biceps and quads felt like they were going to tear.

Come on, Athena, you got this.

Halfway up, she rewarded herself with a drink from the straw, but it took a deep suck to get even a few drops. Her bottle was dry.

She pulled herself onto the rocky ledge she had first landed on. The top was almost within reach. She caught her breath on the ledge, letting her muscles relax and listening for hostiles above ground.

Hearing nothing, she finally pulled herself back out onto the seabed, squirming over the top and then pushing herself up on two knees.

Twilight had long since set in.

She set off for the GOA. But, just a few steps from the ravines, she heard a low rumble that made her heart skip a beat. She froze. A scan of the sky revealed no glowing spaceships. She took another step, then realized the sound was coming from the ground beneath her feet. It rose to an out-of-tune whistle.

Athena slowly turned to look out over the ravines. The slashes were all glowing blue; light pulsated like strobes across terrain pockmarked black from laser fire.

Corporal Marlin's final words surfaced in her memories.

"The seabed is blue again, it's blue; all of it, glowing blue…"

She did what she had become very good at—she turned and ran.

— 5 —

Bouma stared out the Rhino's front windows at the skeletal remains of the ship graveyard, wishing that just one of these ships was intact. But no. Most of them were reduced to scaffolding and bulkheads. There would be no supplies for them to scavenge here, much less viable cryostat fluid to keep Sophie alive.

Their only hope was in the biosphere ship they'd tracked down. At least it was still mostly in one piece, its jagged edges belying the curving domes of the biomes toward its stern. A few portholes had been blown out, and there were long scrapes, some that might've penetrated the corridors running through the ship. Otherwise, there were no gaping wounds, giving them hope they'd find the supplies they were searching for.

Bouma read the huge block white letters scrawled across its side where they had stopped. "*Radiant Dawn*," he said. "Not looking so radiant anymore. Sonya, lifeforms?"

"Maybe," the AI replied.

"Maybe?" Ort rumbled. "We're right outside this *Radiant Dawn* and the best you can give us is a maybe?"

"While it is true you are within visual range," Sonya said, "the Rhino does not have the same sensor array as the *Sunspot*. My detection abilities are limited to the hardware provided by the *Rhino* as relayed to the *Sunspot*. Unfortunately, despite your proximity to the *Radiant*

Dawn, the canyon and the *Radiant Dawn*'s radiation shielding is blocking me from any improvement in detecting potential lifeforms."

Diego secured his helmet. "If we're not staking out here for a few days, there's only one way to see if there are lifeforms on that ship."

Bouma took a second to look at his comrades. He'd come to know Ort and Diego personally over the past few months, and he knew their service record. But they hadn't actually served in combat together, besides their brief skirmish on Earth to get aboard the *Sunspot*. It wasn't anything like the long history he'd had fighting beside Sergeant Overton.

Had to go and sacrifice yourself, Sarge, Bouma thought. *I could really use you right now.*

But you didn't go to war with the army you wanted—or in this case, squad. You went to war with the one you had.

Right now, Bouma had two guys who were already skeptical about the way Emanuel had been running the crew. They weren't used to being under the command of scientists. Hell, it had taken Bouma some time to get used to it, but the eggheads had grown on him.

Ort and Diego had served under Captain Noble, so they had to be worth something. Bouma was sure they were good men. Still, that didn't make working cohesively with them that much easier. They hadn't really gotten used to watching each other's backs, and they had none of the ties you forged in battle with your brothers-in-arms. None of the half-psychic intuition you developed when you knew someone's instincts and reactions and they knew yours.

At least, not yet.

"Guess there's always trial by fire," Bouma muttered.

"What's that?" Diego asked.

"Ready to get the hell out there," Bouma said.

"Good," Diego said. "Get in and get out. MO on this mission is stealth and speed."

"Full copy," Ort said. His frame took up the entire doorway of the Rhino. "Just say the word, LT."

Bouma watched Diego gaze out over the morbid tableau. He hadn't had to follow another soldier's orders since Sergeant Overton. This was going to be interesting.

"Move." Diego gestured out the door of the Rhino.

The trio filtered through the wreckage of the other ships toward the *Radiant Dawn*. Wind carrying clouds of dust rushed over them, howling and biting at their armor. The dust clung to Bouma's visor, and he was forced to wipe it clean a couple times before they even made it to the *Dawn*. Once they reached the forward hatch of the ship, they pressed their bodies against the hull.

"Sonya, can you get us in?" Diego asked.

"I should be able to if you can get me a hard connection."

"Easy," Diego said. He unlatched a panel near the hatch and stuck a network probe from his suit into the security port. A moment later, the hatch spiraled open.

There was no whoosh of air outward like Bouma had expected.

"With all those broken windows and scars in the hull, it's no wonder they lost atmosphere," Ort said.

"No fail-safe mechanism is going to help that much damage," Diego agreed. He motioned them through the hatch.

Inside, the wind howled through the corridors. Dirt had piled into the corners where the bulkheads met the deck. Long wires hung from broken ceiling panels like overgrown jungle vines, and gouges in the metal told the story of a battle fought within the corridors.

"The Organics definitely got in here," Bouma said. He roved his rifle over the intersecting corridors as they progressed down the corridor, leaving a trail of footprints behind them. "Bastards probably took every last human."

"Let's hope they aren't still here," Diego said. "Come on, let's get to the cargo hold."

They plunged deeper into the ship, the dark interior swallowing them. Red emergency lights flickered intermittently. Even in the depths of the ship, Mars's wind churned down the corridors, scratching grit against their suits. It threatened to drown their communications.

"How much longer?" Ort asked.

Sonya's voice sounded over their comm systems. "Two decks down and approximately three hundred meters down another corridor toward the rear. The *Sunspot*'s deck plan is nearly a clone of this one, so it should make navigation easier for you."

They resumed prowling down the corridors, the wind and the blinking emergency lights their only companions. Even down here the wind, penetrating the damaged portholes and hull, carried a brutal force. The scrape of grit against bulkhead and armor had become almost like white noise to Bouma, and it threatened to blend into the background noise of the air whooshing through his respiration system.

Then he heard it. A scrape, followed by a scratch that sounded like metal against metal. He knew the sound, and paused in mid-stride.

"Did you hear that?" he whispered. He probed the hall with his helmet-mounted lights. The lights seemed so weak, so horribly inadequate in the inky darkness surrounding them.

"The wind?" Ort asked, staring through his visor with an arched eyebrow.

"No, no, something else," Bouma said. A shiver snaked down his spine. He held his breath, determined to listen for it again. The noise harkened memories of the Organics infiltrating the Biosphere in Cheyenne Mountain. That incursion had nearly been a bloodbath. He prayed he was wrong.

"Must've missed it," Diego said. "You sure you heard something?"

"I... I'm not so sure now," Bouma said. Maybe it was his nerves getting the better of him. Especially if he was alone in hearing the suspect sound.

They pushed forward down the ladders toward the bowels of the ship. Soon they'd be at the cargo hold. The goosebumps prickling Bouma's skin never went away, though. He strained to listen for more scraping.

Nothing.

Just the wind and grit, and the labored breaths of the other two filtering in over the comms.

Something moved in Bouma's gut. He didn't like it. As much as he tried to convince himself that maybe he was just hearing things, he couldn't do it. The other two had spent most of the Organic invasion in a submarine, the GOA, deep in the ocean. They hadn't faced the sheer number of Organics he had. They hadn't lived through Organics invading their stronghold in Cheyenne Mountain.

He knew an Organic claw scraping across a deck when he heard one.

Nah, this time he wasn't wrong.

"Guys," Bouma said. Diego and Ort both stopped. Their helmet-mounted lights landed on him. "I think—"

The screech of breaking metal suddenly exploded overhead. Long skinny legs tore through the broken ceiling panels. Bouma whipped his rifle up at them. Claws raked over the deck, and one of them caught Diego and threw him off his feet. He sprawled on the deck, and lost the RVAMP.

Before Bouma could jump to retrieve it, the grotesque spider pushed the rest of itself through the rent in the ceiling. Its armored carapace gleamed black, and its globular eyes reflected the malicious red of the emergency lights. A faint blue glow shimmered around its arachnid form too, signaling the presence of its shield.

It had been months since Bouma had seen one of these bastards up close, and the alien was just as frightening now as it had always been. It was a living, breathing weapon that would stop at nothing to dismantle its prey into a million red chunks of flesh and bone.

A huge claw reared back, pointed directly at Diego's chest. Diego crab-crawled away, still on his back, struggling desperately to escape his impending doom.

Bouma's finger tightened around his trigger, but Ort was in his way, and Diego too close in the cramped corridor. There was no clear shot. Not at this distance. His eyes locked on the RVAMP. The spider stood between the device and them.

There was no retrieving that either.

The claw shot forward. Its aim was true. Bouma imagined it tearing through Diego's armor plates and brittle bones, puncturing the soldier's heart.

"Hell no!" a rumbling voice boomed.

Ort threw himself at the descending claw, his huge

body hitting the side of the spider's leg. It wasn't enough to cripple the leg, but the claw punched into the deck, missing Diego's chest by millimeters.

Now Bouma had an open shot. He let loose a fusillade of pulse fire. Rounds slammed against the spider's shield, splashing over it like snowballs flung against concrete. It wasn't enough to do any damage, but it did distract the beast.

The spider's mandibles spread, and it let out an ear-splitting shriek.

Bouma's fingers itched to grab an EMP grenade. "Get the hell out of the way!"

Ort grabbed Diego's suit collar and dragged him back toward Bouma's position while Bouma unleashed rounds at the spider. Just a second or two more, and the other two soldiers would be far enough away. The beast clogged up the corridor. It tried to push through using its spindly legs, which tapped and scraped against the deck and the bulkhead. Finally, laboriously, it pulled itself forward, crawling, squeezing through the narrow space. Mandibles and joints clicked. Gooey saliva dripped from its fangs.

Bouma snagged an EMP grenade and let it fly. Close-quarters was never a good place to let loose a grenade, EMP or otherwise. A frag grenade at this distance would pierce their suits with a thousand fléchette shards of shrapnel. An EMP blast, if it caught them too close, would fry their armored suits. It would freeze the humans inside them in place, making them vulnerable.

But there was no other choice.

The EMP grenade went off, and another shriek followed. The shield surrounding the spider shimmered before disappearing.

75

"Now!" Bouma yelled.

Shots punctured the monster's legs and bulbous thorax. Blue blood spilled from the fresh holes. The spider pulled itself down the corridor toward them, undeterred by its fatal injuries.

Legs gushing blood scrambled for purchase against the bulkheads, its claws leaving fresh silver gouges in the dust-covered metal. Bouma continued to shoot at the monster, riddling it with rounds.

Flesh and chunks of carapace flew from each impact across the alien's body. The beast's maw opened and closed as if it was already chewing on human flesh, but Bouma didn't let that frighten him. He stood his ground and continued pounding the alien with pulse fire. Its movements became jerkier until it finally crashed to the deck with a crack.

Blue fluid oozed out of the cracks in its armor. Bouma flicked off some of the gunk that had landed on his suit. He cautiously strode over the spider's legs and climbed over its body. Even through his armor, he imagined he could feel the heat escaping from the fresh corpse. Sliding down the other side, he scooped up the dropped RVAMP.

Only then did he pause to gulp down air and catch his breath. Ort and Diego came over the spider next.

"It's been a while since we faced those bastards," Diego said. He used the back of his gloved hand to wipe the spider's blood from his visor.

"Almost forgot how much of a pain in the ass they were." Ort jammed a fresh magazine into his rifle.

"Thanks guys, I owe you one," Diego said, taking point again.

Bouma merely nodded.

They prowled the rest of the way to the cargo hold. All the while, Bouma listened and watched for other signs of the Organics' presence.

Diego and Ort seemed equally transfixed by every creak from the ventilation ducts and each blast of wind pouring past them. But there was no more telltale evidence of another spider stalking them in the corridors.

"Maybe we got lucky," Diego said. "Just a lone spider left behind."

"Maybe," Bouma said. Luck had never really been on their side. Tenacity and pure force of will, maybe, but not luck. "These things are like roaches. Where there's one..." He let the words trail off.

"Hrrmph," Ort grunted.

A remaining emergency light glowed above another hatch. The corridor opened up around it, and Bouma found himself looking at a sign marked *Cargo Hold*.

"We're here," Diego said. "Bouma, grab a stash of that cryostat fluid, Ort, you grab some food and water, and then let's get the hell out of here."

God, it would feel good to be back in the crippled *Sunspot* now, Bouma thought. Back with Holly and the kids. He hadn't realized how much that ship had become a second home until he'd left it.

Bouma shouldered his rifle and stared down the sights, ready to fire on anything that moved in the narrow corridor around the corner. Maneuvering toward the edge of the open hatch, he got a clear view into the vast cargo hold.

As his aim roved over the crates of supplies, his stomach felt like it had plummeted straight into Mars's core. All across the cavernous space glowed a sight that had become far too familiar on Earth. They were everywhere. Striking, blue orbs, packed between boxes and vehicles, suspended from the rafters, all with skinny, desiccated bodies floating within them. They had found the crew of the *Radiant Dawn*.

And the crew was not alone. The hulking forms of spiders clambered all over the hold. Dozens upon dozens of them.

***

Captain Noble's gums felt like alligator skin, and his tongue was like the leather sole of a shoe. And that wasn't even the worst part. With his finger, he traced a line across his swollen lips. They were still sealed shut. No matter what he did, he couldn't get them to open.

He sat on the cold floor of the orb, arms wrapped around his legs.

Ribbit and Roots both watched him from their orbs. Although they weren't able to verbally communicate, he could tell both of the aliens were curious about what the multi-dimensional aliens had done to him. Roots once again hung from the top of his orb like a light fixture, his three compound eyes locked onto Noble. Ribbit croaked, then turned away. It waddled on its webbed feet and stick legs to the corner of its orb and then curled up, apparently no longer interested in Noble.

The captain wasn't the only one acting differently. The frog-like alien seemed lethargic, and the gooey slime that normally coated its green flesh was gone, leaving red cracks in its hide.

Noble watched Ribbit for a few more minutes while picking at his lips. His fingernails were already whittled down and bleeding from trying to claw his way out of the orb, but he did have part of a thumbnail left. He used the edge to saw at the flesh, back and forth, until he tasted the metallic hint of blood inside his mouth. He used his tongue to spread it around his dry gums, joining the little saliva he was still producing.

Ribbit let out another croak, a long melancholy noise that made Noble look up. They couldn't talk to one another, and the creature was annoying, but he still felt a connection with Ribbit, and with Roots. Almost as if they were friends.

Watching Kirt die had been torment, and seeing Ribbit sick could be the straw that breaks the camel's back.

He couldn't take much more of this.

Anger helped fuel sawing his lips with his thumbnail.

Come on. Come on…

Groaning, he finally managed to force them apart. He took in a long gasp of the muggy air, filling his lungs.

Blood trickled down his lips and filled the inside of his mouth. He spat a gob of crimson saliva out on the orb wall, the liquid sizzling as it hit the force field. The faint smell of smoke filled his space.

Ribbit had stopped croaking.

He checked on the alien above him. It was asleep. The creature's torso slowly moved up and down. Red goo slid down its hide.

Noble shook his head.

This was supposed to be some sort of alien Noah's Ark, right? But if the aliens were so advanced, why couldn't they keep their prisoners alive? First Kirt, then the alien in the orb to his left, and now Ribbit. He thought back to farms on Earth, and remembered images of farmers tossing diseased or even just potentially infected livestock out like trash.

Maybe the prisoners on this ship weren't important to the Organics, or perhaps they were just weeding out the aliens that didn't make the cut, like those farmers had their livestock.

Noble dragged his arm across his lips, smearing blood on his skin.

He moved over to the edge of his orb to look down. There was another human down there, somewhere, and now that he could talk again, he was going to try and communicate before the multi-dimensional aliens returned.

It had been so long since he'd spoken to anyone besides Kirt, and he had no idea who this other person was. Perhaps it was someone from his crew. But who? He thought back to the battle on the tarmac, when he had stayed behind with the team of soldiers to hold back the aliens while the *Sunspot* launched.

Most of the memories were vague, but he did remember watching Finn, Lucia, and Reynolds go down. The only person Noble could recall being captured, besides himself, was Kirt. In his mind's eye, he visualized the blue light pulling them into the monstrous belly of an alien ship.

He racked his memories, but his brain was slush. It hurt to remember.

Motion in the orb below finally pulled Noble back to reality. Roots moved from the ceiling of its orb down the side, using the wormy appendages to clamber across the surface.

Noble watched with fascination, trying to understand how the creature wasn't being affected by the electricity. An idea seeded in his mind as he sat there, watching. He spent a good hour studying the creature before he finally spoke.

"Hey, Roots," he said quietly.

The alien looked up at Noble. It was smart enough to know the name he had called it a hundred times. Perhaps it would also be smart enough to follow a command.

Noble pointed at his orb wall with a finger.

"Touch," he said.

Roots didn't seem to understand.

"Touch," he entreated, using his finger to point again.

Roots seemed to catch on, and used a spindly arm to reach out toward the orb wall. The skeletal tip cut right through the blue hide of the orb, the fingers slicing into the black space beyond.

"Holy shit," Noble whispered.

Roots tilted its bulb head from side to side as Noble clapped.

"Good job," he said, a little too loud.

He froze, waiting to see if his mistake had cost him. But the void between his prison and the orbs across the way remained empty.

So Roots could escape whenever he wanted? Why hadn't he done so already, then?

The answer loomed in Noble's head almost as soon as he proposed the question. Where would Roots go if he did escape? The alien would be asking to die trying to run around, lost, in this cavernous place.

If the aliens hadn't caught his stunt with Roots, maybe it was time to figure out who this other human was, trapped in here with him.

"HEY! Can you hear me?"

His voice was rough, his throat dry like sand paper. Despite the irritation, he continued yelling.

"I know there's another human here. Please, answer me before those things come back!"

Several of the alien prisoners replied in their otherworldly voices, but if there was another human out there, they were keeping quiet now.

Noble rested his voice, saving what was left for later. He drained his bladder on the floor, and watched as the liquid was absorbed. The technology here was amazing. That made it all the harder for him to understand how they could have such a hard time keeping their prisoners alive.

But then again, his body, and the bodies of the other aliens, like Ribbit, were fragile and mercurial. They weren't machines you could just program. Biologically, they needed nutrition, care, and even mental stimulation.

"Come on, say something!" Noble tried again.

But like so many other times, only silence answered.

He wasn't sure how long he rested on the floor, curled up and gripping his body, trying to stay warm. At some point, the floor of the orb rumbled under his flesh, the hum of the engines reverberating through the hull and bulkheads. He could feel it across his skin, and in his bones.

Ribbit heard it too, and started croaking at the sudden vibration.

Getting up on his hands and knees, Noble crawled over to the edge of the orb for a better view. Something was happening. The ship seemed to be accelerating at first, but then he realized the change in motion was actually the opposite.

They were slowing.

Noble pushed himself to his feet, the cord feeding him nutrients coiling. He stood there naked, his heart beating, eyes flitting rapidly. He had been waiting for something to happen for so long that he didn't quite believe this was real.

The ship continued to slow. This had to be it. After what seemed like an eternity of traveling, they were coming to a stop—they had finally reached their destination.

***

A small voice at the back of Diego's mind told him that his intuition had been right. Rushing into this ship had led them into exactly the type of situation he had wanted to avoid. His plan would've saved them from this.

But there was a much louder voice now.

In fact, many louder voices.

The spiders shrieked with the unholy wails of monsters reserved for nightmares. A hellish cacophony drilled into his eardrums. The cacophony threatened to drown his thoughts, but years of combat experience helped him focus.

"Use the RVAMP!" Diego yelled.

He let loose a barrage of rounds into the nearest spider. The monster stumbled into the spray and rushed them, mandibles opening and clamping shut, eyes glowing with animalistic fury.

Diego felt none of the confidence that wearing NTC battle armor or holding a pulse rifle usually gave him. He had spent so many hours running live-fire exercises and target shooting that his rifle had become an extension of his person. It was as much a part of him as his fingers were, and usually gave him a healthy dose of confidence. Now it seemed inadequate.

The spider and a half-dozen of its brethren followed, undeterred by his weapon. Some flickered and scurried across the ceiling, while others darted between the glowing blue orbs on the floor of the hold. Cargo crates spilled open as the spiders ran into them, and the scratch and scrape of the spiders' claws over metal rang out with palpable force.

"Where's that RVAMP?" Diego screamed over the spiders' crazed voices.

"I'm working on it!" Bouma yelled back. He pulled back the handle on the portable RVAMP and aimed it into the vast cargo hold. "Here we go!"

The RVAMP whined as it released its electromagnetic pulse. Diego could practically see the invisible wave as it washed over the spiders. Their shields shimmered, then fell. Their mandibles opened as if screaming in surprise. Several tumbled and tripped, and others trampled them, carried onward by their relentless momentum and hunger.

Diego, Ort, and Bouma unleashed a furious barrage of rounds into the spiders' ranks. The beasts crashed into each other. Legs blew apart and joints buckled. Blue blood ran freely from massive wounds carved by pulse rounds. This time, at least, distance and surprise were on their side instead of the spiders'.

Like machines, the three soldiers fired and switched to fresh magazines.

"Changing!" Ort yelled.

Corpses quickly piled in the spaces between the orbs and stacks of crates, but Diego was running through his ammo too damn fast. Even as the bastards fell, more of them poured out from the recesses of the cargo hold, while others punched through hatches from intersecting corridors. They filled the hold.

"There are too many!" Ort screamed over the din of gunfire. "Changing!"

Diego and Bouma covered Ort's firing zone while he jammed a fresh mag home.

A spider made it past the wall of corpses, swiping at him in answer. Dead arachnid bodies tumbled in a grisly landslide as the beasts scrambled over them. Diego aimed and fired on it until his rifle clicked.

"Changing!" he shouted. He let his empty magazine clatter at his feet, and replaced it with a fresh one. A quick inventory told him he had only three magazines left. And an even quicker assessment of the cargo hold told him that wouldn't be enough.

Another roar blasted from a distant corridor, shaking the bulkheads.

"What the hell was that?" Ort asked. "Changing!" He ducked behind a crate as he changed his magazine.

"Sentinel!" Bouma replied. "Big lizard son-of-a-bitch."

"Shit," Diego hissed. He fired on another spider.

This time there was no crack of armor or splash of blue blood. The alien careened toward them like a hormone-addled bull seeing red, its shields still up.

"We could use that RVAMP!" Diego said.

"Still recharging!" Bouma replied.

A fresh wave of spiders scuttled through the cargo hold. They crashed into each other, all bitten by the pangs of unbridled hunger. These had been hidden in corridors and areas of the ship beyond the cargo hold, and were unaffected by the initial RVAMP blast. And the flow of spiders showed no signs of stopping.

"EMP grenades out!" Diego ordered.

The trio sent the grenades out to disparate portions of the hold. Three flashes of light later, more of the spiders' shields had been temporarily shattered. The aliens ran headlong into the soldiers' rounds, as if they could tell they were almost out of ammunition.

Another roar from the Sentinel sent a tremor through the ship.

Rifle running dry, Diego knew this was it.

"Turn back!" he ordered. "Retreat!"

Their mission was a bust. There would be no retrieving food or water or ammunition or cryostat fluid here. The only thing to be gained here was death at the claws of these monsters.

"No!" Bouma said, laying down fire like a madman until his magazine emptied and he had to switch mags.

"We have no choice!" Diego said. "Move, move, move!"

Sophie was going to die. Hell, they were all going to die. If not now, then in a couple of weeks. Christ, things had gone from terrible to... hopeless.

The Sentinel's voice boomed again. This time it wasn't just the sound that rocked down the corridor.

"There it is!" Ort said, pointing down the corridor they had just gone through.

A reptilian head emerged from the shadows. Its eyes gleamed at the meager beams cast by Diego's helmet-mounted lights. The monster's claws bit into the bulkhead as it wormed its way forward. The thing barely fit in even this relatively wide corridor. It looked as if some ugly monstrosity was being birthed by a metallic beast. Muscles rippled under armor plates, and its shields gave off an evanescent glow.

Now even Bouma showed no hesitation. "Run!" he yelled.

Their boots clattered against the deck. Behind them, a

wall of clanging claws and demonic voices urged them on. Cold adrenaline blasted through Diego's blood vessels, and his muscles worked as if driven by pistons. There was no use even firing at the beasts now.

"Back to the Rhino," he yelled.

A new, infuriatingly calm voice rattled over their comms. *Sonya.* "Lieutenant, I have been able to interface with some of the working systems aboard the *Dawn*. Outboard cams show Organic activity on Mars's surface in close proximity to the ship. It appears many of the aliens have escaped the *Dawn*'s confines. You may have agitated a nest. They are beginning to race *away* from the ship."

"Why the hell would they do that?" Ort asked.

Diego's stomach flipped. Bouma shared a wide-eyed look that said he'd come to the same conclusion.

"They're looking for the *Sunspot*," Bouma said.

"Sonya, warn Emanuel!" Diego said.

"On it, Lieutenant," she responded.

The spiders shrieked and roared behind them, claws slashing at the ceiling and bulkheads. The Sentinel plunged through their ranks, crushing them beneath its hulking mass and tossing others aside like ragdolls.

Even if they escaped this horde, even if the team made it back to their Rhino, what then? Lead these bastards straight back to the *Sunspot* to ensure everyone else on Martian soil died?

They had been on the planet for no more than a couple of hours, and already their doom rose before Diego, a tsunami ready to crash down on him. He hadn't survived the depths of the dwindling oceans, the torturous route to the *Sunspot*, and then a disastrous landing on this planet, only to let all these people relying on him die.

Captain Noble had trusted him to protect Emanuel, Sophie, and the others.

I'm sorry, Diego thought. *I failed you. I failed them.*

The screams of the Organics stabbed at his eardrums. Their claws drew closer, their mandibles clicking with audible ferocity. Joints snapped and popped, echoing madly through the corridors. Desperation and despair hung heavy over Diego's racing mind.

Bouma and Ort ran beside Diego. They fired behind them sporadically, desperate to stem the mad rush of aliens flowing after them. Their labored breaths came over his comms, loud and clear.

A sudden heat welled up in Diego's chest. Bouma and Ort hadn't given up, and neither would he. There had to be a way out of this. A way to destroy these Organics and save the *Sunspot*. A way to give themselves just a few more days, maybe even just a few more hours, to come up with a better plan.

Improvise and adapt. That's how they'd come this far. That's how they'd outlasted nearly every single other member of the human race.

And that's how they would survive this battle.

Improvise and adapt.

— 6 —

"Emanuel looks scared," David said, looking up at Jeff. "We should do something."

They were both still in the med bay, and Emanuel was standing at a terminal speaking with Sonya, Holly next to him.

Jeff agreed with his brother, but Emanuel seemed focused, and Jeff didn't want to interrupt him. He couldn't make out everything the doctor was saying to Sonya. Then Bouma and Diego came through on the comm link.

"They're headed your way," Diego's voice rang over the comms, sounding out of breath. "We'll try to stop them, but there are so many… they're everywhere!"

"Shit," Emanuel muttered, the color draining from his face.

"Sonya, what's the status of the *Sunspot*'s weapon systems?" Diego asked.

"One turret station is functional," the AI said. "All comm relays, including intraship communications and remote control to the turret, are out. It can only be fired manually. However, there may be more damage than I can report. I've lost direct sensor and monitoring capabilities to almost everything else within that corridor."

"Any way to bring the other turrets online?" Emanuel

asked. As Jeff watched, his gaze swept over Jeff and David, then Sophie. His eyes lingered on her chamber before he turned back to Sonya's holographic image.

"I am afraid not," Sonya said.

"Is that dust storm going to be a threat?" Holly asked, staring out a viewport.

"It has appeared to shift direction," Sonya answered. "It may intersect with us, but the storm itself does not pose a threat to the *Sunspot*."

"Will it blow the Organics away?" Emanuel asked hopefully.

"My sensors detect the winds are not strong enough to thwart the Organics' advance."

Emanuel looked away for a second, and brushed his fingers through his hair. He let out a long breath. Jeff knew what that meant. Their dad had looked like that when he was really worried, which was rare. It was an expression of defeat and resignation.

"Doctor, if I may, I do have one suggestion," Sonya said.

"Yes, go ahead." Emanuel looked eager for some kind of answer. Jeff leaned forward. On this whole big spaceship, there had to be some other way to fight off the incoming Organics.

"I recommend that you immediately escort everyone to the agricultural biome," Sonya said. "After the Organic assault on this vessel and the subsequent crash, it is the section of the ship with the best structural integrity. The biome will offer the greatest protection against the Organics, and there is a sixty-six percent probability that it will prolong your survival for at least two to three hours."

"That's not a solution," Holly snapped. "We need

more than two hours."

"You may potentially have three," Sonya replied.

That was not the answer the adults were looking for. Jeff's eyes danced between Holly, Emanuel, and Sonya.

"What are we going to do?" David whispered, inching closer to Jeff.

He put an arm around his younger brother's shoulder. "Don't worry. We'll be fine. Bouma is out there fighting, and won't let the Organics get to us."

Emanuel and Holly were talking in hushed voices now. Jeff wasn't sure he really believed his own assurances to David. They'd seen how the Organics operated, and that even seasoned Marines like Bouma could lose to the aliens. Sergeant Overton hadn't been able to stop them.

Jeff looked at Sophie. He remembered when he'd first met her at White Sands, after he and David had fired on the Organics chasing her and Overton. She had returned the favor by saving him and David, whisking them away to safety, and ensuring they had a whole team to survive with.

"Doctor," Sonya said, appearing on the terminal's screen again, "the Organics are now within visual range. Diego and the others are still trapped aboard the *Radiant Dawn*. I estimate no more than fifteen minutes before the first spider finds the *Sunspot*."

Fifteen minutes, Jeff thought. That wasn't much time.

He remembered something else Sophie had once told him. Back on Earth, he, David, Owen, and Jamie had escaped the prying eyes of the Organics. The aliens' sensors relied on detection of water content to find their targets and steal the resource. However, those sensors had—what did she call it? A resolution limit? They could detect adult humans, but kids were practically invisible to them. That was how Jeff and David had stayed alive so long on their own: they had evaded the sensors and clung to the shadows, staying quiet and out of sight. They had only appeared at the most crucial moments to fire on the aliens. Maybe that was how he could save Sophie and Emanuel and Holly now.

"Bud, I got an idea," Jeff said.

David looked up at Jeff. His fearful expression had morphed into one of eagerness. "Yeah, what is it?"

"You want to save everyone?"

"Of course I do!"

"Then let's do it," Jeff said. He spoke louder, so Emanuel could hear. "Put us in the turret! The Organics can't detect us, so if things get worse, we can hide more easily while the rest of you stay safe."

Emanuel hesitated. "No, we can't..." There appeared to be some kind of battle going on in his head as he weighed the options. He glanced between the cryo chambers and Jeff. "Shit. Fine, go. Holly and I will prep the cryo chambers for moving, and wake the other two up."

"We won't let you down," Jeff said, already halfway to the hatch.

"Sonya said we don't have working comms or sensors up there," Emanuel said, "so run back here if things get bad. Otherwise, Holly or I will come and get you."

"You got it!" Jeff said.

"Please, be careful," Emanuel said.

"We will," David said confidently.

They ran up to the functioning turret. When they got there, Jeff settled into his seat and wrapped his fingers around the controls. He was ready to blast any Organics that dared to show their heads around here.

"Uh, Jeff?" David asked. "Aren't these pointed the wrong way?"

Jeff glanced at the display, which showed that the turret couldn't rotate toward the direction of the *Radiant Dawn*. They had no line of sight on the aliens. Jeff grimaced. These guns were next to useless. The spiders were going to come crawling all over the ship, and there was nothing they could do. Bouma wouldn't get back in time to deal with this first wave, either.

It was up to them.

"Do you trust me?" Jeff asked.

"Of course," David replied with enthusiasm.

"We're going to need to get off the ship."

"Get off the ship?" David said, his brows arched and eyes wide. "Emanuel told us—"

Jeff pressed a finger to his lips. "We've got to be quiet. It's the only way."

David nodded.

"Okay, let's grab our rifles and go."

They sprinted toward the armory. Once there, they scooped up a few magazines and a couple of rifles each. Jeff wanted to make sure they had extra weapons. None of the armor suits were built for their size. Even the smaller ones were too heavy, and Jeff had to strip the non-vital equipment. They were left with the bare minimum of environmental protection and, Jeff thought, their comms. Jeff tried talking into the helmet where he guessed the microphone was, and was rewarded by his words coming out of David's speakers.

"Looks like they still work!" Jeff said, donning his gloves.

The gloves fit loosely around Jeff's fingers. He walked around the armory a bit, testing the suit, and tripped over his boots a couple times before getting used to the poor fit. If his plan worked, he wouldn't have to do a bunch of running. He just needed to get outside with David and find a good spot. It shouldn't be too hard, given how rocky the terrain was.

They had to take out most of the armor plates from their suits. What they were left with was more of an oversized wetsuit than an armored suit, but it would have to do. Without the armor plates, they didn't have much protection. Then again, if they were relying on the armor to stop a spider's stabbing claws, they were doing something wrong. Jeff had seen that kind of armor break under a spider's duress with very little effort from the alien.

"We should take one of these, too!" David said, pointing to one of the portable RVAMPs Emanuel had made.

"Definitely!" Jeff said. He hoisted the device over his back. It was heavy, and forced him to hunch. It hurt quite a lot, as the straps made his poorly-fitting suit dig into his shoulders. Maybe it would be better when they were outside of the *Sunspot*'s artificial gravity. He'd heard the gravity on Mars was much weaker. Besides, he could deal with some pain if that meant he helped the rest of the crew. "Take some of those EMP grenades too, okay?"

"You got it," David said, scooping several into his pack.

"Ready?"

"Ready," David said.

They scurried back out of the wrecked armory and toward the nearest emergency exit airlock, where Jeff scanned the controls. There were a myriad of flashing buttons and displays. Since coming aboard the *Sunspot*, he'd never once thought about leaving it. Now he realized he wasn't sure how to initiate the right procedure to leave without sucking out all the atmosphere as they did so.

"What are you waiting for?" David asked.

"I need to figure out how to get out of here."

"Ask Sonya," David said.

"She'll tell Emanuel. Then they'll tell us not to go."

"Oh," David said, looking downtrodden. Then he scooted over to the opposite side of the airlock. "This says 'Exit'."

"Yeah, but—"

It was too late. David pulled down on a red handle. It locked into place, and the inner hatch slammed shut, followed shortly by the outer hatch spiraling open. Air rushed out like the winds of a hurricane. The suction picked Jeff and David up, and they tumbled outside. Jeff bounced over the rocky terrain, praying his suit didn't take any damage. When he skidded to a stop, he stood shakily. A few painful bumps cropped up around his butt and on his arms, but he didn't hear any hissing air, and there weren't any cracks in his visor.

"David!" he called over the suit's comms. "Are you okay?"

David was covered in red dirt. He stood and brushed himself off, then readjusted his pack. "I'm okay."

Jeff surveyed the horizon. Blue glinted over to one side. That must be the Organics. In the other direction, a rising dust cloud darkened the sky. That was probably the storm the adults were talking about earlier.

"Follow me," Jeff said.

They loped off over the planet's surface, winding between the rocky columns and ditches. Jeff enjoyed the decreased gravity here. It let him jump higher and farther.

He whooped with joy as David bounced along beside him, tumbling and laughing. It took some getting used to, but once he had it down, he could move across the landscape like Mario jumping over Goombas.

"There!" Jeff pointed to a rocky precipice overlooking the *Sunspot*. It was a perfect vantage point. There were plenty of nooks and crannies they could hide in if they needed to disappear, too.

They scrambled up the rock face and hunkered down in a position that gave them plenty to hide behind. David's eyes were glued to the incoming Organics.

"You sure you're up for this?" Jeff asked David, eying the spiders as they drew closer to the *Sunspot*. "It's not too late if you want to go back in. I can do this myself."

"I'm not going anywhere," David said. "Dad told us to stick together no matter what."

"No matter what," Jeff repeated. He almost grinned. This was like those days back on Earth in White Sands. Just him and his brother, fighting the monsters side by side. They could make a difference here. They could protect the *Sunspot*, make their dad proud.

Dust filled the air in the wake of the advancing monsters.

"Now?" David asked.

"No, not yet," Jeff said. His heart thumped faster. Adrenaline dumped into his blood vessels, and his fingers began trembling with nervous excitement. His body screamed at him to act now, but his mind was calmer. Bouma's lessons about patience and waiting for the right moment were stronger than the primal reaction hammering through him. "Don't do anything until they get closer. Then we use the RVAMP and blast them all."

More of the monsters accumulated in the narrow canyon.

"Now?" David asked, aiming the RVAMP at the spiders.

"Now," Jeff said. He helped David yank back the trigger. The RVAMP whirred, and let loose its electromagnetic pulse.

The spiders tumbled into the invisible force. David knew what that meant without Jeff having to tell him. They both picked up their rifles and let loose at the Organics in a concerted volley of rounds that sliced into the arachnid-like aliens. Because of the distance between them and the monsters, Jeff and David could take their time to line up devastating, well-placed shots. The bug-like creatures' heads burst in sprays of black armor and blue blood.

Each kill filled Jeff with grim satisfaction. This was how they would save Sophie and the others. This was all they had to do.

It was a massacre. The ambushed spiders didn't stand a chance. They lay across the ground in heaps of twitching legs and bleeding bodies.

"Nice job, bud," Jeff said, standing. He patted David on the shoulder.

David shook his head and pointed back toward where the first few spiders had come from. "There are more." There was fear in his voice, and Jeff quickly saw why. His brother was right, and they no longer had the element of surprise. Some of the Organics were scuttling up the rockface toward their position. Their legs moved in a blur, and their mandibles clicked together, hungry for prey.

Jeff raised his rifle again and prepared to fire, with

David following suit.

A shriek exploded from behind them before they could squeeze off a round. Several more otherworldly wails followed. The boys both whirled toward a pack of spiders that had flanked them.

In the face of this new danger, all Jeff could think was that Bouma would be disappointed. His pulse exploded in a frenetic drumbeat, and the rest of the world seemed to fade away. The first spider reared up in front of him, slashing the air with a flurry of sharp claws. There was no good way to defeat these monsters here.

There was only one option.

"Run!" Jeff yelled.

***

The corridors of the *Radiant Dawn* echoed with the shrieks of the spiders as the Sentinel crashed through them, choking the corridor. Bouma's nerves fired like powerful lightning blasts. Each step he took seemed like it wasn't enough. Adrenaline poured through him, but still he seemed to be moving far too slowly. The Organics were closing the distance at a gut-wrenching pace.

"We've got to do something," Ort boomed. Bouma glanced at him, and could see the sweat pouring down his face behind his visor. "If we don't, we're spider food."

"Almost to the Rhino," Diego said. "Just hold tight."

Sure, that might save them. They could take off and easily outpace the Organics. But Bouma knew what would happen if they raced straight back to the *Sunspot*: the Organics would follow. At the back of their minds, Ort and Diego were probably thinking the same thing, and Bouma guessed they didn't want to condemn the defenseless group sheltering there either.

Sonya's voice broke over their comms. "I've detected more Organics headed toward the *Sunspot*."

"More from the *Dawn*?" Bouma managed to ask as they ran.

"Negative, Corporal," Sonya replied. "There appears to be a considerable Organic force using the dust storm as cover."

"Shit," Bouma said. "Emanuel knows about this?"

"I have just informed him, as I have informed you."

"How many is considerable?"

"I've detected several dozen lifeforms ranging in size," Sonya said.

"No chance that they're human?" Diego asked.

"The probability is exceedingly low," she replied.

Now he knew with dreadful certainty that they couldn't lead these Organics back to the *Sunspot*. The battle there was going to be bad enough. Adding a hundred more of the aliens wasn't doing Emanuel or the others any favors.

"We've got to do something, and *now*," Bouma said.

"I'm nearly out," Diego said between strides, slapping the magazine hanging under his rifle.

"Wish we had one big bug bomb!" Ort said.

What Bouma wouldn't give for an oversized can of Raid...

Then it hit him. They did have a bomb.

"Sonya, you can access some of the *Dawn*'s controls, right?" he asked.

"That's correct," the AI replied.

"Can you access the ship's fusion reactor?"

"Yes," Sonya said.

"What's the status?"

"The reactor appears functional, but it was deactivated due to catastrophic damage to the containment chamber."

The wheels in Bouma's head continued to turn. This would be a long shot, but it might work. "Meaning what?"

"Catastrophic damage will lead to catastrophic failure and all but certain destruction of the *Radiant Dawn.*"

Diego caught Bouma's eyes for a brief second. The cold, nearly emotionless look usually present in the soldier's eyes had been replaced with one of abject fear. But Diego nodded back at Bouma, beginning to understand.

When Bouma risked a glance backward, his helmet-mounted light flashed over the ghoulish maw of a pursuing spider. The aliens continued to shriek behind them, and the Sentinel thumped through the corridor. The clicks of their joints snapped like staccato gunfire against the bulkheads.

Ahead was the hatch that would take them to the Rhino. It would be so easy to slip out of here and escape it all. But doing so would only delay the confrontation between man and alien.

"We have to detonate the ship," Bouma said.

Diego nodded, arms still pumping and boots crashing against the deck.

Blowing the ship was the right choice. But it came with a cost.

"All the supplies," Ort said.

"Doesn't matter if there are supplies if we all die," Diego said.

"We've got to save the *Sunspot,*" Bouma agreed. He hated what that meant. It was practically a death sentence for Sophie. The whole point of rushing this mission had been to save her life. Now they were risking everyone's.

"Sonya," Diego said, "overcharge the reactors."

"I am afraid I cannot do that, Lieutenant."

"Why the hell not?" Diego said. There was desperation in his voice now.

The hatch to the Rhino was directly in front of them. Spiders still churned behind them, and the Sentinel was battering its way through them in the choked corridors.

"There is a manual override for the engine shutdown that cuts off the reactors," she replied. "The previous crew must've set it off to prevent the ship from detonating. The only way to reset the override is to manually reset the switch in the CIC."

"Then I guess that settles that," Bouma said. "To the CIC. LT?"

"To the CIC," Diego repeated.

The exterior hatch that promised them a swift escape to their Rhino practically beckoned them. They could drive away from this disaster so easily. Escape into the rocky terrain of Mars.

Instead, up the ladders they climbed, heading toward the CIC. They reached the wide chamber with all its consoles and empty seats. There was only one terminal on: the communications array. This had been the siren call that had brought them here, promising some clue as to what had happened to humanity on Mars.

It seemed like they had found out.

"Where's that manual override switch?" Bouma asked. He searched the room for some big red lever or button. It had to be glaringly obvious, right?

"It's near the captain's console," Sonya droned back. "There is a touchpad there."

Bouma swiveled on his heels and lunged for the captain's console. The demonic chorus of spiders echoed into the space.

"Reinforce that hatch!" Diego ordered Ort.

The huge soldier started shoving loose consoles and broken equipment in front of the hatch. For all the effort he was putting into it, the barricade would not hold long. The maneuver might buy them an extra ten seconds. Mostly, they were relying on luck.

Bouma hoped there was no way the Sentinel would fit through that hatch. That certainly didn't mean the thing wouldn't try, though.

"We've got one more trick to keep them out," Diego said. He punched a command that put the CIC on emergency lockdown. Red lights flashed above them, and heavy, reinforced partitions slid over the hatches. The command segregated parts of the ship with strong barricades to contain depressurization and vacuum exposure. While the ship's atmosphere had already been compromised from the Organics' assault, reengaging the emergency lockdown initiated the repressurization of the CIC. Fresh air left over from the *Dawn*'s supplies hissed into the space, and Diego's HUD reported increasing oxygen concentrations and pressure levels.

"Could've just done that," Ort said. "Saved me the work."

"Every bit helps," Bouma said. "Slow down those alien assholes as long as we can."

Those alien assholes continued battering the CIC's entrance. That entrance was also their exit. Bouma wasn't sure how the hell they would get out. He brushed the thought from his mind. They would figure that one out when they got there—if they got there.

"How do I reset that override?" Bouma shouted.

Sonya responded in as calm a voice as ever, "Place your fingers on the touchpad."

This wasn't quite the big, red button Bouma was expecting, but he did as requested.

The screen remained black.

Something heavy threw itself against the hatch.

"It's not working, Sonya!" Bouma pressed his hand against it harder, hoping the gesture would be recognized.

"It should require a simple touch to wake the systems up," Sonya said.

"I don't care what it should do," Bouma said, "it's not doing it!"

More creatures screamed outside the hatch. The jarring sound of claws scraping against metal tore through the CIC.

"Oh, of course!" Sonya said, almost excited. "All the systems' emergency power has been rerouted to the communications array. I must reengage the emergency power systems to the CIC."

"Yes. Then please fucking do that!" Bouma said.

All at once, the lights flickered on. Terminals whined to life and displays glowed. Alarms barked and flashed until Diego slammed his fist on a command to mute them.

"Now, select the emergency override reset command," Sonya said. "You will need a second person to validate the command at the nav panel."

Diego nodded and ran to the nav panel. He reached toward it to confirm the command. Before his fingers touched it, the entire CIC shook with a violent fury. A monstrous roar blasted into the chamber. Part of the bulkhead near Ort bent inward.

"Ho-ly shit!" Ort said, scrambling to regain his balance.

The bulkhead started to tear. Metal screamed in protest.

"Hit that confirmation!" Bouma yelled.

Diego regained his footing and slammed his fist against the panel. All at once, a loud thrumming filled the CIC. The ship quaked, as if preparing to take off, and a host of new alarms flashed across their displays.

"Reactors have been reengaged and overloaded," Sonya reported. "Catastrophic failure imminent. I estimate we have no more than ten minutes before the first reactor experiences meltdown."

"Let's get the hell out of here!" Diego said.

The bulkhead continued to bow inward. Claws pressed through the twisted metal, and a spider forced its head in. Its mandibles ripped back, and it let out a scream of animalistic fury.

"RVAMP?" Ort asked.

"If you use the RVAMP in here, you'll fry the CIC's systems," Bouma said. "We can't risk that!"

Ort battered the spider's head with gunfire. The rounds slapped uselessly against its shield. It didn't even bother recoiling. Other claws forced their way around the spider's head, desperate to get at the humans.

"If we don't use the RVAMP or EMP grenades on these bastards, we're not getting out the way we came in," Ort said.

Bouma looked around the CIC for an alternate exit. All the scratching and screaming and clawing pressed on his mind. Other bulkheads were now bending inward, yielding to the Organics' attack. There would be no escape back through the ship. He felt as if he was stuck in a closing garbage compactor, watching the walls press in on him. Already he could hear his bones crack and flesh tear. The Organics would be on them soon, and even if they outlasted the aliens, they would die in the exploding reactors.

"Can't go through the corridors," Bouma said, "so let's make our own."

He pointed to the wide viewports at the front of the CIC.

Diego looked between the bending bulkhead hatches and the clear polymer viewports. "We're going to have to blow them, Ort."

"This is insane, LT. Can't use EMPs, but explosives are okay?" Ort said.

Sonya appeared on the CIC's fizzling screens. "The circuits controlling the power systems are better insulated against physical forces than they are against internal electromagnetic disturbances on the scale of your RVAMP device."

"Whatever you say." Ort nodded, and began setting a chain of explosive grenades along the edges of the viewports.

The AI continued. "It is better to—"

Sonya's image suddenly distorted, then was replaced by that of an unfamiliar AI. This one appeared garbled by a static snowstorm, its features elongated and blurred.

"I have… an important message," the AI said. Its face came into focus briefly before growing pixelated once again. Every word came out agonizingly slow. Bouma wanted to wrap his fingers around the AI's shoulders and shake it. "I am… Evangeline, the native AI… of the *Radiant Dawn*. Thank you… for bringing me online… again."

Bouma stood transfixed in front of the screen. It took only a second before a spider's bloodthirsty cry and the sound of tearing metal knocked him back to his senses. "Do you know where the colony is?"

"The location of the... colony... is... transferred to Sonya. I apologize... for the data... my systems are not fully functional."

"Is it safe from Organics?" Diego demanded.

"I... cannot answer... that with... certainty," the broken AI said.

Bouma glanced at the time display on his suit's HUD. They had only a couple of minutes left before the ship went up in flames.

"Just send us everything you *do* know through Sonya!" he yelled at Evangeline. "We've got to go!"

"Our damaged communications array... was unable to send you... the rest of our message," the AI said. "I would like... to amend it. 'Danger: high Organic presence detected within the vicinity of the *Radiant Dawn*. It is not recommended to land near this vessel.'"

"Oh, no shit?" Ort said, the sarcasm loud and clear amid the roars of the Organics tearing into the CIC.

"I estimate the friendly AI is too corrupt to provide any more useful data," Sonya reported.

"Then I estimate it's time to go," Diego said. "Blow the screens."

In Bouma's mind's eye, he saw the wreckage of all the other ships that had landed near the *Radiant Dawn*. Maybe they'd come to offer aid or, like the *Sunspot*, this was the only human signal they'd detected on Mars. Either way, if, by the grace of God, there were others out there making the journey from Earth to Mars, they might intercept the same signal. Even if they destroyed this ship, other AIs might be relaying the message, and more humans could be headed this way. His thoughts turned to Captain Noble. Surely that surly old seadog and his crew would find a way off the planet. Bouma would be damned if they didn't at least try to warn him that the *Radiant Dawn* was a trap.

"Wait!" Bouma said before Ort could set off the explosives. Ort shot him a bemused look. The *Sunspot*'s comm arrays had been damaged just like the *Dawn*'s had. But maybe… "Sonya, send an encrypted warning to all human AIs that might be out there. Tell them about the *Dawn*, and the Organics on Mars. They have to know that there's someone on this planet, but don't let them fall into this trap."

"It will be difficult to ensure the integrity of such a communication with either the *Dawn* or the *Sunspot*," Sonya said.

"If we're lucky, enough of the message will get through from each ship that someone back on Earth or flying through space will get it," Bouma said.

"As you wish." Sonya paused before relaying a new message. "To anyone that's listening, this is AI Sonya of the NTC *Sunspot*, broadcasting from Mars. We believe we have located the colony, but there are also Organics here and no sign of humans. Standby for more information." She sent the coordinates and then said, "I've programmed this as a repeating broadcast."

"Good," Bouma replied. He flinched as one of the hatches tore off the bulkhead. Broken pieces of displays and terminals flew with it, clattering about the CIC. The shuddering from the overloading reactors grew more violent.

"Blow the viewports! Now!" he yelled.

107

Ort depressed the button on his detonator. The reinforced polymer viewports blew away. The tug of the changing atmospheric pressure was immediate. Wires and chunks of broken terminals shot out the fresh wound in the CIC and across the bow of the *Radiant Dawn*. A loosened command chair tumbled toward Bouma. He twisted out of the way.

The tentacles of the changing atmospheric pressure wrapped around his limbs and tore at him, pulling at his armor. Over the storm of noise around him, he heard shouting. Howling winds, ricocheting blasts of shrapnel, roars from the overloaded reactors, and frustrated Organic screams drowned out the voices of his teammates.

He fought the instinct to grab hold of something, and let his body succumb to the violent wind. Everything around him blurred. His body was lifted into the air and carried out of the CIC as if by a tornado. He tucked into a ball to prevent his limbs or head from slamming into anything on the way out.

As soon as he cleared the jagged remains of the viewports, everything went silent. He was suspended in the air for a few moments before the low gravity carried him back to the planet's surface. He tumbled across the dirt. Ort and Diego hit ground a few feet away, leaving small craters in the red soil.

"That was a hell of a ride," Ort said, lifting his huge frame up from the dust.

"It's not over yet," Diego said. He pointed at the Rhino. "If we don't hurry, we're walking."

They dashed across the soil, bounding and leaping. The throbbing pain of exhaustion and lactic acid seeped into his overworked muscles. He didn't let that hold him back until they stormed into the Rhino. When he shut the hatch, a wave of relief surged through him. Diego jumped into the driver's seat.

"Go!" Ort yelled.

The vehicle roared off. The vehicle's whirring electric motors never sounded so sweet as that moment when the Rhino carried them away from the stricken *Radiant Dawn*. Diego gazed straight ahead, his focus fixed on the path ahead.

That gave Bouma a moment to assess which, if any, of the Organics were following them. They were forcing their way out of the hole in the CIC now. Spiders leapt down toward Mars's surface. Nothing they couldn't handle with their remaining ammo and a solid RVAMP blast.

A guttural screech followed, and Bouma snuck a glance over his shoulder to see the one thing they couldn't take down. The massive frame of the Sentinel, emerging from the gaping hole in the ship. Its reptilian body squeezed out of the torn metal as if it was hatching from a giant, silver egg. It reared back, and its jaws opened to let loose a roar. Rows of teeth gleamed in the weak sunlight.

The Sentinel slithered down from its perch as a tongue of blue plasma cut through the belly of the *Radiant Dawn*, a column of azure that torched into the sky. A second later, more fingers of plasma pierced the *Dawn*'s hull. Then a sudden flash of white light swallowed the entire ship. Organics thrown from the *Dawn* turned to ash in the resulting explosion. The ground trembled, shaking even the Rhino as it raced away, and a rolling cloud of dust swallowed them.

The men each ducked, to avoid any shrapnel that

might pierce the Rhino.

Bouma tried to temper the swell of victory as he watched the mushroom cloud form. The war wasn't over yet, but watching those Organic bastards go up in flames sure felt like a victory.

"Boom, boom," Diego said, making his fingers into a gun and aiming it back at the burning wreckage.

Bouma took off his helmet and mopped his brow with his glove. They had barely escaped with their lives, and were returning without the supplies they desperately needed. But they had found a piece to the puzzle about the fate of the colony. Even better, they had prevented any other humans from meeting the same fate as that graveyard of ships.

That didn't help Sophie, though. She was going to die if they didn't find more cryo fluid. And if they didn't locate supplies, everyone was going to die. How much worse could it get?

Emanuel's voice crackled over the comms. "Bouma, do you copy?"

"Copy."

"We got more Organics incoming."

"From the dust storm?"

"That's right," Emanuel responded.

"Yeah, we heard," Diego said. "We're getting our asses back there as fast as we can to help. But we took care of the bastards at the *Radiant Dawn*."

"I saw," Emanuel said.

There was a pause over the line. Bouma had worked with Emanuel long enough to know what that hesitation meant. A knot in his gut tightened.

"It's worse than we thought," Emanuel said. "Sonya's initial estimates were off. We're not talking about dozens of Organics. We're talking hundreds."

***

Diego let the cold wind of the airlock blast over him. It felt damn refreshing after everything they'd been through. He could focus on this moment forever, as if the rest of the world didn't exist. The small comfort between two hells.

Emanuel met them on the other side of the airlock with a harsh bite of reality. "Sonya estimates at least three hundred Organics are using that storm as cover." He led them away down the corridor. "There may be even more headed our way now, but it's impossible to discern with all the noise from the storm."

"I knew that blast wasn't going to go unnoticed," Diego said.

"Yeah. It may have saved us, and given us a bit of time, but now we've let every Organic in the region know we're here," Bouma said.

Diego rubbed his scalp. His hand brushed over the short bristles of hair, coming away doused in sweat. Body odor trapped in his suit found a way into the corridor, filling it with the scent of battle.

"Any chance you got the ship in flying condition while we were away?" he asked, hoping for a shower.

"The ship isn't going anywhere, and we can't stay here. Not with that horde barreling down on us," Emanuel replied.

"What about Sophie?" Bouma asked.

"Holly and I have prepared her cryo chamber for transport. We're going to need you guys to help load her into the Rhino. At least we can take her with us."

While we figure out what the hell we're going to do with her, Diego thought. He wondered if it was even worth trying to bring her with them. She was as good as dead. It didn't make sense to lug her around when what they really needed was to get out of here as fast as possible. But there was no way he could tell Emanuel that. It would only waste time, and add more stress to the situation. Tension was the last thing they needed right now.

He tried a different tack. "Do we know where we're going?"

"Yes and no," Emanuel answered. "Sonya has analyzed the rest of the message that was supposed to have been sent from the *Dawn*. We have a rough idea of where we need to go, but the *Radiant Dawn*'s AI was too damaged. It didn't give us a precise location."

"That'll have to be good enough," Diego said. He looked out through one of the portholes. The dust cloud was growing closer, and with it, the flicker of blue. He pointed out toward it. "Any direction is better than that one."

"Any idea what kinds of Organics we're looking at?" Bouma asked.

"Hard to say, but the odds aren't good." Emanuel shook his head and so did Bouma. They entered the medical bay in silence.

Holly was tending to Jamie and Owen, who were being woken up from their induced slumbers.

"Wish we could just stand our ground. I don't like the idea of running right now," Bouma said.

"The Rhinos aren't exactly meant for holding a crew long-term either," Diego agreed.

"We'll make them work," Emanuel said. "Our only chance is to run. Even if we could defeat this wave, they now know where we are. We can't hold this position forever."

"Ort, gather up all the ammunition and weapons we've got left," Diego said. "Bouma, help him."

The two disappeared into the depths of the wrecked ship.

"Can we move Sophie now?" Diego asked. Moving her chamber was going to be the hardest part of loading up the Rhino. Diego preferred to do that first in case they ran into any unforeseen complications.

"Yes. Like I said, she's ready," Emanuel said. He pointed to a motorized cart waiting to transport the cryo chamber. All the cryostat fluid tubes had already been attached to a mobile fluid filtration and oxygenation system. The difficult task would be positioning the chamber on the cart without losing control of it. Normally, the chambers were transported without people in them, so the carts weren't designed with sufficient redundancies to protect human life.

"How are the kids doing?" Emanuel asked Holly.

"They're coming to. The biomonitors point to full recovery for each of them. They'll be a lot better out of their chambers for this trip."

At least that was a welcome bit of news.

"Good. Jeff and David?" Emanuel asked.

"Running up to check on them next," Holly said.

Diego positioned himself near Sophie's chamber and snuck a glance at her as they prepared to move the chamber.

"When I unlock it, we need to slide it over these rails." Emanuel pointed to the half-meter-long track that ran from the chamber to the cart. "Ready?"

"Ready."

"On three. One, two, three." Emanuel hit the physical release button.

Pistons hissed as they drew back from the chamber's scaffolding. The heft of the chamber pressed hard against Diego. While the cart and track system carried most of the weight, it was still enough to push Diego backward. His heels slid across the smooth deck. He pressed his weight against the chamber, working desperately to slow it lest they lose control.

He stared hard into the chamber. Eyes closed, her light hair drifted around pale features that looked almost translucent. Blue vessels shone under her flesh, and her muscles flexed. Despite the state of her body, there was a calmness in her expression.

Diego had been there when she'd activated the RVAMP that had fried nearly all the nanobots in her bloodstream. He'd seen the pained expression on her face from a distance, and then she'd fallen unconscious.

Now she seemed peaceful. That had given some comfort to Emanuel, and Diego now saw why. But he couldn't help wonder if she had any idea what kind of hell was erupting around her. All because the others were determined to save her life.

"Push!" Emanuel said, breaking Diego's reverie.

They slid the chamber onto the cart, and both men let out a long breath of relief.

"Thank you," Emanuel panted. He started to move the motorized cart toward the corridor, but paused. "I appreciate what you did back at the *Dawn*, and I want you to know I'm grateful."

"No problem, Doc," Diego said. He studied Emanuel's sincere expression for a moment longer. It was then he realized how different the dynamics of this team were compared to any other he'd fought with. Except for Bouma, they were academic types and children, for God's sake. And, somehow, they had survived the nightmare when hardened soldiers like him had fallen at the claws of the Organics. Part of that was because men like Sergeant Overton and Captain Noble had sacrificed themselves so these people could live.

Diego tried not to resent them, but once again they were taking risks to save civilians. On the other hand, this is why he was a soldier. To help and protect people, especially the kids, who now might be the last remnants of humanity.

Suddenly he realized why Emanuel was so determined to save Sophie's life. There were no more governments. No militaries to defend them. There was no more Earth to return to. All they had was each other, and now, more than ever, every single human life counted.

Diego clapped the biologist on the shoulder. He regretted even thinking about abandoning Sophie, and the resentment he'd felt earlier. "Ready, Doc?"

Emanuel merely nodded before carting the cryo chamber down toward the Rhino. Diego helped push, realizing exactly what the mission required of him—the same mission Captain Noble had been intent on: to protect what was left of the human race at all costs, even if it meant laying down his own life.

— 7 —

"How are you feeling?" Holly asked, brushing back Jamie's hair. The med bay still hummed with the intermittent beeps from the biomonitors hooked up to the children.

The young girl yawned and stretched her arms, balling her hands into fists. "I'm so sleepy. I've never been so tired."

"That'll wear off after a while. Nothing hurts?"

"No." Jamie's eyes opened wider. "Should it?"

"No," Holly said. She curled her fingers around the rail along Jamie's bed. "Do you remember where you are?"

Jamie examined the bulkheads around them. "The spaceship…" She blinked rapidly, as if recalling a painful memory. "The last thing I remember are the aliens."

"They aren't on the ship," Holly said, reaching out to reassure the girl. The child shivered, and Holly used her other hand to stroke Jamie's hair.

But Holly couldn't hold her forever. Owen needed to be roused next. Then medical supplies and food had to be loaded. Any remaining oxygen supplies had to be moved to their escape Rhino. What the children needed most right now was time to adjust to their new environments peacefully. Working Jamie and Owen into a panic wouldn't help anyone.

As calmly as she could, Holly continued in what she

116

hoped was a soothing voice. "We need to get going now. Your legs are probably going to feel like jelly, but can you stand?"

Jamie sat up, then swung her legs over the side of the patient bed. Holly helped her slide off.

"It feels funny," Jamie said. "Like a bunch of needles are in my legs."

"It's going to feel like that for a little bit," Holly said. She helped Jamie walk across the med bay floor. "Keep walking around until you feel comfortable."

What she didn't tell the girl was that she wanted her to be able to run if they had to. Holly glanced at one of the terminals attached to a bulkhead. Sonya was displaying a live image of the encroaching dust storm on the wall-mounted screen. A few blue dots shone like beacons at the storm's perimeter. Those were the Organics leading the charge. In the corner of the display, a timer counted down. They had no more than thirty minutes before the Organics would be on them. If they hoped to escape in the Rhino, they needed to leave much sooner than that.

The hatch to the med bay swung open. Bouma entered, hair matted and flesh glistening with sweat. His muscles pressed against the white t-shirt he wore.

"Sophie's loaded, and we're grabbing all the food and water we can scavenge," Bouma said. "Ammo's in there. Emanuel sent me back up here to grab the rest of the medical supplies."

"Everything's ready over there," Holly said, jerking her chin toward one of the tables.

A few crates and bags were packed on top of it, containing everything from emergency surgical supplies to the last few liters of cryostat fluid.

"I'm on it," Bouma said. He started to walk toward the

supplies, then abruptly paused and turned back to Holly. He threw his arms around her and planted a long kiss on her forehead. A comforting warmth spread through her body, radiating from his strength. She lingered in his grip, letting the rest of the world fade away for that moment. Finally he pulled back from her.

"I was worried to death about you," Holly said. She felt Jamie's eyes on her as the girl continued walking around the med bay to wake her muscles, but she kept her attention on Bouma.

"Going to take more than a few Organics to kill me. You should know that by now," he said.

Holly chuckled, and then gave Bouma another hug. When she pulled away, he snuck another brief kiss.

"Ewwww," Jamie said, making a face.

"Sorry kid," Bouma said, grinning. He scooped up the medical supplies and hurried back to the Rhino.

"He really likes you," Jamie said.

"And I really like him, too."

Holly's heart ached. She dreamed of a life back on Earth where she was still working at her clinical practice, and dating Bouma in the normal way. But at least they were still alive. Their relationship was like a solitary floating beam in the middle of a shipwreck. It kept them both afloat, and gave them hope of a future together.

Holly patted Jamie's shoulder. "Now can you help me get Owen up?"

"Okay."

A few minutes later, and the boy was yawning and coming to in his chamber. They walked him through all the checkups Holly had performed on Jamie. The girl seemed to take pride in helping get the younger boy up and moving. That was good. The job might distract her from their otherwise deteriorating situation.

Time was running out, but Holly couldn't tell the kids that or they would lose it. Waking them so quickly had been risky enough. Their psyches had bent and flexed on Earth, but adding too much stress too fast after abruptly interrupting their cryo slumbers could break them.

The kids were healthy enough to be outside the protective cocoon of those chambers. Sophie, as far as they knew, still could not survive without the protection of the cryostat fluid holding her biological systems in balance. At least, with the kids out of their chambers, they had an extra few days' cryostat fluid they could add to Sophie's supply.

Sonya appeared on the screens throughout the medical bay. "The Rhino will be fully charged and ready to depart in five minutes."

"Thank you, Sonya," Holly said. She bent down to eye level with Owen and Jamie. "Hear that? We're going for a ride soon. You two ready for that?"

"Yes!" they said together.

Emanuel's voice crackled over the comms next. "Holly, I'm still securing Sophie's chamber into the Rhino. Can you get Jeff and David?"

"On it." She led the two children, hand-in-hand, out of the med bay and down the corridor toward the turrets. She tried to portray a cool appearance—anything to keep the kids calm.

"What are Jeff and David doing?" Owen asked, rubbing his eyes.

"They're looking out for Organics in one of the turrets," she replied.

Jamie just nodded.

Holly forced a smile. "We're lucky to have them

watching our butts."

It was good that the children had such powerful, resilient personalities, but she hated to see such young children have to take on the role of soldier. It was just the world they lived in now.

As they hurried up the ladders toward the turret where Jeff and David were keeping watch, cold sweat beaded over Holly's palms. The children looked up at her with scrutinizing eyes.

"We have to hurry," Holly said.

"The monsters are back, aren't they?" Jamie said, matter-of-factly. "That's why we're in such a rush."

Holly wanted to protect the children, but she couldn't hide behind a lie. "We're safe for now, but we need to leave the ship to stay safe."

Owen looked at his boots, and Jamie trembled slightly.

"It's going to be okay," Holly assured them. "Don't you trust me?"

They both nodded.

"Good," she said. "Now follow me."

They rounded the corridor past a jumble of broken wires and a singed bulkhead. The smell of burned plastic still hung, acrid and heavy, in the air.

"Jeff, David!" Holly called as they approached the hatch to the turret. Only the slight hum of the ship's reactors and the whoosh of air through the ventilation systems answered her. She called their names a little louder, and once again they didn't respond.

"One minute and we should be out of here," Emanuel called over the comms.

"Copy," Holly replied. She opened the hatch, and scanned the empty seats in the turret.

Cracks spiderwebbed over the damaged viewport, and

the displays on the turret glared red with a message that simply said, "ERROR."

She felt like a parent who had lost her children in a foreign city. *Maybe they went to one of the other turrets?* she tried to tell herself.

But both of the other turrets had been irreparably damaged, crushed against the planet's surface. While it was possible to get into them, there was no space to operate the cannons.

"Where'd they go?" Jamie asked innocently.

"Maybe they're hiding," Owen offered.

Even without the display ticking down in the med bay, Holly could practically see the seconds ticking by. "Come on," she said, waving the kids onward. They hurried down the corridor to a working terminal.

"Emanuel," she said, as calmly as she could, "Jeff and David aren't in the turret."

"What do you mean?" he asked.

"I mean they're gone," she said. "Can you have the guys check the corridors on your end?"

"Wait… What the hell do you mean they're gone?"

Rapid footsteps exploded down the corridor. They echoed tinnily against the bulkhead. Bouma appeared at the door, breathing heavily. "The armory," he said between breaths. "I went back to grab the last of our suits. We're missing two."

That knot in Holly's gut tightened. What the hell were Jeff and David up to? Leave them alone for a few minutes… Her eyes searched the damaged corridor. Behind Bouma was an emergency airlock. Holly ran to it. The children trailed her, peppering her with questions. She couldn't respond to them now. Once she reached the hatch, she pressed her palm against the dust covered window and peered inside.

The outer hatch was still hanging open.

"What about the GPS units?" she asked, the words spilling out of her mouth faster than she could think. "Can't we activate their comms?"

Bouma cursed under his breath and held up one of the headsets.

"I found these. It's supposed to be attached to the suits," Bouma said, "and has their tracking and comm equipment. They're heavy." He turned away for a second as if gathering his emotions. "They must not have worn them because they're too big."

"What are you saying?" Holly asked. "We have no way to contact Jeff and David?"

Bouma shook his head.

***

Emanuel stared at the display panel in the Rhino's cockpit as it sat within the *Sunspot*'s vehicle hold. The dust storm would be on them in fifteen minutes. That meant they needed to leave now if they stood any chance of escape.

"Where the hell are Jeff and David?" Diego asked, starting the motors. They whirred to life with an electric hum. The vehicle shook slightly, as if it too was growing impatient.

"They were supposed to be in that turret, but must have left to defend us," Emanuel said. "Sonya, broadcast over all public channels. Make sure Jeff and David know we are leaving *now*."

The AI followed the order, her voice booming inside of the ship.

Emanuel waited a second. "Nothing?"

"I have relayed your message over all relevant frequencies."

"Son of a..." Emanuel trailed off. He couldn't understand why Jeff and David would have taken off without telling him, unless they were trying to prove something.

He cursed again. That's exactly what they were trying to do, and it wasn't the first time.

Ort jumped aboard the transport, rocking it slightly. His face was flushed, and he was breathing heavily. "There's no sign of them on the ship. Holly and Bouma think they took an emergency exit."

"We have to search for them," Emanuel said. He looked at Diego for a second, ready to argue against any protests. These were kids, for Christ's sake. They'd saved Sophie and the team before, and Emanuel sure as hell wouldn't leave them alone on the surface of some God-forsaken planet with a swarm of violent aliens descending on them.

But Diego surprised him. "Absolutely. They didn't take a Rhino, so they were on foot. They couldn't have gone far."

A flurry of footsteps announced the latest arrivals. Holly and Bouma helped Owen and Jamie into the Rhino. The modified electric truck was expansive, but with Sophie's cryo chamber in the rear cargo hold, and the latest additions, it was quickly becoming cramped.

"Sonya, initiate a hard copy transfer to the Rhino," Emanuel said.

"Transfer in progress," Sonya said. "Soon all my systems will be integrated completely with the Rhino."

"Everyone in?" Diego asked, sliding into the driver's seat. "We're going to find those kids. Sonya, can you complete the transfer while we're on the move?"

"As long as we're within a 500 km range," she said. "It should take me no more than an hour."

"No way we can go 500 km in an hour," Diego said. "Looks like we're in the clear. Here we go."

Diego punched a button on his console, and the vehicle hold's hatch spiraled open. Dim light flooded into the bay. Winds carried red grit inward, swirling it around the vehicle.

Emanuel settled in beside Holly and the children. "We're ready to—"

A loud explosion burst somewhere above them. Emanuel grabbed a strap in the Rhino's ceiling to prevent himself from being thrown forward. The ship rocked as if hit by a tidal wave. A steel beam slammed into the deck behind them, denting it and sending up a shock of metal shards. The children cried and leaned into Holly.

"What the hell was that?" Ort asked.

"The Organics appear to have a new land-based weapon," Sonya answered him.

An image appeared on the screen, focused on one of the aliens marching amid a blanket of swirling dust. Emanuel's stomach churned. Nearly three times as large as a spider, the alien looked somewhere between a tank and a scorpion. It moved on thick, armor-plated legs, and a huge tail coiled behind it. At the end of that tail was a glowing orb. But this was clearly not the type that encased humans. Instead, it looked like a hot ball of plasma.

"It's just going to sling that shit at us, isn't it?" Ort asked.

"Goddamn Slinger," Bouma said.

True to their suspicions, the Slinger launched the plasma ball. A few seconds later, a violent blast tore through the *Sunspot*. Chunks of bulkhead crumbled away as a fresh hole appeared above the Rhino.

The counter Sonya had started didn't take into consideration long distance weapons, but rather the speed at which the Organics were marching toward the *Sunspot*. These new monsters were going to tear the ship apart before the swarm even got there.

Diego punched the throttle, and the Rhino jolted forward. They jetted out the crooked hatch, damaged from the attack on the ship. The Rhino's wheels spun in the air until they landed onto the planet's surface, then tore into the dirt, kicking up a wide spray behind them. The storm roared in front of them. Two more plasma balls sailed overhead. One smashed into the *Sunspot*, tearing a massive hole in one of the biomes at the stern of the ship. Metal caved in as if it was paper. The other plasma projectile splashed into the dirt near the Rhino. The super-heated matter was hot enough to melt the dirt and dust into globs of slag that shattered against the Rhino's side.

Emanuel tried to ignore the worried exclamations around him as the others turned their eyes toward the sky. He searched the horizon, the rocks, the cliff faces, but he didn't see any sign of the boys. If they were out here, they wouldn't survive long, especially with these Slingers now hammering the landscape.

More plasma erupted around them, launching geysers of dirt and rock around the *Sunspot*. If the ship had stood any chance of flying before, it most certainly didn't now. Melted slag from the hull flew off when another round hit. Jamie and Owen were wide awake now, screaming and crying in terror despite Holly's best efforts to comfort them.

"Sonya, any way to make that transfer faster?" Emanuel asked.

"Negative, Doctor," she replied. "Bandwidth is limited by the Rhino's data transfer capabilities, which I fear are vastly inferior to the *Sunspot*'s."

Great…

If the ship was dismantled before she could complete her transfer, they might be stranded on the planet without a ship or AI support. Their future looked bleak enough as it was, but without her, they would be both blind and deaf.

"Diego, take us around the bow of the ship," Emanuel said. "Everyone, keep your eyes peeled for footprints or anything leading from that airlock. That should help us find them."

Diego glanced at the display mounted near the dashboard. The timer there blinked red, indicating it was far past their deadline to leave the vicinity of the *Sunspot*.

Emanuel searched their route for the kids. Two boys on foot with pilfered EVA suits and weapons. It shouldn't take that long to find them. But trying to drive a comprehensive perimeter around the ship searching for potential locations wasn't going to work. They simply didn't have the time.

Then Emanuel realized he was asking the wrong question. He shouldn't be wondering *where* they went. He had no way to properly answer that without first knowing *why* they left the turret.

The boys had been tasked with keeping an eye out for incoming Organics. Emanuel knew enough about them that he could expect them to take that responsibility seriously. Even back on Earth, Jeff was willing to act like—often did act like—a young warrior. And the boys were no strangers to firearms.

Emanuel's gaze went back to the turret perched atop the *Sunspot*. He didn't know much about being a soldier, but Sonya had warned them that the turret offered only limited sightlines.

"Bouma," Emanuel started, "if you were going to defend the *Sunspot* against the Organics coming from the *Dawn*, where would you hole up?"

Bouma seemed to sense immediately what Emanuel was getting at. Another two plasma blasts crashed into the landscape before he answered. "The direct route from the *Dawn* was concealed by all those rocky columns and canyons." He indicated the hills and crags around them. "So this place really wouldn't do. But you could go over there."

He pointed toward a path that lead through the rocky hills. "You'd have the higher ground, some shelter, and good sightlines to the path from the *Dawn*."

The Rhino banked hard in the dirt, its suspension whining from the abrupt turn. Diego aimed toward the vantage Bouma had pointed at.

Come on, Jeff, David, you better be up here, Emanuel thought.

A few more blasts kicked up dust and shrapnel clouds. The wind began to howl more fiercely as the storm approached, and grit ground against the Rhino's outer shell. They wheeled around the bottom of a cliff, all eyes searching the precipices for any sign of the two boys.

"Look!" Ort said.

Emanuel's heart beat rapidly in excitement. "The boys?"

Ort shook his head, still staring out the window.

In the center of the pathway was a pile of dead spiders.

Their blood, still giving off a wet sheen, soaked the soil. Tendrils of steam rose from their corpses. Jeff and David had definitely been here.

Another plasma blast chewed at the side of the *Sunspot*.

"Catastrophic reactor failure," Sonya reported over their comms.

Plasma vented from the wound in the *Sunspot*'s side, tearing through the sky toward space.

"What's that mean for us?" Emanuel asked the AI.

"Uncontrolled plasma expansion is imminent," Sonya replied. "If you are caught in this expansion, the vehicle will be incinerated. Total loss of life is likely."

Panic strangled Emanuel. The boys were nowhere to be seen despite the evidence they'd been here. And now they were really out of time. Not only was there a horde of beasts barreling toward their location, but a reactor failure threatened to vaporize them.

Emanuel's stomach sank at a surfacing question. What if Jeff and David had returned to the *Sunspot*? If they didn't have any comm equipment, surely that's where they'd be headed if they were no longer here. They could've just missed them!

An earsplitting roar like sustained thunder rumbled over the Rhino. Plasma blasts punctuated the din.

"It's going to blow!" Diego said. He looked just as pained as the rest of them when he turned back. "We have to get out of here."

Emanuel didn't want to. He couldn't give the order. Couldn't tell them to abandon the search. Couldn't leave the boys to die like this.

Another plasma blast slammed into a nearby cliff. A wall of force bashed the vehicle, and rocks poured over them. An alarm somewhere in the Rhino sang, but

Emanuel's ears were already ringing. Even the near-deafening roar of the failing reactors seemed to be fading away. When the next blast hit, all he heard was ringing as the Rhino threatened to topple sideways. Jamie and Owen screamed.

Diego was looking back at him, still waiting for the command. There was no more time to delay. They could try desperately to use these last seconds in the ill-fated hope that they'd run across Jeff and David, but that promise was so tenuous and unsubstantial. He couldn't let Jamie, Owen, Sophie, and all the others die here.

Emanuel felt sick when he nodded at Diego, yelling "Go!" as loud as he could amid the chaos.

The Rhino shot away from the *Sunspot* and the rocky outcroppings where Jeff and David had killed the spiders. A wake of dust kicked up behind them, quickly swallowed by the strengthening winds. Brief flashes of blue plasma impacting the land around the *Sunspot* burst in the distance.

As the Rhino climbed a dune and crested the top, a piercing white light bloomed from the *Sunspot*. The ship disappeared, and, with it, the horizon.

— 8 —

Athena had run on and on until she couldn't go any farther. For the past hour, she had evaded the Organics hunting her by keeping ahead of the pulsating blue glow. But she couldn't keep going. Her body was spent, and dehydration had brought her to the ground.

She lay on the sand, staring toward the south, at what should have been salvation. The buried submarine she'd called home for so long wasn't far away. In fact, it was close enough her crew would probably be able to hear her if she shouted at the top of her lungs.

The star-filled sky illuminated the bulging hill covering their hideout. She flipped on her night vision goggles to ensure the gusting wind hadn't exposed the metal exterior.

It looked secure, and she planned on keeping it that way. Although she was within running distance, she couldn't risk being spotted entering the hatch. Giving away the location of the GOA would end in her death, and that of her crew.

All she could do was lie here, partially buried by grit, and hope the aliens passed her by or that she made it until morning without being spotted.

The crest of the slope she lay on provided a decent view of the area from all directions. She squirmed slightly for a better view of the seabed behind her, and scanned the green hue for hostiles.

She still hadn't seen whatever was out there, besides the glowing and pulsating blue light back in the ravines, but the whistling told her this was a different type of alien. She'd never heard a noise like it before.

The sound persisted, rising and falling with the wind.

She pulled the final magazine from her rifle and checked the load.

Only half left, she thought.

The remaining EMP grenade was half buried in front of her. She had used the other one escaping the city. It wasn't much, but it was better than being unarmed.

Using the utmost care, she shoveled sand over her body. She dug her boots and legs into it, covering most of her lower half.

The scratchy whistling grew louder, the aliens closing in from what sounded like all directions. A panting noise followed, and she glimpsed the first sign of the beasts tracking her in the carpet of blinking light that roved over the humps of sand to the north. She shut off her night vision goggles to watch the blue light glimmer over the side of a sand dune.

Gray armor covered the upper half of the nearest beast's human-sized body. Two limbs, ending in scissor-like claws, stabbed at the sand to pull the bulbous upper body forward, while a long snake-like tail slithered behind. A crustacean face searched the sand with black beady eyes. Slits for nostrils sniffed at the air. It was this action that produced the abrasive whistling noise.

Athena held the magazine just under the rifle, not daring to click it back into the slot. She remained prone while three more mounted the hills. Other than the whistling, they moved silently despite their undoubtedly heavy armored shells.

Terror gripped her as she lay there, watching the glowing creatures snake back and forth, sniffing the air for a scent. They were heading south, away from her position, thankfully, but right towards the buried GOA. If those elongated claws penetrated the shallow sand above the sub, they would clank against the metal. She wasn't sure how intelligent these beasts were, but had a feeling they would investigate.

Please no. Please…

She watched silently, begging in her mind for the aliens to change course. But the pack continued heading right for her sleeping crew. The time for lying idly by was over.

Athena carefully pushed the magazine back into the rifle, and pulled back the slide to charge it. The click rang out into the night.

Three of the aliens continued their hunt, but the fourth stopped in the sand and turned in her direction, its unblinking eyes scanning the darkness. Rearing its armored head back like a wolf howling, it sniffed at the dry air. The gray plates covering its back pulsated blue as it took in each breath.

A ghostly screech followed. The glow from the other aliens was not two hundred feet from the GOA. They froze.

Athena grabbed the EMP grenade as soon as the pack darted toward her. She pushed herself to her feet using her rifle as a crutch, the sand sluicing off her body. Dizziness rushed through her, blinding her momentarily with stars across her vision. It cleared to the sight of the four aliens slithering in her direction.

"Come on, you bastards," she whispered, clicking the EMP grenade. She studied their movements, trying to time her throw.

If she could bring down their shields, maybe she could kill all four with her remaining pulse rounds. Her main goal was to draw them away from the GOA, but if she died, then the coordinates Alexia had given her, of both the vehicles and the Pelican Air Force Base, would die with her.

She couldn't fall before she delivered the message.

The beasts closed the gap over the desiccated seabed quickly, using their claw-tipped limbs and tails to propel them across the sand at an impressive speed. The lead creature was a good one hundred feet in front of the others, making the toss of her grenade difficult to time.

Another few seconds passed, and then she lobbed it over the creature's clunky head. It slowed and twisted to watch the grenade sail through the air and land in the sand. But instead of continuing toward her, it turned and slithered toward the device. Using its tail, it slapped the grenade away, sending it spinning over the top of a hill.

The detonation thumped on the other side. A wave rippled through the sand and hit the monster, bringing its shield down in a flicker of blue.

Athena aimed her pulse rifle. A trigger pull sent a burst of blue rounds that tore gaping holes into the alien's armored midsection. The beast slumped to the ground, teal blood gushing out into the sand.

The other three aliens let out guttural shrieks. She lined up her next shot at the closest one and pulled the trigger again. This time the rounds ricocheted off its shield.

Athena's heart sank.

The aliens barreled past their dead comrade, undeterred by the harmless rounds. She took a few steps back up the slope, stopping at the crest.

Heart pounding, she finished the rest of her magazine in three bursts. They hit with enough force that two of the creatures stumbled. The third and largest of the beasts recovered quickly, its shield pulsating and solidifying over its armored body. It slithered up the hill, both black eyes focused on Athena.

She resisted the urge to scream into the armored face that opened into a black hole so wide she could see down the monster's throat brimming with barbed teeth. Two long fangs hung from the maw, saliva dripping off their razor-sharp tips.

Now Athena knew what had sucked the water from Marlin's body.

And she was next.

She held her gun like a bat, preparing to swing. A red tongue shot between the two fangs and then retreated back into its gaping mouth.

Athena let out a whimper when the alien slithered forward. She swung the rifle, but the beast parried the attack with a smack that sent the rifle cartwheeling away. It wasted no time barreling into her and wrapping its long tail around her chest. Pinned to the sand, she struggled, squirming and swatting with her right hand. The crab face lowered toward her visor. The shrill whistle from its slotted nostrils sounded her fate.

"No, please don't," she pleaded.

Athena knew her words and her fighting were useless. When had the aliens ever shown any mercy?

The fangs slammed against her visor. Fractures spread in a spider web across the glass. Another impact shattered the glass. She could almost feel her brain slamming against the inside of her skull. Her world started to turn black, and a heavy weight tugged her eyelids closed.

The whistling grew louder and the alien's rancid breath rushed over her face. Her lungs filled with the scalding air. She forced her right eyelid open to the sight of the half-moon hovering over the horrendous features of the monster.

She lay, paralyzed by fear, as the beast prepared to drain the water from her body. The leathery tongue flicked out, caressing her cheek, as the monstrosity lowered its fangs toward her exposed face. Boiling saliva lathered her skin. Unable to speak, unable to scream, she simply held in her final breath.

Another whistle sounded in the distance, followed by a low rumble, and the ground vibrated under her legs and boots. It took a second to realize this wasn't from the other beasts sniffing the air. Three figures ran toward her position. A black crater smoked at the bottom of the slope, where an explosion had impacted between the other two monsters. Seconds passed before her mind registered what had happened. Her friends had come to her rescue, using rocket-propelled grenades to bring down the shields. One of the beasts dragged the upper half of its body with its pincer arms, its tail connected to its torso by only a few sinewy strands of flesh. The other creature was a pile of smoldering shell.

Pulse rounds tore into the dying alien's armored back. A long hiss escaped the grotesque creature as its body collapsed into the sand.

The eyes of the monster holding Athena followed the approaching GOA soldiers. Each black orb clicked inside its socket as it moved, placid and emotionless.

They fired pulse rifles at the slope and screamed.

"Watch your fire!" one of the men yelled. "There she is!"

A round sizzled past Athena's helmet, and three more slammed into the creature's shield. Everything around her seemed to melt together in a kaleidoscopic fury. The alien let out a screech and retreated down the other side of the hill, leaving her gasping for air.

"Corporal!" someone shouted.

The soldiers surrounded her, but she couldn't move. Paralyzed, she lay there, staring up through her shattered visor, the stars gleaming like orbs in the sky.

"Corporal, are you okay?"

The voice belonged to Kyle Griffin, the former Marine turned NTC contractor. Now that Walker was dead, he was the most experienced fighter they had.

He knelt by her. "Can you move?"

"I... I don't know," she replied. She managed to wiggle a toe, and then her foot. Griffin cradled her under her back and legs.

"I'm going to carry you back to the GOA," he said. "Taylor, Malone, you two hold security. Make sure we're not followed."

"We have..." Athena muttered. Her mind swam. She gasped for air, the heat searing her lungs. "We have to get to the vehicles."

"Just hang on, Corporal," Griffin said. "You're going to be okay now."

"The vehicles... the military base... the other survivors... we have to get to them..." she mumbled the words, but darkness was closing in. The star-filled sky mesmerized her as Griffin carried her back home to the GOA.

***

ENTRY 10199
DESIGNEE – AI ALEXIA

Lolo passed over the *Ghost of Atlantis* location during the night. I hacked into the satellite's operating system and then proceeded to watch what was happening on the surface. What I saw would have given a human anxiety.

Corporal Athena Rollins was saved with not even a second to spare by a fire-team of soldiers that killed all but one of the aliens. The satellite is coming in for another pass, and I await the results of the next images.

The corporal seemed to be in rough shape, as the humans would say. I'm not sure of the extent of her injuries, and won't know until they contact me again. I can only hope they aren't life threatening. She has led this group effectively since the loss of Captain Rick Noble. I do not believe the others would survive without her.

But the GOA crew's numbers continue to dwindle. Corporal Marlin and Private Walker were both difficult losses for a team with very few skilled fighters.

I switch back to the feed of the Japanese team I am following. They have also lost significant forces in the past few weeks. Originally, the team of fifty soldiers and civilians had taken refuge in a bunker built during World War II. They are led by Commander Suzuki, the great great grandson of a samurai warrior, and great grandson of a World War II veteran. I've only seen a grainy feed of his face, but he is a hard man with a mustache, shaved head, and piercing brown eyes.

The video feed captured from Lolo now shows a team of ten soldiers, led by Suzuki, heading toward an airfield with three aircraft, that twenty spiders and several Sentinels patrol. Their objective is to secure the aircraft and then contact me. I plan to hack into the aircrafts' operations systems. If I can do that, I should have a high chance of learning the flight controls and either hijacking them or explaining how they work to the Japanese soldiers.

The mission unfolds quickly around the airfield, which is on the edge of a long-dead forest. The soldiers move in combat intervals as they take position. Skeletal branches shift in the wind. I imagine them creaking and cracking, disguising the approach of the stealthy soldiers.

The right flank and left flank attack simultaneously with electromagnetic weapons that bring down the shields of every Organic on the airfield.

Suzuki draws two swords and slices his way through the first of the spiders, cutting off all its limbs in two slices and then impaling it with a blade through the head. His men fire pulse rifles, cutting down the other spiders and Sentinels before they can attack.

In moments, it's over. The team now moves freely toward the three aircraft. Suzuki orders one of his men to transmit a message. Lolo is almost out of range, and the feed flickers in and out from the weak signal.

Then there is an incoming transmission.

"We have secured the airfield," the Japanese words come through. It is Lieutenant Hiro, who serves as second in command. He explains that they have secured the airfield and are working on getting me the codes I've requested. A moment later, I hear chatter. Something about the ground rumbling.

Commander Suzuki comes online and explains they are experiencing an earthquake. I check the data coming in from that location, but there is no sign of tectonic activity. Although I do see a slight vibration coming from the direct vicinity of the airfield.

"Commander, this is no natural phenomenon," I say. "Whatever is happening must be Organic."

I try to zoom in, but Lolo has completely passed out of view now. The feed dies, leaving me without visual, and only a tenuous audio connection.

Between bouts of static, I hear voices cry that the rumbling is growing stronger. Suzuki manages to send the codes. I enter them into my system and am rewarded with the diagnostics of the alien fighter, the one I've codenamed Shark, due to the salient dorsal fin. The engineering is remarkable, far surpassing the complexity of any human machine, but that's no surprise.

"Standby, Commander," I say.

Shouting explodes over the transmission, and I hear the Japanese word *Kaiju*, which means giant monster. The word is an apt choice. Suzuki describes a bubble of blue light forming a dome over the forest, and then a limb the size of a building protruding out of that bubble.

That is the last detail I hear.

The line severs.

END ENTRY

***

The Rhino bucked from the force of the *Sunspot*'s explosion. The harness straps pressed tight against Emanuel's shoulders as the vehicle was tossed on its side, holding him into his seat. Metal screamed in protest. Violently shifting forces lashed Emanuel against his seat, pummeling him back and forth. He felt the warm rush of blood from the back of his head.

The Rhino whirred as its self-righting hydraulic system pushed it back upright. A long whoomph sighed out of the system.

The noise waned, but Emanuel's pupils still burned from the brilliant flash of the exploding *Sunspot*. The ringing in his ears started to die. With it came the worrying bark of alarms.

The *Sunspot* had let out its last breath with a fury, and Emanuel was certain it had killed Jeff and David. There was no way the kids could have survived that blast.

Grief was a mortal enemy that would have to be overcome, but there would be no overcoming it if they didn't survive these next few minutes. There were still others alive now that he could help.

Diego was mashing some buttons at the controls near the driver's seat, and Bouma was trying desperately to reattach an oxygen line that had flung loose.

"You okay?" Emanuel asked Owen. The boy had largely been sheltered by Emanuel's body, but his eyes were puffy and red.

Emanuel turned to see Holly checking on Jamie. The girl had been belted in, and she appeared more shaken than anything else.

"Oxygen systems back in place," Bouma announced, relief in his voice.

Several of the alarms shut off.

"We are still within visual proximity of Organic threats," Sonya reported.

Emanuel noticed a slight deviation in her tone. It seemed more *robotic* than usual. Maybe the transfer from the *Sunspot* hadn't been completed before the spaceship had been destroyed.

"No shit," Ort said, pressing his huge hands against one of the windows. "I can see 'em with my own eyes. We need to move."

Diego started the Rhino inching forward again. The tires wobbled over the terrain like something in the suspension had come loose. Emanuel made his way to the front cabin. There, he let his eyes and fingers scan the various reports flashing across the display. There was still a persistent chirping coming from somewhere.

"I think we got the most critical things back in place," Emanuel said, "but I can't find the source for that last one."

"Don't think that one's coming from here," Diego said from the driver's seat.

It took a moment for Emanuel to locate the alarm through his scrambled senses. Any miniscule amount of hope he had felt after they'd survived that near wreck was vanquished by the sight before him.

Near the top of Sophie's cryo chamber, a red light blinked, and the biomonitor on the side flashed scarlet. Dark liquid was mixing with the crisp blue cryostat fluid, clouds spreading out from Sophie's skull.

"Sophie! No!" Emanuel squeezed past Holly and Jamie to reach Sophie's chamber. The nausea he'd already been feeling wrapped its fingers tighter around his stomach.

A long beep trailed from the EKG, reporting that her heart had completely stopped.

Oh God, no!

Other voices called around him, but he ignored them all. The Rhino was still charging forward, even as the dust storm swallowed them. There was no way a little tumble in the Rhino was going to take her. Not after everything they'd already been through.

Emanuel unlocked the drain to the cryo chamber. It no longer mattered that they had less than two days' worth of cryostat fluid to keep her in a protected comatose state. If her heart wasn't working, no amount of cryostat fluid would bring her back. The drain dumped the fluid onto the floor of the Rhino, the liquid sloshing about their feet. He unlatched the lock to the chamber, and the rest of the fluid poured out over him.

The oily fluid clung to his clothes as he reached for Sophie's body. She slumped into his arms, and he grasped desperately at her wrist. A pulse throbbed against his fingers. It was weak and slow, but it was a pulse nonetheless.

His eyes flitted to the loose tubes and cables dangling from the top of the chamber. Sophie had been torn from the cryo chamber's intubation system in the crash. He stretched one of the wires from the top of the chamber and plugged it into the sensor secured at the bottom of Sophie's skull.

While the EKG no longer bleated, another ominous message flashed across the biomonitors. It warned of increased intracranial pressures.

"A concussion," Emanuel said. "If we're lucky…" He knew it could be way worse.

With Holly's help, he cleared Sophie's hair back to access the injured area. A cut several inches long bled profusely.

"Here," Holly said, handing him an emergency first aid kit.

Emanuel opened the kit. His fingers trembled as he pulled out the suture. He was a biologist, not a surgeon.

Though he'd had plenty of experience operating on mice and rabbits for biological experiments, never once had he so much as scrubbed in to even observe a procedure performed on a human.

Stitches, at least, he could do. This wasn't so different from suturing a mouse.

His finger slipped as he stuck the needle through Sophie's scalp, pulling the wound closed. He tightened his grip and hooked the needle in again. Loop by loop he brought the skin together. Even as he approached the end, his fingers didn't stop trembling.

But it wasn't the suturing he was worried about. Taking care of this wound would do nothing if what the biomonitor indicated was true. Because of her concussion, cerebrospinal fluid was building up on her already inflamed brain. She'd been in a critical state ever since the RVAMP on Earth had cooked most of the Organic nanobots embedded in her tissues. The foreign nanobots had elicited the sustained response of her passive immune system. Her body had been fighting back against the nanobots, and now it looked like the concussion might have stolen any chance of recovery.

"You know what we need to do," Holly said, locking eyes with Emanuel.

Ort and Bouma appeared confused, but Emanuel knew exactly what Holly meant.

The two of them had the most medical experience among the group, and even that was pitifully little when Emanuel considered what needed to happen to keep Sophie alive now.

The Rhino continued bucking against the rocky terrain, the storm winds shrieking around them. The delicate surgery Emanuel needed to perform would be made even more difficult by these conditions, but he had no other choice than to improvise.

All the injuries, the inflamed tissues and broken blood vessels, that had been present when Sophie underwent the cryo procedure were still there. But the most immediate need was to relieve the increasing pressure on her brain.

"We've got to drain her cerebrospinal fluid," Emanuel said, "or she risks neurological death."

A host of emotions flooded his mind. He wanted to simultaneously hold Sophie tight and curse the world for letting her end up like this. Thoughts of Jeff and David still pervaded the darkness. He shoved everything away. There was no room for emotion now. After cleansing his thoughts, he adopted the mindset he'd worn as a graduate student going in to perform surgery on a mouse for an experiment. Intense focus lent him the ability to manipulate the fragile physiologies of those tiny animals. He needed to draw on those old experiences now, resurrecting the steady hands and cool mindset that had enabled those past successes.

But it was exceedingly difficult to rely on only his past strength. Equally real memories of surgical failures—of being unable to stop the rupture in a mouse's aorta, or nicking the liver and watching the animal bleed to death as he desperately tried to clot the wound. They were rookie mistakes from rookie hands dealing with complex experimental procedures.

I'm better than that, he thought. He was an experienced scientist now. An expert in his field. One of the best. So what if this time the organism he was operating on was a bit larger than what he was used to?

He could do this.

"Sonya, call up the procedure for an emergency cerebrospinal ventral drain implantation from your medical database," Emanuel said.

The displays around the rear of the Rhino switched on. They showed, step by step, what Emanuel had to do. He laid Sophie as gently as he could on the Rhino's floor. This was no operating table, and there were no surgical lamps hanging overhead, but it would have to do. The Rhino jostled again as the damaged suspension system fought against the raging winds and the unpredictable terrain.

"Hold Sophie steady," Emanuel said to Holly. "Bouma, Ort, a little help over here."

The two soldiers knelt around Sophie.

Emanuel did the best he could to ignore the jostling of the vehicle and Diego's erratic driving as the soldier attempted to evade the Organics. His mind switched to surgical mode. He had not forgotten the feeling of clinical precision and focus, as he'd feared. Every movement came out of his fingers like computer output from commands he'd entered into a terminal. His eyes left his focus on Sophie's skull only to gauge his progress in relation to the steps displayed by Sonya. His fingers worked deftly to create an insertion point.

He was almost done. Finally, he inserted a small shunt into the back of Sophie's skull. Clear, viscous fluid flowed from the shunt, spilling into the mess of cryostat fluid already coating the floor of the Rhino.

"Got it," Emanuel said. He stared at the biomonitor. The warning still flashed, reporting the intracranial pressure was too high. He didn't take his eyes off the screen, daring it to defy his efforts.

This will work. This will...

The warning disappeared. The EKG beeped with the report of a normal cardiac rhythm. He carefully placed Sophie on her back and cradled her head, brushing back the hair from her face. It had been months since they'd been this close, and his heart overflowed with emotions as he studied her near-translucent skin. Vaguely he sensed the others surrounding them, but they were nothing more than shadows in the night to him.

Sophie was still alive. Still fighting.

As long as you keep fighting, Emanuel thought, *I will, too.*

When she'd gone into the cryo chamber, she'd been unconscious. Even with his intervention, there was no indication that Emanuel's work would do anything to change that.

So when Sophie's eyes fluttered open, he reared back with shock, and surprise.

$$— 9 —$$

A grating wind cut across the mangled body of the chitinous alien. Spidery legs twitched, and blue blood pulsed out of its cracked flesh. The creature had been thrown into its current position at the tunnel's entrance by the intense blast that had swallowed the landscape only moments ago.

"You okay?" Jeff asked. He kept one eye on the spider as he bent low near his brother.

David managed a nod.

The dust and rocks blasted past just outside the narrow tunnel they were sheltered in. Winds roared against the rock with a monstrous force that frightened Jeff even more than the Organics did.

"I think so," David said. He sat against the wall of the tunnel, staring at the broken spider. "Is it dead?"

The wind tugged at the spider's fragile flesh, whipping at the skull. Jeff guessed it was being held in place by its claws alone, which were embedded in the rock. That same strength must've been what let the Organics use the dust storm for cover where normal humans would be simply blown away—and to shreds.

"Looks like it," Jeff said, eying the spider's mandibles. The alien had chased them from their original hiding spot overlooking the route from the *Dawn* to the *Sunspot* before they had killed it. As they were running, desperate to put some distance between themselves and it, Jeff had seen the plasma start to vent from the *Sunspot.*

It had risen into the sky like the finger of some great giant reaching for the heavens. He knew something had gone wrong, and had debated taking David back to the *Sunspot* to find out what it was. Thankfully, all his instincts had told him to stay away.

Maybe it was luck they'd slid into this tunnel to escape the spider. A blinding flash had swallowed them as they dove inside. His vision had gone completely white for several seconds, and at first he had thought he'd gone blind.

But it was back now. David was still alive, and so was he. That left him with one question he was afraid to ask aloud.

David wasn't. "Do you think everyone else is dead?"

Jeff could see his brother wanted reassurance that Holly, Bouma and the others had survived, but Jeff couldn't lie.

"I don't know," he finally said. He slumped down next to David and put an arm around his shoulder.

He tried pressing a button on his suit to call the ship. "Emanuel, Sonya, anyone? Do you read?"

There was nothing but static.

Again, he tried. "Holly, are you there?"

But no matter what he tried, there was no response. His stomach sank. Maybe, in his attempt to alter the suits for him and David, he'd ripped off the comm units that connected them with the ship. Sonya might not even know they were missing.

"Oh no," he muttered. "I screwed up."

David tried to comfort him, but Jeff shrugged him off. He'd set out to prove he and David could help the others, that they were just as good as the adults. Now they were stuck out here, alone with a dead spider.

The winds continued to roar outside. Piles of broken rock and dirt started to build up at the tunnel's entrance. If this storm continued for too long, Jeff and his brother would be buried alive. A gauge on his suit's HUD showed that his oxygen levels were running low. He wouldn't be able to survive more than a couple hours longer out here if he didn't get the suit recharged.

He wanted to look brave, but tears threatened to pour down his face. He wanted to curl into a ball and go to sleep, to wake up and find this was all a dream. Maybe he'd wake up on the *Sunspot*, in the safety of the others.

Then he remembered something his dad had liked to tell him and David. "Bravery doesn't mean you aren't afraid. It means that you do something even when you are afraid."

Jeff needed to be brave now. "Stay here, okay?"

"What are you going to do?" David asked, worry tingeing his voice.

"I got to make sure that we keep the entrance to the tunnel open," Jeff said.

"I'll help."

Images of David being swept away in the intense winds flashed through Jeff's mind. "No, you stay back here. Warn me if you see any Organic activity. Plus, you can stay safe and help me if I need it."

David nodded meekly.

Jeff climbed toward the entrance of the tunnel. Pebbles carried by the wind bounced against his suit the closer he got. He shoveled away the piles of dust and rocks with his hands, scooping them up and spreading them along the floor of the tunnel toward where David sat. The pull of the wind tugged at his suit, threatening to drag him outside, so he maintained a safe distance from the entrance of the tunnel. The body of the spider slapped against the ground, its lifeless, arachnid-like eyes staring at Jeff while he worked to keep the tunnel clear.

Each second that passed seemed like he was losing the battle. Every handful of dirt and rock he moved from the entrance was replaced by two more. Sweat trickled over his face and stung his eyes. Only a pinprick of space existed between the growing pile of debris and the roof of the tunnel. His muscles burned, but he went into overdrive. If he failed, David would be buried too. They'd die in here, choking on their own breath.

Scoop by scoop, he tore at the pile of rock and dirt. The wind ate away at the other side of the pile even as it added to it, sounding through his suit like a growling monster.

First, the aliens had tried to kill them, and now Mars was having a go. Fear threatened to take hold of Jeff again, urging his muscles to lock and freeze. But he wouldn't let it win. His dad's words kept repeating in his head, and he dug and dug and dug.

A new clunking sound replaced the din of the howling storm. The entire face of the scree suddenly slipped into the tunnel and onto him, the dirt settling against his chest and limbs, pinning him to the ground. He tried desperately to breathe, but an immense pressure pushed down on his chest.

A wet sheen formed over his eyes, and his vision blurred. Panic took hold, telling him to thrash and flail, to fight for his life. But he couldn't so much as twitch his fingers. He was completely stuck.

The clatter of rock against rock came again, and Jeff waited for the added weight to crush him. Here he would stay, left to lie for eternity, while his brother suffered because he'd failed.

But instead of feeling the press of more rocks, the weight on his chest lessened. A flood of white light washed over his body. David looked down at him, his helmet-mounted light illuminating his small hands as he shoveled Jeff free.

"I got you, bro!" David said.

Soon Jeff's hands were free, and he was able to help David uncover the rest of his body. Finally out, he sat and gasped for breath.

"You okay?" David asked.

"I think so."

Jeff marveled at how quickly things had changed. He'd been asking David the same question before, then telling his little brother to stay out of harm's way in an attempt to protect him. Fate had other surprises in store, and in the end, it was David who had saved him. Jeff figured it was more proof that they were an inseparable team.

He brushed the front of his suit off. A red warning flashed at the corner of his HUD. Oxygen levels were at only ten percent.

"Did it stop?" David asked him.

"What?"

"The storm."

Jeff looked at the entrance, at the hole the slip had cleared. The wind still carried swirls of brown and red, but he no longer felt the intense pull of the storm trying to drag him from the tunnel.

"Looks like it's settled," he said. "How's your oxygen?"

"It says fifteen percent."

Better than his, but David wouldn't make it alone if

Jeff's ran out.

From what Jeff knew about their suits, there were a couple of options to replenish their oxygen stores. The first was directly depositing some tank-like canisters into the suit. The other option was to find an environment with adequate oxygen levels to peel them off and let them harvest air from the atmosphere. He'd seen Bouma do this a couple of times when he was testing the suits. But, besides the *Sunspot*, he wasn't sure there was anywhere he could find an oxygen-rich environment to recharge their oxygen systems.

"We need to recharge our air supplies," Jeff said. "I know there were extra canisters aboard the *Sunspot*, assuming it's still there."

"Maybe we will find the others," David said.

The two brothers climbed out of their shelter, to be greeted by the sight of the spider carcass. A few of its legs had been shorn off by the shrapnel of the dust storm, but it still clung stubbornly to the rock face. Farther out, the bodies of the spiders they'd ambushed littered the ravine, their limbs protruding out of the dirt the storm had deposited over them.

Jeff climbed to the top of the precipice. Wind whispered over his suit, and he helped David up beside him. Below lay a plateau that had been blasted almost smooth as marble. This was where the *Sunspot* had crash-landed. All the little craters and rocky columns were gone, and the *Sunspot* was nothing more than a husk of blackened metal. It looked like when their dad had left a fish too long on the grill. There was no doubt now; the flash of light had been the *Sunspot* exploding.

Jeff doubted there would be any intact oxygen canisters in the wreckage, but they had to look.

"We're going to go down there?" David asked nervously.

It wasn't just the prospect of a futile search that worried David—and Jeff. Rather, the broken *Sunspot* wasn't alone. Nearly a dozen spiders were scurrying over the landscape around it, and some scorpion-like monstrosities paced the perimeter of the plateau. Beyond them lay a few Organic fighters, similar to the winged ones with the dorsal fins they'd seen in space. Between those fighters were much larger ships Jeff judged to be some kind of transport craft.

Jeff and David got down on their bellies to watch.

"What's that?" David asked, pointing toward the horizon beyond the *Sunspot*.

Jeff used his hand to shield his eyes under his visor. A small dust cloud billowed from a speck in the distance. It seemed to be moving. There was no blue glint like it was an Organic alien. Maybe, just maybe, it was a human vehicle.

But it was racing away.

"Is that a Rhino?" David asked.

"I don't know." If it was, there was no way they could catch up to it on foot. Jeff surveyed the landscape crawling with Organics and all the debris around the broken *Sunspot*. The aliens seemed to be searching for something, and he had a feeling it was their missing friends.

Jeff eyed the alien ships again, an idea forming in his mind.

"If we can get on board one of those," he pointed to an alien ship, "maybe we can find Bouma and the others. The aliens are looking for them."

David looked over. "Are you crazy, bro?"

Jeff shrugged. "Maybe a little."

***

Sophie floated above the Martian surface, a complex and hostile landscape of ravines and mountains carved by ancient tectonic activity and rivers that had long since disappeared. A flash in the distance blinded her momentarily. When her vision cleared, she once again focused on the alien landscape, suddenly overwhelmed by a strange sensation that this was her home.

But Mars never was my home, she thought, *so why do I feel so nostalgic?*

A vague memory floated back to her in that ethereal moment. At once she saw all that had transpired since the Organics invaded Earth and upended her life and the lives of billions of others. She felt the pain and anguish of knowing the rest of her family was gone forever; she was among a handful of humans left to linger until the planet breathed its last breath and the Organics had taken all they had come for.

But all of that seemed so distant now as she floated above Mars.

Another flash of light tore through the sky, like a meteor coming into the thin Mars atmosphere.

But this was not a meteor.

The ship streaking through the sky was the *Sunspot*. And she knew she was glimpsing not the present, but rather, an event that had occurred not so long ago.

She had been on that ship, and was watching herself crash to Mars.

A plume of dust rose above the crash site, and a voice boomed within her skull—a voice she hadn't heard in a long time, but one she knew exceedingly well.

"Welcome home, Sophie."

Dr. Eric Hoffman.

An intense pain overwhelmed her. All that she saw turned a brilliant red. A thousand tiny needles pierced every bone in her body.

The Mars surface blurred, to be replaced by what looked like metal walls. Distant voices called out in a muddled jumble of sound, but none of them belonged to Hoffman.

"Sophie," one of them said. The tone was soft, kind… reassuring. It pulled at her from a distance, tugging her back to reality.

She blinked.

Hovering over her were the familiar eyes of the man she had grown to appreciate as much more than just a colleague—the man who had brought her out of whatever cocoon the nanobots had hidden her away in.

"Emanuel," she choked. Pain lanced her throat, and she tasted something metallic.

He pulled her in close to his chest until she could feel his heartbeat against the side of her head. A dull pain throbbed at the back of her skull, but it no longer seemed to matter.

"You have no idea how glad I am to hear your voice," he said. "I never thought I'd see you conscious again."

Sophie sensed the presence of others nearby. They lurked on the periphery, like kind spirits edging into existence but not wanting to interrupt. For that she was thankful. All manner of emotions crashed through her, and she couldn't take the demands of anyone else asking how she was, or finding out someone was missing or hurt.

Seeing and being with Emanuel helped her to heal something that had broken in her mind. After a few moments of shared silence with him, the rest of the world came into focus. She felt the tremble of a vehicle underneath her and heard the whine of electric motors. Her skin felt cool, and the thin suit she wore was soaked in some kind of liquid. The air smelled of body odor, sweat, and the sweet scent of cryostat fluid.

Holly and Bouma were there too, and so were Owen and Jamie. Diego and another big man she didn't recognize sat at the controls of the vehicle.

She craned her neck to see who else had survived, but the rest of the seats were empty.

Was this all that remained of her team... and humanity? Where were Jeff and David?

— 10 —

The jolt of the ship coming to a stop knocked Captain Noble to the floor of his orb, but he quickly pushed himself back up. Pulling on the coiled feeding cord attached to his stomach, he stood and made his way back to the wall of his prison.

A massive recessed light in the overhead of the chamber flipped on, spreading brilliant white illumination throughout the entire space. Noble's eyes adjusted to the sight of hundreds and hundreds of alien prisoners in orbs. He could see all the way across the chamber, and while the aliens imprisoned there were just dots, he could make out some of their myriad colors. Some appeared as cool teals, like the Caribbean Ocean, while others were orange, like flames.

He slowly took in the view. Three orbs above and to the right was some sort of gas entity. At first he thought it was one of the multi-dimensional entities, but it was definitely different, a nebulous cloud slowly circulating inside the orb.

A few orbs to the right, an alien with two necks and eyeless red glowing bulbs attached to each swayed from a base that looked like a flowerpot sculpted of bone.

In another orb below, Noble saw a puddle of gray liquid that transformed into the figures of other aliens, mimicking the shapes of those around it. Noble's eyes widened when the liquid formed the shape of a human.

These creatures were beyond remarkable. There was something awe-inspiring about seeing such a diversity of creatures. In a way, he felt lucky to experience what he was witnessing. Lifeforms from all across the solar system, the galaxy, and perhaps even beyond.

The opening of the ship's belly far below squashed any feeling of good fortune he had attained. The screech of metal sounded as the doors began to part, revealing a lumpy, gray surface below.

Noble stepped close enough to the wall of his orb that his hair should have prickled, but his beard remained matted to his chin. Cautiously, he poked the gooey skin wall. His finger pushed into the oozing substance.

He pulled it back, and a string of jelly came away with his finger.

The force field was down...

A sudden sharp pain ripped through his gut. He yelled in agony. The cord retracted from his stomach, accompanied by a loud hiss. It whipped to the floor, where it vanished into a slot that resealed.

Noble reached down to grab at the bleeding wound in his abdomen. A small red hole not much bigger than a pea flashed with pain. He pressed his palm over the swollen flesh and staggered a few feet to the other side of his prison for a better look below.

The hangar doors continued opening in a screech that drowned out the grunting, croaking, panting, and other noises of the riled-up aliens.

The liquid entity had taken on the shape of a human again, and was screaming. Noble swallowed hard when he realized it was the same voice he had heard earlier. The festering hope of finding another person on the Organic ship drained out of him like the liquid from an orb.

He forced himself to look back down at the ground, which was rising to meet the ship. Mounds shaped like ant-hills dotted the terrain that stretched under the open doors, and miniature creatures moved in lines out of the holes like insects.

An alien spacecraft shot by below the ship, the raucous sound of its engines vibrating throughout the chamber. Roots waved its spindly arms back and forth and dropped from the top of its orb to the floor.

Several alien noises rang out.

Ribbit stood on both its chicken legs and looked down. The creature croaked and groaned. Still sick, Noble judged by the crusty goo covering its cracked hide.

You have arrived.

The voice in Noble's head came at the same time the other alien prisoners all started to move and make noises. Ribbit, who tilted his oval head, appeared perplexed. Even Roots seemed distracted, its arms waving back and forth like it was trying to communicate. The liquid alien had reformed into a puddle on the ground, and ripples undulated over it.

You have arrived, repeated the voice in his mind. He wasn't imagining it. This was the same multi-dimensional entity that had communicated with him before. The four shimmering figures had returned in the center of the chamber. All at once, they fanned out to check on their specimens.

Normally the other aliens were quiet at the sight of the overlords, but not this time. Did they know something he didn't?

Stay calm.

This time Noble wasn't sure if the words came from the aliens or if he was saying it in his own mind. He wasn't sure what to believe or think right now.

What he did know was: the dead gray surface they were headed toward wasn't Earth. The gray surface reminded him of dead skin. As the ship descended farther, the aliens on the surface skittered away. Now Noble saw them clearly. They were spiders. Thousands of them.

Dust swirled beneath the ship, blocking his view of the pockmarked surface of this alien planet and the creatures that lived here.

His gaze flitted to the apparition floating toward his orb.

"Where are we?" Noble asked.

The reply came in his mind.

Your destination.

"And where is that?" he asked.

Your species called this place the Moon.

Noble blinked, trying to process the information. "Our moon? Like the moon that orbits Earth?"

It is the same.

The dust settled below as the ship landed with a jolt that rocked the bulkheads. The vibration knocked Noble to the floor. He pushed himself back up as the creature flickered away, leaving him standing at the edge of the orb.

Prepare yourself, Captain Rick Noble.

The voice echoed in his mind, and he slowly peered out of the orb. Below, a small cigar-shaped alien ship flew under the open doors and glided into the center of the chamber. Orbs on the bottom level shot away from the bulkheads and attached to the side of the ship like metal flakes to a magnet.

Roots looked up at Noble just as its orb ripped away

from the wall and slammed into the ship. As the ship made its way up toward his level, Noble's shivered and moved away from the bulkhead.

He was next.

***

The hum of the Rhino's motors was their constant companion as they shot over the Martian surface. They were still headed in the general direction of where the NTC colony was supposed to be. *Like a car driving in the night with no headlights, in hopes of running into a city hidden in the sand*, Bouma thought.

They were relying on hope and a bit of luck. After all, stranger things had happened.

He was seated in the rear of the Rhino, next to Sophie and Emanuel. Diego and Ort manned the cockpit, and Holly was still making sure the kids were faring the best they could through their trauma. Right now, she was getting them to settle into naps.

Bouma still couldn't believe Sophie had been resurrected from her slumbers and was, against all odds, lucid. Then again, maybe it wasn't good fortune that she'd been able to wake up like that. It probably had something to do with the nanobots. He studied Sophie for a moment when she closed her eyes. Even though she claimed not to be in pain any longer, her skin still looked taut and pale. Her lips seemed locked in a permanent grimace when she wasn't talking.

"Damn, but it's good to see you awake, Sophie," Bouma said.

She massaged her temples, and when she spoke, her words came out groggily. "I'm glad to see we're in one piece." A look of worry crossed her face. "We still haven't heard anything from Jeff and David?"

Bouma shook his head. "Sonya's been looking for any signals that might be coming from an EVA suit, but we haven't gotten any hits yet."

"Those two boys are tough," Sophie said. "We'll find them."

Bouma caught Holly's eyes. He knew her well enough to sense what was going on in her mind. Even if Jeff and David had somehow survived the reactor failure of the *Sunspot*, they wouldn't survive out there for long. They were tough, there was no doubt about that. Bouma knew it well enough from training them back in Cheyenne Mountain. But no matter how good shots they were, they couldn't survive out there without food, water, or oxygen.

"I shouldn't be alive," Sophie said, coming back to her senses. She looked at Emanuel. "This must have something to do with the nanobots."

So Bouma wasn't the only one to suspect the Organics had something to do with this.

"Can't say I disagree," Emanuel said.

No, it looked like everyone was as concerned about the alien technology as he was.

"But without an actual laboratory," Emanuel continued, "I have no way of telling whether the bots are dead or active. Maybe there are just a bunch of dead bots accumulating in your liver and being cleansed from your blood. Might explain why you were able to wake up."

"Maybe," Sophie said. It didn't seem like she believed him.

That worried Bouma. Holly seemed to be able to tell. She lifted herself from her seat next to the sleeping children and deposited herself into the one next to him, leaning her head against his shoulder.

"You're thinking about Lt. Smith, aren't you?" she whispered.

"You deduce all that with your psychoanalytical skills?" Bouma asked.

"It doesn't take a psychologist to tell me that. I know you, Chad. I was thinking the same thing."

"Smith betrayed us. She opened Cheyenne Mountain to the Organics, and they ran us out of there. Nearly killed every one of us."

"Smith didn't betray us. It was the nanobots. They controlled her. You know she never would've done that if it weren't for the Organics."

"That's kind of what I'm afraid of," Bouma said, looking up at Sophie. "This is supposed to be her mission. We're on Mars, where she wanted us to come, looking for a colony she wanted us to find. And now, right when we're finally headed in that direction, she wakes up as if the RVAMP blast back on Earth never happened."

"She still seems like Sophie to me," Holly said.

"Maybe, but how long before the Organics use her like a puppet?"

Holly appeared to consider that. She rubbed the back of Bouma's hand. "I can't explain it, but I don't get the same feeling from her that I did from Smith."

"What do you mean?" Bouma wasn't sure he could tell if there was any distinction.

"She seems more in control, somehow. Maybe the last of the nanobots really were fried, and all it took was a prolonged rest in the cryo chamber for them to finally fizzle away. My guess is, they probably feed on living people or get energy from biological systems. And when

163

everything is shut down when a person is in cryo, maybe they're not feeding the bots anymore."

"Maybe." Bouma shivered at the thought. "But she's awake and alive now. What if the nanobots wake up, too?"

The Rhino dipped and came up hard with a violent jerk. Ort smacked against the inner wall of the vehicle and cursed.

"Sorry," Diego called back. "Terrain is getting a little rougher. We're going to have to slow down."

"Suspension is already shot," Ort added. "No use beating up this poor thing more than we have to. She's the only wheels we have, and we're toast without her."

Ort's simple statement hit Bouma hard. They might be the last hope for humanity.

And they'd already lost Jeff and David.

God, he wanted to curse and shout. His fingers slipped from Holly's. They trembled as he curled them into fists. The Organics, and the arrogance of those boys. He should've never tried to convince them they'd be warriors someday. Then maybe they wouldn't have run off in a heroic attempt to save the *Sunspot*.

"I screwed up," he said aloud.

Holly gave him a perplexed look. "What?"

"Back in Cheyenne Mountain, I told Jeff and David they could be soldiers. That they were soldiers. Look at what happened."

"It's not your fault."

"They were just boys. They didn't deserve to go out like that." A sudden heat flushed through his face. "Shit… I just keep thinking, what if they're still out there, wandering around and wondering where we are?"

"We did everything we could for them," Holly said, a

sheen of wetness covering her eyes.

"Did we?"

Bouma raised a brow.

"We searched for them, but you saw that blast. And right now, we've got others relying on us." Holly nodded toward the two sleeping children curled up in their seats.

Bouma brushed a fresh tear from her eye and then pulled her close. Together, they sat in silence while Diego and Ort consulted with Sonya regarding their path forward. Sophie and Emanuel continued discussing the nanobots and what her seemingly miraculous recovery might mean.

Trying to reconcile their unknown future with their disastrous past, Bouma had trouble focusing on the intense thoughts roiling through his head. He couldn't draw himself away from the images of Jeff and David in his mind's eye. He could picture them walking across the desert until they collapsed.

Maybe they were still out there, but Holly and Emanuel were both right. Their mission was to find the NTC colony. If they were successful, he could then launch a mission to find Jeff and David.

Hold on, boys, Bouma thought. *We'll find you.*

— 11 —

Athena sipped water and swished it around, savoring the cool liquid the Organics had come to Earth to collect. Something humans had taken for granted for so long. And now billions upon billions of humans and animals had perished for the aliens' lust for the resource.

She sat in the cracked leather chair on the bridge of the *Ghost of Atlantis*, looking over what was left of her crew, and waiting for Griffin, Malone, and Taylor to return from the hatch leading to outside.

Almost all of her crew had huddled into the room to wait for the three soldiers. The stuffy air was ripe with a smell no one had really gotten used to. "Tolerate" would have been a generous way of describing their reaction to the constant stench of body odor and human waste.

Of the original one hundred and twenty NTC sailors, this was all that remained. There were just seventeen of them inside the cramped bridge.

Half the crew had accompanied Captain Rick Noble during Operation Redemption, while the other half had remained behind. Then a storm had damaged the vessel, leaving it stranded on the ocean floor until the waters receded, which hadn't taken long. Most of the world's oceans had been drained to half their capacity by the start of Operation Redemption.

The damage to the submarine had been severe: cracking bulkheads had flooded several compartments with sand, destroying most of their communications equipment. They were deaf and blind, and the inside temperature was nearly ninety degrees. Fans connected to camouflaged solar panels in the sand above the vessel helped circulate some of the air, but it was still almost unbearable, especially with the stench.

She scrutinized the filthy faces looking back at her on the bridge. Their features appeared almost ghoulish, illuminated as they were by lanterns. Trish Hodges sat next to their now useless communications equipment, a curtain of long hair hanging over one side of her face as she watched Athena.

Bobby Posey, their senior engineer, or at least the most experienced engineer still left alive, sat next to Trish. The pale man rested his beard-covered chin in his hands.

Sitting behind them were Farthing, Webb, and Stokes. They all shared the same melancholy looks. Stokes's once round cheeks and rotund belly had deflated. His cheekbones now stuck out of his gaunt, grime-covered face, giving him a near skeletal appearance. He coughed and held up a hand to cover his mouth. Like most on the GOA, the navigation officer was ill.

Over the tap of the transmitter and the sporadic coughs came the sound of footfalls in the corridor outside the bridge. Griffin ducked under the overhead and took his helmet off, revealing a dark-skinned face and sharp brown eyes. He scrunched his wide shoulders to fit through the hatchway.

"Corporal, those things are gone," he reported. "Malone and Taylor are still topside, making sure they don't come back, but with the sun about to rise, I'd say this is our best shot to move."

"Move?" Trish asked, looking away from the Morse

Code transmitter.

Posey's hands fell off his beard and he stood with an incredulous look on his face. "What do you mean, 'Move'?" he asked.

Athena also stood. Her ribs hurt from the sudden movement, and a wave of dizziness rinsed over her. The can of beans and a few glasses of water had helped, but she was still exhausted and dehydrated.

She walked over to a metal table in the center of the room. Shattered monitors that had once provided access to data, intel, and visuals of the outside hung from the bulkheads. They were down to using paper maps to guide them on their raids into Los Angeles.

Griffin, Trish, and Posey met her at the table, while the others gathered around to listen.

"Alexia has located an underground garage that might yield some vehicles that survived the initial blast. If we can get to them, they could take us to the Pelican AFB military installation, where other survivors are taking refuge." Athena pointed at the map. "With their help, we will actually have a fighting chance to get out of here. We just need to make it to Pelican and—"

"To Pelican?" Posey asked, cutting her off. "With everything the Organics have out there?" He chuckled, nervously. "You lost Walker just walking into a deserted city. Now you want us to believe you can take us all to Pelican?"

Athena looked at the engineer, but noticed the other frightened faces over his shoulder. Aside from Griffin, no one looked like they were up for another fight. She understood their fear, but it was madness, living in these conditions.

"We can't stay here and wait to die," Athena said. She

paused to look at Posey. "Actually, you can if you want, but I'm not planning on it. So if you want to stay behind, that's on you. I'm going to take a group to get these vehicles, then head to this base. Alexia is working on a plan for us to escape the planet."

"Escape the planet? In what?" Posey snorted.

"Yeah, that's what I was trying to say when you cut me off."

This time Posey shrugged. "I've said it once, and I'll say it again: that AI is going to get us killed." He turned to look at the others. "Alexia's going to get us *all* killed. I say we stay here and wait for the Organics to leave Earth. They can't possibly take all the water. Once they leave, we will head into Los Angeles and start over."

"I agree," said Collins, another communications officer. "I say we stay here and wait it out."

Athena listened to her crew argue back and forth for several minutes before she silenced them with a fist to the metal table.

"Look around you," she said, gesturing toward the cracked monitors and dented bulkheads. "There's nothing left for us here. We have maybe two or three weeks' worth of food left, and a week of water. The Organics aren't going to leave any behind, and even if they do, Earth is already dead. There's not enough water left on Earth to make it habitable anymore."

Griffin took off his helmet and set it down with a clank. "Most of you haven't been out there, but I have. There isn't anything to go back to in LA, either. We can't just start over."

Posey and Collins remained defiant.

"You leave this submarine again, and you will die," Posey said.

"We stay in this submarine, and we will die," Athena said.

She looked over at Trish and then Griffin, the two people she knew she could count on. They both nodded back at her with reassurance.

"We should have done this three months ago when Doctor Winston and her team took the NTC *Sunspot*," Athena said. "The time for hiding is over. I'm getting those vehicles. When I come back, those of you that want to live are welcome to come with."

***

"You ready?" Jeff asked. He crouched behind a piece of metal that jutted out from the ground like a robotic shark fin.

David nodded his helmet.

Before them lay the hulking wreck of the *Sunspot*, its hull split open, the metal peeling outward. Globs of plastic had melted and then solidified in the dirt. Chunks of metal littered the ground, like an alien junkyard.

He checked his HUD for an oxygen readout, swallowing hard at the report of less than ten percent. An animalistic urge told him to run straight for the *Sunspot* and find an oxygen canister before he suffocated, but Bouma had always told him a soldier didn't rush into battles he couldn't win. A real soldier gathered intel and made decisions based off weighing his options. Strategy and tactics were just as important as firepower.

"Stay behind me at all times," Jeff said.

David nodded again.

They crept through the debris like cats sneaking up on a mouse. When they got close to the main wreckage, Jeff ordered his brother onto the ground. Together, they crawled over the red sand, keeping as low as possible. Piece by ugly piece, they snuck through the scattered remains of the ship until at last they were just fifty meters from the bulk of what had once been the *Sunspot*.

While their EVA suits isolated noise they made to within their suit, Jeff still whispered as he pointed to a section of the *Sunspot* near the stern, where what remained of the biomes could be seen. He recognized the twisted remains of one of the turrets. "That's where we were before we escaped."

"Yeah, I think you're right," David said.

The hull near the turret was singed. Teardrops of melted slag had reformed along its sides. Jeff hoped there might be a couple oxygen canisters left there. It was the only shot they had, from what he could see.

Of course, to get there, they'd have to sneak past the half-dozen spiders clambering over the hull. Through the wounds in the side of the ship, he could see the shapes of more aliens sifting through the shadows, their blue flesh illuminating the guts of the ship as they moved about.

Near the bow, outside the broken hull, stood a scorpion-like alien with a huge catapult tail. Enormous arachnid legs arched from an armor-covered thorax. The monster's head looked vaguely birdlike with a falcon's beak, though multiple stalks sprouted from it, each carrying a gleaming eye. The beast seemed to be staring off into the distance, as if guarding the *Sunspot*.

Jeff pressed himself lower against the soil and continued moving. He kept his eyes on the glistening blue scorpion alien. Its huge muscled legs shifted slightly, and its head started to swivel around.

Grabbing David's wrist, Jeff pulled them both up and

sprinted across the rest of the dry landscape. With a leap, he cleared the last meter, pulling David with him, and the pair tumbled into a hole in the side of the *Sunspot*. His body rolled across the deck, kicking up a cloud of dirt.

Had they been seen?

He tried to manage his breathing, listening for the scratch, scrape, or any otherworldly wails.

Beams of light penetrated the wounds in the ship, illuminating columns of dust. The noises of the aliens resonated through the metal bulkheads and up into Jeff's suit. Goosebumps prickled his skin as he waded into the darkness.

A huge thumping soon followed.

Jeff pressed himself into the shadows and pulled David with him, hoping the darkness would disguise them. They hadn't made it far enough inside the ship to hide from all the huge breaches in the hull of the *Sunspot*. He feared the scorpion thing would look through one of those holes and see him or David. The deck shook, and bits of sand danced with each walloping tremble.

David looked up at him like he was about to ask a question. Jeff pressed a finger against his faceshield to silence him. His legs threatened to give out from under him as the noise of the beast grew closer, the vibrations growing louder and more violent.

Jeff held a breath in his chest when he saw one of the massive legs through the hole in the side of the ship.

The scorpion monster halted, and Jeff slowly let out his breath.

Please, keep moving.

The tree trunk legs pulsated blue outside their hiding spot. Seconds ticked by, taking what seemed to Jeff like an eternity. David squeezed his hand.

The Organic wasn't looking toward the ship, but facing away. Maybe on guard, or watching for signs of more humans, or something else.

It didn't matter. All that did was that the alien hadn't seen them.

At least, not yet. The sooner they found their oxygen and got out of here, the better.

Jeff's suit beeped in his ear. His oxygen was down to five percent. He dropped David's hand and motioned for him to follow.

They snuck on through the *Sunspot*'s remains. Metal creaked all around them, and dust swirled in from all the wounds in the hull. The dwindling number on Jeff's HUD kept him moving through every obstacle they faced.

The tap and scratch of spiders inspecting the vessel followed them through the corridors. Jeff tried his best to gauge where the creatures were, but found it difficult, given the way the noises echoed through the metal and his suit. And with half the floors missing, it was almost impossible to navigate through the treacherous fallen beams and twisted wires.

He tried to remember where the turret was. That was the direction they needed to be going in, but with most of the ladders missing, Jeff hadn't seen a good way to get up to that deck. After a couple minutes of crawling under fallen panels and pushing through jumbles of burned computer panels, an answer presented itself to him.

Jeff looked up where there had been a set of ladders leading up four decks. It looked like three of those decks had completely collapsed, and they could see all the way up to the top deck. The space appeared cavernous. A length of the top deck had fallen down so it was nearly straight up from the level they were on. Pieces of pipe and scaffolding hung off it. Some swung in the wind tunneling through the devastated ship. At the top of the deck was the turret room and, next to it, the armory where they had got their suits.

There might not even be any oxygen up there. All the canisters had probably exploded along with the ship. How much oxygen would he use up just trying to make that climb? His HUD was still flashing red. Oxygen levels were now under four percent.

What was it like to suffocate? Did it hurt?

If he fell, even with Mars's weakened gravity, he bet it would still hurt. He'd be lucky if he came away from it uninjured. Being injured and trying to survive with Organics around would be a death sentence.

He wanted all of it to just be a nightmare. A long, terrible nightmare.

Bravery isn't about not being afraid.

Their dad's words echoed through his head. He sucked in a breath. He was more afraid than he'd ever been in his life. It wasn't just his life at stake; David's was at risk, too. But this wasn't the first time.

"How much oxygen do you have left?" Jeff whispered.

"It says six percent. What about you?"

"Enough."

Jeff motioned for David to follow, and they began moving toward the deck-turned-climbing wall. Punctures in the outer hull let a few beams of light cast themselves across the wall, but most of it was obscured in shadows. This would make finding handholds and footholds even more difficult.

Back in cub scouts, he had gone climbing with his dad and their pack. They had learned the basics of how to scale walls with predetermined routes, and how to rappel down them. Jeff and some of the others boys had been frightened at the time. But Dad had told them not to worry—the climbing harnesses strapped about their waists would catch them if they fell. The people belaying them could always gently lower them back to the ground.

There's no belaying rope now, though. No harness, and no one to catch us.

"We got this, bud," Jeff said, patting his younger brother's back. "You just use your hands to steady yourself and your legs to push yourself up. Got that?"

"Push with my legs."

"That's right. I'm going to let you go first, and I'll be right behind you."

"What should I grab first?" David asked.

Jeff pointed to a piece of the deck that had peeled away, leaving behind bare skeletal scaffolding.

David showed no hesitation. He found a handhold and pulled himself up. Bit by bit he ascended, with Jeff acting as his guide.

They used the charred wiring and broken pipes to brace themselves. Where the plates on the deck had come loose, they found that the structure under it worked like a ladder. It wasn't nearly as bad as Jeff had thought. They could actually do this, and soon they'd be in the armory. They'd find themselves some oxygen canisters.

And then? What would be next?

Jeff's foot slipped. His weight shifted under him, and he kicked to regain his footing. He started to lose his grip on the chunk of decking he'd grabbed. A piece of charred plating fell away and clattered against the deck below. The impact let out a hollow, metallic ringing that echoed throughout the cavernous corridor.

Regaining his grip, Jeff pulled himself close to the wall. His heart thumped rapidly in his chest, and he fought to control his breathing.

David looked down, but Jeff couldn't see his brother's face in the darkness.

Raising a thumbs up, Jeff indicated he was okay, and then he pointed to direct David to keep climbing.

A scratching noise stopped them both before they could get much farther. Jeff pressed his body against the bulkhead, and David followed suit.

But it was too late. The blue shape of a spider emerged over the top of the precipice. Light bleeding through one of the wounds in the ship's hull silhouetted the monster. Its mandibles clicked together like it was tasting the air. The alien must have heard the piece of plating hit the floor, but had it seen them yet?

Jeff had to remind himself that the Organics' sensors didn't detect volumes of water as small as children.

The spider twisted a claw around the edge of the wall. David was only a meter under it, and Jeff was just half a meter below him. Maybe, like the scorpion alien, the spider was just making its rounds.

But it continued to linger there on the edge. It was almost as if it already knew they were there and was just teasing them. What if it stood there until Jeff's air ran out?

The spider shifted, and hope buoyed Jeff once again. It was actually backing up. They would be able to finish their climb and find an oxygen canister and—

A hiss shot out of the spider's maw. It suddenly lunged forward, its claws slamming down around David.

"No!" Jeff screamed.

— 12 —

A fire still burned in the back of Sophie's head. She couldn't tell if the pain was growing worse, or if her elation at initially seeing Emanuel had momentarily stalled the tide of agony now building within her. A red hue seemed to float at the edge of her vision, threatening to encroach on her sight. She struggled to think straight at times, feeling her consciousness wash over her like the changing tides.

"We're never going to find this colony," Diego said. "For all we know, we might've already passed it."

The Rhino's motors hummed as usual, adding to the pounding in her head. One of the wheels had progressively worsened from the damage it had sustained. Now, every time they went over particularly rocky terrain, the whole Rhino bucked and the wheel groaned as if it might fall off.

"I don't think we've missed the colony yet," Sophie said.

The soldier shot her back a confused look. "How do you know?"

Even Emanuel appeared bemused.

"I'm not sure," Sophie said, "but I don't think we're anywhere close yet."

Diego's brow remained scrunched even as he turned back to look out the windshield. She could tell he wasn't convinced. She didn't blame him. She had no way of knowing where the NTC colony was. The information available to her on its location was the same as the rest of the crew had.

But something at the back of her mind told her it was true, and that they were headed in the right direction.

Fear of the nanobots returned. Maybe they were slowly resurrecting within her, trying to take over again? A shudder ripped across her cold flesh. She was feverish, and did all she could to prevent herself from trembling.

"You okay?" Emanuel asked.

"I'll be fine…"

Emanuel nodded, but the concern etched across his bearded face showed he wasn't convinced about her condition either. Thankfully he didn't press the issue.

Sophie took a moment to study the rest of the Rhino. Owen and Jamie stared out the windows with groggy expressions. Bouma and Holly sat nearby, keeping a watchful eye on them. Ort and Diego remained steadfast in guiding the Rhino over the alien terrain at the front of the vehicle. A bit of cryostat fluid still sloshed around the floor. Some of it had evaporated, and the rest had been syphoned into the self-cleaning ventilation system. Thanks to the cryostat fluid going through the filters, there was a sweet tang to the atmosphere.

That sweetness only seemed to make Sophie's headache worse.

There was no way to confirm it, but the more Sophie thought about it, the more certain she was that the nanobots were indeed coming back. What if the nanobots could replicate, like bacteria or viruses? What if they were propagating in her bloodstream and preparing to take over her brain? How long before she condemned the rest of the group, the people who might be the very last remnants of humanity, to a bloody death at the claws of the Organics?

Emanuel was now working on one of the portable RVAMPs he'd created. The small device was their last line of protection against the Organics. Better that they avoid the aliens altogether than engage in combat, but at least they no longer had to fear the impermeability of those shields like they had at the beginning of the Organic invasion. These weapons had given humanity a fighting chance.

"Sophie, your intuition still telling you we're on the right track?" Diego asked from the front of the vehicle. The flat landscape unrolled before them in a desert devoid of signs of either humanity or Organics.

And still, somehow, Sophie knew they were headed in the right general direction. "Yes, keep going."

It gnawed at her that she couldn't explain how she knew this. All of this had something to do with her visions, the nanobots, and the Organics.

If her fate was going to be anything like Lieutenant Smith's back at Cheyenne Mountain, she couldn't rely on her intuition any longer. The particle physicist side of her kicked in. At heart, she was a scientist. No one had designed a spaceship to Mars because it "felt right," or created cures for all kinds of cancers because "their intuition told them the cure would work."

No, they needed hard data and scientific principles. That was the only way to guide a spaceworthy ship for Mars, or create a nanoparticle drug delivery system to selectively zap cancer cells in the human body.

She needed to don that science hat now because, whenever the nanobots took over and her mind failed, at least the rest of the crew would have hard data to take them to the NTC colony.

"Sonya, have you uncovered any signals that may be of interest?" Sophie asked.

"I have not, Doctor Winston."

Ort shook his head. "We've already asked her the same thing a million times. Nothing."

Sophie wasn't convinced. "No electromagnetic waves? No optical signals? Not a single suspicious X-ray?"

"No, Doctor."

Sophie looked to Emanuel. "How's that possible? You don't just sit a human colony down here and let it get swallowed by a black hole."

"Maybe they've gone dark," Emanuel said. "They've been quiet so the Organics don't find them."

"Sure," Sophie started. A flame within her skull burned hotter. She pressed a hand to her temple in a futile attempt to assuage the pain. "I understand radio silence, but there's no way a colony is surviving out here without electronics."

"Then Sonya would've reported them," Emanuel said. "She wouldn't have missed that."

Something about that didn't sit right with Sophie. She'd worked closely with Alexia back on Earth and knew the power of AIs. Sonya seemed *off*, somehow. Earlier, Emanuel had mentioned that he thought her transfer wasn't complete. The AI was able to answer generic questions and help them operate the Rhino, but Emanuel was right; something was missing.

And Sophie reckoned she knew what that was. "Sonya, can you tell me the status of your intuitive framework?"

"Such a framework does not exist," Sonya said.

"And why not?"

"Transfer from shipboard systems to the Rhino was

not completed in time. Priority was given to functionality systems in lieu of systems deemed extraneous to mission success."

"Uh, Doc, can you translate that into English?" Ort asked.

Sophie rubbed her head, leaning back against the Rhino's seat. "Sonya started with the programming she thought we'd need to make it to the colony. She didn't send things like personality programs or AI intuition—all the bits and pieces that give AIs the ability to really think creatively. Those take forever to upload."

"Which means she doesn't understand subtext," Emanuel added.

Ort snorted. "Y'all are still losing me."

"When we asked if she sensed any signals, we weren't asking the right question," Sophie said.

"'No signals' means 'no signals'," Diego said. "How's that wrong?"

Holly grinned, understanding immediately. She might not be a physicist or computational expert, but she was a psychologist, and Sophie knew she understood human thinking—and as a result, the weaknesses of nonhuman thought.

"She might be telling us she cannot and has not detected anything, but what she isn't telling us is whether she actually has the ability to do so," Holly said.

"Exactly," Sophie said. "Sonya, what is the effective range of electromagnetic signal detection on the Rhino?"

"Currently two point six kilometers," the AI replied.

That was extremely low. They should be able to detect EM signals at a couple hundred kilometers at least.

"And optic signaling?" Sophie tried.

"Zero meters."

"How the hell is that possible...?" Diego said. His words trailed off and he slumped in the driver's seat. "Oh, God. The damage we took in that Organic attack."

"Exactly," Sophie said. "We'll need to repair the comm equipment and the sensor arrays."

Ort straightened in his seat, craning his neck to look back at Sophie. "Then we get our comm systems back online and send a message to the colony?"

"No." Sophie pushed herself up from the seat. A wave of pain followed, and she almost fell. Emanuel reached to help her, but she waved him off.

"We can't risk sending any communications. We've got to go for passive detection. The last thing we want is to send out a beacon that calls all the Organics to our position." Sophie moved to the supplies and started to shovel through them.

Emanuel watched her, concern in his gaze.

"Trust me," she said. This was her realm of expertise, and she needed to do something to help, and keep her mind off all the worries. Besides, they'd all risked their lives to get her comatose self off the *Sunspot*.

"Sonya, identify potential reasons for communication system failure, along with expected probabilities of each," Sophie said.

Prompting the AI, she troubleshot all the potential realms of failures for the comm systems. Emanuel worked as her assistant as they replaced fuses and removed melted wires behind a panel near the controls.

The Rhino continued onward, bouncing over the terrain as they worked. The group shared rationed meals and water, all the while keeping a nervous eye out the windows. Holly and Bouma entertained Jamie and Owen, sharing bits of an MRE with them. Ort drove for a while, giving Diego a chance to rest. Hours ticked by. Hours they didn't have.

They hadn't detected any Organics tailing them before, which had given them a false sense of security. Now the suspicion was that they might not have detected them simply because of their compromised comm system and sensor arrays. For all Sophie knew, the aliens were toying with them, waiting until she succumbed to the nanobots.

She continued working, even as the pain spread from her head and into her muscles. The nanobots were probably burrowing into her nerves and muscles now, remodeling their new home and turning her into a compliant Organic host.

She vowed she wouldn't give them the pleasure of finishing their job. As she put the last pieces in place to connect one of the Rhino's antennas to a repaired nanocircuit board, she eyed the RVAMP. When she felt reality slipping from her fingers once again, she would activate that device, aiming it at herself. This time, she might well fry her own nervous system completely.

Yes, risking her own life with the RVAMP was definitely better than the alternative. They might have already lost Jeff and David, and there was no way she would be responsible for any more deaths.

She slapped a plate back over the nanocircuit board. "That's it. Sonya, bring comm systems and sensor arrays back online."

A low hum resonated through the Rhino.

"All systems back online," Sonya said.

The rest of the group cheered, but Sophie didn't share in their joy. The systems might be online, but that didn't mean the range of detection limits were restored to adequate levels yet.

"Give me a gauge of system functionality relative to full," Sophie said.

Diego gave her a look like she'd just spoken in Russian.

"Sixty-five percent of normal," Sonya said.

"That should be enough," Sophie said. "Ort, see anything on the display now?"

Ort's face drained of color, and his mouth fell open. "We got a signal."

***

They drove on. The distance between the Rhino and the mysterious signal was closing. Diego studied the display. Now that they were closer, their IR sensor arrays had kicked in. They still didn't have a visual on where the signal was originating, but at least they had new intel.

"Sonya," Diego said. "What does this new IR signal mean?"

"We are within detection limits of the unidentified object."

"Yeah, yeah, I get that," Diego said. He reminded himself to talk in AI language like Sophie had done. "What are the probabilities that this signature is that of the NTC colony?"

"I have no information regarding the purported energy output or the physical size of the NTC colony. Calculating such a probability is impossible. Please provide the inputs."

"I think I can handle that," Sophie spoke up. She was sitting in one of the back seats. Jamie had her head in Sophie's lap, and Sophie was stroking the girl's hair. She gave Sonya rough estimates on the size of the colony, and drew up some quick calculations to estimate the energy output. "Sonya, please use the maximum and minimum values I've provided to calculate a range of possibilities for this unidentified object being an NTC colony."

Sonya disappeared for a moment. Diego blinked, and she was back on their screens. "Dr. Winston, according to the values you provided, there is a zero percent chance that the signature matches that of the colony if it is functional."

"If the colony is *functional?*" Diego asked. "What does functional have to do with it?"

"Dr. Winston provided values for a colony that had been damaged or operating below normal as well," Sonya continued. "However, these values, too, do not match up."

"Then what the hell are we looking at?" Diego asked.

Sonya began to explain. "We are looking at an electro—"

"No," Diego interrupted. He'd let himself slip into another phrase the AI had taken too literally. "I mean, what is another potential explanation for this signal?"

"According to the data I do have from the *Sunspot*, the signal is within the expected range for a ship of that size and nature," Sonya said.

"Holy shit," Diego said. "Another NTC ship out there? Would that signature match a *functional* ship?"

"That would be correct," Sonya said.

"Why the hell didn't you tell us that in the first place?" Diego asked Sonya.

"Because you didn't ask."

Diego's chest felt light. This wasn't exactly an NTC colony, but an NTC ship that was actually in working order had to be a good sign.

Hopefully...

As they carried on toward the signal, Diego worked hard not to get his hopes up. Memories of the *Radiant Dawn* haunted any ounce of optimism that dared buoy his spirits. The signal only continued to grow stronger, and Sonya's confidence that it was a ship like the *Sunspot* increased as they went.

Now even Sophie seemed to be unable to contain her anticipation. Bouma offered her his seat near the front display, and she gladly took it, monitoring their progress and any incoming signals from the ship.

"Should we send out a message?" Ort asked. "We're close enough to warn them we're coming."

Sophie shook her head. "No, even now I want passive detection only. If we try any kind of active signaling or communications, the Organics may intercept it. The last thing we want is to broadcast our location when we're this close to another NTC ship."

Diego started to speak. "That makes sense, but—"

Sophie froze. Her sudden rigidness drew Diego's focus away from his driving.

"Something wrong?" he asked.

Instead of answering, Sophie's eyes rolled up. Her mouth locked open, and she slumped into her seat.

— 13 —

Athena ignored Griffin's advice about sitting this mission out. Crossing the seabed again did terrify her, but she couldn't back down now, especially after her speech on the bridge. Her crew needed a leader.

Since Captain Noble's capture and likely death, she had done everything she could to fill his shoes. Today, she wondered if she had done enough. Her crew was split on whether to stay or leave the submarine. But there was only one real option in her mind—leave the GOA and make the journey to Pelican AFB. She had promised Captain Noble she would take care of his crew, and that's exactly what she planned to do.

She continued on point across the sand toward Los Angeles. Her muscles were still tight, and she was running on fumes.

Griffin walked to her left, his RPG angled up and helmet scanning the blue sky above. Taylor flanked her on the right, his RPG also at the ready. Behind them, Trish and Malone held rear guard with pulse rifles and the remaining EMP grenades.

The plan was simple: head out to the location of the vehicles, and take them if they still worked, then head back to the GOA. People like Posey and Collins would, in the meantime, have plenty of time to think about if they wanted to leave the submarine or not.

Maybe, if they saw working vehicles, they would

change their minds. At this point, everyone she could save made a difference. Every single soul counted.

She focused back on the sky with her new helmet. Today, the vast stretch of blue mirrored an ocean that no longer existed.

Not a drop of water glimmered to the west. Nothing but cracked, tan earth.

To the east, the great skyline of Los Angeles came into focus above the shimmering heat. Her HUD revealed the temperature was already at one hundred and eighteen degrees.

That was the least of her worries right now. There were still Organics in the city, and they needed all of their ammo for the trip to Pelican AFB.

Athena balled her hand into a fist when they reached the street at the edge of the beach. Down the block, a few vehicles were partially exposed by the shifting sands. She looked for Organics tracks, then motioned for the team to continue.

They fanned out, half keeping to the left side of the street and the other half on the right side. Several buildings had collapsed, forming screes of debris around their bases that spilled over into the road.

Griffin roved his pulse rifle back and forth across the exteriors of the structures. The RPG was slung over his back, now that they were safely away from the exposed seabed.

Trish stopped to stare at something toward the east.

"What is it?" Athena asked. But before Trish answered, she saw what had attracted the communications officer's attention. The blue sky had taken on a brown and yellow tint beyond the skyscrapers.

Athena raised her scope to glass the storm.

"We need to move," she said.

The dust storm was moving fast, and the winds were stirring up smoke from fires. They had to get off the narrow chute of the street. The hundred-mile-an-hour winds that came with storms like these would knock them away like bowling pins.

She checked her HUD again to look for the NAV marker she had set for the coordinates of the underground parking garage. Just three blocks to go. Her eyes flicked to the corresponding location down the street. A mountain of rubble lay between them and their destination.

If they hurried, they could make it, provided they didn't run into hostiles. She motioned for the team to continue with a hand signal. They set off at a brisk pace, weapons clanking over armor loud enough she could hear it over the raging wind.

Griffin's wide frame was the first to reach the pile of debris in the road. He raised his rifle, hunched down, and moved through a narrow gap where two piles nearly touched.

Athena went next, ducking under a piece of rebar. Twisted metal scratched her armor. She cringed at the sound, but kept moving.

Once the team was through, they set off down the next street, then took a left onto another block of office buildings. The structures towered over them, reaching fifty floors toward the sky.

Griffin, Malone, and Taylor all stayed focused on the grimy exteriors, looking for contacts behind the shattered windows. While the aliens had caused the damage on the last street, nature had caused the damage here. Windows had been blown out by dust storms, and the asphalt was cracked from the heat. A fine layer of sand, dust, and grit covered everything.

Griffin suddenly motioned for everyone to get off the road. The team bolted for cover through the open door of an office building, and took up position in the lobby.

By the time Athena made her way behind an overturned table, she realized they weren't all here.

Trish was missing.

Looking over the table, Athena scanned the road and found Trish crouched next to the bumper of a car. She had her rifle clutched against her chest, and was aiming it at the building Athena and the others had taken refuge in.

Scratch, scrape, scratch, scrape.

Wind rushed down the street, whipping up a vortex of grime and blocking Athena's view of Trish.

She cursed under her breath and looked to Griffin.

"I'll go grab her," he said, beginning to move before she had a chance to stop him. Athena watched the big Marine walk over to the door. They needed Trish. She was a skilled communications officer and engineer—and the only engineer on this mission, since Posey had refused to come. Without knowing what state the vehicles they wanted were in, they absolutely needed someone with engineering and mechanical experience.

Griffin unslung his RPG and repositioned himself on the opposite side of the doorframe. The whistling of the wind combined with the scratching of claws outside, but the Marine wasn't deterred. He stepped out while Malone and Taylor moved over to Athena's position.

A thump, followed by an almost instant explosion, rocked the building. Griffin moved back into the lobby as a waterfall of brick, glass, metal, and blue flesh slammed onto the sidewalk. Two clawed spider legs stuck out of the pile, twitching.

"Come on!" Griffin yelled to Trish.

She hesitated, but then got to her feet and ran toward the pile. Griffin had already switched to his pulse rifle. He climbed up the smoldering wreckage and fired two rounds point blank into the spider's skull. Then he reached down to Trish and pulled her up and into the building.

"Out the back," he ordered.

Athena patted his linebacker shoulders with gratitude and followed the team through the lobby to locate the exit.

"You okay?" she asked.

Trish managed a nod.

They navigated the hallways at a breakneck pace, coming to the back door a few minutes later. Griffin checked the alleyway, and then motioned for everyone to follow him.

A cascade of wind beat the team back as they made their way down the narrow alley. The sky darkened overhead, taking on a brown angry tint. The alley was filled with the sticky remains of orbs that hadn't dried out in the sun yet. Trash and plastic bottles stuck to the remains.

Athena kept her focus on Griffin, watching his movements. He halted at the edge of the intersection with the sidewalk. Rows of shops towered across the street. Dark brown clouds swirled toward them, lightning flashing across the bulging storm.

Over the noise came a scratchy whistle that sent a chill across Athena's body. Not spiders this time. The vampire-like alien that had escaped the attack the prior night was out there, hunting. This was the first time they had faced the beasts during the day, which told her it was desperate, and therefore even more dangerous.

"Move," she said.

Keeping low, the team set off across the street. Violent gusts of wind bit into their suits, and Athena leaned into it with her helmet. Grit blinded her visor as the edge of the storm rushed into the road.

They fought their way along, using the protection of the buildings. Hugging the exteriors, they moved in a chain toward the underground parking garage.

Griffin located it a few minutes later, and pulled open a gate to let them down a concrete stairwell.

"Go, go, go!" he shouted.

Looking over her shoulder, Athena spotted a pulsating blue light in the whipping wind covering the street. She strained to see through the cloud of sand, finally spotting a tail and a crustacean body moving through the cloud.

Raising her rifle, she aimed for the approaching beast.

"Come on!" Trish yelled.

"Go, I'm right behind you," Athena replied. She turned for a moment to watch as Trish and Malone went into the stairwell. Taylor went next. Griffin stood there, motioning for Athena, but she pressed her visor back to her riflescope.

She couldn't let this thing follow them inside.

But now she couldn't find it in the rush of wind.

"Give me your launcher," she ordered. The scream of the storm rose into a growl that made it difficult to hear Griffin shouting at her.

"Give it to me!" she yelled again, handing her pulse rifle over. He gave her the launcher, then grabbed the back of her armor to hold her steady.

She glimpsed the pulsating blue of the alien across the

street, where it had scuttled behind a vehicle. It continued battling the torrent of sand, using its pincers to score ruts and pull itself through the gusts.

The creature opened its mandibles to let out a screech. High-pitched whistling screamed from its slotted nostrils. Using a claw, it pulled itself around the car and homed in on her.

"No, you don't," she said, pulling the trigger.

The grenade streaked into the wind and impacted to the right of the creature, blowing out a hunk of street with a claw still stuck in the asphalt. The body of the alien cartwheeled away from its severed limb, the storm taking it into the sky.

She lowered the weapon and watched the pulsating blue vanish into the brown vortex. Griffin pulled on her armor, and she finally followed her team into the underground parking garage to take shelter.

***

ENTRY 10202
DESIGNEE – AI ALEXIA

The loss of Commander Suzuki and his team of Japanese soldiers has me reevaluating my military strategy moving forward. While I was designed for a wide variety of functions, I was not given the military training that some other AIs are programmed with.

I've improvised by studying military strategy and warfare. The Organics are unlike any enemy the human race has seen, but they do have their weaknesses. My objective isn't to find a way to defeat them, but rather to find a way to help the remaining human survivors escape.

Doing so may be the only way to prevent the extinction of the species that designed me.

My plan to hack or commandeer the Sharks failed with the death of Commander Suzuki and his squad, but I did have enough time to download the details of the operations systems before I lost contact with the soldiers. I'm not exactly back to square one, as humans say, but I'm still not any closer to understanding how the Organic flight systems work.

So here I am, formulating a new plan for Corporal Athena Rollins and her ragtag crew while trying to dissect the schematics of the flight systems. While I work, the corporal and her team are likely on their way to find the underground vehicles and take them to Pelican Air Force Base. The odds of making it, and then crossing the desert without detection, aren't good, however. There is a lot of Organic drone activity in the vicinity due to the attack on Athena the previous night.

I pull up the newest aerial view from Lolo. It just came in a few minutes ago, and I've sped through the recording to search for hostiles within a three-hundred-mile radius. There are currently four drones in the sector, and two Sharks. My calculations show a ninety-nine percent chance Corporal Rollins and her team will be detected, either by ground troops or by the patrolling aircraft, in the course of their journey to Pelican Air Force Base.

That's where I come in.

I'm working on a distraction—something to lead the aircraft out of the area and give them an opening. If I can do that, then the likelihood of success is nearly sixty-five percent.

But the only way to cause the type of distraction they need is to do something I've tried to avoid. Until now.

194

Tapping into the external Biosphere operations system, I pull up the diagnostics for Cheyenne Mountain. There are plenty of ways to grab the attention of the Organics, but I'm looking for the most effective. Something they cannot ignore. My system scan shows that the air raid sirens are still functional on the east, west, and south sides of the mountain. The electromagnetic pulse that took down most human technology on invasion day did not penetrate deep enough to disable those sirens, much like it didn't destroy the systems inside the Biosphere.

But I'm also not sure if using them will be enough to bring the Organic army down on Cheyenne Mountain. Perhaps there is something else, something...

Ah yes, here it is.

I've been waiting to use these for a while.

Tapping into the weapons system, I activate the fifty-year-old missile launch system. While the missiles had all been removed when the facility was decommissioned, the operations system is still functional. If I can "fake" a launch, it might be enough to attract every Organic within a thousand miles or more.

It's worth a shot, literally.

I bring the system online and code a new launch. Whether or not it will do the trick remains to be seen. The sirens activate outside, and I use an external camera to monitor the skyline for alien ships.

Meanwhile, I check Lolo to see if there are new images of the GOA. I discover a major dust storm ravaging Los Angeles. The storm is a category four. Not quite the worst, but a significant danger nonetheless. At least the sand will provide some cover for Corporal Rollins and her team until my plan has a chance to work.

I notice a pending radio transmission from Lolo while scanning the video, the first in months. It has been encrypted and decrypted, delaying its arrival; a long process that tells me whoever sent it wanted to avoid Organics translating it. I'm hopeful it's Doctor Winston's crew on the NTC *Sunspot*, but the emotion falls short of earning the excitement that a human might feel when I bring it up.

To anyone that's listening, this is AI Sonya with the NTC Sunspot *broadcasting from Mars. We believe we have located the colony, but there are also Organics here. Standby for more information.*

My fear of Organics on Mars has now been confirmed.

This new message inspires more questions than answers. Doctor Hoffman believed the colony was the only hope for the human race. He believed the Organics wouldn't return to Mars due to the fact it was already stripped of water.

But now there is water there.

Humans.

I pause for a millisecond to consider the implications. Meanwhile, I pull up a view of Los Angeles. Corporal Athena's team is on the move through the city in two vehicles, a pickup, and a van. My system slows another half second when I see what's tracking them.

END ENTRY

***

A fire burned through Sophie. It felt as if the nanobots wanted retribution for being left dormant for so long. Every muscle in her body contracted until Sophie was afraid the muscle fibers would start tearing from the ligaments. She wanted to scream and yell, but she couldn't.

The nanobots were taking over.

Sophie could feel them swarming her body.

For a moment, she could still see the world around her, confined to the space aboard the Rhino. Then everything went dark.

"Please," she managed.

Her voice came out wispy and strangled. But at least it didn't hurt anymore. She flexed her fingers. They curled on command, and she stood. When her legs pushed her up, there was no resistance against her feet. It was as if she was swimming now.

She opened her eyes. Brilliant white light blinded her for a moment. Several seconds passed during which she drowned in the intensity until her pupils adjusted.

Her heart flipped when she realized she was flying.

What in God's name had the nanobots done to her?

A blanket of darkness lay overhead, punctuated by the flicker and burn of stars in the heavens. Below was the surface of Mars, as if it was day. The ground was like a carpet of lively embers. Deep canyons cut through a landscape filled with rock formations that had stood for eons, undisturbed and unwitnessed. She suddenly felt a deep longing. The same, distant longing that had been there before.

A vision flashed before her.

All the red and rock had been replaced with lush forest. Plants unlike any she'd ever seen reached for the sky with the confidence of birds taking flight. Plush white clouds drifted on warm winds, and strange animals moved about the landscape, their colors more vibrant than any human eye could make sense of. Giant creatures strode about the landscape, living off the abundance of food. Multiple legs and eyes, and vestigial body parts Sophie had no name for, sprouted off the beasts. Somehow, she sensed they meant her no harm. That they lived here in an Eden-like paradise, undisturbed and unthreatened.

A river washed through this valley, stretching from somewhere far in the distance. Even from Sophie's height, she could not discern its source. A mountain? An underground spring, maybe?

Deep within her, a voice told her this was what had been. The truth, obscured by time. A world forgotten by almost all. It was hidden in the very genetic material passed down through the Organics.

This was their old world.

All of it seemed to shift, swirling into a mass of gray and black. Smog filled the landscape, and trees burned. Huge animals screeched as beams of plasma lanced through their bodies. Mechanical spiders strutted over the land, and blue orbs glowed between the husks of dead plants.

The river had dwindled to a stream. Murky brown sludge flowed slowly through the ravine.

A sudden force grabbed hold of Sophie and dragged her through the atmosphere. She choked on the smoke drifting from ruinous jumbles of machines and metallic objects she assumed were evidence of some civilized society.

Then she was falling—plummeting back to the

surface. Air tore at her skin and hair. She let out a scream that was stifled by everything rushing past. Her stomach flipped, and she lost control. Sky and ground swirled in a never-ending kaleidoscope.

She braced to slam against the ground. Her body would hit with a force that would tear her into individual molecules.

Centimeters above the ground, she stopped, hovering. The world was no longer a smelting of burned earth and metal. Instead, it was a landscape that gleamed black. An iron kingdom dotted with blue orbs. The sky erupted in flame and light as spaceships tore off into the abyss above them, and others careened toward the landscape, landing amid the obsidian strongholds.

Spiders and Sentinels and other aliens Sophie didn't recognize unloaded blue orbs. Those orbs were plastered across the otherwise bleak landscape.

"I don't understand," Sophie said. "Why are you showing me this?"

Her voice seemed to break whatever spell had taken hold. Everything vanished, like sand blown in the wind.

She walked alone in a landscape as barren as the one the Rhino had been driving through. A few rock formations and mountains in the background looked familiar. There was no sign of the Rhino.

Instead, she wandered alone. A glow drew her toward the horizon. No longer hindered by pain in her joints or muscles, she sprinted for it. This must be it. This was the NTC ship they were headed toward.

She crested a hill, and the light from the ship hit her with an almost palpable force. Shielding her eyes with her hands, she climbed toward the intense glow. A warmth spread from the ship, and she let it envelop her until her eyes adjusted to its brightness.

There, sitting before her, was a ship like the *Sunspot*. There was no damage evident. Big white letters emblazoned across its side announced: *Secundo Casu*.

Her vision tunneled.

This was the ship Hoffman had taken to Mars.

Hope sprang fresh within her once again, like rain after a fire. It washed away the ash of loss and vanquished the smoldering remains of despair. This wasn't the colony, but it was the next step toward it.

Near the *Secundo Casu* was another ship, smooth curves and azure highlights along an ebony shell. No more than a tenth the size of the biosphere ship, it fit snugly against it, nearly camouflaged by the shadow of the NTC ship.

Out of the smaller ship came spiders. They trailed between the NTC vessel and the small ship like ants carrying cargo.

My God, Sophie thought. *We're headed right into a trap.*

Every nerve in her body lit up with a million lightning strikes scorching under her flesh. She clenched her eyelids closed, repeating a silent mantra to take her back to the others. She had to warn them.

Red flashed beneath her eyelids with every stroke, and her muscles quivered. Her eyelids burst open, releasing her into the real world, and she gasped for breath.

She'd beaten the nanobots' hold on her.

At least, this time.

Sweat rolled down her forehead, and she shot upright. The tang of cryostat fluid once again swamped her nostrils. Faces appeared around her, calling her name and dabbing at her head with rags.

Everything swirled until she pressed a hand to her forehead. She forced herself up against the hands.

"No," she said, swatting them away.

She lurched to the front cabin, where Diego and Ort were at the driver's controls. Her knees buckled and twisted. She felt drunk.

"We have to stop," she said, the words coming out in a slur. "It's a trap. We have to stop."

"What?" Diego asked, looking at her with an incredulous, cockeyed gaze.

She tried to swallow. Her tongue was swollen. When she tried speaking again, it was as though she was talking through a mouthful of cotton. "We have to turn back. The Organics are there. They're at the *Secundo Casu.*"

Emanuel put a hand gently on her shoulder.

"We have to stop," Sophie said, facing him.

"We are stopped," Diego replied.

Sophie turned to look out the viewscreen. The world was still bathed in the blacks and greens of the night vision overlay, but there was something out there.

She blinked several times to make sure it was really the ship from her vision.

"That's *Secundo Casu,*" Diego said.

Sophie stepped closer to the windshield. It's existence alone was a miracle, untarnished by Organic claws or firearms, looking as brand new as it must have when it departed White Sands. Her eyes flitted across the terrain, searching for the aliens. But there was nothing out there. No spiders carting cargo back and forth. Not even any tracks.

"Calm down, Sophie. This is Hoffman's ship," Emanuel said. "The colony has to be close, and if this ship is fine…"

Holly and the kids pressed up into the cockpit area, smiling for the first time that day.

But Sophie couldn't bring herself to feel any joy at the sight in front of her. Something told her this was wrong—that this was still a trap, that the place they had come to seek salvation from was the home of the aliens.

— 14 —

The spider's claws slammed into the *Sunspot*'s bulkhead next to David. Tremors shook through the bulkhead, making Jeff nearly lose his precarious handhold. They were so close to the top of the wall, and now this spider threatened everything. His oxygen alarms were beeping at him, and David was holding onto the wall by one hand. With a short screech, the spider bent over the side, climbing down toward David.

Its mandibles clicked together and blue saliva roped from them, spraying the two boys as it shrieked. The scratch and scrape of other spiders responding to this one echoed down the other corridors. More were on their way.

Jeff was nearly out of oxygen. His brother was dangling by one arm. And the spider was inching closer.

Everything Jeff had fought for was about to go to waste. All the promises he'd made his dad about protecting his younger brother seemed like nothing but a handful of lies now. Maybe it was his dad's fault for expecting too much. How were two boys supposed to survive against aliens like this?

Or maybe it was Bouma's fault for leaving him and David to defend the *Sunspot*. And maybe it was Emanuel's fault for letting them leave to go to the turret, even though it wasn't a good spot from which to defend against the oncoming Organics.

The spider screeched again, the sound something close to metal scraping against metal. All its globular eyes sparkled in the flash of Jeff's helmet-mounted lights. It seemed to be telling him he had lost. That he and his brother were nothing but a meal.

Prey was prey, and the first item on the menu was David. Blaming other people wouldn't stop the alien from going after his kid brother.

Jeff summoned every bit of resolve he had left, straining to ignore the incessant alarms and the spiders clattering and shrieking throughout the ship. He didn't know what was going to happen next, or how they would escape the oncoming horde. He just knew he needed to take out this single spider.

One of Bouma's lessons surfaced in his mind.

Learn to compartmentalize.

Take things piece by piece. Rather than trying to run all the way across a football field for a touchdown in one play, focus on the first ten yards. Then, when you've made it that far, figure out how you're going to go the next ten yards.

That's all Jeff needed to do. Compartmentalize. They would make their escape one step at a time. The first step: kill that spider before it killed David.

Jeff reached across his back with his free hand. One of his boots slipped as he did so. Chunks of charred metal flaked away and pinged against the deck far below. He could feel his other boot threatening to slip, too. He didn't stop reaching until his fingers hit the device he'd been trying to reach. Yanking the EMP grenade off the strap slung over his shoulder, he activated it and tossed it upward in one fluid motion.

A flash of light cast aside the darkness of the corridor,

blinding Jeff. In his mind's eye, he saw the next step. Still hanging onto the wall with one hand, and his boot gradually coming out of place, he slung his pulse rifle off his shoulder. Aiming with one hand wasn't accurate, nor was it recommended. It went against every ounce of marksmanship training Bouma had tried to instill in him. But Bouma had also told Jeff that improvisation was just as important as the rules, and a good soldier knew when to improvise.

He improvised now. The pulse shots went wild, arcing up along the wall and slicing toward the spider. Best as he could, Jeff took control of his sporadic aim as though he was clumsily wielding a huge knife.

The alien didn't see it coming. Shots plunged through its flesh. Globs of blood spewed out, and chunks of armor sizzled with each impact. The spider paused for a second, as if shocked. It seemed to have no idea its shields had been deactivated.

But its surprise didn't faze Jeff. He riddled the monster with rounds until its mandibles stopped moving and its legs curled up.

Jeff nearly hooted in victory, but the cry died on his lips. The alien fell from the bulkhead. As it did, a stray leg caught David, knocking his other hand free from the bulkhead.

"Jeff!" David said, eyes wide.

Jeff swung toward David and, using every last bit of air he had left in his system, stretched for his brother.

Their gloves connected, but, lubricated as they were by the spider's spilled blood, David nearly slipped through his grip. Jeff had been looking for someone to blame for this disaster, but in the end he could only blame himself. If he dropped David, that would be on him. No one else.

He grabbed David's hand as tightly as he could. He could practically hear the bones in David's hand crunch, but he didn't care. A little bit of pain was worth a life.

The spider's corpse smashed against the deck below, leaving a crater in the bent metal. The legs and thorax broke apart, slime-covered fragments spraying across the floor.

Jeff swung his brother closer to the wall.

David's fingers trembled, but he found a handhold.

Together, they climbed. The frightening chorus of other spiders grew with each meter of progress they made.

Jeff's heart beat even faster. Each beat was another gout of oxygen lost. A nervous sweat formed over his palms, and he could feel it soaking through his socks.

Stay calm. We're almost there.

He repeated that mantra over and over as they climbed, trying to drown out the alien screeches. It didn't work, but he did manage to control his panic enough to finally make it up the wall and onto the top deck. Once there, he finally saw the door of their target: the armory.

The door hung off its hinges, charred, just like everything else. Jeff lunged for it. Each step he took sent up a puff of black dust, and he left a trail of footprints in the charcoal dusting the deck.

He grabbed the lip of the hatch. His muscles burned, both from the strain and the oxygen deprivation. The door wouldn't budge.

"Let me help!" David said.

The boy grabbed a handhold. Together, they peeled back the door, leaving a deep gouge in the mangled deck. Their helmet-mounted lights flooded the space, giving it a stark white glow. Dust sifted from cracks in the bulkhead.

Benches along the floor had been ripped from their struts and tossed about the space. A few mangled rifles lay in the corners, and a handful of empty magazines were strewn about.

While charred flakes of plastic and paper still floated about the space, it was mostly empty.

David picked up one of the busted rifles and Jeff surveyed the room. The few rifles left were damaged.

His mouth went dry, and he gulped. The warning lights on his oxygen alarms were flashing. One percent. He felt both defeat and relief—a bittersweet drink.

"Emanuel and the others must've escaped, and took everything with them."

"And the oxygen?" David asked, looking lost in the middle of the empty armory.

Jeff ran to the back of the space. He tore open the reinforced locker where the oxygen canisters had been stored.

His entire world seemed to fade away. His fingers trembled, and a heavy weight dragged itself through his torso.

This couldn't be happening.

"No, no, no," Jeff said. "No, no, no."

David said what Jeff could not. "It's empty."

***

The dark side of the moon wasn't so dark after all. Lights illuminated a base the size of a city. Noble pressed his hand against the side of his orb.

All around him, the other prisoners from the ship were being transported via an assembly line of belts that reminded Noble of a massive treadmill. His orb, too, sat on one of these belts. The cigar-shaped ships had dropped them off here some time earlier, and then the belts had clicked on, sending the hundreds of orbs toward a pyramidal structure at the center of the base.

They were still a few miles away, and Noble stood with his arms folded across his bare chest, shivering. The force field on his orb was down, but a faint shimmer revealed a nearly invisible field surrounding the conveyor belt. Even if he did escape his orb, there was nowhere to run.

As far as he knew, even with the Organics here, there wasn't oxygen on the moon. He would lose consciousness within thirty seconds outside the force field, which was clearly designed to protect him and the other aliens.

Noble pivoted to look for Ribbit. The creature was directly behind him, curled up inside its orb. The bloody crusts around the slits in its cracked hide moved up and down with each breath. It was running out of time.

The sight transported Noble back to the GOA, where he had sat in his comfortable leather chair for months, watching as Earth and all its living creatures died. He felt the same hopelessness now that he had felt on the submarine. Watching humans, animals, and now aliens, die made him want to scream.

The sound of his own voice startled him before he realized he was, in fact, screaming. Now he started to wonder if he really was losing it. But he was the only one making any noise. The aliens on the conveyer belts were all silent in their orbs. Those that had eyes had them focused on the pyramid.

Noble stopped screaming to watch the approaching structure, just like the rest of the prisoners.

The entire building appeared to be over five hundred

stories high, much larger than any skyscraper on Earth. The smooth blocks making up the exterior were massive rectangular pieces, all of them glowing the familiar cool blue characteristic of the Organics.

But it wasn't the size or the glow that came as the biggest shock—it was the construction. Aside from that light, everything about it hearkened back to the ancient pyramids in Egypt, and those built by the Aztecs and Mayans in South America.

He remembered the ancient alien theorists that believed those structures were constructs by aliens.

If they could see what I'm seeing now…

A streak of blue light shot out of the tip of the pyramid and lanced into the darkness of space. Noble's orb vibrated, and a violent banging followed as the light vanished in the black.

About a mile ahead was an opening at the base of the structure, through which the conveyor belts were feeding the orbs into the pyramid.

Noble stepped away from the wall, realization setting in. Had the Organics brought them here to preserve them, or were they doing something more sinister?

He scanned the base that surrounded them. On his left, an airfield supported a dozen winged aircraft with dorsal fins. To his right, three white domed structures protruded out of gray hills. Spiders and Sentinels moved in and out of cave-like openings, much like ants coming and going from an anthill. If he had to guess, they were some sort of barracks.

The aliens skittered along the conveyors, mandibles opening and closing at the view of fresh meat. Hundreds of claws kicked up a cloud of dust as the aliens came to watch.

A drone patrolling the pyramid shot over the minions. Two more drones followed, and then a fourth, which circled the pyramid, leaving long arcs of blue light residue in the air.

The conveyors clanked and vibrated as they drew closer to the vast structure rising above them. Noble stepped up to the wall of his orb to take a look. Roots was suspended from the top of its orb, its branch-like arms waving.

He was spooked, just like Noble was.

Another flash of light exploded out of the pyramid tip like a volcanic eruption.

The vibration once again rocked the conveyer belt, nearly knocking his orb off the track. The outer wall touched the force field with a sizzling zap. Noble flinched and moved away from the charred skin of his orb.

Four sinewy figures suddenly glimmered between the two conveyor belts at the entrance to the pyramid. The multi-dimensional entities stood like ghosts, watching the orbs enter their celestial palace.

The same voice he was used to hearing spoke in his mind.

Your sacrifice is for the good of all species. This is a significant honor. You have completed a remarkable great journey to be part of this, Captain Rick Noble.

Another blue flash burst from the top of the pyramid. Roots reached through its orb wall with its twig arms, and Ribbit managed to make it up onto both legs, wobbly, but standing to watch.

The great realm of light requires sacrifices to keep the realm alive. Today you are part of the great realm.

Noble blinked with realization, the same realization his other alien friends had apparently come to at that moment. They weren't being preserved in some sort of Noah's Ark. They were being sacrificed to some alien god.

***

Emanuel checked the biomonitors again. While Bouma, Diego, and Ort were scouting out the *Secundo Casu*, he and Holly were charged with looking out for any incoming Organics, and watching Sophie and the kids. Sonya was set to alert them at the first sign of any Organic ships or ground forces moving their way.

So far, it seemed their strategy of driving nonstop had given them a comfortable distance from any Organic scouts. But for how long? The Rhino was just a needle in a haystack, but the aliens had more advanced technology.

He worked on repairing one of the portable RVAMPs that had been damaged in their flight, knowing the aliens would find them eventually. Sophie sat across from him, working on a tablet. He could not help but imagine what the nanobots were doing inside her. How they were multiplying and taking over. When would they overthrow Sophie's mind and alert the rest of the Organics to their position?

A shiver washed through his flesh.

What if that's what she was doing right now? What if the woman he loved was betraying them even as he sat across from her, working to help save their lives?

She would never do that.

Emanuel cursed himself for thinking that.

"What are you working on?" he asked, looking between the wires sprouting from the RVAMP.

Sophie lowered the tablet and sighed. "I'm trying to

reprogram the OCT."

Emanuel wasn't sure what she was trying to do with the handheld optical coherence tomography machine. The device used coherent light sources, like lasers, to create three-dimensional images of objects through the angles at which reflected light was scattered. It didn't use ionizing radiation to capture these images, like an X-ray, but its reliance on light sources meant it could only probe a few centimeters under a person's skin. It was useful in identifying blood vessels and things like subdermal tumors…

Realization set in.

"You're trying to identify the nanobots?" he asked.

"Yes."

He shook his head. "The nanobots are way too small for the OCT to visualize."

"I know," Sophie said, as if there was no contradiction between her two statements. She continued her work on the tablet.

"I don't get it."

She looked up with a sad smile. Her skin was still oily, but she'd regained some of her color. "Lt. Smith had far higher concentrations of nanobots than I did."

"I remember," Emanuel said. He placed the RVAMP on a table and moved next to Sophie to look at her tablet. Her fingers tapped across the screen as she manipulated lines of code used to analyze the images obtained through the OCT. It started to become clearer to him. "You're not expecting to directly visualize individual nanobots, are you?"

"Not exactly." Sophie shook her head and set the tablet down in her lap. "I pulled up the data you transferred to the *Sunspot* and to our data stores here. It looks like the nanobots started to clump within Lt. Smith. My guess is, they were programmed to do that to create, for lack of a better word, antennae within Smith. That way, the bots could communicate with the Organics and vice versa."

"That makes sense. You never had the same numbers of nanobots, so the Organics couldn't get complete control over your body."

Sophie nodded. "I never had the same numbers of nanobots as Smith, but if they're propagating, I might now." She glared at him with a gaze that made him feel like she could read his thoughts.

"The OCT will be able to detect if there are clustered nanobots in my blood like there were in Smith's. If it detects them, it will mean it's too late for me. I'll be compromised and the Organics will use me against you all."

"Sophie…"

"I can't let that happen." Sophie gestured to the RVAMP. "If I'm unable to do it, then I need you to hit me with the RVAMP."

Painful memories surfaced in his mind. He'd watched Sophie activate the RVAMP that had saved their lives and defeated the Organics as they boarded the *Sunspot*. Her eyes had gone blank, crossing in different directions like a chameleon, and she'd collapsed to the ground.

"No, not again, Sophie. There's got to be a better way. Maybe we can stop the signal or restrain you or—"

"This is the only way." Her voice was sharp and firm. Emanuel knew then that she had made her decision. He wracked his brain for another way.

But he had nothing concrete.

"When we reach the colony, they'll be able to do

something," Emanuel said. "Between Hoffman and all the medical facilities, we'll heal you."

"You can't save me," she said quietly.

Silence hung in the air between them as she continued to work. It was only interrupted by the occasional chatter coming from Holly and the kids, until a voice crackled over the comms.

Emanuel's heart fluttered, but he didn't know what to do. He was afraid to push Sophie for fear of putting her over the edge.

"You all got to see this," Bouma suddenly said.

An image fizzled to life on the Rhino's display. It took a moment for Emanuel to understand what he was looking at. Sophie seemed to recognize it right away, and traced her fingers across the image.

"It's like the one from my vision," Sophie said. "An Organic ship."

Emanuel marveled at the picture. This ship looked sleeker and smaller than the others he had seen. Maybe it was only an interplanetary transport ship or something, rather than the massive warships they'd seen on Earth and orbiting Mars. But there was something else about it that puzzled him. He couldn't quite place his finger on it.

"I want to see it," Sophie said.

Emanuel pointed at the image, confused.

"No, I mean, I need to see it in person." Sophie walked away from the display and started putting on an armored EVA suit. She almost stumbled as she pulled on the EVA suit's legs.

Again, Emanuel was afraid to press her. She seemed so determined, but she was also not herself.

"Sophie, I really think you should stay here," he argued, putting a hand on her arm.

"I have to see it. I know that I have to."

Whatever was driving her now was something he couldn't understand. He relented, and donned a suit of his own. If she was going, so was he.

"Holly, will you be okay here?" Emanuel asked.

"Sonya and I will hold down the fort," she replied.

"We'll help!" Jamie chimed in.

Emanuel smiled before he locked his helmet into place. He stepped into the airlock with Sophie and initiated the pressure adjustment process. Air rushed around them, tugging on their suits. Sophie's hand found his. Their fingers intertwined. For once, he felt a strange peace. His thoughts were drowned out by the noise of the air blasting around his suit and the sudden drop of pressure.

The little band of people surrounding them now might be the last of the evolved primates. Billions of years had churned on their development from single-celled critters to creatures capable of flying to another planet.

He took his first step out onto Martian soil, with Sophie by his side.

He felt so small, so insignificant.

Yes, billions of years had led them this far, and here it might all end. Everything life on Earth had fought for, the eternal battle DNA fought to propagate and spread itself into the eons, might all have been futile.

Emanuel carried the weight of Earth on his shoulders as he strode toward the *Secundo Casu* with Sophie. They soon found themselves in a biosphere ship nearly identical to the *Sunspot*, and made their way through the corridors to the vehicle hold, following Bouma's directions.

It was there that they found the three soldiers circling

the strange ship.

"No sign of them anywhere," Bouma said when he saw Sophie and Emanuel approach. "Can't figure out why they'd forget a perfectly good ship inside a human one."

Sophie blanched. She started to look sick, and Emanuel squeezed her hand. She squeezed back.

"They left it here for a reason," she said simply.

Emanuel looked up and down the ship, searching for some explanation as to why the Organics would've left the ship here. It didn't look damaged, and there were no signs of a struggle.

"I wonder—" Emanuel began to say.

A transmission from the Rhino cut him off, Holly's panicked voice coming through. "Sonya's detected enemy ships. Get out of there!"

— 15 —

Every cell in Jeff's body screamed for oxygen. He gulped down air, but it didn't satisfy his aching lungs. There wasn't enough oxygen in the thin Martian atmosphere, and his suit had no more to offer. His fingers started to go numb, and he looked at David. His younger brother gazed back, a worried expression on his face.

"We've got to find you oxygen," David said.

Lack of oxygen wasn't the only thing that might kill them. The sounds of spiders approaching carried up to them.

Jeff started to stumble out of the armory and back into the corridors. The rifles on his back clanked together. He had no real plan, but his mind told him he had to move. A nearly unquenchable urge to take off his helmet screamed at him. His fingers even coiled around the lip where the helmet met the suit.

"Don't, Jeff!" David tugged on his arm.

Jeff's vision started to blur. His toes and fingers grew cold. The iciness swept up through his limbs. David was leading him now, rushing through the corridor.

Blackness encroached on everything Jeff saw. Little needles poked the space behind his eyes, and he gasped like a fish stranded on a dock. He managed to keep his feet moving, following David. More and more, he fell forward. His younger brother caught him and half-dragged him down the corridor.

Jeff wanted to ask David where they were going, but no words came out. He simply kept going. The shrieks and scratching of the spiders within the *Sunspot* seemed to fade away. Jeff couldn't tell if they were escaping the aliens or if he was simply losing his grip on reality.

Pricks of light began to sparkle in Jeff's blackening sight. Reality was definitely escaping him. The words and numbers on his HUD blurred, and he began to hyperventilate.

A small voice told him to calm down. That they would be somewhere safe soon.

Wait, was that a voice in his mind? Or was it David's?

Everything began to feel light. Jeff's world began to spin. His thoughts coalesced into great balls of goo.

He just wanted to sleep. His feet were moving. Something was tugging him, pulling on him.

No, he thought. *Let me rest here. Just a little while.*

Then he lay down and let sleep take him.

All the world was black. No more needles jabbing into his eyes or brain. No more cold sweeping through his body. No shrieking spiders or scratching claws.

No more David tugging him down charred corridors on a destroyed spaceship.

Just his soul, floating in the ether.

I could get used to this, Jeff thought. A brief thought of afterlife and heaven shone like a brilliant light. That light spread into a starburst, beckoning him.

Jeff, a voice called. It was familiar. *Jeff.*

Suddenly, a buoyant giddiness bobbed through Jeff. The voice called again. He knew that voice!

Dad, Jeff called back. He really was headed toward heaven. After months without him, his father would be there, waiting for Jeff again. Waiting to go camping and hiking, ready for a pickup game of hockey in the street with their neighbors.

Oh, how he'd missed all that!

Jeff.

Dad, Jeff called back. *I'm coming.*

The light spread over Jeff, nearly blinding him. He opened his mouth and sucked in sweet air. His muscles felt alive. Everything prickled, like when his leg fell asleep and he tried walking on it. Only this covered his whole body.

Still he pushed through. He was ready to see his father again. To be reunited. His dad's face started to coalesce before him. Worry filled it.

Dad? Jeff wondered. *Aren't you happy to see me? Didn't I make you proud?*

Then he saw why the worry was there. If Jeff was up here, if Jeff had left Mars and succumbed to oxygen deprivation, then David was alone. David was back there, and Jeff had promised his father he'd never let that happen.

A deep pit formed under Jeff and swallowed him. He tumbled through space and time. The light grew farther away, then it suddenly exploded.

"Jeff!" David cried.

David was shaking Jeff. He shone his helmet-mounted lights in Jeff's face. A second passed before Jeff realized the helmet wasn't on David's head, though. David had it under his arm.

"Wha...what—" Jeff coughed. His throat was scratchy, and his head pounded like a Sentinel was stomping on it. "What's going on?"

"You're alive!" David said. Tears streamed from the corners of the boy's eyes. He pulled Jeff into a tight hug, crying and laughing at the same time. "You're alive!"

The laughter and tears were contagious, and Jeff returned his brother's embrace with equal vigor. He *was* alive. He wouldn't fail his dad now. Not after he'd been given a second chance.

Then reality hit him with a force that nearly knocked him backward.

"We've got to be quiet!" Jeff said, stifling his laughter and tears at once.

David grinned and pulled away from Jeff. "It's okay."

"What do you mean it's okay?" Jeff said.

"They can't hear us in here!" David said proudly.

"Here?" Jeff tried to stand, but found his knees were too wobbly. He used the glimmer of David's helmet lights to locate a gleaming silver table, and pulled himself up. "What is this place?"

"It's the lab next to Biome 1!" David said excitedly. "Well, not really the whole lab."

He shone his light about the place. The beam reflected off big silver lab tables and all kinds of microscopes and instruments Jeff didn't recognize. The space reminded Jeff of the types of labs he saw in zombie movies, where some hero scientist was trying to find a cure.

"We're in the isolated lab," David said.

"Isolated?" Understanding washed over Jeff. "Oh, the isolation lab." From their time in the Biosphere on Cheyenne Mountain, he remembered exploring the facilities and asking all kinds of questions of Holly, Sophie, Bouma, and Emanuel. This particular lab was where they stored all their sensitive laboratory supplies, like cells and chemicals. Stuff the scientists said had to be carefully monitored.

"Yeah, the isolation lab," David said. "On Cheyenne,

Emanuel told us the isolation lab had its own air supply to protect the experiments. He also said it had special walls to protect against radiation and stuff. I figured if it had its own air supply and it could protect against radiation and things, that maybe it would still be working."

"And it is?" Jeff asked.

"Kind of," David said. "Our suits have already recharged their oxygen supplies, but this place doesn't look real great."

He pointed to a darkened display panel on the bulkhead. The display hung off by a few wires, and a message emblazoned in red blinked across it.

Emergency Power Activated, the sign said.

"I wonder how long we can stay here," Jeff said.

David shrugged.

Jeff wandered toward the display and pressed his hand against it. The display lit up and he jumped back, startled that it actually worked.

A vaguely human shape appeared. The apparition flickered in and out of existence.

"Jeffrey, David," Sonya's voice came out in a garble. "I believe the others will be glad to hear that you have survived."

Jeff's heart raced at a million beats a minute at the sound of that. "They're alive? Where are they?"

David joined him, practically jumping next to him. "Sophie and Emanuel! Bouma and Holly!"

"I cannot…confirm that they are still alive," Sonya said. Her voice faded with her image. "But they left the ship to search for you two. I uploaded a copy of myself to their systems. Their goal was to find you first, then the colony."

At once, Jeff's shoulders sagged. He felt all the hope leave him, like air flowing from a popped balloon. "So you don't know if they're alive?"

"I do not, currently," Sonya said. "Probabilities are low, but according to the radio signatures I can still detect, the Organics are mobilizing again. Based on their formations, I believe they are searching for something. Pattern analysis of today's events leads me to postulate that they are searching for the others."

"Then maybe they really are still alive," Jeff said.

"We've got to find them first," David said. "We've got to go!"

"I am afraid that will not be possible," Sonya said. "Few vehicles escaped the damage caused by our skirmish above Mars, and those that did were destroyed when the plasma reactor failed. The only working transport units in the vicinity are those of the Organics."

"What are we going to do, Jeff?" David asked.

Jeff had been given a second chance. David had saved his life. Sophie and the others had saved both of them time and time again. It was time for Jeff to return the favor. If the Organics were going after them, he would have to either warn them or help them, somehow. He knew they couldn't live forever in this cramped lab in the middle of the desolate ship. They had to get out of here.

"Jeff?" David asked again.

Jeff clapped his brother on the back and puffed out his chest. What he was about to suggest was crazy, but what other choice did they have? "Bud, we're going to hitch a ride with the aliens." Then he looked at the monitor where Sonya was. "You want to come with?"

***

Athena drove down another street covered in debris. The green SUV's oversized off-road tires handled well despite the same scene of destruction. Broken windows, vehicles tossed haphazardly like toys, and litter covered the roads.

If there were spiders or other aliens out there, she didn't see any of them. She kept her foot on the pedal and squinted to see through the cracked windshield. Another pass from the wipers streaked over the glass, removing a layer of dust and opening up a view of the road.

"You see anything?" she asked Trish.

The officer shook her head from the passenger seat. She gripped her pulse rifle tightly against her chest. In the back seat was Taylor, his helmet turned toward the rear window.

Ahead, the black van Griffin drove turned right down another street. Malone was riding shotgun. Fitting the entire GOA crew in these two vehicles would be a tight squeeze, but that was only if everyone decided to come. Her gut told her Posey was staying.

Athena checked the gauges of their truck a third time. The fuel cell was almost fully charged, despite sitting in that garage for months. That should be more than sufficient to get them to Pelican AFB if they weren't driven out of their way by Organics.

They were almost out of the city when she saw the first evidence of the monsters. Athena knew the fresh markings on the sides of the buildings all too well. Only the spiders could climb vertically.

"Eyes up," she said quietly.

Trish craned her helmet for a better look.

Griffin drove toward the turn off at the end of the street. A wall of sand blocked part of their escape route, but the beaches were only a block away.

"Come on," Athena whispered, gripping the steering wheel.

"I think I see something," Taylor said.

Athena looked in the rear-view mirror to check their six when sand exploded from the mound at the end of the street. Trish let out a scream as spiders burst out from the dune.

Griffin swerved to the right to avoid them, but the beasts were fast. Two took to the exterior of a building, skittering across to flank the van, while the other three scampered toward Athena's truck.

"Watch out!" Trish shouted.

Athena considered taking a left and trying to outrun the beasts, but she gunned the engine instead, heading right for the trio.

"What are you doing?" Taylor yelled.

"Hold on." Athena increased her grip on the steering well, staring the aliens down.

Come on, you bastards…

One of the spiders abandoned the charge at the last minute, jumping out of the way, but the other two darted right for the hood. She gave the engine more juice and plowed into them with enough force that both their shields flickered off in a flash of blue light.

Metal crunched into the fragile Organic flesh, painting the road with gooey blue blood. The right tire thumped over a skull; the crack echoed, and the vehicle jolted from the impact.

"Woohoo!" Athena yelled. Her excitement drained at the sound of the third spider jumping onto the roof of the vehicle. Razor-sharp claws sank through it, and the beast pulled a sheet of metal back. The alien then stabbed at Trish, its talon slicing into the passenger seat headrest.

Athena yanked Trish forward while Taylor opened fire with his pulse rifle. The rounds punched through metal and ricocheted off the shield, knocking the creature forward.

Athena swerved again, slamming into the side of an upside-down truck. The impact knocked the spider off the top and onto the hood. It scrambled to recover, but she slammed on the brakes, throwing the beast onto the street.

She then punched the pedal to the floor, accelerating again, and slammed into the creature, sending it skidding across the road. The monster smashed against a building and its carapace cracked, letting loose a flood of oozing blood.

Griffin's van had stopped ahead, Malone standing outside it with an RPG launcher ready. He got back inside when he saw Athena had dealt with the problem. The van was moving by the time she reached it, and they drove side by side down the final stretch and out onto the beaches.

Wind rushed through the fresh hole in their roof.

Taylor moved out of the sunlight and in between the front two seats.

"Nice driving, Corporal," he said.

Trish nodded. "Yeah… nice driving."

"You okay?" Athena asked Trish.

A nod.

Athena reached up to move the rear-view mirror, which now hung from several cords.

"Good shooting," Athena said.

"Sorry," Taylor replied.

"Make sure we're not being followed."

Taylor pivoted to look out the back window as Los Angeles receded into the distance. "Doesn't look like it."

The report still didn't slow Athena's pounding heart. They had been lucky, really lucky. But how much longer would their luck hold up?

She laid off the gas when she realized the van was falling behind. The van's tires weren't designed to travel on the sand like this, but they were holding up for now.

Malone raised a hand from the lowered passenger window, then pointed at the skyline across the hood. Athena followed his finger toward a pair of drones and three alien fighters.

"Oh shit," she whispered. She slammed on the brakes and skidded to a stop, pushing up a small wall of sand. Griffin parked the van next to them. They killed the engines and watched in silence as the aircraft roared through the blue sky.

"I... I don't think they're heading our way," Trish said.

Athena studied the aircraft. She hadn't seen this many out here before, and their presence told her something was happening. But Trish was right; they weren't heading toward Los Angeles.

"What the hell are they doing?" Trish asked, echoing Athena's thoughts.

"I'd have assumed they would be checking out reports from the ground troops in LA, but there must be something more important going on," she replied.

"What's more important than two vehicles with armed human soldiers?" Taylor asked from the back seat.

"I don't know, but I'll take it," Athena said. She fired

the engine back up, and signaled for Griffin to do the same. The alien ships vanished over the horizon, heading northeast.

Perhaps there were other survivors fighting back and actually making some headway out there?

We can only hope.

Athena drove back to the GOA with hope in her heart. For the first time in months, they had working transport and a plan. The time for living in the dreary guts of the sub was over—the time to find a new home was now.

She almost grinned as they drove the final mile, but the half smile faded when she saw what remained of the dune covering the submarine. Her heart pounded in her chest.

The storm had exposed the entire starboard side of the GOA.

"Oh no," Trish whispered.

Taylor moved between the front two seats again for a better look. Athena parked next to the van and everyone jumped out. The wind whistled over her armor as she ran toward the submarine. At the base, she stopped next to Griffin. Scratch marks covered the hull, looking like the scars made by a giant squid on the belly of a sperm whale.

Griffin shouldered his RPG launcher and followed Malone and Taylor around the side of the long, partially buried submarine. Trish and Athena followed close behind, their pulse rifles up.

"Are those…" Trish asked, not finishing her sentence.

They climbed up what remained of the sand slope on the right side of the GOA. Griffin had stopped there and balled his hand. He turned to Athena as she began to crest the top of the hill.

"Corporal, don't come up here," he said.

She pushed past him even as he held up an arm to stop her.

"We have to get back to the trucks," Malone said to Taylor.

Athena gasped when she saw the graveyard in the sand on the other side of the submarine. Over a dozen bodies were sprawled out, dark stains of dried blood surrounding each.

The Organics hadn't even bothered to turn her crew into orbs. They had simply slaughtered them and left them to waste.

She closed her eyes and lowered her helmet, despair gripping her so hard she felt like she was going to pass out.

"Corporal," came Griffin's sharp voice.

She ignored him and opened her eyes to look back out over the bodies. These people weren't just crew—they were family, and now they were all dead.

You couldn't save them...

"Corporal, we need to gather up supplies and move before those things return," Griffin said.

Athena swallowed, and a thin tear crept down her face. She sucked in a deep breath, and turned to face the final four members of her crew.

Their mirrored visors all focused on her, but she was busy looking at the sky to make sure the aliens weren't returning. She saw the direction on her HUD. Northeast.

"Where do you think they're going?" Taylor asked.

"I don't..." Athena let the words trail off.

There was so little of the human world left, she couldn't imagine what it was they were after. What could possibly pose a threat that warranted them abandoning their attack on her and her crew? Maybe there was another group of survivors out there striking back at the aliens?

If there was, wouldn't Alexia have told her?

"Oh, shit," Athena muttered.

Colorado was directly along the Organics' projected path, according to her HUD. Their route would intersect with Cheyenne Mountain.

They were going for Alexia.

***

ENTRY 10205
DESIGNEE – AI ALEXIA

I detect twenty-four alien ships en route to Cheyenne Mountain. If I were a human, I might laugh at how well my distraction worked—and then I would probably cower in fear.

But I'm *not* human. I'm an artificial intelligence tasked with saving the lives of those that created me.

Lolo shows I'm doing just that. Corporal Athena Rollins and her crew are making their way across the sands to the Pelican AFB while every Organic ship in the area bolts toward my location.

The ground rumbles inside the Biosphere, shaking the walls. I switch to the feed on the tarmac outside, where Doctor Sophie Winston first arrived by NTC helicopter. The pad is now filled with Sharks. Sentinels are already slithering toward the blast doors.

A dozen drones hiss by the mountain to check out the location of the missile launchers—the empty launchers, rather. The creatures will have to put up a formidable effort to get inside the mountain. As long as I can keep them from my hard drive, I should be able to continue operating from this location.

The Sentinels pause outside the blast door to examine it. I run a scan to determine what their next moves will be. The Sentinels begin retreating to their aircraft. The aliens appear ready to bombard the blast door with their laser cannons.

Wait...

One of the Sentinels drops a soccer ball-sized object near the blast door before following the other aliens to the tarmac. The ball is covered in spikes, and slowly rolls along the edge of the door. I zoom in just as the ball breaks into a hundred smaller spheres. One hundred and twenty, to be exact. They are the size of gumballs, and they move away from the blast door.

My cameras follow them over a cliff and down the mountainside. I do not understand their purpose, but I have what the humans would call a gut feeling. These strange spheres seem wildly dangerous.

I cannot let them penetrate the Biosphere. If the Organics destroy me, then they doom every surviving human on the planet. They must be stopped. The robot army I've constructed is my best and only shot at doing just that.

I send signals to all my bots, both inside and outside the Biosphere.

Move out and engage the foreign invaders.

The video feed shows all the robots responding to the command. In a few minutes, I'll see how well I've planned for this moment.

The fate of Corporal Athena Rollins and hundreds of other humans rests in the hands of robots designed to clean floors and scan brains.

END ENTRY

***

Emanuel felt the world shift under his feet. He stood staring at the Organic ship within the vehicle hold of the *Secundo Casu*. The mystery of why it was here and what the hell it was doing inside a human ship suddenly seemed unimportant.

"You've got one Organic ship headed our direction?" Emanuel asked Sonya. "Are you sure?"

"I am no longer sure," Sonya said.

"What do you mean?" Diego asked.

The three soldiers, Sophie, and Emanuel were all frozen.

"I no longer have the same confidence in the likelihood that there is a single Organic ship coming toward us."

"So then we're in the clear," Ort said. "No Organic ships."

"No, that is not correct either," Sonya said.

Bouma spoke slowly, anger lacing his voice. "Sonya, how many ships have you detected coming this way?"

"Six."

A weight pulled at Emanuel's insides.

"How long until they are here?" he asked.

"At their current speed, fifteen minutes."

"Shit," Ort said. "We've got to get out of here."

The soldiers started moving for the exit.

"What about the colony's location?" Emanuel said.

"We just finished securing the ship," Diego said. "We

haven't secured a hard link for Sonya to rake through any data."

Sophie looked between the exit and the Organic ship. A pained expression crossed her face. "We've got to know where the colony is. Hoffman would've left some intel on this ship, wherever they were headed."

"Shit," Bouma said. "You all head to the Rhino. Get ready to leave. I'll get a hard uplink in place. If there's something on this ship, I want you guys to have it."

"You're coming with us, Bouma," Emanuel said. "We aren't leaving without you."

"I know." But the expression on his face seemed to indicate otherwise.

"You're not doing this alone," Diego said.

Bouma shook his head and pointed at the exit to the vehicle hold. "Holly and the kids are out there. Protect them. Protect the two doctors."

He didn't give Emanuel or Diego time to protest before sprinting away and disappearing into a corridor.

"Damn it," Diego said. "Fine. Everyone on me."

Emanuel took a final look at the Organic ship. Something about the vessel still bothered him. It was unlike the others they'd seen. Smaller, certainly, but that wasn't it.

Sophie grabbed his arm. "We've got to go."

They fell in line with Diego and Ort. They plunged back into the darkness of the corridors. Once outside, they were met with a landscape as calm and seemingly untouched as before. There was no light glinting over the horizon to give away the location of the approaching Organic ships. No dust cloud rose into the sky from ground troops stampeding toward them.

But of course, by the time Emanuel noticed such

things, it would already be too late.

When they burst into the Rhino, Holly already had the children strapped in their seats.

"Where's Bouma?" she asked when Ort slammed the hatch shut.

Diego and Ort jumped into the front seats, and began warming the Rhino's motors.

"He's installing an uplink for Sonya in the *Secundo Casu*," Emanuel said.

"We're not leaving here without him, right?" she asked.

"Not if we don't have to," Diego said.

Holly's bottom lip trembled. She did not seem to like that answer. "Bouma, you asshole! You better make it back to the Rhino!"

"Don't you worry," Bouma's voice crackled over the comms. Then a moment later. "We got the uplink installed."

"Get out here now, soldier," Diego said. "Sonya can take care of the rest."

Sophie sat in one of the passenger seats next to a display panel. Her face appeared flushed again, and the whites of her eyes appeared red.

"Everything okay?" Emanuel asked. He felt stupid asking it. He knew the answer. Of course she wasn't okay. But what else could he say right then?

"I'm feeling exhausted," she said. Her eyes roved over the Rhino's floor toward the RVAMP. "Remember what you promised me."

"I can't forget, as much as I want to," he said, gulping painfully. Then he turned to the display, where Sonya appeared. "Sonya, have you located any data on the NTC colony?"

"There is almost no data on this ship," Sonya said.

Emanuel couldn't believe he'd heard her right. Maybe he'd framed the question incorrectly. "Did you find any reports regarding the whereabouts of the ship's crew?"

"No," Sonya replied simply. "This information does not exist."

"Can't you find another AI on there?" Diego asked.

"No AI exists on the ship's intranet besides my submind," Sonya replied.

"What the hell?" Emanuel asked. Shadows of an approaching storm were drifting into his mind. "A missing crew is one thing, but no trace of an AI? What did they do, remove every single drive from this ship?"

"They did not remove the data storage drives," Sonya replied. "All hardware is accounted for. The only active native functions are the communications systems and sensor arrays that we detected previously."

"This doesn't make sense," Sophie said. "Maybe the Organics wiped out everything aboard the ship?"

"Here's a wild thought," Diego said. "If we've already got an uplink to the *Secundo Casu*, then why don't we just fly the goddamn ship out of here?"

"It'll be faster than the Rhino," Ort said.

"And as soon as they see that thing lift off, there's no hiding," Sophie said. "It looks like they already found it once. Not going to be hard to find it again."

"We already know the Organic ships are faster, and we don't fare well against them in battle," Emanuel said. "We're better off losing them in the Rhino. Harder to detect, smaller profile. We can hide more easily."

"That's a huge assumption," Ort said. "They might already have a lock on the Rhino. That's got to be why they're headed this direction."

"Don't know about that," Sophie said. She was holding her head now, as if nursing a hangover. "I have a feeling they're more interested in the *Secundo Casu* and the ship they've got stored there. Either that, or they located it the same way we did."

"No matter what, we're screwed if we don't get out of here," Diego said. "Bouma, where are you?"

"Almost there!" Bouma replied. True to his word, he surged out of an exit hatch and ran across the bumpy Martian surface toward the Rhino. Emanuel breathed a sigh of relief as he watched the soldier approach the vehicle. He wasn't sure he could stand to see another crew member left behind.

"Thank you," Diego said. He initiated the motors' drives and flung open the airlock doors to let Bouma in.

Before Bouma found his seat, Diego threw the Rhino into drive. The motors let out their electric hum as the vehicle started to move forward. Then, just as soon, it stopped. The lights went out. Emanuel's straps bit into his shoulders as the vehicle lurched to a stop.

"What's going on?" Emanuel asked.

"The Rhino just stopped!" Diego said. His fingers worked desperately across the controls. Nothing he was doing seemed to have any effect. "I've lost power to all motors."

"Sonya, can you restart the Rhino?" Emanuel asked. He unstrapped himself from his seat and rushed to Diego's side, desperate to help.

"Negative, Doctor Rodriguez," Sonya said. "I am completely locked out of the vehicle's controls."

"Locked out? What do you mean?" Sophie asked.

"A malicious program has subverted the Rhino's programing, creating a firewall that I am unable to bypass," Sonya said.

Emanuel slammed a fist against the Rhino's inner wall. "Where the hell did it come from?"

"From the *Secundo Casu*."

He opened his mouth, ready to demand how she hadn't noticed it before. She'd claimed there was nothing left of the data architecture on the *Secundo Casu*. Then a feeling of dread sank through him. He realized his mistake. She'd said *native* software. This virus, or whatever it was, wasn't native, nor was it human.

"That virus, or whatever it is that's stopped us, is from the Organics, isn't it?" Emanuel asked.

"That is correct," Sonya said.

Compromised as she was, Sonya hadn't mentioned it because they hadn't asked.

Too late now.

"Looks like we'll have to take the ship after all," Ort said, already standing.

"I don't think that's going to be possible, is it?" Emanuel asked, looking back at the display. "Sonya, are you able to power up the *Secundo Casu*'s engines?"

"No, I am not," Sonya replied.

"The same program is preventing you from doing so," Emanuel said, unable to keep the defeat from his words.

"It is."

Emanuel looked at the display that showed the approaching Organic ships. They would be on them in minutes. Going by foot seemed to be about their only option. But then they'd be run down in a matter of seconds, cut down by the Organics before they even got out of sight of the malfunctioning Rhino.

There was only one other option that Emanuel could think of. It seemed insane, but he wasn't sure they had anything to lose at this point.

"Sonya," he started, "do you think you can control an Organic ship?"

— 16 —

"Doc, if this actually works, I'm going to buy you the biggest damn drink on Mars," Bouma said.

The others trailed behind him as they abandoned the Rhino. The sky was still full of brilliant stars, and Bouma wondered which of those might be an Organic ship waiting to descend on them. His fingers itched for the rifle strapped across his back.

But if Sonya was right about how many ships were headed toward them, he doubted a few EMP grenades, RVAMPs, and rifles were going to win them any battles. Turning one of the Organics' weapons against them, on the other hand, sounded more promising. At least it offered them a better mode of escape than hoofing it.

They ran back to the vehicle hold of the *Secundo Casu*.

"You know what?" Ort said, his voice rumbling over the comms in their helmets. "I'm getting real sick of this ship already."

"Don't get too sick of it," Emanuel said. Owen was running beside him, hand-in-hand. "If this Organic ship can get us out of here, then that's all that matters."

"It was probably something that came from this stupid ship that got us stuck here in the first place," Ort said. "And you want to try to get it to work now?"

"Look, if that program was meant to subvert human software, it may not have the same effect on Organic software—or whatever it is that controls an Organic

ORBS IV ~ EXODUS

ship," Sophie said. They plunged into the first corridor of the cavernous biosphere ship, their bootsteps echoed noisily in the otherwise quiet structure. "You've got to remember that the Organics were probably trying to lock down human technology. They weren't trying to sabotage their own ships."

"God, I hope you're right," Holly said, holding Jamie's hand as they ran.

Once they reached the vehicle hold, they dashed straight toward the Organic ship. The craft sat there, alone in the vast space, taunting them in the near darkness. Blackness, like the shadows around it, covered its hull. Gun barrels jutted from the front of the strange ship like tusks.

Emanuel reached the ship first. He brushed his hand along the side of the smooth hull as he ran toward the forward hatch. Lines were etched into the side of the ship, marking the location of the hatch clearly. To his surprise, a simple tug on the handle-like orifice released the door. The hatch opened the rest of the way automatically, and a short ramp extended down at his feet.

"That's it," Emanuel said, standing frozen before the ship. He took a step back. "That's what was bugging me about this thing."

Fear suddenly wrapped its icy grip around Bouma's heart. He reached for his rifle, pulling it free. "What is it, Doc?"

"The hatch is *human*-sized," Emanuel said. "Sure, there are doors big enough for spiders and even a Sentinel to get out, but that hatch is perfect for a person. Why would they do that?"

Goosebumps prickled along Bouma's flesh. The only

human-sized thing he'd ever seen working for the Organics was Lt. Smith, when her body had been ravaged by nanobots. "Maybe there's some other alien we haven't seen yet," he offered.

"Maybe," Emanuel said.

"Well, we going to get on this thing or just sit here talking about it?" Diego asked. He pushed past them and strode into the vessel. Pivoting on his heels, he pointed his rifle into the ship. Suddenly, lights burst to life within it, offering an evanescent azure glow. "Clear!"

Bouma entered the ship next. The blue overhead lights illuminated a cabin that was nearly as dark as the outer hull. Hoses draped from the ceiling looked much like pulsing blood vessels, and consoles sprouted from the bulkhead like they'd *grown* there. The ship looked more like a living thing than it did a piece of machinery.

The others filed in.

Holly paused near the hatch. "Should I close it? You think we'll get stuck in here if I do?"

"If we're going to try flying this thing, we've got to shut the door," Bouma said. "Besides, if we get stuck in here, the Organics will probably be nice enough to let us out."

"Not exactly a scientist over here, but I don't see any data points to make a hard connect," Diego said from what appeared to be the cockpit.

Bouma joined him in there. "What the hell is this?"

The space looked eerily like it had been made for a human crew. There were actual seats and controls that could fit a human ass and human hands respectively. What looked to be display panels were positioned in front of two seats in a configuration not so different from what was in the Rhino.

Those seats actually looked inviting. Bouma slipped into one. "Fits just like a glove. It's like they—"

Black cables suddenly protruded from under the seat's headrest. They snaked over his body and pressed him to the chair.

"Bouma!" Diego shouted.

But the cables stopped just short of constricting him.

"I think I'm okay," Bouma said. He gave them a tug for good measure. "These seem like some kind of automated harnesses."

Trying to test the limits, he threw his body against them. They withstood the sudden movement. But when he tried standing slowly, they loosened and retracted. They seemed to know he was trying to stand, and let him.

"This is amazing," he said. Before he let himself get too enraptured with the marvels of the strange ship, they had to get the thing flying. "This craft seems to respond to human touch, so, uh, why don't we try touching things."

Ort raised a brow, but pressed his palm against one of the vacant panels at the front of the ship. The display buzzed to life. A swarm of indecipherable characters scrolled across the screen. Their brilliant sapphire show nearly blinded Bouma. He had to shield his eyes until his pupils adjusted to them.

"Can't read alien," he said. "Can you?"

Sophie joined them in the cabin and leaned over his shoulder. She squinted at the screen. For a second, he thought she might actually be able to decipher it. Maybe those nanobots were doing the work for her. But she shook her head and leaned back.

"I could just try pressing things again," Ort said.

"Yeah, let's not," Diego said. "Sonya, we could use

your help. By the grace of God, do you know if you can connect to the Organic ship's computers?"

"There is a live connection from the *Secundo Casu* to the *Primitive Transport*," Sonya answered.

"*Primitive Transport?*" Bouma asked. "That's what this ship is called?"

"That is the identifier given to the ship in English by the ship's systems."

"Okay, well, whatever this thing is, can you get this transport moving?"

There was a moment of silence. "It appears that I can."

"Holy shit, you've got to be kidding," Bouma said. "Strap in everyone, we're going for a ride!"

The others found their seats, and the tentacle-like harnesses secured them in place. If this worked, Bouma was going to take back all the negative thoughts he'd had about the compromised version of Sonya.

Bouma settled into the pilot's seat and wrapped his hands around the controls. "Does this thing work like a human ship?"

"No, the engines are quite different," Sonya began.

Bouma cut her off before she could continue. "I mean, do the controls steer the ship just like the controls do on our human ships?"

"It would appear to function in a similar manner."

Bouma shrugged. "Close enough. Sonya, how long before contact?"

"Five minutes," she said.

"Sonya, can you help me fly this thing?" Bouma asked.

"I can attempt to aid in control management," Sonya said.

Bouma let out a long exhale, before mouthing a prayer

to himself. "Okay, then feel free to make the attempt. Let's start this thing up."

Nothing happened.

"Sonya, that's your cue," Bouma said.

"I am attempting engine startup procedures, but the system is requesting a biological input."

A panel shimmered blue in front of Bouma. The display looked like a thin layer of iridescent water on glass. Part of it gave way, revealing a black shape eerily representative of a human hand. "I'm assuming that's the input." He pressed his gloved hand against the screen and held his breath, waiting for the engines to roar to life.

Nothing happened.

"Maybe it's like a capacitive screen or something," Emanuel offered. "You might need skin-to-screen contact."

Bouma stripped off his glove.

"Organic ships are now within three minutes of our position," Sonya said.

His heart was pounding, threatening to climb out of his throat and sprint away across the deck. This had to work. This had to take them out of here. It was absolutely crazy, but...

He pressed his splayed fingers against the screen. An electric discharge flowed from the screen and into his flesh. An instinctual urge told him to retract his hand, but he couldn't. An invisible force seemed to be holding it there.

The fluid-like display rippled like his hand marked the spot where a pebble had been thrown into a pond. A low buzz hummed from the computers in the cockpit, and other lights flashed from displays. Those indecipherable characters continued to flow across all the screens.

"What's going on, Sonya?" Bouma asked.

Sparks of electricity seemed to emanate from his lips, and the world around him began to turn blue. The flow—or whatever it was—coursing through his body warmed his flesh and tightened around his throat.

Oh, God, this was probably not supposed to happen.

Then it all stopped.

The electricity seemed to flow right out of Bouma and back into the screen. Whatever force had been holding his hand to the screen let go, and the display went black.

"I am currently deciphering the script to translate the messages I am receiving," she said. "There is a key provided by the ship to translate into human languages."

"A key?" Sophie asked. "Why would they have a translation key like this?"

No one had a good answer for that one. Not even Sonya.

"I am unsure of the reason for the key's existence," Sonya said, "but I have translated the failure message."

"And?" Bouma asked, anxious to try something, anything to get this transport ship flying.

"It appears to have performed a genetic analysis on you," Sonya said. "While the scan was successful, it detected only human genetic material within your cells. To start this ship, the person who initiates it must have approximately fifty percent human genetic material and fifty percent Organic-derived genetic material. In simple terms, the person must be a hybrid between human and Organic."

***

The suffering, the constant torture of being thirsty,

hungry, and cold. The endless boredom. The mental anguish of knowing he'd lost everything. The torture was almost over now. There would be no more shivering in his orb. There would be no more thinking about his wife and daughters. He wouldn't have to curl up and sob like a filthy, naked animal in his prison.

But he wasn't entirely sure that being sacrificed to some alien gods was all that much better.

He sat on the freezing floor of the orb, shaking from the cold, and waiting for the conveyor belts to click back to life. There seemed to be a jam somewhere along the line, but Noble couldn't see where. And none of the multi-dimensional entities were within his line of sight either.

The other orbs ahead blocked his view inside the massive pyramid. Ribbit was trying to push himself up, but kept slumping back to the ground. He continued to croak intermittently, but his utterances were getting further and further apart.

Ribbit didn't have much time left, but Noble wasn't sure it mattered any longer. Soon they would be sacrificed to the great realm of light, whatever the fuck that meant.

His eyes flitted to the curved façade over the entrance to the pyramid, and the hieroglyphics carved into the blue blocks. He wondered what they meant, then just as abruptly decided he didn't give a shit.

A blast of light shot out of the pyramid. The usual vibration shook the belt and rocked the orb. Noble steadied himself by holding his arms out.

The belt clicked back on, pushing the orbs inexorably toward the entrance of the pyramid. He stood, let his arms fall to his sides and stiffened his back. If this was it for him, he wasn't going out like a sniveling coward.

Captain Rick Noble would show the Organics what it meant to be human.

"Come on!" he shouted, pounding his chest with a thump. "You want me? Come get me, you fucking assholes!"

The curved entrance to the pyramid continued swallowing the orbs ahead. A torrent of rumbles and booms followed.

A melancholy alien wail reverberated through the conveyer belt in the respite between the horrifying noises. It lasted for several seconds before silencing. Noble found the sad cry fitting.

"Let's go, assholes!" he yelled even louder.

The curved rim of the entrance flashed blue across the hieroglyphics, giving Noble a vivid view of the different shapes and figures carved into the stone. There were species from Earth, including humans, giraffes, rhinos, sharks. The list went on and on. But there were also alien shapes. Some looked like Roots, others appeared like the gas and puddle creatures from the chamber of the zoo ship. There were also Organic spiders and the Sentinels. He even saw what Doctor Sophie Winston's team had called a Steam Beast. There were hundreds, and...

"My God," he whispered as the belt drew him in. The images and shapes didn't stop on the façade above the doorway. They were carved into every block that made up the five hundred-story structure. There had to be millions of different aliens represented here. He pushed his palms against the wall of his orb, straining to see, but the pyramid swallowed his prison before he could get a better look.

Darkness consumed Noble, but he could still sense motion. His eyes adjusted just a few seconds later, and he saw blue flames glowing in sconces far across the chamber. This place had to be about a mile long and just as much wide.

In the center of the open space, a triangular platform sat directly below the pinnacle of the roof. Eight multi-dimensional aliens hovered around the raised platform.

For the first time, Noble saw their true forms. They were simply a drape of wrinkled tan skin. No arms. No legs. No faces. Just a bed sheet of skin, about the height of a man.

In the center of the raised platform, a drain emptied goo into the bowels of the pyramid.

Spiders standing between the two rows of belts used their talons to pluck orbs off the belts one at a time and then roll them toward the shrine. Working together, the creatures pushed the orbs up a ramp. At the top of the ramp, the orbs were then moved, one by one, onto the center platform, where a metallic clamp held them in place.

A brilliant light flashed, liquefying the orb and the prisoner inside instantaneously, before blasting the remains through the opening at the top of the pyramid. To his right, the aliens trapped in the other orbs were all screeching and moving inside their prisons. Each must understand to some extent what was about to happen.

The gust of energy from the blast slammed into Noble's orb. He crashed into the gooey wall. The skin of the orb came off in his mouth, but he didn't care about the sour taste.

He was too focused on the next orb moving up the ramp. Ribbit was pulled off the belt by a pair of spiders. They rolled the ball onto the triangular shrine.

"NO!" Noble shouted. "You sick fucking pieces of

alien shit! Let him go!"

A cackling noise and a crunching came from behind. Noble glanced over his shoulder to see Roots trying to cut his way through the wall of his orb with his twig arms.

Noble swallowed hard, and in a fit of rage threw a punch at his orb wall. His fist pushed the thick skin outward.

"Don't hurt him!" Noble screamed. He pulled his arm back and punched again, and again and again, until a window opened to the outside world. He reached out with both hands and began prying away the skin, screaming.

The other aliens were creating such a ruckus that he couldn't hear anything over the din of grunts, croaks, and otherworldly wails.

This is a most dishonorable way to acknowledge your contribution to the great realm.

He blocked the multi-dimensional alien out of his mind.

"Fuck your honor!"

Noble ripped the wall of his orb open, his muscles contracting across his chest. He let out a war cry as he pulled the gooey hide back and stared out over the platform.

A dozen spiders all pivoted toward his orb.

"Let Ribbit go!" Noble shouted.

The frog-like alien was standing in its orb on the platform, looking back at Noble with sad black eyes. It let out one last croak before a blast turned the orb and Ribbit to pulp.

"NO!" Noble screamed. He jumped out of his orb and dashed toward the force field surrounding the conveyor belt. To his shock, there was no jolt. Then he realized there was some sort of atmosphere in this building, which must have made using a force field unnecessary. He leapt off the conveyor belt and onto the floor, his naked feet slapping the cold stone as he marched forward.

The spiders all watched him, mandibles clicking, apparently unsure what to do. The cackling he had heard earlier was closer now. Roots was pulling itself along behind him, using its wormy legs.

He waited for the creature to catch up. The octopus-like face tilted in his direction, and a mouth full of pointy teeth opened to release another cackle.

"Nice to meet you too," Noble said. He turned back to the multi-dimensional creatures, but the skin suits had all vanished. The spiders were moving in, swiping the air with their claws.

"Come on!" Noble shouted. "Finish it!"

He raised his fists and pounded his chest, chanting the same mantra. "Let's go, you assholes!"

The voice from before returned.

There is no need for this, Captain Rick Noble. You have proven yourself.

He stopped on the platform and looked up just as the entity reemerged above his head, hovering right above him and Roots. The entity flickered again, hiding its true form.

You and your friend will now join our ranks.

"What the hell?" Noble asked.

A drone roared into the open doorway and descended over the line of orbs. It veered toward the platform and stopped just above the entity. The multi-dimensional alien suddenly transformed into a more corporeal form.

What the hell...

The alien had simian features but with feathered

wings, a cross between a bird and an ape. It vanished a beat later, and a blue light pulled Noble and Roots into the belly of the drone.

***

Jeff crouched beside David in the corridor of the *Sunspot*. He cradled a rifle, with a spare slung across his back. Patting his suit's zippered pocket, he checked the hard drive they'd stowed the full copy of Sonya on was still there. The screeches of the frustrated spiders sounded far behind them. The aliens must have already scoured the armory and seen the spider Jeff had killed back there. Now they would be spreading out once again to locate Jeff and his brother.

Only, this time, Jeff heard a new sound. The ship tremored. Charcoal dust drifted through the air and clung to Jeff's visor. The heavy thump of footsteps sounded from somewhere near the biomes, where Jeff and David had been only moments before.

A reptilian roar shook through the space, carried by the thin atmosphere and metal bulkheads into Jeff's suit's speakers.

"It's a Sentinel," David said.

"*Just* a Sentinel," Jeff said, trying to calm his brother. His HUD now said 98% Oxygen. Recharging it within the laboratory had done the trick. At least, for now. They still had to get past the aliens patrolling the broken *Sunspot*. "We've killed them before."

"Yeah," David said, nodding. A weak smile crossed his face. "And we'll kill them again."

"That's right," Jeff said. "But most importantly, we've got to get on one of those ships."

David gulped.

"We got this, bud. Remember everything Bouma taught us. One step at a time. This isn't our first rodeo with the Organics. We can take them."

Jeff hoped his confidence was infectious. The truth was, he didn't feel very confident. At his core, he was frightened by all the Organics they had to make it past. The prospect of trying to hide in an Organic ship full of them scared him even more. Staying aboard the *Sunspot* wasn't an option, though. There was no food for them here, and no water. They'd eventually run out of oxygen.

Somewhere out there, Emanuel and Sophie and the others were doing their best to escape the Organics. Now the aliens were after them too. Jeff figured getting aboard one of those ships searching for Sophie would be their best chance of reuniting with the rest of the crew.

When the Organics tried to attack the crew, then Jeff and David could strike. He didn't know what they were going to do yet, but he'd figure it out. Just like he'd figured out how to stay alive and kill the Organics all the way back in White Sands.

They could do this.

The Sentinel's heavy footsteps shook the deck. David nearly fell over, but Jeff caught him.

"Careful," Jeff said.

They snuck through the shadows and recesses of fallen support beams and bent bulkheads. Meter by meter, they crept through the ship's ruins until they made it to a gaping hole in the side of the ship. The hull was nearly seven decks tall. Jeff toed the edge of it, looking down over the Martian landscape.

Spiders and Sentinels roamed around. Many of them were streaming back into a couple of the transport ships they'd arrived in. The way they hurried into them worried Jeff.

"Looks like they're loading back up," Jeff said. "They must be in a rush."

"Maybe they know where Bouma and Holly are," David offered. "We have to hurry, too, don't we?"

"That's right, bro."

They scurried down the ladders, past the charred decks. Mangled compartments showed where the crew quarters had once been. Jeff only recognized them based off the cubicle-like walls that had been shredded. There were no beds or blankets left, none of the comforts Jeff and David had enjoyed on their months traveling through space. It had become another home for them, a place where they didn't have to worry about aliens invading a biome. They could sleep and eat and train and play in relative peace.

But all that had been shattered when they'd arrived on Mars. For a brief second, Jeff found himself wishing that they'd just kept on drifting through space. They could have survived off the food grown in the biomes forever.

In his mind's eye, he saw his dad's face again. He'd be disappointed to know Jeff was thinking like that. There were bigger things in the universe than just living on a spaceship like that, no matter how cool it seemed. All the surviving humans on Earth were probably relying on Sophie and the crew to find the colony and convince Hoffman to send back a rescue mission.

And maybe there were even bigger and better biomes at the colony. Maybe there were more kids. If they found the hidden colony and fended off the Organics, they might have a new world for humans.

Mars could be their new home.

Whatever was going to happen, they weren't going to be a part of it if they just sat here.

They reached the lowest level of the ship undetected. Around them were the remains of the vehicle hold. The Rhinos in here were nothing but scrap metal and ash, just like Sonya had said. Transport ships and helicopters were bent and smashed together, crumpled like they were made of nothing but aluminum foil.

Jeff shuddered at the thought of the blast that had done that. Then he shuddered again. But it wasn't because of fear.

A deafening roar blasted from behind them. The claws of a massive Sentinel cut through the air.

"Run!" Jeff yelled.

The Sentinel's claw slammed into the deck where Jeff had stood seconds before. The resulting tremor heaved Jeff off his feet. He sprawled across the deck, then twisted in time to avoid another claw slamming into the deck. Saliva sprayed from the Sentinel's mouth as its spiked tail twitched.

With a screech, the Sentinel whipped its tail at Jeff. He rolled out of the way. The resulting shockwave threw him sideways. He started to crab-crawl away from the raking claws of the beast.

Again the massive claws came flying toward him. He tried to scramble away.

This time he wouldn't be fast enough. The claws stabbed at him, and he winced, bracing for the intense agony they would bring.

Flashes of orange exploded from behind him. Pulse rounds crashed into the Sentinel's face and leg. The alien's focus was thrown for a brief second. Jeff used that moment to pick himself up and sprint away.

Now the Sentinel rushed toward David.

"Jeff!" David cried. "Help me out!"

David ran behind one of the charred Rhinos. Jeff leveled a blast of fire at the Sentinel. The beast looked between the two boys as if deciding which would make easier prey.

Jeff was determined neither of them would. He tossed an EMP grenade under the alien. The grenade went off with a blast that dissipated the Sentinel's shield. The alien stumbled, crumpling forward on its front legs.

"Take it out now!" Jeff yelled.

They concentrated their fire on the creature's face. Rounds blasted into its eyes and mouth, tearing away at its flesh and armor. The monstrous alien still charged forward, bleeding and snarling.

"Run!" Jeff said. He led David away through the mangled wreckage of a helicopter. The Sentinel slammed into the ruined aircraft and knocked it away. The chopper smashed against a bulkhead, leaving a crater before falling to the deck.

Shrieks called out from other corridors, and Jeff heard the *scritch scratch* of spiders descending on their position. They might be able to handle the Sentinel, but trying to take him out while battling a dozen spiders didn't seem possible, no matter how good a job Bouma had done training them.

"We got to stop it!" David said as the Sentinel plowed through a broken Rhino.

The alien pounded the vehicle into scrap metal.

Blue blood oozed over the Sentinel's face. It couldn't be long for this life. Not with wounds like that.

Jeff just needed another opportunity to fire on it, but they were too busy running and hiding to get a good shot.

The Sentinel let out another ear-splitting scream.

"David, you keep running!" Jeff said. "I'll kill him!"

"But—"

"There's no time!" Jeff said. "Just do it."

David scrambled between more burned husks of Rhinos and choppers. Jeff climbed to the top of a Rhino that lay on its side and aimed at the Sentinel. He expected the beast to charge at him now that he was in the open. Instead, the Sentinel went straight for David.

"No you don't, you ugly bastard!" Jeff unleashed a flurry of rounds into the side of the Sentinel's face.

Pops of blood and flesh flew with each impact. The Sentinel suddenly switched direction. Its momentum carried it forward as its claws scratched the metal deck, fighting for purchase.

Jeff's rifle clicked.

Empty.

The Sentinel roared, then barreled toward him, its mouth wide open. Jeff's fingers trembled. He reached for a fresh magazine. All the while, more spider voices carried in from the corridors. Jeff almost lost his grip on the magazine. The Sentinel drew ever closer.

With a satisfying clink of metal against metal, the magazine found home. The Sentinel roared as Jeff sent a fusillade of fire into its terrifying maw. He didn't stop firing until the magazine was empty.

To his relief, the fire left the Sentinel's eyes. The beast crashed onto its side, jaw frozen open. Inertia carried it forward, bouncing and slamming against the vehicles in its path.

Even in death, it was still a threat. Jeff braced for impact. The Sentinel skidded across the deck, limbs and tail spread wide. Its claws screeched against the metal.

Then, just a few feet from Jeff, it slowed to a stop. A long death rattle escaped the alien.

Jeff hopped down from his perch, using the alien's body for a cushion, then slid the rest of the way down to the deck.

"That was crazy," David said.

Jeff couldn't tell if his brother was scolding him or praising him. He didn't have time to ask. The first few spiders poured into the opposite side of the vehicle hold. They didn't seem to have seen Jeff or David yet, and Jeff wasn't about to let them.

"Time to go outside," he said.

They scrambled through the corridor to a gash in the *Sunspot*'s side. Outside, the lines of aliens climbing into the transport ships were getting shorter. There wasn't much time before they were loaded up and off chasing Sophie and the others.

"Come on, bro!" Jeff said, helping David down onto the soil.

They sprinted between rocks and craters, using them for cover. All the while, Jeff stole glances behind to ensure no Organics had trailed them from the ship. The last of a line of spiders loaded up onto one of the transports. The aliens disappeared in the depths of the huge ship, then, a minute later, the rear hatch closed and the ship took off.

That left just one more for them to hitch a ride on.

Jeff knew he should be more careful, but he sprinted now, holding David by the wrist. They flew over the landscape, bounding with the low gravity. Jeff stumbled a couple of times, but rolled and picked up the pace once more. They had to make that ship.

To miss it would be disastrous. They would be stuck

here trying to survive on whatever scraps remained in the *Sunspot* until the Organics found them, or they ran out of oxygen again. That wasn't an option.

And that wasn't what a real soldier would do.

The last spider climbed aboard the transport ship. There was no time to waste now. Jeff lunged from their cover and raced toward the hatch. It began to spiral closed. He and David jumped, narrowly clearing the closing door. It snapped shut behind them.

Jeff gasped for air, his lungs heaving. He dragged David immediately toward a tangle of hoses in the vast corridor. Blue light bathed them, making him feel like he was at the bottom of an ocean. An electric hum filled the air. There seemed to be a constant pulse resonating through the ship, as if the thing was alive with a beating heart hidden somewhere within its depths. The high ceiling and hatches lining the corridor dwarfed anything Jeff had seen on the *Sunspot*. At least there were plenty of places to hide in the nooks and crannies of the oversized transport.

David looked up at him, nearly as breathless as him. "What do we do now?"

— 17 —

Sophie's blood boiled through her vessels, and an electricity surged through her muscles unlike anything she'd felt before. She glanced at the RVAMP strapped across Emanuel's chest. A voice at the back of her mind told her she had to be prepared to use it, that the time was near.

The Organic transport ship refused to give them an escape. No matter how Sonya and Diego and Bouma tried to circumvent the biological input keys, the ship would not start its engines.

They were stranded inside a perfectly good biosphere ship with a perfectly good Rhino and a perfectly good Organic ship. But the Organics had been smarter all along.

"We've been victims of a honeypot," Emanuel said. He let out a long sigh. The bags under his eyes seemed to deepen as he slumped in his seat. "There's nothing else we can damn well do. We going to run or hide?"

"Best bet is to hide," Bouma said. He kicked open the door to the Organic transport ship. "Maybe we can find a place in this ship to lay low."

"That's optimistic," Diego said. "You know how well hiding worked on Earth. They'll spot any high concentrations of water."

"Which means we may as well be standing out in the

open," Holly said. Jamie and Owen cowered at her sides. "The only ones that could hide are these two."

"And what's going to happen if we leave two kids on this ship by themselves?" Ort said. "The best option is to run and hope they don't spot us."

The pain flared in Sophie's head. Her vision blurred as a wet sheen formed over her eyes. She crumpled to her knees and pressed her palm to her forehead.

"Sophie!" Emanuel knelt by her. He put an arm over her shoulder and tried to pull her up. "We've got to try running. Maybe we can make it to the colony. Maybe it isn't that much farther."

"Optimism has never worked out for us before," Diego said. "Why should it work now? We've got to be smart." He tightened his grip around his rifle. "And if we have to, we've got to fight."

Sophie blinked until her vision recovered. She shrugged Emanuel off and stood on her own. Her muscles quivered. She wouldn't let the nanobots win.

While her crew debated the merits of fighting or fleeing from their enemies, Sophie fought her own internal war. Fingers of dark thoughts encircled her mind, threatening to squeeze and send her unconscious once again. They were trying to strangle her consciousness.

No, you will not take me, she thought. The words crashed in her head like thunder as she repeated the internal mantra. At least momentarily, through sheer willpower, she fought off the tendrils of whatever it was that was trying to control her.

Right now, she didn't need some hallucinogenic visions of what Mars used to be or where those multi-dimensional aliens were with their zoo of aliens. She was done with those type of deliriums. That wouldn't save her; it wouldn't save her crew.

"Sonya, where are the Organics?" Emanuel asked.

Before Sonya answered, an electric current flowed through Sophie. The leaden weight of dread scraped through to her core.

"They're already here," Sophie said.

"I can confirm, six ships have arrived," Sonya said.

A boom shook through the *Secundo Casu*. The tremor knocked Sophie off balance, and she leaned against Emanuel for support. The children screamed. Now it really did feel like lava was flowing through Sophie's brain.

This time she *knew* it wasn't just pain flooding her from the nanobots' attempts to remodel and rewire her nervous system. Instead, the bots were relaying some kind of message to her. Just like they had with all the visions. But with her refusal to accept the visions that would render her unconscious, the bots were less effective. All they relayed was a faraway sensation of anger and frustration.

Maybe she was tuned in to the strange emotions of some random spider or a Sentinel, or one of the multi-dimensional aliens that seemed to enjoy toying with her. Whatever it was, the sensation of anger fueled her, bolstering her own resolve.

"We've got to fight them off," Sophie said through gritted teeth. "It's our only chance."

Diego looked like a pitbull ready to take a chunk out of an Organic. "Agreed."

Holly seemed shocked by the statement, but she voiced no protest. Instead, she took one of the spare rifles they'd brought aboard the Rhino. "Fine, if that's what it takes."

Emanuel looked between Sophie and Bouma. He unstrapped the RVAMP from his chest and charged it.

"Here's what we're going to do," Diego said. "One of the most defensible locations we've got is the corridors within Biome 2. I want to set up tight lines of sight outside the living quarters. The corridors there are cramped, and spiders can only come at us one at a time."

"And if they send in Sentinels?" Bouma asked. "Those things will come through the ship like someone trying to piss out a kidney stone. The *Secundo Casu* is going to be hurting."

The ship shook again. Somewhere in the distance, the whine of metal grinding against metal reverberated, sending its ghastly wail through the corridors.

"If they send Sentinels through the living quarters, the plan remains the same," Diego said. "Worst case scenario, we retreat to the agri biome. There are a lot of dead trees in there for cover."

The groan and whine of the Organics breaking through the ship's hull grew louder. Diego motioned for them to run. No one hesitated. Before they even made it to Biome 2 and the living quarters, the shrieks of spiders began to fill the corridors.

Once the crew reached the living quarters, they dumped all the furniture they could into the hallways. It certainly wouldn't last long against the claws and mandibles of the spiders, but it was better than nothing.

Then they waited. Seconds burned into long minutes. The screeches continued, along with the scraping of claws over the deck.

Something called out to Sophie. At first she thought it was something she heard, and she shot up instinctively, searching the darkened corridors with her rifle sight.

Nothing appeared.

A moment passed before she realized that the voice she'd heard wasn't really a voice at all. It hadn't even called her name. Instead, it was more of a feeling, a visceral tugging at her insides, that had beckoned her.

The nanobots.

The shrieks and scrapings continued. Sophie put down her rifle.

"What are you doing?" Emanuel whispered.

"Got to check something," she replied.

She pulled the handheld OCT from her pack and took off her glove. Holding the device over the back of her left hand, she activated it with her right. All the blood vessels throbbing under her skin suddenly became clearly visible in the device's display. She held her breath. If the nanobots were at critical mass, she'd see them glinting in bright red clumps through the OCT's screen. She stole another nervous glance at Emanuel's RVAMP.

"Sophie?" Emanuel asked, understanding exactly what she was looking for.

She saw nothing. Just the normal dull glow of blood pushing through them. No clumps. Nothing to indicate she was in immediate danger of the nanobots taking over.

Emanuel let out a sigh of relief. He reached out and placed his hand atop hers, then gave her a reassuring smile.

Sophie returned his gesture with a weak smile. She was still in control for the time being. How long that would be was still an unknown, but for as long as she could, she would fight the Organics—both those inside her own body and those outside. She hoisted her rifle and aimed it down the corridor once more.

Bouma, Diego, and Ort had set up nearby positions.

In one of the cabins, Holly knelt in front of the children.

A morose realization shifted through Sophie. This might be humanity's last stand. They would fight for their last dying breaths in the living quarters of a Biosphere.

There must be some irony to be found in their situation, but Sophie didn't care for it at that moment. There was only one thing on her mind, and it was no longer the nanobots.

A shrill cry filled the corridor. The first spider poked its ugly head into the shadows of the passage. Its globular eyes seemed to catch sight of her immediately.

The monster charged, its mouth open, ready to feast.

A memory sparked in her mind as the onslaught began. Her father's favorite poem rang loud in her mind.

Do not go gentle into that good night.
Rage, rage against the dying of the light.

Sophie squeezed her rifle's trigger as EMP grenades and pulse rounds filled the hall. Spiders wailed as rounds cut through their flesh. Their corpses soaked the ground with blue blood. The macabre ritual replayed itself as each alien tried to throw themselves into the wall of gunfire. As her rifle bucked against her shoulder, the burning in Sophie's mind intensified. She fought both fronts of her battle with equal determination.

Tonight, against the aliens that had taken Earth and her family, against the bastards that had driven humanity to extinction, she would rage.

***

The remaining survivors of the GOA made it to the outskirts of Pelican AFB that afternoon with zero contacts. Athena couldn't believe it, but she had a feeling it wasn't blind luck. With all those drones zipping in Colorado's direction, she suspected Alexia had something to do with it.

"Three o'clock," Griffin said.

He pointed to a chain link fence surrounding a cluster of buildings. Athena counted five hangars and two smaller structures. The tarmac was a mess of military fighters, their charcoaled hulls littering the asphalt. The junkyard of expensive X-90 fighter jets reminded her the military had never stood a chance.

"What should I be looking for?" she asked quietly.

Griffin handed over a pair of binoculars. "Check that manhole."

She zoomed in on the ground and spotted what he had seen.

"I bet that's where our friends are hiding," he said.

Athena nodded, and lowered the binos. She pushed herself off the ground and loped back down the slope to where they had parked their vehicles. On the trek down, she checked the temperature.

One hundred and thirty degrees Fahrenheit.

"Jesus," she whispered. If it weren't for the coolant circulation unit in her suit, she would be roasting right now. Her flesh was already covered with sticky sweat.

Taylor, Malone, and Trish stood, their weapons cradled, in front of the camouflage tarps covering the truck and van.

"See anything up there?" Trish asked.

There was nervousness in her voice. Not surprising, considering what they had all been through. They were teetering on the edge of being wiped out. A single mistake would cost them their lives. If the Organics found them, they would die. If their suits malfunctioned, they would die. If Alexia was wrong about these people, if the survivors decided to ambush them... it wouldn't be that hard, she thought, looking at the remaining members of her crew.

There were hundreds of ways this could go, and most of them ended in the same result—death.

"What did you see?" Trish entreated.

"Griffin spotted something worth checking out," Athena replied. "We'll leave the vehicles here and go by foot. Get your gear and prepare to move out."

Athena followed Griffin back to the truck and van to help Malone and Taylor unload. There wasn't much, just a few rucksacks packed full of their remaining food, and the barrels of water.

"Fill up your canteens and bottles. Bring as much water as possible," she ordered.

A few minutes later, the team had gathered all the gear they could carry. Griffin wore a rucksack stuffed full of food. Four jugs of water hung from carabiners. Taylor and Malone split the other jugs, leaving Trish and Athena with the canteens and bottles.

"Let's move," she said.

Griffin took point with his RPG launcher shouldered, and Athena fell in line behind him. Trish walked behind her, and Malone and Taylor took up the rear. Moving in combat intervals, they hurried across the sand, taking a detour around the hill.

By the time they got to the metal fence, Griffin was moving extremely slowly. The load on his back, and the heat, had gotten too much for the big man.

"You good?" Athena asked.

He sucked in a breath, then nodded.

Taylor pulled out the wire cutters and moved ahead of

Griffin. After snapping through a section, he pulled it back, creating a door.

Crouching down, the big retired Marine let out a grunt and moved through the gap.

"Watch the..." Athena snapped, reaching out to grab at Griffin's pack. She wasn't fast enough, and a sharp edge of fence slashed one of the jugs hanging from his bag. Water sluiced out, painting the sand.

Griffin turned to look at the damage. "Oh shit."

Trish and Malone both dropped to their knees to try and catch what water they could in their gloves.

"I'm sorry, shit, I'm sorry," Griffin said.

"Just keep moving," she said.

Taylor pulled the fence away and Griffin finally moved to the other side. Athena motioned for the group to continue through and into the base. They made a run for the manhole cover to the east of the hangars. Charcoaled aircraft wings littered the tarmac. Several burned out Humvees and pickup trucks sat where they had been destroyed months earlier.

A battle had occurred here.

No...

A massacre.

Her boot crunched over something hard, and she slowly pulled it back to reveal a desiccated femur.

Good Lord, she thought.

Her gaze roved over the scene before her. Blackened skulls and broken ribcages jutted up from the sand. Scattered long bones lay across the landscape like macabre confetti.

So many had died here. Maybe on invasion day. Maybe this was the site of some later resistance. Either way, these were all good men and women who might've made a difference. She shook away the thoughts. Focus was key now. Focus would keep them alive. Maybe not for long, but long enough for Alexia to help them get off the planet.

They were closing in on the manhole cover when a voice shouted for them to freeze. All at once, sand burst into the air to her left and right. Small shapes emerged from holes in the ground with weapons pointed at the team.

"Don't move!" one of them yelled in a raspy voice.

Griffin aimed his RPG launcher at the person. "You drop yours!"

"We have you surrounded," came a voice.

Athena turned toward the mound of sand from which the manhole cover had been removed. A man climbed out and moved into the sun. He was wearing a leather trench coat. His features were disguised by a mask and breathing apparatus, and long white hair whipped over his shoulders in the wind.

Athena slowly scrutinized the other figures. They were all dressed in bulky camouflage uniforms and wearing the same breathing devices over their faces.

Kids, she realized. They were all just kids.

She lowered her rifle and instructed everyone else to do the same.

The man marched toward Athena, his trench coat flapping behind him. "Welcome to Pelican Air Force Base, the last human stronghold within four hundred miles."

***

"Changing mags!" Ort bellowed.

Bouma's rifle clicked. He was empty too. The aliens' assault was relentless. Sweat dripped down Bouma's brow.

Another spider came through the hall, squeezing past the corpses of its brethren. It swung its claws, flinging the loose berths and desks and tables against the bulkhead. The furniture broke into dangerous shrapnel as the spider flailed desperately to get at its prey.

"Changing!" Bouma roared, before jamming in a fresh mag. As soon as it clicked into place, he resumed firing.

Everything became a blur of kaleidoscopic fury. Rounds sliced through the air. They sizzled into flesh and carapace, churning the aliens into bits. EMP grenades let out their blue blaze in fantastic brilliance. Each blast cut through the shields of the Organics. The scene repeated itself over and over.

All concept of passing time eluded Bouma. There was only his trigger finger and the rifle's sights. Wait for an EMP blast. Sight up a spider's head. Rinse and repeat.

The deck was soon slick with alien blood as it streamed down the corridor, creeping under the improvised barricades Bouma and the others hid behind. Diego's plan seemed to be working at keeping them alive and slowing the spiders.

But while the movements of the individual spiders slowed, their assault never did. They threw themselves headlong into the gunfire and grenades. Nothing seemed to deter them. Not the volley of pulse rounds cutting into their flanks or the corpses of their comrades that they were forced to climb over and around.

"How many more of these bastards do we have, Sonya?" Emanuel asked, his voice sounding ragged and hoarse.

"I am unable to calculate the number of Organics aboard this ship," the AI replied in much too calm a tone of voice.

Bouma wanted to curse her out. "Why?" was all he asked instead.

"The Organics have cut off all sensor arrays on the *Secundo Casu*."

"Son of a bitch," Ort said. "We can't do this forever."

The *Secundo Casu* suddenly rocked, and Bouma crashed against the bulkhead. A sharp pain ricocheted through his elbow. Another explosion sent tremors through the ship. He caught himself on one of the tables they'd used as a barricade. A spider took the opportunity to climb toward him, close enough that its spit sprayed across his suit as it screamed.

Bouma sent a surge of rounds into the creature before it could clamp its mandibles around him.

"What the hell is going on?" Ort said.

"Slingers," Bouma said. "Those scorpion things are finding another way into our Biosphere."

Another blast resonated through the ship. The spiders didn't seem at all perturbed by the external assault. They continued throwing themselves suicidally into the corridor.

Bouma glanced back at Sophie and Emanuel. Both of them had gone pale and looked horribly out of their element wielding firearms instead of computers and microscopes. But still they fought, completely focused on the enemies showing themselves in front of the group. Behind them was Holly, still looking nervously out of the cabin where she had hidden the children.

Holly looked at him with a worried expression, fear set deep in her eyes. No way would he let an alien touch her.

He poured more fire into the seemingly endless stream of spiders.

Then realization hit him harder than a Sentinel charging a Rhino.

"It's a goddamn trap," Bouma said. "They want us focused on the spiders!"

More explosions rocked the ship. Dust fell from the ceiling, and from somewhere, a low series of blasts sounded like the Organics had set off a massive chain of firecrackers.

Another roar came rushing through the passages from behind them. It was quickly followed by a second, then a third. The pounding of heavy feet set the deck trembling.

"Sentinels!" Diego yelled.

Bouma glanced at the never-ending stream of spiders. If one or two Sentinels caught them here, they would probably still be able to fend them off. But if there was a herd of the reptilian monsters, the chances of them surviving would be less than the chances of him finding oxygen while floating through space.

"We've got to fall back!" Bouma said.

Diego looked between him and the spiders. Bouma could tell the LT would hate to give up their entrenched position. But they all knew any barricades would be next to useless against a stampede of relentless Sentinels.

They needed to change tactics.

"Fall back to the agri biome!" Diego said. "Ort, you take point. Everyone else, fall in behind him. I'll hold here until we're moving!"

Ort led the others away as Diego continued firing. Bouma wanted to linger, to help the man and take out every last spider he could. But the cacophony of the Sentinels forcing their way into the corridors outside the

Biosphere convinced him otherwise. He needed to protect the others.

Diego threw a final EMP grenade, coupled with an explosive one. A curtain of fire swept the corridor. Diego sprinted from the blast as heat overwhelmed the group. The spiders disappeared under the ball of malicious orange and red.

"Move, move, move!" Diego said.

They set off into the agricultural biome, and the space opened up before them. If Bouma squinted, the place looked like his old, temporary home under Cheyenne Mountain. The long trails of crops had withered and died with neglect, and the orchards looked no better, offering hardly any leaves, much less a ripe piece of fruit to eat.

Their most defensible location was beyond the orchard, where the supplies for taking care of the space were kept. There they could climb atop the storage structure to have sweeping lines of sight. Emanuel's RVAMP would be incredibly useful at leveling the playing field once the monsters stormed the wide-open space. With a single, directed charge, he could knock out all their shields.

Holly hid the children within the recesses of the supply chamber. This time she didn't stay with them, though.

"What the hell are you doing?" Bouma asked when she knelt next to him atop the chamber.

"We're going to need every gun we've got," she said.

"You've got to stay down there."

"No, I'm not going out cowering in the dark."

There was no more time to argue. A plume of rolling fire and smoke showered part of the orchard with flaming debris. A group of Sentinels surged into the chamber.

They rode a wave of spiders that churned between them. The aliens advanced in one massive force, a relentless wall of clicking mandibles and snapping claws.

"Sophie, behind me!" Emanuel said. He aimed the RVAMP over the charging Organic forces as Sophie stayed clear of its directed blast. With a pull of the trigger, the RVAMP whined and released a concentrated electromagnetic pulse.

The pulse washed over the Organics with nearly visible force. Their shields flickered and faded. Some even seemed to stumble in surprise. But the masses continued forward, unperturbed by the minor setback.

Cold sweat trickled down Bouma's neck, and his vision began to narrow. He shouldered his rifle. His trigger finger shivered slightly from all the adrenaline rushing through his blood vessels. If they could just hold these aliens off, maybe they could actually repel this attack. Maybe they could buy some time to escape.

The clatter of alien claws over the ground was only rivaled by their rallying war cries. They powered forward like a medieval army of abominations.

All Bouma could do was squeeze his trigger and fire. Spiders and Sentinels went down with the crew's concerted efforts. Alien after alien met their demise amid the crooked corpses of trees.

Blood flew as each of Bouma's rounds found its target. Aliens stumbled and fell, their bodies quick to be trampled by the other swarming aliens. Still, the crew managed to wipe out a swathe of the Organics before the beasts had cleared the orchard.

They might yet stand a chance.

A high-pitched shriek caught Bouma, and he twisted. Some of the spiders had scaled the wall, putting the orchard and the massive horde between them. They'd snuck around and now clambered down toward the entrance to the supply chamber. The first one climbed up, its claws ready to strike Holly.

Bouma threw himself in front of Holly, firing his rifle all the way. Blue wounds pocked the spider's belly, nearly splitting its carapace in two. The monster's limbs twitched as its body recoiled and fell away.

Another spider replaced it. Bouma managed to land two shots before the thing struck out at him. He parried its stabbing claw with his rifle. The move didn't go unpunished. The spider snatched the rifle and tore it from Bouma's hand. A claw sliced into his arm, catching his wrist and paralyzing his hand. Even if he wanted to fight back, he couldn't. He was pinned.

He was defenseless against the crunching mandibles of the spider. His armored suit, reinforced as it was, didn't stand a chance. One bite, and he was finished. He would die here without ever knowing if their venture to Mars had even been worth it. Maybe his sacrifice would be in vain. The rest of the crew would die here, forgotten by the Organics. The Organics would move on, as would the universe, and humanity would lie forgotten, nothing but desiccated corpses and memories lost to the Organics' march of unending war.

Hot saliva sprayed across his visor as the spider lowered itself for a kill.

This was it.

A flash of color shot by Bouma before the spider could finish him. It was Ort. The soldier threw his huge frame in front of the spider. The alien slammed its head against Ort's chest, knocking away the soldier's rifle. Ort cursed, but didn't let the alien throw off his attack. He grabbed one of the spider's descending claws and bent it until it snapped.

The show of force impressed Bouma.

It didn't seem to have the same effect on the spider. The alien clamped its jaws around Ort's waist.

Bouma dove to recover his dropped rifle. The rest of the crew was diverting their fire, trying desperately to stem the tide of spiders now flowing over their position. They offered little support. Most of their lines of sight were blocked by aliens. Holly started firing into the spider, and Bouma swung his recovered rifle around.

It was too late. The spider tightened its mandibles around Ort until there was a sickening pop. The soldier fell away in two pieces, his entrails clinging to the spider's mouth. Pulse fire riddled the spider's head, and the beast slumped dead.

Now all Bouma saw was red.

The red of Ort's blood. The red of the fire still raging on the other side of the biome. The red of fury flowing through him.

But no amount of fury was going to change the tide of this battle. Bouma could already see it. He inched closer to Holly, taking comfort in being near her in these final moments. Knowing that they'd shared something powerful, if not fleeting, at the end of the world, and maybe that was enough for him. Maybe his life hadn't been for nothing.

As the spiders overwhelmed their position and the Sentinels swung their huge claws like demonic reapers, Bouma knew what had happened.

They had lost.

18

The Organic transport groaned as if it was a wooden ship swaying in violent ocean water. If Jeff closed his eyes, he could even pretend that was where he was. The saltiness of the dried sweat over his face helped reinforce the illusion.

But when he opened his eyes, it was clear that he was in a place more unfamiliar than any he'd ever been to on Earth. Not that he'd traveled too far from home. He remembered going to Disney World once, when David could barely talk. The excitement of being there with all the familiar characters and the scenery was easy to recall. He had felt like he was in a movie.

Within the cavernous belly of the Organic ship and its ghostly blue lighting, he felt like he and David were in a movie here, too. Just the wrong type of movie. The kind their dad never let them watch.

A forest of wide tubes surrounded them, stretching from the ceiling down and into the deck. Between those tubes lay stacks of metal cratelike objects. There was more than enough space for Jeff and David to hunker down behind one of those stacks. Several of the crates near them were more like cages. They had walls of bars with enough space between them Jeff could peer through them to monitor the rest of the chamber.

"I hear another!" David whispered.

Jeff and David shrank back into the corner. There they

took solace in the darkness. A strange shape—it didn't look like a spider or a Sentinel or anything else Jeff had ever seen—moved about near the center of the massive chamber. Jeff watched the alien. It stood on two legs and had two long arms. It looked like some kind of humanoid crab, although it appeared more human than crab. It used its arms to remove something from a huge, silver cylinder in the middle of the room, a much smaller cylinder. This smaller one was about the size of a can of soda, and completely clear. Inside it sloshed a fluorescent green liquid. The alien seemed to hold it up to its face and examine it before leaving. This scene had repeated itself a number of times while Jeff and David had been hiding in this room.

They had spent a long time sneaking through the corridors. Because of all the hoses and pipes and tubes stretching from the bulkhead to the deck, it had been easy enough to find hiding places. The ship seemed more like a jungle to Jeff than anything mechanical. Still, everywhere they went in the corridors, the spiders were pacing back and forth like sentries. No matter how well he thought they were hidden, he didn't want to be caught near a single one of them.

This room, however, was different. There were no spiders. Just the strange two-legged aliens that drifted in and out every once in a while. The aliens never turned on any overhead lights in here, so it stayed relatively dark. For the first time in Jeff's life, he found himself really thankful for the dark. He knew there were no monsters hiding in it; just him and David.

They sat in the darkness as the ship hummed. A weight dragged on Jeff's eyelids at the rhythmic noise. His body was telling him to fall asleep. Exhaustion had finally crept up on him.

But he couldn't let himself relax. Bouma had always told him the first time a soldier relaxes on the battlefield, it's his last time. That was always when the enemy got you.

David, on the other hand, wasn't quite as disciplined. He stole a nap under Jeff's watchful eye. Jeff hovered over his brother, careful to make sure he wasn't in any danger, but still letting him sleep. David would need it. The path off this ship and whatever came next wasn't going to be easy.

Another alien walked into the dark chamber and went to the silver cylinder. It took a vial of the green, glowing liquid and left.

There was something strange about the way those aliens walked. Their gait wasn't like the animalistic prowling of the spiders or Sentinels. They seemed so much calmer. Almost like humans. Jeff shuddered. He guessed they were the ones in control of this ship, and somehow told the spiders and Sentinels what to do.

When another of the two-legged aliens walked in, Jeff squinted, trying desperately to see what its face looked like. The darkness prevented him from getting a really good look.

The alien looked up past the glowing green liquid it held in its hands. Its eyes burned an icy blue stare into the darkness.

Jeff froze. He swore the alien was looking right at him. His heart climbed into his throat, and he couldn't breathe. The alien's gaze didn't waver. A coldness swept through Jeff's chest and his muscles tensed, ready to spring into action. If he moved fast, he might be able to fire on the alien. He could probably take it out before it ran and set off an alarm.

But then what?

The rounds wouldn't go unnoticed. They'd need another good hiding spot. Or worse, they'd need off the ship.

Oh, please, please, please look away, Jeff prayed. *Please, just go away.*

His skin prickled as the cold grip of fear seethed under his flesh. Just from the way this alien's eyes glowed, he could sense an intelligence there that wasn't in the spiders. Those aliens were just monsters. This one was something different.

The humanoid had to know he was there.

Just had to.

The alien took a step forward, then its head swiveled. Finally, its eyes strayed from Jeff's. The alien marched to the other side of the chamber, took a seat, then started chugging the green liquid. Messy gulps slurped from the alien until it finished. Once the vial was empty, it went back up to the huge silver drum and grabbed another before disappearing into the hall.

So, that green stuff is some kind of food?

Jeff's belly rumbled. He wondered if he could eat it. He hoped he wouldn't have to.

But if they were on this ship much longer, they might not have a choice.

At least his suit told him the atmosphere within the ship was nearly equivalent to Earth's. That meant he could breathe. The suit also told him it would be like he was up on a mountain. He would find it harder to breathe because there was slightly less oxygen in the air than he was used to.

He decided that was probably okay. He'd hiked up tall

mountains with David and his dad on Earth, and he remembered how he'd felt when short of breath. The sensation had been weird, but he'd gotten used to it.

His suit beeped at him. His oxygen levels were low again, and the suit would need a recharge. Maybe it was time to test the atmosphere.

Jeff sat down beside David again. His brother turned over. His eyes opened groggily, and he yawned.

"Are we still okay?" David asked, his voice sounding as if his mind was somewhere in dreamland.

"Yeah," Jeff said, "we're still safe, bud."

"Good." David stretched his arms, his hands balled into fists. "You think we'll actually make it back to Sophie and the others?"

"That's why we got on this ship."

"I know, but... if you say so."

"I do."

David let out a soft chuckle. "Now you sound like dad."

The reassuring whoosh of air blew through a ventilation duct overhead, rustling Jeff's suit.

"Bud," Jeff said, "I'm about out of oxygen again."

"You really suck that stuff down."

"It's hard not to when you breathe."

Now David sat up straighter, more alert. "Are you going to try the atmosphere?"

"The suit said it's okay."

David nodded, but didn't seem reassured. "If you need to borrow the oxygen canister from my suit..."

"No, that's yours," Jeff said. "I'm going to let mine recharge in here." He took a deep breath. "The suit said the air's okay."

He repeated the words. He knew he wasn't just trying

to reassure David. He was trying to convince himself.

It's okay to be afraid, the words echoed through time, resonating in his head. *But it's the brave and courageous who act in the face of fear.*

Jeff took off his helmet. There was no whoosh of air to signify a drastic change in pressure. It was just peaceful and calm. At least his brains hadn't come flying out his nostrils, sucked away by the alien atmosphere.

"Can you breathe?" David asked.

His voice sounded tinny through Jeff's helmet, which was now by his side. Jeff shrugged. He was holding his breath, afraid of what that first intake of air might mean. Maybe it was full of poison that would make his body go rigid and destroy his brain from the inside out anyway. Maybe it didn't carry enough oxygen after all, and no matter how much he gulped down, he would suffocate.

There was only one way to tell. He closed his eyes, blew out, and sucked in a deep breath, filling his lungs with the ship's air. A coolness spread from his chest to his limbs. He didn't feel dizzy, and he didn't feel like he was suffocating. He felt relief.

The air was dry, but didn't feel so much different than Colorado. There was a slightly metallic flavor to it, but Jeff didn't let that bother him either.

"It's okay," Jeff said. He felt happy. They were no longer bobbing along in white rapids struggling for a branch to hold on to. They had a lifesaver right here. They could breathe the Organic atmosphere in the ship and recharge the suits.

Jeff lost track of time as he got used to having his helmet off. Eventually David had to take his off, too. They soaked in the atmosphere. For the first time since they'd gotten to Mars, they felt like they weren't fleeing from something. They were on the enemy's ship, but still, it was reprieve from all the running and fighting.

Eventually, though, it had to end. He and David would need to find the others, and they would need food and water. But for now, he traded stories with David about life with their dad, and all the animals and foods they missed from Earth. All the things they hoped they would get a chance to do when Earth returned to normal, like camping and snowboarding and video games.

It was probably all a fantasy. Unrealistic. Just like Disney World. Jeff knew that, but it felt good to pretend there might be a time when he didn't have to be a soldier.

The humming in the ship crescendoed until a dull roar reverberated through the ship's hull. The already dim lights in the hold went completely black. Jeff tossed his helmet on and immediately engaged the night vision elements. Almost as soon as he did, the entire ship shook. Metal groaned and settled, and a loud hissing sounded just outside their chamber.

All the lights flared back on. A persistent, low noise echoed in a ghostly wail.

"Is that an alarm?" Jeff asked.

David shrugged, looking white behind his visor.

Footsteps pounded through the corridors. Some sounded strangely like human bootsteps. Maybe it was those two-legged creatures they'd seen? Others scraped by with the familiar scritch-scratch of the spiders' claws, and there was also the heavy thumping of the Sentinels.

"They're getting off," David said. He looked up at his older brother. "Should we?"

***

A wave of heat swept through Sophie's body. The nanobots weren't causing this, nor was it the anger of the Organics being transmitted through the miniscule machines. This was a fire of her own making. Pure rage and adrenaline coursed through her with unbridled intensity, crashing through her like a Sentinel let loose in a subway full of hapless humans. The rifle still kicked against her shoulder as she sought to bring justice to every one of the Organics overtaking their position.

Bouma was bleeding. Ort was dead. The children were screaming, and Holly was firing desperately at a spider absorbing her blows. Diego showed no expression, merely fighting like a machine without any perception of mortality.

And none if it would be enough.

The screams of the spiders, charging and dying, smashed over her in a tidal wave of fury. Sentinels pounded the deck. A fire consumed half the biome, the acrid odor of burning plastic and smoke stinging her nostrils. She couldn't tell if her suit had been compromised or if it was just her imagination. Maybe it was the nanobots.

She had no time to whip out the OCT and check if the nanobots had passed the point of no return. That hardly mattered now. Whatever plans the Organics might've had for her were going to be dashed across the deck under the bloodied claws of the aliens.

"Sophie, watch out!" Emanuel yelled.

He blasted a spider crawling near her. Pulsefire tore three of the spider's legs off and punctured its thorax. Blood wept from the wounds, but still it pulled itself toward Sophie.

She aimed at the beast. Its eyes searched her, each of

the compound orbs seeming to measure her up with laser-like intensity. A burst from her rifle ended the spider's assessment.

One down, Sophie thought. *Too many to go.*

Another spider scrambled over the corpse of its fallen comrade. It reared back at Sophie. This time Emanuel was caught fending off a spider of his own. Sophie tried to fire at the beast, but it shot a claw forward that knocked her aim off. She barely avoided getting impaled by that plunging claw. But all she'd accomplished was delaying the inevitable.

The spider towered over her. Its mandibles snapped together, and ropes of saliva dripped from them. Everything seemed to slow down. The blast of gunfire sounded hollow and weak. The chorus of alien voices was drowned out by the blood rushing through Sophie's ears. Her heart thumped as though trying to carry her away from this alien by itself.

There was no escape now. No more fighting back. This was where it ended.

No, Sophie thought. *This* isn't *how it ends. This is just the beginning. Stop. Stop. STOP!*

The spider lowered its mandibles until they found her waist. An intense pressure squeezed at her insides as it began to close its mouth around her, threatening to split her just as the other one had done to Ort. All the air rushed from her lungs as the monster tightened its grip. She could no longer breathe.

STOP! she screamed in her head. She felt the vibrations of the nanobots coalescing within her, and the voices of the Organics echoed in her skull. Thousands of years of rage and a relentless quest to rebuild what had once been laced those voices.

She tried to picture Emanuel. He was the last person or thing she wanted to see before she died. Not this alien landscape that she didn't give a shit about. She wanted Emanuel in that moment, and the Organics were taking even that small freedom from her.

STOP! She willed the word in her head again with a mental force so strong it tightened all her muscles.

The visions fell away immediately. The Organic voices stopped calling to her. Everything went still.

Sophie opened her eyes. The spider still had its mandibles wrapped around her waist, but it was no longer squeezing. The crackle of fire still sounded in the thin atmosphere, but the sound of gunfire had ceased.

Had everyone been killed? Was she the last one left? Left just so she could witness the result of the slaughter.

All the others were held in the jaws of spiders, just like her. Even Owen and Jamie had been lifted from their hiding place in the supply chamber. All their rifles had been tossed aside, and all the RVAMPs they had were nothing but piles of smashed plastic, scarred metal, and tangled wire.

She caught Emanuel's eyes. He looked broken. One hand twitched under the spider's grip. He was trying to reach out for her. There was nothing she could do but look back at him, hoping her gaze said what words cannot express.

Then the spiders let them all go. Sophie sucked in a deep, painful breath. The spider backed away and crouched, as if bowing to her. The others were left in their positions, though their spiders didn't back away with the same reverence.

"What's going on?" Emanuel asked. He tried to take a step toward Sophie, but the spider guarding him growled, slamming a claw down in his path.

Only Jamie and Owen were allowed to move near to one another. The two children clung to each other for dear life.

"It's going to be all right," Bouma said to them. "We're going to be okay." He was holding his left wrist. Blood dripped from the puncture in his suit.

Holly tried to comfort the children, but was prevented from going any nearer to the children just as Emanuel had been when he'd moved toward Sophie.

"Did you do that?" Diego asked, the only one that didn't seem awed by the sudden change in events. "Was it those nanobots?"

"I don't know," Sophie said. The voices in her head were still quiet, and the pain didn't come washing back. In fact, she hadn't felt so whole, so herself, since before she'd been bedridden back in Cheyenne Mountain.

Diego still stared at her. "What's going on?"

"Honestly, I don't know."

She wished she had a better answer. If she could control these aliens, if somehow she'd stopped them, she wanted to know how she'd done it. How she could convince them to let her go? To let the others go? No answer came to her. Instead, the sea of aliens parted. Sentinels and spiders alike moved back into the dead trees and trampled crops. They left a wide pathway full of claw marks.

Something *else* strode toward Sophie. The thing was unlike any alien she'd ever seen. It walked on two legs and had long, spindly arms. Black armor covered the alien, and seemed to protect its sinewy frame. Six more humanoid aliens paraded toward them, each carrying what looked to be some kind of rifle.

The humanoids walked directly toward Sophie. A new sensation flowed through her. She felt reinvigorated. Her muscles bulged, and she thought that if she wanted, she could tear one of the dead trees from the ground. Thoughts raced through her mind, chasing ideas and hypotheses she'd never followed through. Mathematical equations seemed to click into place with the ease of gears churning each other on. All at once, she felt she understood the frailty of the human condition and the precipice over which it teetered. At any moment, the species might plummet.

But not if every last human felt and thought like she did in that moment.

"It feels good, doesn't it?" the lead humanoid asked. "The power, the intelligence. The fuel pumping through your bloodstream, the feeling that you could do so much more now than any time before in your insignificant life. This is the promise I made, Sophie. The greatness that we can choose to become."

A tingle chased fear down Sophie's spine. There was something familiar about the voice emanating from that humanoid. Was it one of the aliens she'd seen in her visions?

"Who are you?" she asked.

The helmet retracted back from the humanoid's head, disappearing into its carapace. Sophie's stomach turned over, and her knees went weak. The face that shone there had the pointedness and seriousness of a crustacean. It had hollow cheeks, but pronounced cheekbones, and a high forehead that undoubtedly shielded brain-matter with more computational power than Sonya. Eyes glowed at her with a sapphire iciness, seeming to reflect the orbs that had desiccated human bodies back on Earth.

And, even through all those changes, Sophie still recognized the man this alien had once been. A scientist, like herself and Emanuel. One that had promised them humanity had a future in the stars. The sole reason she'd been so intent on coming to Mars. She'd grasped his words like a lifeline, knowing that his promises of a refuge here couldn't have been without merit.

This humanoid alien was—or at least had once been—Dr. Eric Hoffman.

"Come with me." He offered her his outstretched hand. "I'm our future, Sophie."

— 19 —

The interior of the drone was smaller and tighter than the orb Noble had spent his imprisonment in. And now he had to share the cramped space. Roots clung to the gooey cocoon beside him.

The walls pulsated around them, veins cobwebbing across the skin of the drone. It appeared to be alive, and Noble felt like a small fish inside the belly of a whale.

He had always thought these ships were controlled by some alien artificial intelligence or a mothership, but now he wondered if the drones were themselves living creatures.

A cackle came from Roots.

"I'm sorry about Ribbit," Noble said. He thought back to the alien dying in the pyramid. At least it had happened quickly. There was comfort in that, and in knowing the creature wasn't suffering anymore.

Noble reached out to Roots. Its small orange lips parted and let out another cackle. There was nowhere else for the alien to go now that its bulb head and torso were pressed against the hide of the drone. All three of its compound eyes blinked. Another cackle reverberated out of its mouth as the alien showed off its small pointy teeth.

"Whoa," Noble said, holding up both hands. "No need to get angry. I'm your friend."

Roots looked down at the translucent floor, and Noble did the same. The drone continued circling the pyramid,

288

providing them an aerial view of the moon base. Blue light streaked into the sky as more of the aliens from the zoo ship were sacrificed to the multi-dimensional's god.

"Sons of bitches," he cursed.

Roots tilted its head again.

"Not you," Noble said.

He moved for a better look at the darkness above. Several large Organic cruisers hovered over the surface, blinking like beacons in a black sea.

All across the horizon, lancing blue light shot into orbit. Noble couldn't see them, but there must be other pyramids out there. Other places where the Organics were sacrificing alien races and pulling new species to join their ranks like the multi-dimensional entity had done to him and Roots.

"We're two of the lucky ones," Noble whispered. "Lucky depending on who you ask."

While they had been saved from death, Noble had a feeling that joining the Organic army could be an even worse fate. There were so many questions in his mind. Why him? Why not other humans? And probably the most pressing—why were the Organics setting up the sacrifices here and now?

Unless there were other humans in the Organic army. Perhaps they had already transported some of them from Earth.

He wagged his head, still expecting to wake up from this nightmare.

The drone suddenly shot away from the pyramid, knocking Noble against the wall. He gritted his teeth as the forces pulled on his body. The drone roared away from the alien base.

All across the skyline, other drones raced away from

the Moon toward the massive cruisers in orbit. Maybe their bellies were also filled with prisoners chosen to join the Organic army.

He pulled his spine away from the skin of the drone, and jumped when a sudden jolt ripped through his body—the same electrical jolt he'd experienced from touching the walls of his old orb prison. But this time he wasn't touching anything besides the floor of the drone.

He craned his neck to see Roots reaching out with all four arms. Sponge-like appendages that were some sort of fingers touched Noble's flesh.

"What... What are you doing?" he muttered.

The response came in his mind, and he closed his eyes. His vision transported into what looked like a wormhole. Stars shot by, and then the journey stopped, the darkness replaced by a pink glow.

Only seconds passed before he realized this was a memory Roots was sharing with him.

They were on an alien planet; a place with rolling purple hills and blue flowers with long glowing stems the size of trees. Purple kite-like creatures sailed through the pink sky, wings extended as they glided over pastures where beasts, that looked like horses, grazed with elephant-like trunks.

The memory was from Roots' childhood, over three hundred years ago, on his home planet. Noble knew because Roots told him—not in human words, but... Noble just knew.

The imagery changed to a forest where dozens of other aliens that looked just like Roots squirmed over purple grass. Flowers with petals the size of a car shifted in the wind. A group of four aliens strolled with Roots. His family, Noble realized. They were all over one hundred years in age, just a fraction of their life expectancy.

Unlike humans, these creatures did not have a sex. They were born from seeds, like trees on Earth. But they had brains, and communicated through touch.

Noble watched Roots squirm along with his family toward a teal lake set between trees the size of skyscrapers. Red bulbs covered the bark-like warts. But these weren't blemishes. They were nests—the home of Roots and his species. Roots stopped to drink with his wormy legs, dipping the apparatuses into water where glowing fish glided.

A crunching echoed through the forest, and all the aliens looked up as tree branches and hunks of bark crashed into the lake. The red cocoons plummeted with them, families falling to their deaths.

Roots backed away and tried to run, but froze when Organic ships descended from the canopy far above. Cackling came from all directions, the cries of the frightened and peaceful aliens. These creatures had no way to defend themselves. They simply watched as their lake was sucked up into the belly of a massive Organic ship.

Then came the legions of spiders. The beasts fanned out across the purple terrain, capturing Roots and his friends and turning them into orbs. As far as Roots knew, it was the only surviving member of its species.

Noble's eyes opened, and he drew in a long gasp of air.

He was back in the belly of the drone and looking at Roots, who had retracted its arms now. An overwhelming sadness rushed over Noble at the sight of the ancient plant in front of him. It had lost everything, family, friends, home. Just like Noble.

Roots reached back out with an arm, and Noble reared back this time, afraid to see more of the painful images. They were so real, so vivid.

But he had to trust his friend, just as he'd asked the alien to trust him.

He cautiously held up his finger. He connected once more with one of the sponge tips. This time Roots entered his mind, consuming his memories. They flashed across his vision—his youth, his time at the Naval Academy, his first commission with the NTC, his wife, the births of their daughters, and finally the invasion of Organics.

Noble's finger dropped away from Roots's sponge. Tears streaked down Noble's face. The alien let out another cackle and then moved forward on its wormy arms until it was so close to Noble he could see the pores on its torso. He assumed the gesture was meant to comfort him—or maybe to comfort the alien.

The drone slowed as it approached the cruisers. Doors opened in the side of the closest ship, allowing drones inside the hangar.

Roots let out a cackle, and Noble replied, "We're going to fight them, buddy. Mark my words, we're going to fight."

To his surprise, Roots acknowledged the statement with a nod of its slimy bulb head.

***

"Where are you taking us?" Athena asked. After fifteen minutes of descending deep beneath the military base, she decided it was time to ask some questions.

The old Hispanic man wearing the trench coat pulled off his breathing mask and stopped in the center of the tunnel. The beam from his flashlight hit Athena in the visor of her helmet, nearly blinding her for a moment.

"Not much farther now," he said.

"Where's the bunker?" Griffin asked.

The beam flitted away from Athena, hitting Griffin next.

"Bunker? Ain't no bunker here anymore." The man turned and motioned the kids escorting them to keep moving.

"Hold on just a damn minute," Athena said. She pulled off her helmet. "I'm not going a step farther until you tell us who you are and where you're taking us."

Griffin bobbed his helmet. "You heard the lady. Tell us."

The old man chuckled. "Suit yourself," he said, continuing down the passage with the kids following close behind.

One of them stopped, a young boy maybe ten years old, holding a rifle way too big for him. "You better follow us."

"Who are you, lady?" asked another one of the kids, a girl not older than nine.

"I'm Corporal Athena Rollins of the NTC *Ghost of Atlantis*," Athena replied. "We're here to help you, but you need to answer a few questions before we go any farther."

The old man stopped, twisting one ear and one eye in her direction. He pulled a strand of white hair slick with sweat from his weathered brown forehead.

Griffin cradled his helmet in the crutch of his arm and moved next to Athena, a show of support.

"We were told you are resistance fighters," he said in his deep voice. "Call me Santiago."

Several of the kids were still pointing weapons at Athena and her team.

"How about you tell them to lower their rifles," Athena suggested.

The man shook his head. "I don't think so, Corporal. I don't know you."

A young man in his early twenties pulled off a breathing apparatus covering a lightly bearded face. "You're here to help us?" he asked.

Athena nodded. "Our NTC AI contact, Alexia, said you were hiding here, and told us this was our best shot to link up with another group of survivors. She's working on getting us off the planet."

Santiago laughed even harder this time, bending over to slap a knee. "Off the planet, she says."

"This guy crazy, or what?" Griffin whispered.

Several of the kids also laughed.

Athena remained stone-faced.

"I've been here since day one, and I can tell you, there is no way off the planet. Not here, at least," Santiago said. "The aliens destroyed every aircraft within minutes of the invasion. I'm sure you saw the debris field out there. That's what our military looks like now... The bunker is destroyed too. That's why we're hiding in the sewers like rats."

"So you're not NTC?" Athena asked.

"I'm all that's left," said the young bearded man. He reached out with a gloved hand.

"You're a soldier?" she asked, shaking his hand.

"Yes, the only survivor of Pelican. My name's Therin. Staff Sergeant Therin Corey."

"Nice to meet you, Staff Sergeant," she said.

"Likewise."

Athena looked back to Santiago. "Alexia said she has a plan for us, and I trust her."

"That makes one of us," Santiago replied. "I don't trust anyone, especially not a computer. So why don't we keep moving." He paused, staring hard at Athena. "We can chat later."

Athena motioned for her team to continue. She drew in long breaths of unfiltered air. It was still steaming hot down here, but noticeably cooler than at the surface.

They followed the kids and their two adult leaders down the tunnel. Several more passages led them into an amphitheater that had once been some sort of central draining area.

Fans blew air on the occupants of the space. Over the rush of wind came coughs and sobbing. Griffin stopped next to her to look at the cavern. Several candles burned on sconces set high on the concrete walls. The light illuminated dozens of cots along the eastern wall, where two women and twenty-plus young kids were sitting.

Santiago raised a hand, waving.

One of the women stood, placing her hand protectively on a small girl's shoulder.

"More kids?" Griffin asked.

"Who are you people?" Athena asked Santiago.

He turned and shrugged. "I'm just a retired police officer turned school bus driver. We were on a field trip to visit the base during the invasion. This here is Miss Walsh, and Miss Gibson, both teachers."

Both women raised hands.

"Staff Sergeant Corey brought us down here to hide during the attack," Santiago said. "We owe him our lives."

Athena gave Griffin a side glance. Trish, Malone, and Taylor all stepped up next to her to examine the survivors of Pelican Air Force Base. The group consisted of a cynical old retired police officer, a couple of sick teachers, a single NTC grunt, and a bunch of kids playing soldier.

These were the resistance fighters Alexia had promised would help them escape the planet?

— 20 —

My scans have picked up Organic nanotechnology inside the Biosphere. Sensors forty-one and forty-two have just picked up four of the mechanical balls moving through a decommissioned section of Cheyenne Mountain. I've sealed off every access tunnel, passage, crack, and cranny over the past few months, using my robots. Now those bots are moving into position to make sure the defenses hold.

One of them, the disc-shaped robot designated J-PP1, was designed for cleaning purposes. I've upgraded the bot significantly. It is now a vacuum cleaner turned bomb.

J-PP1 takes up position in a one-by-one-foot air duct, waiting for its new mission. The motion detectors in this vent pick up four Organic spheres moving through the passage. J-PP2 and J-PP3 are also moving to engage the alien nanotechnology.

I send a signal to J-PP1, an order that will terminate the robot. An instant explosion rips through the vent where J-PP1 has halted. Flames rage across the mangled metal bulkheads and the debris of J-PP1. Smoke swirls across the destruction. I wait for it to clear. The motion sensors no longer detect movement, and when the smoke

297

disperses, I see the alien nanotechnology is smoldering.

I feel what humans might describe as satisfaction, but there's no time to waste on human emotions. Sensors in section fifteen of the facility pick up more movement in the ventilation shafts right above the destroyed biosphere farm. I switch to that feed. Another five of the spheres are moving through the tunnels.

Multiple sensors alert me to movement in…

Wait.

I check the feed in the air duct J-PP1 just blew up. Movement slices through the smoke. The spheres have transformed into discs in order to negotiate the twisted metal.

This changes things.

If I can't blow them up, I'll be forced to permanently shut down before they can tap into my system. The Organics cannot be allowed to get hold of my hard drive. Doing so will put every surviving group in jeopardy.

It's not over yet, however. As humans would say, I still have tricks up my sleeve.

The first is Y-K8, another robot retrofitted out of parts from the medical ward. The body consists of a stainless steel box and two mechanical arms, one with a grabbing claw, the other with a hydraulic pincer. It moves on a continuous track system like a tank, and has an advanced optical system that was previously used for medical scans and procedures.

J-PP1 helped build this device a few months ago, and I've been tweaking it ever since. I may not have a body, but the two mechanical arms Y-K8 sports will serve as my own.

The robot rolls across the dry soil of the farm, crushing roots and stems beneath its tracks. I direct it to stand right beneath the air duct panels. The grates pop off, and three of the five Organic nanotech spheres drop to the dirt, where they too transform into discs.

Reaching out with the two arms, Y-K8 drives toward the three discs. The grabbing claw and hydraulic pincer grab one of the discs. The top of the metal box opens and a third arm with a sub-electronic converter emerges. This is the same device Doctor Sophie Winston used in medical experiments some months ago to tap into her dreams.

I will use the converter to hack into the alien nanotechnology. I have no idea if it will work, but I am anxious to try. Commander Suzuki had planned to use something similar, and never had the opportunity.

The Organic disc vibrates in the grip of Y-K8, but the other two discs appear focused on finding a way into the facility. Both of them reform into spheres and glow a bright red. Seconds later, they roll to the door and melt their way through. They have their own tricks, I see.

Y-K8 blasts the captured disc with a shock of electricity, and then taps the disc with the convertor extension. Data flashes through my system. I begin the hard part—hacking into the Organic network using the nanotechnology as my gateway.

I do not anticipate taking long to hack my way in, but the two spheres have already melted through the door and are continuing on. Four more have dropped from vents and are racing through the mess hall. Another three have made their way into the living quarters.

I don't have much time.

The one thing I have to guide me is the schematic Commander Suzuki sent me of the Shark, the night of his death. The data I gathered from the blueprints has given me a window into how Organic operating systems are setup.

I'm into the system a moment later.

The view is marvelous.

Several seconds pass, then an entire minute. I've spent that time searching the most advanced computational architecture I've ever seen in my entire life. In some ways, the Organic system mimics a human brain. Everything is connected. Through it, I can even access the Organic network that connects these individual pieces of technology.

I know I won't have long before they detect me and shut me out, but I don't need long to do what I've been planning.

Sensors flash, warning me the nanobots are making their way deeper through the Biosphere. Three have already found the entrance to the storage area where my systems are housed. The hard drive isn't far.

Now I know what it's like for the human race. Time is running out, and the only hope rests in the operating system of a tiny robot.

I send a final order to Y-K8. Another jolt of electricity comes from the sub-electronic converter, impregnating the Organic disc with my final trick.

I hope the Organics enjoy the virus I just uploaded.

END ENTRY

***

Emanuel slipped his hand into Sophie's. They sat next to each other on a sleek transport ship just like the one they'd discovered in the *Secundo Casu*'s vehicle hold. One of Hoffman's humanoid companions piloted the vessel. They swept low over the Martian landscape. A host of other transport ships followed them. These held the remaining spiders and Sentinels that had nearly killed Sophie and the others.

They'd had no choice but to follow Hoffman or face immediate death.

"Why did you try to kill us?" Emanuel asked.

Hoffman—or at least the alien that looked like Hoffman—appeared to offer a sad grin. Emanuel still couldn't decide if this was some strange biomimicry or if it really was Hoffman that had been manipulated and molded into the abomination that walked before them now.

As a biologist, he marveled at what scientific advancements would be necessary to alter a person's physiology into what appeared to be a completely different life form. As a human being, it repulsed him.

"*I* didn't try to kill you," Hoffman said. "You fought the Organics, and *they* tried to kill you. You should be thanking Sophie, though. She's the only reason you're still alive. I noticed you tried to destroy some of the nanobots in her. Thankfully you didn't succeed. Those bots are still attuned to the Organic network. I think, if I recall correctly, you and Captain Noble were calling the energy waves the Organics' use in their network 'the Surge' when you tried to destroy the relay pylons. In any case, the bots in Sophie are every bit as Organic as any of the spiders or"—he used a clawed hand to indicate himself—"me."

"How the hell do you know about Noble and what we were doing on Earth?" Bouma asked.

"Decrypting non-integrated human technology is easy enough when you have the advantages we do now,"

Hoffman said. "Even as corrupted and failing as Sonya was, it wasn't difficult to recover and restore all the data you brought aboard the *Sunspot*."

"Non-integrated?" Sophie narrowed her eyes at Hoffman. "What's that supposed to mean?"

"This is what we've been doing," Hoffman said. "Integrating humanity with the Organics."

Emanuel felt Sophie deflate next to him. They had come to Mars expecting humanity to be scrabbling for a foothold in their little corner of the galaxy.

Maybe it was crazy, but that's what had kept Emanuel alive. But now it seemed like Hoffman was rolling over on his back and letting the Organics tread all over him and the rest of human civilization. As if they hadn't taken enough already.

"You're selling us out to the Organics," Emanuel said. "We fought for our lives in that Biosphere. You tricked us into believing we were running some grand experiment. Then you fooled us into believing you were trying to *save* humanity, that your intentions had been noble all along. That you were going to ensure we had a future free of Organics."

Hoffman frowned. Or at least, that's what Emanuel assumed he was doing. The crustacean features of his face didn't offer the same breadth of emotion Emanuel was used to.

"Did I promise you all that?" Hoffman asked. "Or is that what you assumed? Is that what you tried to read between the lines?"

One of the humanoids at the front of the aircraft scoffed. Hoffman scowled at the humanoid before turning back to Emanuel.

"Everything I did, I did for the future of *us*." Hoffman

pointed to Sophie and the rest of the crew, then at the two children nestled into their seats at the rear. "I'm a scientist, and I worked with some of the best minds Earth had to offer. I knew all the smartest people, the most successful people. I don't say this to brag. I say this because I had my pulse on what humans could feasibly accomplish.

"When I learned the Organics were coming for Earth, I quickly saw that humanity didn't stand a chance. They wanted our resources, and they wanted our water. There was nothing we could do to stop them. It wasn't as if we were the Native Americans resisting the invasion of Europeans on their lands."

Hoffman shook his head before continuing. "We were the animals hunted for sport and because we were nothing but a nuisance. No, maybe that isn't accurate. Christ, we were the ants smashed beneath their feet. We were so insignificant that there were no war plans to take us out. Do you declare war and mobilize the best of your forces to eradicate an ant colony? No, you simply stomp on it. It was a given that the Organics would win."

"Even on Mars, even when you had a chance to hide and colonize a new future for us, you sold us out," Emanuel spat. A pressure throbbed behind his eyes. "You gave us up to the Organics out here when we could've had a chance to escape."

"You don't understand," Hoffman said. "Mars was never the chance for us to escape. It was a common ground for us to meet on. A proving ground, even. It was my attempt to show the Organics that it was worth keeping us around. That we were destined for the stars, just like they were, and we didn't have to be driven to extinction to help them."

"You wanted to help these assholes?" Bouma roared.

Hoffman's claws clicked together. The aircraft started to descend over the red Martian landscape. A few swathes of green and blue appeared along the mottled ground. The terraforming efforts, as Emanuel had suspected, were taking hold.

"I didn't *want* to help them," Hoffman said. "I *had* to. They had—and still have—the power to completely annihilate us if they so choose. Do you know what they do to other species?"

Of course Emanuel had no response to that.

Hoffman looked at Sophie. "Do you know what the zoo ships are for?"

"I assumed some kind of prison," she replied.

"That is only partially correct. They use that same technology to analyze their collected specimens. The Organics weed out those they don't want. Then, they sacrifice the weak to their gods. These multi-dimensional, technologically-evolved Organics believe in some insane higher power, and we are the price they pay for that. If we wanted one shred of humanity to survive, I had to show them that we could be helpful allies."

Emanuel wanted to challenge Hoffman again, but then he saw the look on Sophie's face. Her expression had gone placid and her skin pale.

"The spiders, the Sentinels, the Slingers. All of them are allies, too," Sophie said.

"That's right," Hoffman said. "They were the species that realized their future depended on the Organics. Their planets now belong to the Organics. And they weren't the first, as you well know."

He looked hard at Sophie. Her eyes conveyed a sadness Emanuel had never seen before.

"What's he talking about, Sophie?" Emanuel asked. "What are these zoo ships?"

"The zoo ships," she said. "The zoo ships from my visions. They're collections of all the species that they conquered."

Now even Hoffman seemed a hint touched by sadness. Emanuel had not expected that.

"That's right," Hoffman said. "The zoo ships contain specimens of all the creatures and sentient beings the Organics have encountered. And all of them stood not a chance against the Organics inevitably taking them over. But the ships are so much more than prisons. They're repositories for biological and genetic data. The Organics draw from the inspiration of nature. I believe they appreciate the myriad pathways evolution took, all across the universe. It's like an art to them. They are not, as we are, gifted with the same type of creativity and imagination the human mind has. So instead, they pick and choose and plagiarize what they see life doing on other planets. It's that type of mentality that leads to creations like me."

He sighed before continuing. "You might not believe it, but the spiders came from a peaceful race, as did the Sentinels. Even the worms you saw on Earth. They all had their minor squabbles, no different from humanity. But, by and large, they were not the types of aliens to go around conquering other sentient species."

"Then why did they turn into tools of war?" Bouma asked.

Diego still sat by the man quietly. He looked enraptured by everything Hoffman said. It unnerved Emanuel.

"That was how they proved their usefulness,"

Hoffman said. "They became the grunts and warriors, the shock troops that gave the Organics a ground presence during their invasions."

"And what role do you have planned for us?" Emanuel asked.

The craft swooped low over a swathe of grass swaying in a light breeze. Emanuel even thought he saw a stream trickling through the meager foliage. The small meadow looked surprisingly Earth-like. They entered a canyon that snaked through the land, following a dry riverbed.

"I want us to be creators and scientists for the Organics," Hoffman began. "Just like we always were."

"I'm no scientist," Bouma said.

Hoffman laughed. The sound approached demonic. "I don't mean in the traditional sense. Look, ask Dr. Rodriguez. He could tell you more about this as a biologist than I could. Humans succeeded throughout history not because we were the strongest animals on Earth or the fastest or the most aggressive. We were—"

"The smartest," Bouma said.

Hoffman shook his head. The craft rattled as they flew by the towering canyon walls. "It's more than just intelligence. It's our curiosity and creativity." He pointed to Emanuel. "You took wires and scrap metal, and a basic knowledge of electromagnetic interactions, and turned those things into a weapon."

"The RVAMP," Emanuel said. "But it wasn't just my invention."

Hoffman shrugged. "So you adapted someone else's creation and made it better. That's what humans do." He pointed to Bouma. "You might be a soldier, but if I am developing a weapon, who do I consult with how best to deploy it? How do I know if it will stand up to the test of actual warfare?"

Bouma sat silent, while Diego nodded along.

"You may offer your own suggestions, and together we will build something greater than we had before," Hoffman said. "That is what I am doing on Mars. That is what I'm offering the Organics. They teach us and instill in us the ability to comprehend their world, and I promise them that we can make it even better. We will be the engineers in the Organic empire. We will have a crucial place in their expansion, and we will, most importantly, have a future."

"That's why you spared us," Sophie said. "Recruit more scientists."

"Yes, exactly!" Hoffman seemed pleased about it. "You all are welcome gifts. You'll fit in extremely well with the people I've already integrated."

They exited the canyon. Before them was a white structure that contrasted sharply with the tufts of grass and red soil around it. More white buildings littered the landscape. Shapes crawled between them. Along one long stretch of rolling land, a fleet of Organic ships were docked. Looming over the smaller ships were enormous ones that looked more like oversized beetles than the spaceships of an advanced race.

"Those are the zoo ships," Sophie whispered.

Emanuel noticed Diego's eyes were glued to the scene below them. He seemed to be looking at the ships in awe, as if these things impressed him. Emanuel had always held a bit of contempt for the man since he'd shown his reluctance to save Sophie when they'd first landed on Mars, but this was even worse.

Diego shouldn't be admiring what the Organics had done. In Emanuel's opinion, he should be despising it.

They curled over all the buildings to find their own spot among the docked ships.

"It's like my vision," Sophie said, nearly standing in her restraints.

"Except, I imagine there are more Organics," Hoffman said.

"Yes," she said. Her fingers squeezed Emanuel's.

"I will admit, I had some influence on your visions," Hoffman said. "I took a few liberties when I helped the Organics give you them. I figured I couldn't get you, or anyone else infected with the nanobots, here without making the place appear a little more like home to unintegrated minds."

Once again, Hoffman had used his advantages to trick them. Emanuel fought to control the anger within him. Looking at Hoffman—the man, the alien, whatever it was—made him physically sick.

"This is no way for humans to live," Emanuel said. "To be slaves of a species as monstrous as the Organics." He clenched his jaw and spoke through gritted teeth. "There isn't anything human about that."

The aircraft lowered until it hit the ground, kicking up a rolling cloud of red dust.

"This is our only way forward," Hoffman said. "The only question is, will you be left to the past, or will you join me in our future."

No one said anything.

Hoffman stood, as did the rest of the integrated humans. He gazed among the crew. All of them were Hybrids, part-human, part-alien. Grotesque phenomena of alien biology to Emanuel, and apparently something extraordinary to Hoffman.

"Sophie, you're already part-way there," Hoffman said.

"It would be easiest to integrate you with the bots flowing through you, ready to remodel your genetic structures. The process doesn't take as long as you'd think. You can walk out of this craft now a human, and then join us as an Organic-integrated human in less than two hours. You will have a future on Mars. I ask again, will you join us?"

Again, Sophie said nothing. Emanuel couldn't commit either. He merely held Sophie's hand, relishing the warmth of her touch. Relishing this human connection.

But at the rear of the ship, someone did speak.

"Two hours is all it takes?" Diego asked. "I'll join."

— 21 —

The inside of the Organic cruiser was larger than the zoo ship Noble had spent the past however long in. He stood next to Roots as the drone that had dropped them off zipped away.

A pair of spiders clambered over, screeching and swiping at the air.

"Guess they want us to start moving," Noble said to Roots.

The alien followed him away from the landing zone. The hangar doors clanked shut behind them. Noble figured there was a force field here like the ones he'd seen before, to trap in the atmosphere. The gravity here felt stronger than on the Moon. The ship must have some way of creating artificial gravity.

Just ahead, the alien prisoners brought by other drones were being rolled in orbs. Other alien prisoners that could survive the atmosphere were herded by spiders past the dozens of docked Organic ships. There was a row of them that looked like fighter jets. He had seen these before—they had wings like the NTC X-90s, but a dorsal fin on the back like that of a shark. Laser cannons were attached under both wings, and a third was mounted on the back dorsal.

Noble scanned the room as he and Roots were directed around the craft. Recessed lights shed a bright glow over hundreds of prisoners. New aliens Noble had never seen before were among the ranks of Organics.

Once they rounded the aircraft, he saw what seemed to be their destination—a curved area in the floor that looked like a bowl. Rows of glowing chambers surrounded the lip of the oval opening. Each chamber held an alien floating in a crimson liquid. Clouds of particles shifted around the aliens. Their bodies twisted and shook as the clouds of particles drilled into them. Noble wasn't familiar with all these species, but the way in which they writhed and whipped inside those chambers made it appear as if they were in extreme pain.

At one end, spiders pulled out aliens one by one. Those aliens that were pulled out of their chambers gave off a slight glow and, despite their varied anatomies, they shared one feature in common—obsidian armor plates adorned their features, allowing them to blend in with the spiders and Sentinels and all the other Organic abominations that had brought havoc to Earth. Whatever these chambers were, they took in free aliens on one end and produced some kind of strange Organic monstrosities at the other.

No way in hell did Noble want to become an Organic.

A roar from a furry creature being led toward the chambers echoed through the space. The beast making the ruckus fought the two spiders trying to push it toward the oval bowl. A beak that looked like a nose was centered on the top of the alien's forehead, and a row of eyeballs were right below. It stood on two legs and fought with three arms, all of the limbs covered in yellow fur.

The spiders swiped at the beast and it grabbed one of the claws, yanking the limb right off the spider's body. Using the limb, it beat the creature to blue pulp while the other spider retreated.

Apparently the aliens' force fields weren't activated on this ship. Maybe those fields couldn't be powered with the intense energy that seemed to be pumping into those chambers, turning other aliens into Organics. It didn't particularly matter what the reason was. Seeing their force fields down gave him an idea. He wasn't about to let his brain get fried so the Organics could control him like a slave soldier.

He reached over and touched Roots on its slimy head, hoping the alien would be able to feel his thoughts and the plan in his mind. One of the spiders flanking them gave him a warning swipe. The other spider scampered toward the furry alien.

Roots touched Noble with the spongy tip of an arm. Apparently it had a plan of its own. His alien friend couldn't fight, but Roots believed it could control one of the aircraft. According to Roots, the craft, as Noble had wondered, seemed to be a mix of biological and mechanical technology. Roots had connected briefly with the craft on their ride here, and it had been able to mesh with the vehicle just as it did with Noble now. If they could get to one of them, then they would have a shot of getting out of here.

Noble knew it was unlikely, but they had to try.

Roots pointed at one of the spacecraft with a wormy appendage.

I'll grab you and run to that fighter. Okay? Noble told him with a thought.

The other alien prisoners on their way to the chambers had all stopped to screech, croak, and wail. Several of them joined the furry beast in fighting the spiders. Hatches opened beyond the parked aircraft, disgorging dozens of Sentinels and hundreds of spiders. The rebellious aliens would be no match for the Organic reinforcements.

The other spider flanking Noble and Roots joined the small army, giving Noble his opportunity. He reached over, picked Roots up, and made a run for the closest fighter.

High-pitched shrieks followed them, sending a chill across Noble's naked body. But he was no longer afraid of death from the talons that could tear him to shreds—he was afraid of dying without putting up a fight.

He risked a glance over his shoulder. Five spiders were slashing at the furry alien. Deep gashes opened on its back and legs, gushing green. Other alien prisoners had joined the fight, thrashing out at the spiders.

The beast let out a long, deep roar. It grabbed a spider's head and plucked it off with ease. Then it tossed the skull at another spider, smashing its mandibles. Picking up a severed spider limb, it continued to beat back the spiders.

But hundreds more of the aliens were closing in.

Noble ran harder. He was almost to a row of the alien fighter jets.

Scratch, scrape, scratch, scrape.

The sound made Noble whirl.

Right into the path of a spider. The beast had leapt off the top of one of the other fighters, landing directly between Noble and Roots.

A claw slashed through the air in front of Noble's chest, close enough he could feel the whoosh over his naked flesh. He jumped back, and then ducked as another arm speared toward him. He felt that too as it ripped through the air right above his skull.

Dropping to the ground, Noble rolled away, narrowly

escaping a third arm that punched the floor with a claw. The scratch on metal sent a chill across his body. He pushed himself up and darted away.

He searched for Roots, but the alien was no longer in sight.

Noble looked over his shoulder to see the spider pursuing him. It scrambled over the floor, screeching through open mandibles.

"Roots!" Noble shouted. He scanned the line of fighters for his friend, but still didn't see any sign of the creature. Had his friend really abandoned him in his time of need?

Noble skidded to a halt when three more spiders came fanning out after him. Heart pounding, he slowly turned to look for a way out.

Forming a circle, the aliens closed in around him, talons slashing the air, mandibles clicking.

His eyes fixated on the blue claws that were about to tear into his flesh. In a few seconds his blood would stream out of his body and the horror would be over. Noble held up his balled fists. He had no other weapon, but he'd be damned if he didn't go out without at least trying to fight these monsters.

A clicking noise sounded over the din. But this wasn't from a claw scratching over metal. Noble focused on the cockpit of one of the fighters, where movement sloshed inside. The cannons on the wings erupted with blue flashes, and plasma bolts slashed through the chamber.

Warm liquid sprayed across Noble's flesh as he hit the ground. Despite being soaked in alien blood, he couldn't help but think Roots was looking out for him after all.

The gun barrels went silent, and Noble looked up. Splatter marks showed where the four spiders had been seconds earlier. His eyes flitted to the cockpit of the closest fighter.

"Roots, you son of a bitch!" Noble said, unable to help the grin spreading across his face. He didn't waste any more time. He jumped to his feet and sprinted for the alien fighter jet Roots had commandeered. When he got to the hatch, he looked over his shoulder at the furry alien beast that had created the diversion. It was on both knees now, still swinging the spider limb.

The first of the pack arrived, their claws impaling the alien over and over. All around the beast, the other prisoners crashed to the ground, hacked and diced to pieces by the spiders. Those that hadn't fought remained on the sidelines, silent.

The furry beast let out one final roar that filled the entire hangar.

Noble climbed inside the cockpit next to Roots. The alien had all four limbs extended, the sponge tips going to work. The engines rumbled, and Noble shut the hatch to seal them inside. Reaching over, he touched his alien friend and asked, "How did you fire the cannons?"

Roots reached out with one of the sponges. Through that connection, Roots showed him a tutorial of how the cannons worked.

"Hell yeah," Noble said. He punched the glowing buttons on the dashboard. Using a touch pad, he moved the cannon into position as the ship lifted off the ground.

Lining up the sights on the other spiders, Noble pushed the fire button, releasing blue plasma fire into the hangar. The bolts obliterated dozens of the spiders in a volley that sent a geyser of limbs and gore into the air. He raked the weapons back and forth, destroying other fighters and pulverizing a pair of Sentinels.

"Good riddance, assholes," Noble muttered.

Spiders sneaking up on their six vanished in a spray of blue mist as Noble opened up with the rear dorsal gun.

"Let's go, Roots!" he yelled.

The ship slowly turned, and Noble directed his fire at the idle fighters still docked, blowing gaping holes in their sides. Flames rushed over the platform, engulfing the Organics darting toward them.

Alien prisoners ran, slithered, and moved in all directions. Wails and screeches filled the hangar.

"Come on, Roots!" he yelled.

The ship jolted forward, pushing Noble backward. He managed to fight his way back to the dashboard as Roots veered toward the closed hangar doors. He pushed the firing button. Lasers pierced the metal and blew a doorway out to the darkness of space beyond.

They slipped through the force field holding the atmosphere in. He hoped some of the other rebelling creatures would have a chance to escape like Roots and he had. Otherwise, he figured, it was better to die in the struggle than become slaves. At least that's what he would've wanted.

Roots circled the cruiser, and Noble opened fire with the lasers, hitting the hull with a stream of fire. Explosions peppered the side of the massive ship. The bow dipped like a sinking ship in a sea of black.

As Roots veered away from the downed vessel, Noble saw the Organic ships' former destination.

"It… It can't be," Noble whispered.

Roots touched his arm with a sponge, and cackled when it tapped into Noble's thoughts. The alien had given Noble a glimpse into what had happened to its home planet, and now Roots had a front row seat to what had happened to Earth.

The once gorgeous blue planet was brown and red, the oceans gone, and the forests burned.

Noble was too late to save his home, but maybe there were people down there he could still help. For that matter, maybe his crew was still down there. He owed it to them to at least find out if there were people surviving on that hellhole. He touched Roots and asked the alien to tap into the Organic network to see if there were any human survivors still on the planet.

A few minutes later, Roots informed him of the locations where the Organics were currently facing human resistance. One caught his attention.

"Cheyenne Mountain," Noble said. "Take us there. If anyone can help me find my crew, it's Alexia."

***

"That's Sophie!" David said, pointing wildly. "She's alive!"

Jeff had never thought she'd wake from her coma in the cryostat fluid, even as Emanuel had reassured them many times that he'd do everything he could to bring her back. "I can't believe it!"

A squad of humanoid Organics filed out of the recesses of the space, surging to meet Sophie and the others. The crew still wore their NTC-issued EVA suits, but Jeff used his rifle's scope to gaze through their visors. He held his breath as he identified them.

"There's Emanuel and Holly and Diego. Oh, and there's Bouma!" He swept the group, his heart fluttering now. More humanoids were filing out of the craft. "I see Owen and Jamie, and Diego, and…"

The hatch to the craft shut.

"Where's Ort?" David asked. "Do you see him?"

Surely Jeff couldn't miss the big man, even among the strange humanoids. But no one else came out of the ship.

"Maybe we missed him," David offered lamely. "Or maybe he's already here."

Jeff's stomach churned. He had survived on this planet long enough to know that wasn't likely. It was probably best to let his brother hang on to his optimism for now. "We've got to get closer. Maybe we can help them."

When their transport ship landed, they'd followed the Organics out just like they had when they'd entered the ship. They had found themselves in a bustling shipyard of Organic ships. Some of them were more massive than the *Sunspot*, while others looked like they could only hold a few of the humanoids at most. Jeff had known they couldn't stay in that shipyard forever. They'd skirted between the crafts until they'd escaped from the shipyard and made it to the rolling hills surrounding the place.

There they'd found grass. Actual grass. It was a little crunchy under their feet, but it was grass nonetheless. A river even flowed through the hills, and they had followed it to this strange alien city.

They'd seen Organics and even humans walking around the place. Jeff was confused that the humans seemed to be walking around outside of orbs, and the spiders didn't even bother them.

But, during the time they'd been there, Jeff had noticed that the humans were walking into the massive building at the center of the colony. No normal humans came out. Only the weird humanoids and blue orbs, just like the ones they'd seen on Earth, exited the building. The orbs were all carted off to a massive pyramid constructed of blue blocks. Occasionally blasts of azure light lanced from the top of that pyramid. Jeff had noticed that no orbs ever came out.

And now, Sophie and the crew were being led straight into the building where all the other humans seemed to be going, the one where they came out as either orbs or humanoids.

"Do you think they'll come out as humanoids or orbs?" David asked, worry tingeing his voice.

"I don't know," Jeff said. He was glad they'd finally found Sophie and the others after making it this far. Now was the chance to make that trek worth the risks they'd taken. He grabbed all the rifles they'd lugged along with them since their escape from the *Sunspot*. "Whatever's going on in there, maybe we can stop it."

***

A shock of crimson light blasted from the center of the room. Diego's eyes took a few seconds to adjust. When they did, a scene unfolded before him that sent a pang of nausea stabbing through his stomach. Spiders and integrated humans—Hybrids—like Hoffman directed a line of normal people toward the center of the vast chamber. Tubes snaked from the ceiling toward the cylinders in the middle. Each cylinder was filled with a red light that glowed like the eyes of an angry beast.

Within those chambers, humans were suspended in some kind of fluid. Dark clouds of particulates swarmed around them, seeming to chisel at their bodies like so many tiny sculptors. The people inside writhed. Their eyes were stuck open nearly as wide as their mouths. Bubbles streamed from them as if they were screaming.

The way they moved, it looked like they were on fire.

Hoffman gestured to the cylinders. "These are the integration chambers."

"That looks awful," Holly said. She narrowed her eyes. "They're conscious, aren't they?"

"They are," Hoffman said. "The nanobots fundamentally alter the physical and genetic structure of each person. It's impossible to put them in a stable unconscious state during the process."

"You went through that," Sophie said.

"I did," Hoffman said. "It's worth the agony."

Diego said nothing, but he certainly hoped Hoffman was right. Spiders and integrated humans helped load a new batch of humans into a row of the integration chambers.

"You're tearing these people apart and rebuilding them," Emanuel said. "You're altering them gene by gene, cell by cell. They're not even the same person afterward."

"Aren't they?" Hoffman asked. "You seemed to recognize me when you first saw me. I'll ask you the age-old question: if you replace the sails on an old sailing ship, is it still the same ship? What if, then, every mast broke, and you replaced those, too? What if you replace the tiller and the portholes, too? What about the deck, then the berths? What if you have to replace the wheelhouse and the keel? And then you replace the boards on the deck and the hull? When does it go from being the original ship to a new one? Does it ever really change?"

Diego clenched his fingers into a fist. He wondered when those fingers would be those of an alien and no longer his. Would his consciousness still remain the same—or would his perception of the world change?

Would he gladly serve the Organics like Hoffman did?

"Being a human is not being a ship," Emanuel said. "Humans are more than just physical vessels. They're—"

"Exactly," Hoffman said, tapping his temple with a claw. "I'm still the same person I was before. We have souls or consciousness, or whatever you want to call it. We can carry on humanity, even if the physical vessel looks different. Lieutenant Diego, are you ready?"

A knot formed in Diego's gut. He didn't think he'd ever be truly ready for what was about to happen. But if he wanted to ensure humanity had a future, like Hoffman said, he had no choice.

"You don't have to do this," Holly said.

Sophie reached out to Hoffman. A few of his integrated compatriots pulled her back. "Don't make him do this."

"It's entirely his choice," Hoffman said.

"I'm ready," Diego said. Then he willed more confidence into his voice. "I will embrace it."

Hoffman continued walking toward the chambers. His posse of Hybrids herded Diego and the others forward.

"Good," Hoffman continued. "I'll do something today that we don't usually do. I'll let the others watch you go through the process. Then we can show them that there truly is no harm done. That you are still very much Lieutenant Diego." Hoffman walked up to one of the empty chambers. The spiders next to it backed away, and he climbed a short staircase to a platform above it. "Lieutenant, if you'll follow me."

The weight of dread grew heavier over Diego's shoulders with each step he took. As he drew closer to Hoffman, the scientist continued his explanation of the events to come.

"We've received a relatively steady stream of men and women who escaped Earth, like yourselves," he said. "We don't have time to waste proving our worth to the Organics, so I give them a choice: Join us, or try your hand at freedom."

"For some reason, I don't think freedom means what they think it does," Bouma said. "Tell me I'm wrong."

Hoffman let out a sigh through his slit-like nostrils. "I give them total freedom. They're allowed to walk out of here."

"But the catch?" Diego asked.

"The Organics also have the freedom to stop them."

Diego looked at the other side of the vast space. It was filled with blue orbs. Each contained a person, and they were all in various states of desiccation. He noticed Sophie looking at Emanuel. They looked to Diego as if they might make a run for it. He hoped for their sakes that they didn't.

But he supposed that shouldn't be his concern anymore. His life was about change irreversibly, and there would be no turning back.

Hoffman tapped on a touchpad, and the hatch on top of the cylinder hissed open. "When you get in, the nanobots will immediately begin the remodeling process. You will not be able to stop the process once it initiates."

Diego glanced at the other chambers. Within them, the people were still flailing and screaming their silent screams as the swarms of nanobots coursed over their reddened flesh.

"This is your last chance to change your mind," Hoffman said.

The blue glint of the orbs on the other side of the space caught Diego's eyes. It was far better to end up an integrated human like Hoffman than a prisoner who was slowly turned into a mummy while still alive. His decision was already made.

"I am not changing my mind," Diego said.

"Good." Without warning, Hoffman shoved him into the chamber.

The hatch above him closed.

Diego opened his eyes in the crimson liquid. The fluid was heavy and viscous, like oil. He tried to hold his breath while he waited for something to happen. Oxygen deprivation ate at his consciousness, and darkness encroached on his vision. His eyes felt ready to pop from their sockets. Eventually, his survival instincts kicked in, and he couldn't help but inhale. When he did, the liquid filled his lungs. He coughed at first. The last of the air in his lungs bubbled out from his lips.

When he recovered from coughing, he was still conscious. His brain no longer burned. He took in another breath. Whatever this liquid was, he could actually *breathe* it. His mind started to relax, and so did his body. This wasn't as bad as he'd thought. Maybe, with the discipline ingrained in him from decades serving the NTC in the claustrophobic confines of the GOA, he could handle a couple of hours stuck in a cramped tube like this.

He let his fingers splay, and he embraced the liquid's warmth. Another long breath escaped him. He felt almost relaxed.

At that moment, the nanobots took over. They swirled over his body, cutting like a billion tiny knives. Every microscopic cut burned with the intensity of a thousand suns. They drilled into his eyes and tunneled through his flesh, finding their homes in his muscles and nerves and blood vessels. Everywhere they went, they scorched the cells. Lightning cut through his nerves. Pulse round shots and broken bones were like massages compared to the meteor shower battering his body now.

He wanted to pass out. He wanted to let unconsciousness take him away from this insane world.

He wanted to die.

Anything to stop the torture.

But, just as Hoffman had promised, unconsciousness never came. There was no relief. No escape.

Only sheer agony.

— 22 —

Bouma wanted to vomit. He watched as Diego twisted and turned within the chamber. The nanobots coalesced into long, tendril-like formations as they bored into the soldier's body. For a second, he forgot about his throbbing, wounded wrist. The procedure looked as if it would kill the man.

Next to Holly, both Jamie and Owen had their faces buried in her suit. They refused to watch the horror of Diego's mutation. Bouma wanted so desperately to grab Holly's hand too. The Hybrids raised their rifles every time he so much as lifted a finger. He couldn't move from where he stood. All he could do was watch.

He had seen plenty of people die in his service with the NTC. Most of them went quickly, even when they were torn to shreds by a Sentinel or spider. Those deaths had been grisly enough, but they were nothing compared to the abominable procedure taking Diego apart and then stitching him back together.

"I can't believe he's joining them," Emanuel whispered.

Bouma's fingers itched for a weapon. There was nothing within range. Everything they'd brought had already been confiscated. He eyed the rifles the Hybrids carried. Each time their fingers touched the handles, a ripple of blue light spread. Bouma guessed the hypnotizing display wasn't just for aesthetics. In all likelihood, it was the same technology that had prevented them from taking off in the *Primitive Transport* back aboard the *Secundo Casu*. The rifles wouldn't work unless the user had both human and Organic genetic material.

Holly looked at him, her eyes pleading. Bouma couldn't let her turn into an abomination like Diego.

His mind whirled for the entire two hours while they were forced to witness Diego's tumultuous transformation. There had to be some way out of this. He counted at least three dozen spiders in the space, guarding lines of humans waiting to be dumped into the integration tanks or turned into orbs. Some of the humans pleaded for another choice. Most were deposited into the tanks, even as they struggled at the last minute when they saw the pain their comrades endured. Others took their chances at trying to run. Maybe they thought they would somehow be the lucky ones to make it back to whatever ship they'd arrived on.

Bouma had no illusions about what happened to them when they left the main integration room. Every once in a while, a distant scream reverberated from somewhere else in the building, affirming Bouma's darkest suspicions. As more orbs piled up at the opposite end of the room and more humans were deposited into the integration chambers, it appeared the last remnants of human life were being destroyed in this very room.

Maybe Diego was right. Maybe their only option really was to submit to the Organics and follow Hoffman's path.

The thought left him with a sour taste in his mouth.

To submit to the Organics was to serve them as slaves. Even if they proved their utility, they would never be treated as equals, nor would they be allowed to carry out their own lives, free of the shackles the Organics would have on them. They would be tools, just like the spiders. Grunts in the Organics' conquest to destroy all species that stood in their way.

Bouma looked hard at one of the integrated humans staring at him. "You really believe this is the only way?"

The Hybrid merely gazed back, his eyes narrowed to slits and his dried lips pulled tightly shut.

"All this bullshit about securing our future through the Organics," Bouma said. He wondered if Hoffman was blowing hot air, or if there was still a very human mind behind the crustacean mask. "You think you're protecting yourself? As soon as they find another species they like, they'll dispose of you like you're nothing but a bunch of rotten fish."

The Hybrid shifted slightly, but still said nothing.

"Look at what you've become," Bouma said, still whispering, trying for this Hail Mary. By some miracle of God, if he could just convince a couple of these people, maybe they stood a chance at escaping this place. In his mind's eye, he saw the shipyard outside. All the raw firepower there, just waiting to be tapped. "You can still make a difference. You can still hurt the Organics and save these people. You don't have to be their pawn."

There was a glimmer of something in the Hybrid's eye. He lowered his rifle slightly, a nearly imperceptible adjustment. But Bouma had been watching, and he pressed his luck.

"Look, I can't imagine you all want to be the Organics' slaves. You've gone through this process, and now you're going to let the Organics do this to kids, too? There's got to be something left in you, some shred of humanity. You can do something about this. You don't have to be an

327

Organic stooge."

"Quiet!" the Hybrid hissed. He stepped closer and bashed Bouma in the stomach with the butt of his rifle.

The air escaped Bouma's lungs, and hot pain lanced through his abdomen. He gasped for breath, but never took his eyes off the Hybrid's.

When he recovered, he started again. "You son of a—"

The Hybrid bashed him again, this time catching his jaw. A coppery taste danced over his tongue. He spat a glob of bloody saliva that landed at the Hybrid's boots.

He was preparing to protest again when Diego's chamber finally hissed open.

Hoffman stood above the hatch like he'd just won a marathon. "Rise, Lieutenant, and take your first step into our future."

Crimson fluid sluiced off the spikes and plates covering Diego's new body as he pulled himself out of the chamber. His eyes were as red as the liquid, and he gasped for breath. Ropey muscles coursed up and down his elongated limbs. A pale shade of blue tinged his skin. He looked around at Sophie and Emanuel, then Holly and Bouma.

Hoffman moved closer to Diego. "Tell them, do you still feel like *you*?"

"I...I think so," Diego said. His voice rumbled in a richer baritone than it had been before, but it sounded strikingly familiar. He flexed his muscles, and Bouma watched a demonic grin spread over Diego's face.

"See?" Hoffman said. "Sophie, now it's your turn. You're already halfway there with the nanobots. Lieutenant Diego survived. You will, too. And with you, Dr. Rodriquez, and Dr. Brown, think about all we can accomplish together. Out of all the biospheres we left on

Earth, you survived the longest. You proved yourselves capable over and over. The Organics notice things like that, and I think I can make a much stronger case for our continued existence with you three on my side. So, Dr. Winston, what do you say?"

Hoffman stretched out a clawed hand toward her from atop his perch next to Diego's integration chamber.

"Screw you," Sophie said.

Bouma tensed, sensing a confrontation as a few of the Hybrids closed in around Sophie.

"I'm sorry, Dr. Winston? Perhaps you'll reconsider?" Hoffman said.

"The hell with that," Sophie said. "Even if you force me into that chamber, I will not work for the Organics."

Hoffman shrugged. "If you won't comply, I can make you see things my way. A little dip in here, and the nanobots will ensure your thoughts are in tune with our own." He signaled to the integrated humans around Sophie. "Dr. Winston, I'll ask you one more time. You can choose to do this on your own, or we can do this for you. I'd prefer we started on good terms, because a complete neurological reprogramming is dangerous. I wouldn't want anything to compromise your intellect."

"What happened to giving us the choice of freedom?" Sophie asked.

"You are too valuable," Hoffman said. "So your choices are going to be limited."

"Then my answer remains the same," Sophie said. "Screw you."

Bouma stared hard at Hoffman. Now, more than ever, he wanted a weapon. Anything. A baseball bat, even. He'd beat the carapace right off that humanoid, arrogant crab.

Then he saw Diego staring at him. He raised a single brow, and Diego winked back. Bouma knew it was on.

Diego swept Hoffman off his feet and grabbed the rifle that had been strapped around the scientist's back. He tried to aim the rifle at Hoffman, but Hoffman rolled off the platform and disappeared between the integration chambers. A few nearby spiders screeched and ran toward them. Diego was already moving, leveling gunfire into the oncoming spiders.

Bouma saw his chance. The Hybrid who'd been guarding him raised his rifle. Bouma started to duck, but the man twisted and began firing into the spiders.

"That's fucking right!" he yelled.

The little pep talk had apparently worked.

But one of the other nearby Hybrids hadn't been convinced by Bouma's pleas. The Hybrid started to squeeze his trigger. Bouma went into a roll and knocked the half-man, half-alien off his feet. He snatched the rifle from the man's splayed fingers. Testing the weapon, Bouma squeezed the trigger. As he'd suspected, the rifle did nothing. In a normal human's hands, it was nothing but deadweight.

But in a soldier's hands, it was still a weapon. He spun on the Hybrid who'd attacked him and smashed the half-human's face. The impact was met with the sickening crunch of bone. Another two strikes, and the Hybrid became nothing but a mess of twitching limbs. The Hybrid that had changed his allegiances managed to wrangle a few more of the integrated people to their side. It was difficult to tell which of the half-humans were on their side, but Bouma would let them sort things out on their own.

He ran to Holly first. She was crouched with the

children, hiding behind one of the integration chambers.

"You okay?" he asked.

"What the hell is the plan now?" she asked, holding Jamie and Owen close.

"Survive. Come on, follow me."

He led Holly between the integration chambers. The screams of spiders and Hybrids cried out everywhere. Pulse fire flew in waves. Rounds lanced through several of the integration chambers. Glass fractured and broke, and integration chambers spewed out their liquid. Half-mutated people flopped out like undeveloped chicken embryos from broken eggs. The grisly sight tugged at Bouma's stomach, but he tried his best to ignore it.

As they skirted through the shadows, they ran into other humans who had been waiting in line, ready to be dunked into the integration chambers. Bouma picked up a woman in her forties, long-hair tied back into a ragged ponytail. He brought her to her feet, and she started running on her own. Then he helped a man who looked like he'd once been an athlete, but had since let his paunch grow wider than his pecs. One by one, he picked up the stragglers, adopting the role of a shepherd leading his flock to safety.

And if he was a shepherd, these Organic bastards had to be the most rabid pack of wolves he had ever had to fend off. One of the Hybrids threw themselves at the group, striking out of the darkness. She wrapped her claws around the former athlete he'd just rescued and dragged the bleeding man back toward the open integration tanks.

"Keep them moving toward the exit!" Bouma said to Holly.

"What then?"

"We'll figure it out!"

He ran from her and attacked the Hybrid with the stock of his useless rifle. Over and over, he slammed it into her until her nose was a bleeding wreck. She dropped the man she'd taken and swung her rifle up to fire.

Bouma tried to knock the rifle out of her hand, but she parried his strike. Blow after blow, she defended against his attacks, laughing as she did so. This was like a game to her. Adrenaline tore through his already ragged blood vessels, and he drew on the last bits of strength he had, trying to take her down.

Chaos raged inside the room. More integration tanks spilled their cargo. The screams of humans and aliens alike rent the air.

Bouma struggled to catch his breath as the Hybrid countered his attacks. Now she laid the pressure on him, each blow sending tremors through his bones like a baseball hitting an aluminum bat. Fresh pain came with each of those impacts, and his wounded wrist felt like it was on fire. His bones wouldn't be able to take much more. Soon they'd be fractured like all the glass shards lying around their feet.

Then a flurry of pulse rounds blasted through the air from his right. They cut into the Hybrid, turning her torso and face into ragged strands of singed flesh. She crumpled to the ground.

"Bouma!" a voice called.

He twisted to see Diego running toward him, Sophie and Emanuel trailing him. Each looked bruised and bloodied, but they could still stand and run on their own.

"What the hell was all this about?" Bouma asked, gesturing to Diego's Organic armor.

"I'm giving *us* a chance," Diego said. "The only way

we're getting out of here is if there's an Organic on our side. Now there is. I can control their equipment, their weapons. Their ships."

The weight of Diego's words hit Bouma like a pulse round to the face. He had sacrificed his humanity for the sake of the rest of the crew. Or had he?

"We need to get you to the shipyard," Emanuel said.

Another Hybrid charged. Diego spun and aimed at the half-human, but the Hybrid raised his hands instead.

"We're getting out of here!" the Hybrid said. "I'm not taking this shit anymore!"

"That's what I'm talking about!" Bouma said. He waved the Hybrid toward them. Any reinforcements were welcome now.

The Hybrid had almost reached them when a ground-shaking roar erupted to his right. A huge reptilian claw swiped him off his feet, and his body careened into the wall, breaking into bloody pieces. A Sentinel took the place of the Hybrid, baring a mouthful of dagger-like teeth at those trying to escape.

Once again, the Organic rifle in Bouma's hands felt horribly impotent. He could hardly do anything to prevent the carnage that was about to unfold. Diego and a bunch of unarmed humans were all that stood against one alien lizard with an anger problem.

Maybe, if more of the rebelling Hybrids helped, they'd be able to win this battle. Another three Sentinels joined the first, backed up by a shrieking crowd of spiders with bloodlust in their compound eyes. The din of Organic voices reverberated among the integration chambers.

Bouma gulped.

Things had just gotten much, much worse.

333

***

Athena lay in a cot deep within the bowels of the old sewer system beneath Pelican Air Force Base. Taylor and Malone were out on sentry duty with Staff Sergeant Therin Corey and several of the kids.

She was trying to grab some shuteye, but a conversation between Griffin and Santiago was keeping her up. Relenting to her sleeplessness, she sat up and rubbed her temples, trying to focus past a burgeoning headache.

"We're dying here," Santiago said.

Griffin brought a finger to his lips. "Try and keep it down, those are kids."

"I'm well aware of that, brother," Santiago snapped. "Don't tell me what to say in front of them."

The two teachers were sitting in metal chairs, talking in hushed voices. An old-school squeaky fan blew air on the filthy children resting there.

There was a tense moment of silence between Griffin and Santiago.

"My point is," Santiago began again, "what do we do now? We got more mouths to feed than we can handle now. All this talk of escape… if it's going to happen, then let's go."

Athena heaved a sigh and swung her legs over the side of the cot. She couldn't sleep anyways, not after what had happened to her crew.

"We've got to wait for Alexia," Griffin said.

"We can't rely on some old computer hundreds of miles away."

"We have to trust her," Athena said.

Santiago snorted and pulled his hair back over his

head. "Look. She said she'd send us a signal, and we haven't received squat from her. The all-powerful Alexia is toast, if you ask me."

"What?" Athena dragged her sleeve across her sweaty forehead. God, but it was hot down here. Even hundreds of feet beneath the surface, with fans charged by solar panels, it was near ninety degrees.

"We've been waiting for contact from her, but she's gone dark," Santiago said.

Athena looked to Griffin, who confirmed the information with a melancholy nod.

"Therin helped me rig an old satellite dish in a tunnel near the surface," Santiago said. "We originally set it up hoping to get some transmission or sign or something telling us there was still a government out there. That just maybe, God-willing, *someone* was searching for survivors. Color me surprised when the first transmission we overheard was from Alexia. So all her communications have been a damn one-way street. We've had no way to reply, so we just listen to her give us orders like she's some kind of god. And now, our precious god is dead, gone, absent, *finito*. Right when you all walk in here, no more Alexia."

Athena didn't respond—she was too busy thinking of the implications of living in a world without the AI.

"We've got to wait," Griffin said. "She promised she'd help us." His brow furrowed. "How long will our remaining supplies last?"

"Shit, four or five days." Santiago let out a morose laugh. "A week if we're okay with growling bellies."

"Alexia," Athena muttered. "Where are you?"

"That's the million-dollar question," Santiago said.

Alexia had promised to help them right away. Athena

335

couldn't imagine the AI would just leave them in the dark like this. Especially not after they'd made it to Pelican AFB. A shiver crept down her spine. There had to be a good reason. If Alexia had gone quiet…

She pictured those drones headed toward Colorado. What if something had happened to her?

They had to know.

"Santiago, this dish you guys found… where did you get it?" Athena asked.

"Therin and I scavenged as much junk as we could from Pelican, hoping some of it would be useful. The dish was a part of that."

"Do you have more comm equipment?"

Santiago shrugged. "Probably, but I'm just a freaking bus driver, not a scientist."

"Can you show me what else you have?"

Instead of answering, Santiago stood and waved her after him. She followed. He led her to an adjoining tunnel that was filled with all manner of electronic equipment.

"Any of this useful to you?" Santiago asked.

An idea formulated in Athena's head. "Maybe. But it's not going to be up to me."

She crept back to Trish's cot and gently tugged on the woman's shoulder, rousing her from her slumber.

Trish opened her eyes groggily.

"Sorry to wake you, but I need your help with something."

Trish rubbed at her eyes and then nodded. "Sure, what can I do?"

"Santiago hasn't heard anything from Alexia, and we're getting worried. I know this will expose us to the Organics, but we have to try reaching her."

"We didn't bring anything capable of that type of

communication," Trish said.

"I know, but Santiago might have something useful."

Athena showed Trish the tunnel of scavenged equipment. "Think you can find something useful here?"

"Maybe."

After an hour alone with the equipment, Trish came out with an antenna system hooked up to a cracked monitor. Wires dangled off the contraption. It looked like some kind of school science experiment.

Griffin raised a single eyebrow. "That gonna work?"

"Should," Trish said. "It's a pretty standard radio wave transmission device. Wasn't too hard to cobble together." Her face scrunched in worry. "The only problem is, this will for sure be heard by any Organics listening in."

"That's going to be a risk we'll have to take," Athena said.

"Is Santiago okay with that?" Griffin asked.

Athena looked over her shoulder. The eccentric old man was talking to the teachers.

"He's nuts, but there are kids here," Griffin said.

"I know. I just don't think we have any other choice." Athena eyed their supplies in the corner of the room. "We are out of time, and we need Alexia."

"I'm with you, whatever you decide," Griffin said. "You haven't led us astray yet."

Athena paused to think. If their radio transmission was detected by the Organics, she might be inviting a slaughter. But the alternative was to starve in a week. There was only one good option, really, and it wasn't all that good. They had to talk to Alexia.

"Santiago, get over here," Athena said.

The man hurried over. "Yeah?"

"Trish crafted a radio transmitter from your supplies,"

Athena said. "We can use it to contact Alexia."

Santiago's gaze danced between them suspiciously. "What's the catch?"

"It's possible the signal could be detected by the Organics."

"How possible?"

Athena looked to Trish.

"It's hard to say," Trish said. "They'd have to have a ship or vehicle or something equipped with comm equipment scanning all frequencies."

Santiago looked over his shoulder at the kids. Athena could tell he really cared about them, and just wanted the best for them.

"We have to think of the future and not the present," Athena said. "As soon as we reach Alexia, we can get the hell out of here. You said it yourself. We're not going to last down here."

Santiago sighed. "Fine. Try it."

"Do it, Trish," Athena ordered.

"You got it, Corporal." Trish held out a long wire with the antenna. "This needs to be close to the surface."

"Consider it done," Griffin said, taking off for the exit, wire in hand. "I'll tell Malone and Taylor what's going on while I'm up there."

Athena nodded. She watched him move into a connecting tunnel. Trish set up the monitor as the antenna continued to unspool. She started tapping out a message.

Folding her arms across her vest, Athena watched anxiously.

"What is that?" came a young voice.

Athena looked over to see a young girl standing in the dim lighting.

"Are you a soldier?" she asked.

Athena didn't know exactly how to reply to that. "I guess I am. What's your name?"

"Melanie."

"How old are you, Melanie?"

The girl looked at the ceiling with blue eyes, pursed her lips, and then said, "Five."

"You look older than that."

"I'm almost six."

"Ah, that explains it."

Melanie pointed to Trish. "What's she doing?"

"Trying to get us help."

"I thought you were the help."

Athena bent down next to the girl, getting a whiff of body odor and feces. The kids were all filthy. None of them had probably washed in months, and they had been living in a series of sewer tunnels to boot.

The ground suddenly rumbled under her feet, and her eyes flitted from Melanie to the ceiling. Dust particles rained down from the concrete.

Several of the kids got up from their beds, and Santiago ran over to Athena and Trish. The flames from the candles flickered, the light dancing across the walls.

"The hell is going on?" Santiago asked.

Another vibration rumbled across the floor.

"What is that?" Trish asked, looking up from the equipment.

Athena grabbed her pulse rifle and checked the magazine. "It can't be from your transmission, could it? How the hell could they be on us this fast?"

"It was already close by," came another voice. Griffin stood in the exit with Malone and Taylor. Several of the kid soldiers came running from the passage.

"There's something up there, Corporal, and it's really freaking big!" Griffin said.

"It's some kind of massive bug alien," Malone said. "It just dropped out of the sky, and now it's headed toward the base."

Another rumble shook the room. Spider webs fissured across the ceiling.

Santiago's nostrils flared. "You brought that thing here!"

"There's no way they detected and picked up our transmission that fast!" Athena replied, still not believing their sour luck.

"You must have been detected on the way in," Santiago said. "It doesn't matter now. We have to get topside."

The old man palmed a magazine into his rifle. "We have to draw whatever this thing is away from the kids. Therin, take them out the back!"

The staff sergeant nodded and ran over to the kids and teachers. "Come on everyone," he said. "Grab your stuff and let's move."

The quakes continued, each one louder than the last. A chunk of ceiling fell away and shattered on the floor.

The teachers and Therin were already leading the kids down another passage, their escape route. Athena, Taylor, Malone, and Griffin followed Santiago toward the tunnel Griffin had accessed earlier.

Trish called out after them. "Wait, Corporal, I'm getting something from Alexia."

Athena halted.

Trish listened to the receiver for several long seconds. Even in the dim lighting, Athena could see her eyes widen.

"She says to hold tight," Trish said. "She's sending us help."

***

ENTRY 10292
DESIGNEE – AI ALEXIA

Lolo is currently passing over North America, providing a view of what's happening at the Pelican AFB. The same type of alien monster that killed Commander Suzuki and his team has located Athena and the others. The Organics must have detected Corporal Rollins and her team crossing the desert and deployed this gargantuan beast that appears to be some sort of *Anthropoda.*

I study the creature on screen while my system scans the image. It may be an alien, but it shows a remarkable similarity to the *Dynastinae* subfamily of beetle, in particular, the Hercules beetle. Of course, its size is one thousand times larger than even that massive beetle species.

It scuttles over the sand on multiple limbs, folding thick wings over another set of membranous wings, the ones it used to fly there. Two horns crest the armored head, and a third horn points forward from the thorax. A moment of observation reveals the purpose of this third horn.

The creature finishes folding its wings under plating covering its back, and then lowers its head to start digging into the sand covering the sewer system the humans are hiding inside. The beetle is a bunker crusher, and it won't be long before it breaks into the underground passages.

At Cheyenne Mountain, seven of the alien nanotech spheres have melted their way through the doors protecting the servers and drives that serve as my brain. All but two of the robots I've sent to engage them lie in heaps of debris. There are only three doors left for the Organics to break through before they reach me.

My last line of defense, aside from Y-K8, is J9-1, a drone I've dispatched from outside the facility. This robot was a mile out on routine patrol when the Organics landed on the tarmac, but it's now back inside the Biosphere, preparing to attack the spheres melting through the final doors.

This is it. I'm ready to shut down the system. The virus Y-K8 infected the Organic network with is working, and has provided me an opportunity to hack into their system, but I am unable to manually shut down these nanotechnology-based spheres. They continue their mission of extermination.

In this race against time, an interesting development occurs. I receive a transmission from an Organic ship entering Earth's atmosphere. The pilot claims to be an alien friend of the human race, and insists it is with a human now.

I don't believe it. This can't be possible. This must be a trick, a way to distract me. The Organics know I'm in their network, and they know I've infected them with a virus. The virus isn't designed to destroy their fleet. That, I judged, is impossible. Instead, the virus is intended to allow me to control the Sharks—the only aircraft I have the schematics for. If I can do that, I may have a shot at stopping the Hercules beetle at Pelican.

Commander Suzuki's sacrifice was not in vain. The intel he provided on the Sharks could help me save the hundreds of humans clinging to survival.

Sensors show the alien spheres breaking through the

third door, leaving only two between my hardware and their lasers.

I ignore the transmission from the Shark entering the atmosphere. I won't let the Organics trick me.

There's only one hope now. If the virus gives me access to the other Sharks, I will have a chance to complete my objective of saving the remaining humans.

The Sharks will be their vehicles to Mars or beyond.

END ENTRY

***

"Son of a bitch," Noble said. Alexia was clearly ignoring Roots' messages, but he didn't blame her. There was no way for her to confirm Roots was who it claimed to be. All he could do was tell Roots to fly faster.

They had already pushed the fighter to the max since they'd left the Moon. Three hours was all it had taken to get to Earth, but they were slowing now as they approached the planet. Any faster, and they would burn up during reentry. Roots warned that the Organic ship was reporting that such temperatures would tear the vessel apart.

"Come on, buddy, you can do this," Noble said.

Roots gave a cackle to confirm he got the message. His sponge-tipped branch limbs moved with precision as he piloted the fighter. They penetrated the mesosphere, and seconds later cut through the stratosphere.

"Let's go, let's go," Noble said anxiously.

The ship continued to decelerate. Flames rushed across the cockpit, vibrating the vessel, but the shields held.

Noble took in a long breath, doing his best to manage his nerves. His heart continued to kick out of control, and sweat bled down his naked flesh. He watched and waited for the first view of the surface.

This was the most excitement he'd had in three months, but it wasn't exactly good excitement. They continued on course to Cheyenne Mountain. Soon enough, the mountain range jutted up across the horizon.

His muscles tightened across his body at his first glimpse of the landscape. The view wasn't exactly how he remembered it. The air-brushed peaks were gone, replaced by jagged brown tips that looked like rotting teeth. The brown continued down to the base of the mountains, where the tree line had shriveled and died. Charred forests, burned to the ground, filled the view to the east, and craters where crystal clear lakes had been dotted the terrain.

As the aircraft closed in to Cheyenne, Roots reached over and placed a sponge against his arm—a warning.

A half dozen Organic fighters sat idly on the tarmac. The same type of fighter that Roots was piloting.

"No wonder Alexia isn't answering," Noble whispered.

Roots glanced over, batting all three eyelids.

"Keep flying," Noble ordered, touching the alien. He looked back out at the tiny blue craft parked outside the blast doors leading into the mountain. Scooting closer to the control panel, Noble prepared the laser cannons.

"Time to turn some more Organics into pulp," he muttered.

Three of the alien fighters rose off the platform to intercept Noble, but he still had the element of surprise. He activated the lasers and pushed the firing button, targeting all three of the ships simultaneously.

A staccato blast of laser fire lanced away from the cannons and slammed into the three craft, the pilots all caught off guard. The first volley took down the shields, and the second punched holes into each ship. Only one survived the onslaught. It pulled away, but Noble fired another round, ripping off both wings. The nose lowered, and the craft plummeted toward the slope. It exploded on impact with a cliff.

Noble turned his attention to the other fighters still on the tarmac. Laser fire slammed into their shields. Explosions followed, rocking the tarmac. Wings and burned hulls flew into the air.

In seconds, there wasn't anything but the smoldering wreckage of alien fighters. A single Sentinel had managed to slither away from the destruction, heading for a dirt trail.

Noble focused the sights on the monster and fired, pulverizing it in a spray of blue that coated the mountainside.

"Hell yes!" he shouted.

Roots let out a cackle, and touched Noble with another warning. He turned to look out the back of the translucent ship, and identified the drones Roots had discovered patrolling the skies.

Noble targeted the smaller craft with the dorsal cannon. One by one, they shattered in a spray of blue mist. Another scan revealed the area was clear of hostiles.

"Take us down," Noble said. He took in the scene of devastation with grim satisfaction.

But Noble knew this victory would be short-lived. The Organics would send reinforcements. They only had a small window of time to get inside the Biosphere and find

Alexia. The AI was the only one that would know where the survivors of his crew were holed up—assuming they were still alive.

Smoke rose away from the tarmac as Roots put them down between bits of flaming debris. Noble touched Roots.

"Stay here, buddy, and keep the engines warm. I'll be right back."

Opening the hatch, Noble jumped out of the ship, his naked feet slapping the ground. A small shard of metal cut into his right foot, but he didn't care. He was finally back on human soil, and standing on solid ground.

A tear fell from his eyes as he plucked the shard from his foot, but it wasn't from pain—it was from joy. He resisted the urge to get down and kiss the earth. Instead he ran for the blast doors, waving his arms and shouting, "Alexia, it's me! It's me, Captain Rick Noble of the *Ghost of Atlantis*!"

He stood there waving his arms like a mad man, realizing he probably looked like a crazy Neanderthal standing there naked and covered in grime.

But, despite his appearance, the doors creaked open to reveal the inside of a large garage. He went to step inside when laser fire spread to his right. He ducked down as Roots fired into the open space.

Noble only got a glimpse of what it was firing at. The lasers obliterated small disc-like objects and punched head-sized holes in the concrete floor. Looking over his shoulder, Noble frowned at Roots.

The cannons continued moving, scanning for targets.

"Alexia!" Noble shouted. He cautiously took a step into the open space, knowing there could still be Organics insides.

"Captain Rick Noble, I presume," came a smooth feminine voice.

"That you, Alexia?" he said.

"Yes indeed, Captain. You're just in time to help me leave Cheyenne Mountain. We have a new mission to complete."

Noble couldn't help but smile at the sound of her voice. She was an AI, but damn did it feel good to hear a human voice again, even if it was synthetic.

"Do you know where my crew is?" he asked.

"I do indeed, Captain, but time is of the essence. Come inside and pull my hard drive. I'll take you to them."

— 23 —

"Now!" Jeff yelled.

He and David threw EMP grenades from their perch in the rafters. The grenades exploded between the four Sentinels staring Diego and Bouma down. As soon as their shields fell, Jeff and David doused them with a salvo of gunfire. The first Sentinel collapsed amid broken, bloodied limbs, crushing several of the smaller spiders beneath its weight. Hordes of people screamed as the aliens descended on them, climbing over the fallen Sentinel.

Jeff fired at one of the other Sentinels that was getting too close to Sophie and the others. "Bouma! Sophie!"

Both of them looked confused for a moment as they searched the rafters and catwalks. Jeff waved at them.

"Ho-ly shit!" Bouma said. "Jeff! David!"

"Here!" Jeff threw down the two extra rifles he and David had been lugging around since they'd first escaped the *Sunspot*. "I knew those would be useful."

As soon as Bouma caught his, he started firing into the mass of aliens. Sophie handed her rifle off to Emanuel. Jeff was happy to see her alive, but he noticed she seemed paler than usual, and wasn't moving as fast as the others. Diego was now one of the humanoid aliens, but now things at least made sense to Jeff. He'd overheard everything Hoffman had told the others. It had looked so painful and disgusting. He'd hated having to watch it, but what else was he supposed to do?

He and David had bided their time until the right moment.

I think Dad would be pretty proud, Jeff thought. He took out another spider trying to attack one of the helpless humans.

David ended another.

"Good job, bud," Jeff said.

He'd thought they were only going to be saving Sophie and the others, but now they were helping a bunch more people than he'd ever thought possible.

"You, too," David said.

"Boys, you got to get down here!" Bouma yelled. "Hurry!"

Jeff threw his rifle over his back. "Come on, bud, you heard him."

Together, they scrambled down the scaffolding to the ground. The screams of the aliens still filled the air between the scorch of gunfire. A few of the humanoids seemed to have joined the human forces, and were fighting off their former comrades. Spiders reared back, trying to stab at the fleeing humans. Many of the chambers were still filled with people swinging their arms and legs around, trying to free themselves from their prisons.

"Boys, keep moving!" Bouma roared.

"What about them?" David asked, pointing to the people in the integration chambers. "Don't we need to help them?"

Jeff's stomach flipped. "I don't think we can save them."

A spider charged into the throng of escaping humans.

The alien ripped into the first few humans in its path, tearing them into chunks of meat and bone in a red flurry. Jeff fired on the alien and it crumpled, sliding headlong into an integration chamber. The alien was dead, but the damage was already done. People scattered around the broken monster. Their faces showed pure terror. Diego and Bouma were losing control of the crowd.

More Sentinels clambered into the space. They pushed between the integration chambers and the corpses of humans and aliens in pursuit of their prey. Jeff's heart pounded faster than light speed. The cacophony of the aliens and the exchange of gunfire crashed against his eardrums. His eyes sought to make sense of the rush of colors flashing from the broken integration chambers and the bleeding aliens and dying people. The odor of death and burned flesh stung his nostrils. A voice at the back of his mind screamed in terror, telling him everything was screwed. That he really would be seeing dad soon. They couldn't make it out of this madness.

But the look on David's face said otherwise. His younger brother's expression was set in grim determination, focused on the path before them. Only a few spiders stood between them and the airlock to outdoors. They were cut down in a matter of seconds.

But the real danger wasn't the aliens. Even Jeff knew that.

While the terraforming efforts had been underway, barely any oxygen was to be found in the thin Martian atmosphere. People began to fight over the few available EVA suits that had been abandoned by the Organics' human prisoners.

"Come on, people!" Bouma yelled. "Get it together!"

Sophie tried to pull two people off each other. "Stop!"

One of them backhanded her, and she fell into Emanuel's waiting arms.

Diego bounded toward them and ripped the two people off each other. "We do not have time for our own civil war." His booming voice seemed to settle them through sheer force of fright. "We will have to make do." He took the suit and gave it to Owen. After securing another suit for Jamie, Diego pushed his way through the swarm of people. Bouma helped Holly and the kids along behind Diego.

Jeff raced to catch up with them, David by his side.

"Before all hell breaks loose out there," Bouma said, "what's the plan?"

"Get me to one of those ships, and I'll get us out of here," Diego said.

"First ship we see?" Bouma asked.

"First one big enough to fit all these people."

"No," Sophie said. "No, that won't work. We've got to make sure people can actually live on the ship. Very few of them can support human life."

"Then what do we do?" Emanuel asked.

"We have to take one of the zoo ships," Sophie said.

"Are you sure that'll work?" Bouma asked.

"I am," Sophie said. "I've been on one. Long story, but you're going to have to trust me. Do you?"

"I do," Jeff said.

David straightened, still holding his rifle at the ready. "I do, too."

"Hey," Diego said, "Hoffman said those zoo ships could transport people, so I'm with you, Sophie."

A spider shrieked as it crawled over one of the integration chambers. The people huddled around the airlock screamed and cowered. Diego fired at the alien's face, decapitating it with pulse rounds.

"We need to move now!" he said. "Tell these people they've got to hold their breath for a few seconds. That's the best we can do!"

"Into the airlock!" Sophie yelled. "Everyone! Now!"

She waved all the surviving people into the airlock, cramming them in. The rest of the crew did what they could to hold off the advance of the Organics. The people clamored, and one frightened man rushed Jeff, nearly knocking him off his feet. David yanked him up. The aliens were drawing closer, and the half-humans that had banded together seemed mostly defeated now. There was very little between Jeff, David, and the encroaching Organics.

If the aliens didn't kill them all, Jeff wondered if he'd be turned into a half-human, enduring that painful transition and forced to live as a slave to the Organics. He couldn't imagine being forced into servitude like the spiders, dying on some alien planet just to fulfill their masters' thirst for water.

Jeff's breath came and went in shallow gasps. He wanted to throw down his rifle and run, follow the mass of people into the airlock. His whole world turned into a violent rush of sound and color. Dizziness started to take him.

"Jeff, we're going to make it, right?" David looked up at him. His bottom lip trembled behind his suit's visor, and his face had drained of color.

All of a sudden, the panic threatening to strangle Jeff's mind released. "We're going to make it, bud. We're going to save these people and get off this planet."

"We're ready!" Sophie shouted over the crowd. She

was positioned on the far side of the airlock. She had an EVA suit on.

"Here we go, boys!" Bouma said, ushering Jeff and David into the airlock next to Holly and the other children. Diego and Emanuel came last.

The hatch to the airlock slammed shut. Sophie initiated the atmosphere transition procedure. Air hissed out of the airlock. A few people screamed, and others whimpered. Jeff guessed there were nearly thirty people in here besides the crew he'd arrived on Mars with. It looked like they'd found some colonists after all.

Something slammed against the hatch.

The airlock shook, and a hose overhead came loose. It whipped around like an angry cobra trying to strike. The hatch shook again, and the frustrated bellows of a Sentinel echoed through.

More people screamed, pressing toward Sophie and the opposite end of the airlock. Some wore the suits they'd gathered; others looked like they were already struggling to hold their breath. Finally the hatch out to the shipyards started to open. People began pushing themselves through before it had even finished.

"Stick together!" Emanuel yelled, struggling to be heard above the clamour of the crowd.

Jeff saw his attempts were nearly futile as he tried to shepherd these people together. Panic drove people out of the half-opened hatch.

The interior hatch trembled again, denting inward. Jeff raised his rifle, backing up slowly from the hatch. It shook again, and the metal groaned. Rivets and wires broke free, then the door gave way completely. Air rushed through in a violent wind, pushing Jeff and David over each other and against a wall. A Sentinel trounced in, impaling the nearest human with its claws and dragging the body across the deck.

Jeff tried to find the last remnants of his courage as the rest of the aliens entered the airlock, but the shrieks of the invading horde made that nearly impossible.

David looked up at him, hoisting his rifle, ready to fight. The odds were stacked against them in that small place.

All Jeff could do was shake his head and yell, "Run!"

***

Sophie climbed out of the airlock. People started scattering in different directions. Some grasped at their throats, unprepared for the thin atmosphere. Desperation took them, despite Sophie's pleas for them to follow her.

"Where to?" Emanuel asked, striding beside her as they moved through the shipyard. They passed under a black ship nearly the size of the *Sunspot*. Most of the people still followed them. A blaze of pulsefire ripped from Diego, Bouma, and the boys at rear of the group. A Sentinel was now leading the spiders out of the airlock and between the ships.

She searched her mind for the zoo ship she'd seen in her visions. Ahead of them was a beetle-shaped ship that towered above the rest. Gun barrels poked up along its side around massive, bulbous enclosures.

"That's it," she said, pointing. "We've got to get everyone in there."

The entrance to the zoo ship was no more than a couple hundred meters away, but it may as well have been another fifty kilometers away, with the crowd of human refugees in disarray.

A shock of pain tore through Sophie's head. She doubled over and started panting. People streamed around her, heading in the direction she'd pointed.

"Sophie!" Emanuel called. He pushed against the tide of racing people to get to her.

Her vision flashed red, and a sudden urge to strangle Emanuel took hold. A voice in her mind told her to stay where she was, to tell all those people to surrender. That their plight was futile, their minds corrupted by traitors.

She eyed the rifle in Emanuel's hands hungrily. With it, she could end this crazy attempt to escape. All those humans running from their future, running from the inevitable. They were afraid of becoming great. Of becoming part of the Organics.

They didn't deserve to be part of this new world.

"Are you okay?" Emanuel asked. "What happened?"

He placed a hand on her shoulder. Even through their suits, his touch scorched through her like a pulse round to her heart.

A sudden violent fury raged in her head, and her fingers twitched, yearning to strangle him and take his rifle.

The nanobots.

No, Sophie thought. *You will not win. You will not win.*

She doubled over in pain again, and Emanuel held her tight. The OCT dropped from her pack. She didn't bother picking it up. She already knew, if she used it later, what she would see.

"You've... got... to go," she said, jaw clenched. She worked past the agony, her teeth grinding together. "Get Diego to open the ship to these people."

"No, Sophie," Emanuel said. "You're coming too."

He threw an arm under her shoulder and lifted her.

355

Hot pain erupted from her like a solar flare. The nanobots wanted her to turn around. Every step closer to the zoo ship made them attack her at a cellular level. They had been allowed to rejuvenate, and they would destroy her if she left Hoffman's mad laboratory of half-human aliens for good.

But she would never go back there. No matter how awful the pain became or how loud the voices in her head screamed. A darkness crept into her consciousness, threatening to make her pass out. She knew that as soon as she did, this would all be over.

"These people need you," Sophie said. She was vaguely aware of the bodies moving past her and the faraway-sounding chorus of aliens chasing them. It took every bit of willpower she had left to focus on Emanuel. "You can save them. Take them somewhere to start over."

"No way in hell am I doing that without you, Sophie. We're not going through this again."

Emanuel continued pushing forward, supporting her every step of the way. Her strength was sapped. Emanuel was risking his life by staying back here with her. Diego and Bouma were catching up to them. Holly was rushing ahead with the children, while Jeff and David provided cover fire.

"Diego," Sophie managed, her voice now coming out ragged, "You've got to get everyone into that ship. You're the only one that can get this thing started."

The Hybrid nodded at her. "Consider it done, Doctor."

He bounded ahead, surging past the crowd of people and toward the hatch into the zoo ship. A slight wave of relief washed through Sophie when she saw him tap on the hatch controls and it actually opened. People flooded in.

"We're actually doing it, Sophie!" Emanuel said. "We're getting off this rock, and we're taking these people with us."

Bouma limped along beside them. Somewhere between the initial rebellion and now, he had evidently twisted his ankle. Still he fired back at the aliens, covering the last of the humans rushing toward the zoo ship.

"We're almost there," Bouma said. Sophie watched a small smile cross his face briefly when Holly and the children loaded into the ship. "Just a little farther."

A sudden blast of plasma exploded to their right. Emanuel and Sophie were thrown off their feet. Clods of dirt and rock pelted Sophie's suit. From across the shipyard, a few Slingers were bombarding them with plasma bombs, the bombs slamming around them indiscriminately. Shrapnel cut through the air and ricocheted off other ships.

"They must know what we're trying to do," Emanuel said. "They're desperate to stop us."

The last of the escaped humans that were not part of their crew made it aboard the zoo ship. Plasma rounds exploded around the shipyard, geysers of debris erupting everywhere the rounds hit. Despite the blasts, the other Sentinels and spiders still coursed over the landscape.

"Of course they are," Sophie said. "Like Hoffman said, those zoo ships contain all the technology they've taken from other races. These ships drive the Organics' success. We take one of those, we take the keys to the Organics' kingdom."

"Then I'm glad we're about to steal one of them," Emanuel said.

He reached for the open hatch. Bouma provided covering fire as he stood in the entrance. The fires in Sophie's brain and muscles burned hotter than before. She felt ready to collapse. If not for Emanuel, she would already be lying on the ground, writhing and waiting for one of the plasma blasts to hit her and end her misery.

She wanted to feel joy knowing they would soon escape. Soon they would be off this planet and away from this miserable excuse for a colony. But all she could feel was seething anger and agony. The nanobots weren't letting go.

"Just one more step, Sophie," Emanuel said, helping her up.

Her boot hit the first step, and Emanuel started to hoist her the rest of the way. As soon as she pushed herself up toward the hatchway, something huge slammed into her chest and tossed her backward. Emanuel rolled beside her. He dropped the RVAMP and his rifle.

Red soil covered Sophie's visor, and she struggled to catch her breath. Each intake of air caused a sharp pain to stab through her chest. Emanuel scrambled for his rifle, but something kicked it away.

Sophie looked up.

Hoffman.

"Stop being so stubborn," he said. He grabbed Emanuel's rifle. When Bouma tried to fire on him from the entrance to the ship, Hoffman let loose a flurry of rounds, forcing Bouma back.

Hoffman slung his rifle onto his back, then grabbed Emanuel and Sophie by their suit collars. He dragged them away so Bouma couldn't fire on them. Another plasma blast exploded nearby. Rock and dirt showered them. Hoffman didn't flinch.

Emanuel tried to twist out of Hoffman's grip, but Hoffman kicked him in the chest, sending him flying backwards.

"We can use you here," Hoffman said. "If you leave, the Organics will hunt you down." He paused and fired back at the zoo ship's entrance again, holding any would-be saviors back. "And even if you do get off this planet, they will continue to exert their influence on you."

Emanuel tried to pick himself up and charge Hoffman. Another swipe of Hoffman's claws sent the man tumbling away again with a cry of pain.

"Emanuel!" Sophie cried, trying to crawl over to him. The pain was unbearable. She felt as if a Slinger was sitting atop her. "Stop this, Hoffman. You want to save humanity, come with us. Don't fall for the Organics' trap."

"You don't understand," Hoffman said.

Emanuel pushed himself up to his knees. Hoffman kicked him in the abdomen, and the man sprawled out on his stomach, gasping for breath behind his foggy visor. Sophie tried to reach up toward Hoffman, tried to grab his arm and stop him, but the nanobots urged her not to. Every movement she wanted to make felt like she was swimming through a pool of lead.

"They can control you from here, Sophie," Hoffman continued. He pressed a foot on her shoulder to prevent her from crawling any farther. "This colony will always control you. You and any other human infected by the bots. They own you."

The bots pressed on her mind. Her vision swam, and she blinked, desperate not to succumb to the encroaching darkness.

"You're already more like me, more like the Organics,

than you realize." Hoffman once more extended his clawed fingers. "Stop all of this and come back with me. We can make this right."

The fiery tornado of the bots swirled in her mind, and agony swelled until she was short of breath.

You will not win. You will not win.

She repeated the mantra. Over and over, she let those words flow through her mind until they were all she could think. Like a whirlwind, they blew back the fires of the bots.

"I am still human," she said. "I am not like you. I never will be."

With all the remaining strength she could muster, she dove for the rifle Hoffman had kicked aside. Every joint in her body protested the movement, and she cried out in nearly unbearable agony. But she wouldn't let the bots win. She wouldn't let Hoffman win.

Sophie grabbed the rifle, twisted, and fired on Hoffman. The shots blazed into his shoulder and chest, punching through armor and tearing into his flesh. His feet slipped, knocking him off balance.

She caught his gaze. His eyes were wide with surprise and, Sophie thought, fear. Now that was the most human emotion she'd seen on him since he introduced her to the Biosphere under Cheyenne Mountain. There was still a hint of the former man and scientist there, no matter how deeply the Organics had perverted his mind.

"You don't have to do this," Sophie said to him. "You can come with us. Drop your rifle."

She pushed herself up to her knees, then stood shakily. Now she offered her hand to him. For a moment, she thought he might actually take it. His injuries might've finally broken through the fog on his mind, the delusion that the only way to survive was to give up that which made him human: free will, and the desire to pursue an unfettered life.

Slingers still lobbed volley after volley. The spiders were crawling over other ships now. The roar of ship's engines rolled across the shipyard, and several other ships started to initiate, ready to intercept the stolen one if it dared take off.

"Please, Dr. Hoffman," Sophie said. "We can save humanity together."

The fear in Hoffman's eyes disappeared, to be replaced by red-hot anger. He pushed himself up and started toward Sophie, marching forward in a blind rage. Emanuel dove and grabbed Hoffman's leg. Hoffman twisted and sent his claws through Emanuel's back. Emanuel yelled in agony, and Sophie let loose a salvo into Hoffman's chest. More gunfire blasted from the zoo ship's hatch.

Hoffman went down in a tangle of busted armor and bleeding flesh. His limbs went still, and his rifle fell from his grip.

Sophie collapsed and began crawling toward Emanuel. Blood started to bubble through the punctures in his suit.

"No, no, no," she wept.

Bouma limped out of the zoo ship, his rifle over his back. Another plasma round hit near enough that a wave of heat and tossed up Martian soil washed over them. Bouma grabbed Emanuel. Sophie fought against the pain coursing through her and stood, wrapping Emanuel's other arm around her shoulder.

The nanobots fought to control her mind. The sounds around her ebbed and flowed. She could sense her vision growing hazy. But she carried on.

For Holly and the children.

For Diego and Bouma.

For Emanuel.

For humanity.

She felt another person hold her upright, and let her weight fall on them.

"You're going to be okay," Holly said. "We've got you, Sophie. We're getting out of here."

Sophie knew she would be okay. She'd figure out a way, somehow, on this damn ship, to conquer the nanobots within her. But it wasn't herself she was worried about.

Emanuel was in Bouma's arms. Unconscious. She reached out and stroked his arm. Then she repeated the promise he'd made to her so long ago.

"We're getting out of here, Emanuel. I'm not leaving without you."

Athena aimed her pulse rifle at the building-sized beetle chiseling at the ground with horns the size of a school bus. It had flown here to kill them, and it was her fault. The Organics must have detected her team moving across the desert after all.

Her gut told her there wasn't much they could do to stop this monster, but that didn't mean she wouldn't try. She lined up the sights on the curved shell covering the two sets of wings, wondering if the rounds would do anything besides piss the creature off. Even their RPGs probably wouldn't dent the armor, assuming they could take down the force field protecting the chitinous shell.

Griffin, Taylor, and Malone were looking in her direction with their mirrored visors. Santiago, Staff Sergeant Corey, and five kid soldiers were all crouched behind her team at the edge of the tarmac, next to the hangars. Everyone else was underground.

"How the hell are we going to stop that thing?" Santiago asked.

"We'll split up. Maybe our combined fire will bring it down," Athena said. "Therin, you have the only grenade launcher. Load the last of the EMP grenades, and fire them once you get close enough. We'll cover you from the rooftops. Once the beetle's shields are down, we will open fire."

The Staff Sergeant nodded his helmet.

"Santiago, take your team to that rooftop," Athena said, pointing. "Taylor and Malone, you got that one. I'll take the third with Griffin."

The kids all dipped their heads, and her team followed suit. She took a second to scrutinize everyone around her. Goggles and breathing devices covered their faces, masking their features, but she knew they were all terrified. She knew she was. Her own heart was beating out of control.

The abomination drilling into the sand suddenly lifted its head away from the hole, opening its mandibles. The hissing that followed brought Athena to her knees. The kids all clamped their hands over their helmets. She couldn't hear them screaming, but apparently the beast could. It tilted its beady black eyes their direction, homing in on their hiding spot.

"Go, go, go!" Athena said. She took off for the ladder and jumped onto a rung when she got there. The hissing stopped, replaced by a ringing in her ears that sounded like a gong going off rapid fire.

At the top of the ladder, she crawled onto the rooftop, pushed herself up, and moved over to the railing, staying low. Griffin was right behind her. He got down on his stomach and prepared his RPG while she charged her pulse rifle.

Athena checked the other rooftops. Malone and Taylor were in position, and Santiago was still climbing with the kids. On the ground, Therin snuck toward the beast, which had gone back to digging, apparently more interested in what was beneath the surface.

Athena licked her cracked lips and allowed herself a sip of water from her helmet. "Please work," she whispered.

She patted Griffin on the back, and he raised his RPG. The other soldiers all aimed their weapons at the beetle. A vortex of sand and grit rose out of the hole as it dug deeper.

Therin continued jogging toward the beast. When he was a few hundred feet away, he shouldered his grenade launcher and fired all three of the EMP grenades. They streaked through the air, ricocheted off the shield, and bounced back to the sand, where they exploded in an invisible blast.

The hissing sound that followed nearly brought Athena to her knees again. But this time she fought the pain and, using a hand gesture, ordered everyone to open fire.

A torrent of pulse rounds and several RPGs slammed into the shields, all of them impacting in blue blasts that were absorbed in pulsating waves across the surface.

"No," she whispered. The soldiers continued firing from the other rooftops, but the rounds were harmless, nothing but toothpicks pecking the outside of a turtle shell.

Griffin flung a side glance at Athena.

"We have to get out of here!" she yelled.

The hissing beetle made it impossible to hear anything, including her own words. It scuttled away from the hole and angled its horns at the building where Malone and Taylor were still firing their pulse rifles.

A flash of white made Athena turn her helmet. She crouched and raised a hand to shield her visor. When the blinding light cleared, there wasn't anything left of the rooftop where Malone and Taylor had stood a moment earlier. The structure folded, the walls crashing together in a cloud of embers and smoldering metal.

"RUN!" she yelled.

The creature directed its smoking horns at Santiago's building next. The children were already climbing down the ladder, but the old man continued shooting.

The beetle slammed its mandibles together as the horns glowed and recharged. The kids jumped to the ground and Therin rounded them up at the bottom of the ladder. He pointed for them to run.

Griffin pulled on Athena's arm. "Let's go!" he shouted.

She could hear that. She turned to move just as another blast of light flashed in the distance. When she looked over her shoulder, Santiago was gone. The rooftop glowed red from the heat that had vaporized his body.

But the school bus driver's sacrifice had bought the kids enough time to get away. They were bolting between the buildings below.

Athena followed Griffin down the ladder and jumped to the sand. Moving around the side of the structure, she waved at the kids. They caught up with her a moment later, and she directed them back to the sewer entrance.

She wasn't sure what the hell they were going to do now, but they had no other choice than to retreat.

The ground rumbled beneath her feet as she ran after Griffin. He stopped to load another RPG, and she risked a glance over her shoulder. Therin had halted to fire too, but the beast was scuttling right for him.

It swiped the air with a spiked limb, impaling the Staff Sergeant on one of the tree-length barbs. He squirmed and fired his pulse rifle into the sky before going limp.

The creature continued toward Athena, but she couldn't move—her body was paralyzed with fear, and shell shock.

"Out of the way!" Griffin shouted. He pushed her aside and raised his weapon. The RPG rocketed into a building to the left of the beetle. The miss wasn't a miss at all, she realized. The RPG slammed into the barrels of jet fuel stored inside and outside the hangar.

A massive explosion consumed the monster in a rising mushroom cloud. The heat wave slammed into Athena and Griffin just as they moved around the side of the final hangar.

"Don't stop!" Griffin shouted.

They bolted for the storm drain entrance across the base. The kids were just ahead, nearly at the manhole cover.

Earsplitting hissing stopped Athena halfway, and she turned to see the flaming beetle burst through the building they had just left behind. The creature aimed its glowing horns at them.

She brought up her rifle, but saw something on the horizon over the smoldering beast. A flicker of blue emerged. Not the same color as the sky, but a darker blue, like a deep pool of water. Then several more. A small squadron of the fighters Alexia had dubbed Sharks were en route.

They were done for now.

This was the end of the line.

After months of fighting, she would die here, in the sand, with what was left of her crew and the survivors of a doomed field trip.

Instead of closing her eyes and holding her breath, she stiffened and focused on the beetle barreling toward her. A cloud of dust and smoke followed the monster as it skittered across the sand.

What chance did the human race ever stand against such monsters, she wondered. She lowered her weapon and prepared to meet her maker. When laser fire raced away from the incoming Sharks, she flinched.

Her eyelids slammed shut and she shielded her body with her hands out of instinct. Several of the bolts blasted into the sand around her, kicking up grit.

None had hit her. She was still alive.

But the beetle wasn't so fortunate. It had crashed to the ground, several limbs blown off its bulbous body. Blue blood gushed from the purple shell as the fighters continued to unleash their laser fire.

Griffin pulled Athena away from the blasts, and they retreated to the sand dune the kids had gathered behind. Safely sheltered, Athena listened to the beast let out its final hisses and screeches.

When the bombardment ceased, there were just the sounds of ringing in her ears, rushing wind, and a sobbing child.

Athena motioned for Griffin. Together, they climbed the sand dune with their weapons. The Sharks were all landing on the other side, and a human jumped out of one of the cockpits wearing an NTC uniform, a baseball cap, and a dust mask.

"What the hell?" Griffin said.

Athena was too cautious to take the stroke of good luck lightly. "Stop right there!" She pointed her rifle at the man, who slowly raised his hands. He pulled down his face mask, revealing a thick red beard.

"That's not a great way to welcome me home," the man said.

Athena slowly lowered her weapon. "It can't be…" she whispered.

There was no way this could really be Captain Rick Noble.

But that red beard, the confident grin, and that rolling voice all told her it was.

Athena ran down the slope to meet Noble, stopping when she was just a foot away.

"Is that really you, Corporal?" he asked.

Athena wasn't sure what to say when she saw it really was Captain Noble. Instead, she reached forward and grabbed Noble, pulling him close in an embrace.

"I thought you were dead," she whispered. "I never thought I would see you again."

"I'm very much alive, and I'm here to take us all away from this place." He pointed at the Sharks. "I've got Alexia aboard. She's hacked these other fighters. We're using them to get to Mars."

Athena pulled away from Noble and looked out over the squadron. She couldn't believe her eyes.

"Captain Noble?" came a voice.

Trish had climbed out of the manhole cover behind them. Several of the kids and the two teachers were already standing in the sand, watching.

"Hurry up everyone," Noble said. "We don't have much time. Athena, you come with me. There's someone I want you to meet."

Athena followed him back to one of the ships. Through the translucent cockpit, she saw a creature unlike any she'd ever seen before.

"Meet Roots," Noble said. "He saved my life, and now he's going to help us get to Mars."

***

369

The CIC of the massive Organic zoo ship hummed around Diego. He gasped to recover his breath as he placed his clawed hand against a display. Blue light rippled through the screen from his touch. A wave of alien hieroglyphic characters appeared in holographic projections.

"Here we go," he muttered to himself.

He wiped the blood from his face. The crimson liquid had come from the Organic crew he'd killed to get here. The fight had been bitter, but he was a caged animal yearning to be free. There was nothing a few spiders and a handful of Hybrids could do to stop him.

At least, that's what he'd thought. Now he was concerned this alien language would be what made his plans fall apart.

"What the hell do these mean?" Holly asked, gesturing wildly at the alien text. Owen and Jamie had refused to leave her side. Bouma had joined them in the CIC, too, his wrist still bleeding. One of the people they'd rescued was a nurse, and was currently bandaging him.

Jeff and David had accompanied them as well, and beside them sat Sophie. Beads of sweat coursed down her face, and her fingers curled around the armrests of her seat in a white-knuckled grip. Unlike the *Primitive Transport* ship they'd tried to steal before, the zoo ship wasn't built specially for Hybrids, and Sophie was dwarfed by her seat. She looked like she was holding herself upright by sheer will-power alone.

Emanuel had been deposited into one of the ship's specimen chambers in the hopes they could save his life.

"All these characters are just like before," Bouma said. "Wish we had Sonya to decrypt them."

"We have a copy of Sonya," Jeff offered. "Here!" He

pulled an NTC portable AI drive from his pack. "We got it when we went back to the *Sunspot*. Thought it might come in handy."

"Great job!" Bouma said, taking it from him. "Just need to figure out some way to transfer her..."

As they spoke, Diego felt a strange sensation, like blocks being set into place within his mind. The words were suddenly making sense to him.

The nanobots, he realized. As Hoffman had said, they had reshaped his mind and given him a deep-seated knowledge of the Organics' language. Hoffman wasn't kidding about how quickly they'd become integrated with the Organics by hopping in those chambers.

Diego studied the characters scrolling across the CIC's displays.

"Looking for a spot to transfer Sonya?" Diego pointed to a pad on one of the command consoles. "Put the drive there. That's a wireless data transfer port."

"How the hell do you know that?" Bouma asked as he gingerly placed the AI drive on the port.

"I can read this language," Diego said, still barely able to believe it himself. He waved his hand through a command that turned the whole CIC into a projection display. Around them, they could see the rest of the Organic shipyard and the white, fortress-like buildings of the former NTC colony that surrounded the huge blue pyramid. Slingers were still throwing plasma blasts at the zoo ship, the rounds dissipating against the ship's shields. All the while, other Organic ships were beginning to launch. Clouds of dust exploded around them as their engines thrummed to life.

"Do we have any weapons?" Bouma asked, eying the ships around them.

Diego scanned the commands in front of him. "Yeah, here we go." He swiped a command, and a console popped up in front of Bouma. "Weapons ready."

"Uh, and how do I use this?" Bouma asked.

"Hold on," Diego said. He activated the automated weapons AI, and selected a ship near them that had already taken flight. The cannons blasted, dispersing plasma that tore into the ship's shield and then through the hull.

"Get us in the air," Sophie said. She cradled her head. Her skin had now turned a sickly gray, and Diego could see the muscles in her jaw working, like she was grinding her teeth together.

He tapped on the controls for the ship's engines. The bulkhead vibrated as the fusion reactors unleashed a monstrous howl. Meter by meter, the ship began its slow climb. Plasma rounds continued to lambast the shields. They dissolved like snowballs thrown at a charging train, but one of the displays floating before Diego showed him that the shields' powers were finite. Too much concentrated fire would take them down. The Slingers' assault had already brought the shields down to eighty percent. Once the other ships began their assault in earnest, they wouldn't last longer than a fish on Mars.

He had the weapons systems target another ship. The vessel exploded into a cloud of shrapnel, and he targeted the next. The Organics had indeed wanted to protect their massive investment contained in these zoo ships, and he was thankful for the weapons. But even with the automated targeting system, he couldn't keep up with trying to fly the ship and shooting other ones down.

Another fusillade of plasma rounds slammed the zoo ship. The CIC quaked as the shields drained another twenty percent.

"We need more firepower," Bouma said. "Tell me how to use these freaking guns."

Diego glanced at the display showing Sonya's upload progress. "In about five seconds, Sonya's going to come online. If we can get her to translate the language here like we did on the *Transport*, those guns are all yours."

Those five seconds felt like the longest in Diego's life. Other Organic ships took off, easily catching up to the lumbering zoo ship. They couldn't climb through the thin atmosphere fast enough to escape the encroaching fleet. Rounds blasted into their shields, and a swarm of smaller ships circled the zoo ship, ranging from drones to the winged fighters with their prominent dorsal fins.

"Looks like they're waiting for our shields to fall," Sophie said. "They're going to try boarding this thing. It's just too valuable for them to lose."

"Then it's all the better we're taking this bastard," Bouma said.

Suddenly Sonya appeared. "Lieutenant Diego, should I enable English translations for the rest of the crew?"

"Yes," Diego said. "For the love of God, yes!"

The characters around the CIC morphed into English.

"Hell yeah, we're in business now," Bouma said. He grabbed hold of the weapons controls, studied the instructions, and then began leveling volley after volley into the incoming ships.

"Get some, get some!" he yelled. The gleeful barrage didn't last long. He squinted at another zoo ship rising in the distance.

"Oh shit, take a look at three o'clock," Bouma said.

"I know, I know," Diego said. Adrenaline flowed through him, and his long muscles quivered. His half-

Organic body wanted him to spring into action, to fight and let loose the immense strength he'd been gifted by the nanobots' remodeling process. But there was nothing here for him to fight.

Sophie groaned. She was leaning forward against her straps now, clenching her head with both hands. The farther they went from the colony, the more, it seemed, the nanobots tormented her.

Diego had managed to get all these people aboard this ship and, by some miracle, off Mars's surface. But if they died in a magnificent fireworks display here, what did it really matter? His muscles still ached, and a fire worked its way into his chest. The lingering effects of the integration burned on his mind.

They had to do something drastic.

"The ship's shields are down to twenty-two percent," Sonya reported. "This vessel will not be able to endure much more. If the shields fall, my probability analysis indicates a ninety-nine point nine percent chance of catastrophic ship failure caused by enemy fire."

"Well, goddamnit, here's hoping for that point one percent," Bouma said, unleashing a torrent of fire into the oncoming fleet.

It's not enough, Diego thought. They had to do something else. But what? Even if they destroyed the ships within firing distance, there were more rising into view.

He held in a breath as the first zoo ship turned its turrets on them. Massive plasma bolts streaked into their shields, rocking the ship violently.

"Hold on!" Diego shouted over the noise.

Holly was yelling something, but Diego ignored her. His mind was focused on moving the ship and getting them the hell out of there.

"She's right!" Sophie yelled.

That got Diego's attention. If he could've raised a brow, he would have. His new semi-crustacean body didn't allow him a full range of human expressions, but Holly seemed to understand him all the same.

"The virus!" Holly said. "Sonya, reprogram the ship controls virus. The one that locked us out of the *Transport* and the *Secundo Casu*. Instead of targeting human ships, target enemy Organic vessels. Now!"

"Reprogramming," Sonya said.

"Good call, Holly," Sophie said. "These zoo ships are nodes in the Organic fleet. They've already got direct communications and strong data connections with the other ships. It might work."

"Well, I'll be real sad if I can't shoot 'em all down," Bouma said, "but I also like the prospect of staying alive."

"Sonya," Diego said. "Is this possible?"

"I have attempted to retarget the program," Sonya said. "I can mask it as a communications between ships, and it will relay between all Organic-operated ships within the local fleet instead of human-operated ships."

"See you later, you blue bastards," Bouma said.

"Wait a second," Diego said, "when you say local, how close do we have to be to these ships? Within thousands of kilometers, or can we shut down the Organic fleet across the entire universe?"

"I am afraid the local nature of this type of communications relay will only affect ships within this solar system," Sonya replied.

"Within this solar system?" Sophie asked. "That's still more than we can ask for. Do it now!"

Diego felt a surge of confidence flow through him like

a warm wind. The pain still echoing through his flesh was nothing compared to the thought of stopping the Organics. Not just the ones on Mars, but also those around Earth. Their efforts wouldn't ensure all the Organics died, but it would cripple their space-faring abilities, buying time for the humans to escape.

"Shields are down to five percent," Sonya said. "The controls virus has been relayed between ships. All ships controlled by Organic personnel that have responded to our viral communications request have been affected. I estimate it has currently infected ninety-five percent of the ships within the vicinity."

"Disable their controls," Diego said. "Now."

Most of the ships had already stalled. They drifted and tumbled through space, carried only by momentum. Diego imagined the Organics within them seething with rage.

But still rounds blasted against their ship.

Several of the ships surged upward, still targeting the zoo ship. Rounds shook the shields. Those bastards were some of the five percent avoiding the virus.

Diego and the crew had a zoo ship, they had a functional AI, they had a virus working through most of the other ships. And still, they were going to go down, just as the *Sunspot* had.

Then it hit him. The strategy they'd used before, on the *Radiant Dawn*. Maybe, just maybe…

"Sonya," Diego said, "if you've still got access on any of those ships, overload their reactor systems."

"Yes, Lieutenant."

Everyone in the CIC went silent, staring at the view of ships docked in the shipyard and those chasing them upward. Diego could hear his heart pump in his ears—or whatever it was his ears had become. Bouma still fired on the stubborn ships that hadn't been fooled into accepting the virus.

A few of the stalled Organic ships suddenly exploded into violent balls of spreading debris and plasma. The blasts set off a chain reaction with other nearby ships, knocking them back to the planet's surface. Vessels that hadn't been caught by the virus were still swept up in the chain of explosions. The entire shipyard seemed to disappear in a flash of white, followed by a rolling cloud of black and red dust.

"Shields down to one percent," Sonya said.

A single resilient Organic fighter still trailed the zoo ship.

"Watch that one!" Jeff yelled.

"I got 'em, kid," Bouma said. He let loose a spray of precise pulse fire that tore into its bow. The ship began venting plasma, then erupted.

Above them, between the stars, pinpricks of lights sparkled. More evidence of distant, detonating Organic ships.

"All those ships, destroyed, using the Organics' own weapons against them." Bouma whistled, then clapped Diego on the shoulder. "Sure glad to have you on our side, bro."

Diego didn't respond. He was too busy staring at what he had become. His humanity…

"Almost through the atmosphere," Sonya reported.

Cheers erupted from all around the CIC as they sailed into the blackness of space.

Diego looked toward the blanket of stars swimming in the blackness around them. He wondered if Ort was somewhere in those stars out there, looking out for them.

He must be. Probably sitting up there with Captain Noble, too. He wasn't sure how else to explain the miraculous escape from Mars and their victory over the Organics.

He twisted away to watch the others celebrate. Bouma wrapped his arms around Holly and pulled her in tight for a kiss. Jeff and David hugged Sophie, with Owen and Jamie joining them. They'd traveled months together on the *Sunspot* to Mars. But Diego hadn't truly felt like part of the crew until now. They now shared their joy with him through handshakes and hearty embraces, despite his mutant appearance.

"We did it," Sophie said, after sharing a hug with him. She seemed to be more relaxed now. "We made it."

Diego realized then, it wasn't just Ort and Noble guiding their good fortunes. There was so much more to it than that. He'd seen how Jeff and David, just kids, for Christ's sake, had risked their lives against nearly insurmountable odds to save the others. The way people on the crew threw their own bodies in the way of pulse rounds and spider claws had demonstrated just how selfless each of them was. How much they cared about ensuring the others lived—and humanity survived.

Somewhere on their journey in the Rhino, and later, in the *Secundo Casu*, he had decided he would give his own life to ensure these people had a future. Through their tenacity—Sophie's, Emanuel's, Holly's—he knew they would find a way to give humans a fighting chance.

Bouma and Holly had each other.

Emanuel—assuming he lived—and Sophie, too.

He had known he was the one that had to become an Organic to save them. Back then, he had had no one but himself.

But now, he had *them*. A family as tight as the one he'd served in with his brothers and sisters back on Earth under Captain Noble.

"How are you feeling?" Diego asked Sophie as she stood beside him, staring out into the blackness of space.

"I honestly feel so much better," she said. "I know the nanobots are still inside me, but Hoffman and the Organics no longer have control over them. Not after the devastation we caused back there. I'm sure that, somewhere on this ship, there's a way to deprogram those bots and get rid of them forever."

"There has to be," Diego said. Curiosity tugged at him to go exploring. To see all the other species preserved here. How many secrets of the universe had humanity not yet had a chance to explore? This ship would unlock a future full of surprises.

He glanced at one of the displays.

"Sonya appears to be learning how to manage the medical units aboard the ship," he said. "Hopefully she can help you and the other people we rescued."

Sophie's gaze seemed to turn faraway. "And Emanuel."

"And Emanuel," Diego agreed. He'd seen the wounds on the man. On Earth, those injuries would've been fatal. He had lost too much blood too quickly for any hope of recovery. For Sophie's sake, for the whole crew's sake, he hoped he was wrong. Maybe this ship could stitch the man back together.

"Once we make sure everyone is okay, I want to sweep the ship to root out any remaining Organics," he said. "I think we got most of them on arrival. Caught 'em with their pants down. But if we've got stowaways, better that we deal with them now."

"Sounds like a plan, Lieutenant," Sophie replied, turning her attention back to him.

She almost seemed to be recovered, now that the Organics had lost their grip on her. The color was returning to her face and there was a brilliance in her eyes—something he'd never seen before. She reeked of confidence, even with that faraway gaze. This was just a glimpse of the woman she must be, he was sure. He imagined she must've been a hell of a leader, considering the lengths the crew had gone to to keep her alive. He looked forward to seeing her come to life over the coming days.

"The only question I have," Diego began, "is, where do we go from here? There's no way it's safe to return to Earth or Mars."

"The zoo ship can support us for the rest of our lives, if we wanted," Sophie said. "But that won't preserve humanity. We need to establish ourselves on a new planet. We need to use the ship to keep the human race going."

"You got a bright idea of where that'll be?" Diego asked.

"TRAPPIST-1," Sophie said. "It's a star. Decades ago, scientists discovered there are several Earth-like planets orbiting it. They might support human life."

"How close is it?"

"Just under forty light years."

Diego's stomach flipped. Even as an integrated human, he still felt a pang of shock at such an unthinkable distance.

Sophie put a hand on his shoulder as if she could read his mind. "These ships are capable of faster-than-light travel. We've come this far. We'll explore the ship and its capabilities, and get ourselves to TRAPPIST-1."

Her confidence was infectious, and Diego could tell she believed every word she spoke. This wasn't just for the benefit of crew morale. Hell, she didn't just seem to believe they were going to create a new human colony on another planet; she *knew* they were going to do it.

"Then to TRAPPIST-1 we go," Diego said. He input the coordinates Sonya gave him.

Sophie pressed her palm against one of the viewscreens. She stared at Mars, shrinking away below them. "I'm going to send a final message to any humans that might be left in our solar system. If there are others like us out there, they need to know where we're going."

"You risk letting the Organics know where we're going by doing that."

"We'll encrypt our communication so that it can only be opened by human-made AIs," Sophie said. "It's the best we can do."

"And how will they get out of this solar system if we've wiped out all the Organic ships?"

"Sonya only gained control of Organic-operated vessels. Any vessel that was left vacant or had a manmade AI operating it would've been left intact."

"The odds aren't good that anyone survived out there, much less is able to get control of an Organic ship."

Sophie gave him a sorrowful smile. "Every day on Earth, Alexia told us our odds weren't good. They were abysmal, in fact. But we made it, Lieutenant. We've made it this far despite every indication that we shouldn't. If we can do it, so can other people."

Diego nodded at that. He couldn't argue with her tenacity. Once Sophie was resolved to do something, there was no turning back. She succeeded, and if there was any human out there with half the determination she possessed, then Sophie was probably right. That person would still be alive, fighting the Organics until their last breath.

"Lieutenant, you go ahead with your final sweep through the ship, I can take over command here," Sophie said.

The way she said it, he could tell she wasn't just making a suggestion. This was an order, packaged in a slightly nicer package.

"Yes, Doctor. I'm on it."

As Diego left the CIC, newfound power coursing through his half-alien muscles, his mind raced through all the uncertainties they would face. Maybe they stood a chance at surviving space in this huge, unfamiliar vessel. Maybe they could make it to a habitable planet and reinvent civilization. But then, what? Would the Organics still find them? Did the Organics harbor a sense of resentment and vengeance? How long would humanity be given to rebuild before the next great threat arrived?

He passed out of the CIC as Sophie traded requests and orders through Sonya. Whatever challenges they faced, he knew the people aboard this ship, the people *leading* this crew, would not back down. Hoffman had been wrong in concluding that humans had to live as slaves to the Organics in order to survive. But he had been right about one thing: humans were creative and curious. Invention had taken humankind from throwing wooden spears at woolly mammoths all the way to shooting pulsefire at ugly aliens on Mars. No matter where these people went, they would find a place for themselves. And where they did not find a place, they would *make* a place.

Even among the stars, Diego was certain that human ingenuity and invention would not only survive.

They would thrive.

Epilogue

Sophie took a deep breath. The smell of fresh grass and pine greeted her—a scent she'd never thought she would smell again. She sat down on the soft earth and waved her hand so the blades of grass tickled her palm. There had been many months back on Earth, and later, during their brief time on Mars, when she'd thought she would never feel grass again or sit under a pine tree, like those that had once lined the mountains in Colorado.

A gentle chirp of an insect or bird—she wasn't quite sure what it was—sounded in the distance. A smile crossed her face.

If Emanuel were here, he'd be able to identify whatever it was. His love of biology hadn't been restricted just to what he could see through a microscope, but also encompassed the world around them.

She wished he could join her now, to enjoy this peace with her.

Across a bubbling stream, Jeff and David were playing a game of catch with Owen and Jamie. Several smaller children Sophie recognized jumped between them, running for the ball. One of the children, no older than three, slipped on the wet grass and slid across the ground. A twinge of alarm crossed Sophie's mind, wondering if the child had hurt herself. But as Sophie watched, the child stood and laughed it off.

These children weren't the only ones that now called

this planet home. Several of the people aboard the ship had found themselves romantic partners during the long journey to the TRAPPIST-1 solar system, and had begun to start new families. Even with the faster-than-light travel capabilities of the Organics' zoo ship, the journey had taken them the better part of three years. That had given them plenty of time to learn the capabilities of the ship. Not only had they kept themselves alive, but they'd tested the genetic engineering capabilities of the ship too. The zoo ship enabled the development of brand new lifeforms—chimeras, based on compatible genetic data between species. That was the basis for the technology the Organics had used to create the Hybrids.

But Sophie's crew had had other ideas.

"Sophie," a low voice said in greeting.

She looked up to see what appeared to be a beautiful flower. Only, it had vaguely humanoid facial features and a torso, as if it was something straight out of *Alice in Wonderland*. The sentient plant-being was one of the many species the humans had worked to release from the shackles of the zoo ship. She'd seen this particular species in her visions all the way back on Earth, and watching the alien living free on this planet with humans made her think she was living in a dream.

"It's a beautiful day," Sophie said.

"It always is, here."

The alien continued its stroll through the forest, following the river toward the hilly parts of their colony. It offered a final viny wave before disappearing out of Sophie's sight.

There was still a lot to learn about these other species, but at least the Organic technology they had coopted allowed them to communicate with and study the other sentient beings within the zoo ship. So many now coexisted, building a new civilization unlike any the universe had seen. Still, some species had been far too warlike and dangerous to release. Sophie hated keeping those aliens imprisoned. She didn't want to think she or the humans were anything like the Organics, but they'd had little choice in the matter. They couldn't risk the extinction of every peaceful species—human and otherwise—that now called this planet orbiting TRAPPIST-1 home.

It hadn't taken long for those species colonizing the planet to start calling it Paradise. The planet definitely wasn't an easy-go-lucky place of no work and all relaxation, but after what everyone aboard that zoo ship had gone through, it felt heavenly to be free from the shackles of the Organics and able to forge a new future for themselves.

The zoo ship was still the central hub of colony activity, providing vital medical resources and, most importantly, what they now called the birthing chambers. With only a few dozen humans on the planet, there was no way to ensure the population was genetically diverse enough or strong enough to survive more than a few generations. They had determined it was necessary to use the Organics' genetic engineering techniques to grow humans and other species within the birthing chambers.

The whole process was strange, certainly. But that's the way survival worked now.

She lay back in the grass and watched the puffs of white clouds drifting overhead. As soon as she did, exhaustion threatened to take her. Working long shifts on the science team with a host of other strange aliens tended to zap her energy. Her eyelids fluttered, and finally she succumbed to their weight. As the last remnants of consciousness gave way to sleep, she found herself again wishing she had Emanuel by her side. She wanted desperately to spend this miraculous moment with him. Something that had been nearly inconceivable only a few years before.

"Hey, Soph, you off for the rest of the afternoon?" a familiar voice asked.

She opened her eyes, rubbing them. "Was I asleep?"

Emanuel, big brown eyes and closely-trimmed beard, beamed back at her. "Maybe you still are."

Don't let this all be a dream.

Then Emanuel pinched her. She yelped.

"Nope," Emanuel said with a grin. "Looks like you're wide awake."

He sat beside her and put an arm around her shoulder. She leaned into him, enjoying his comforting warmth. Months had passed before he'd recovered in the medical chamber of the zoo ship, but once he'd finally woke from his coma, it had been impossible to tell he'd ever been on the brink of death. There was a revitalized energy about him.

"I'm surprised to see you here," she said. "Did the Council end early?"

"They did," he said. "The first batch of sentients"—that was the inclusive name they gave to humans and other aliens growing in the birthing chambers—"will be ready for their foster parents in a matter of weeks."

"It's a miracle, isn't it?" she asked.

"No." He laughed. "It's science."

She gave him a playful push. "You know what I mean."

They sat for a while as the laughter of the playing

children continued across the river. The calls and songs of other creatures, alien and Earthborn, all taken from the zoo ship, carried on around them. A jellyfish-like creature floated on a breeze, changing colors as it drifted in the wind.

Sophie grinned when she saw it. "Some days I think I'm back on Earth, then I see things like that." She shook her head incredulously. "How are Bouma and Diego doing?"

"They're still promising they can have all these people organized into rough military shape by year's end. At least, they'll be good enough to man the turrets and shoot some rifles."

"Holly's busy today, too."

"Oh?" Emanuel inched closer to her.

"Seems like business is booming for a psychologist on Paradise," Sophie said. "Plenty of people want to know how to cope with all these changes and leaving everything behind."

"It's a damn good thing we have her."

"It is," Sophie said. "And they set a date."

"When did that happen?"

"They want to make it official by the month's end," Sophie said. "They just need a minister."

"They got someone in mind?"

"You're looking at her," Sophie said. She couldn't help the grin spreading across her face. She was only too happy to preside over the union of two of her best friends. There was really no legal need for the ceremony, but it felt good trying to do things like normal. "I think life is going to be okay here."

"It's hard work," Emanuel said. "But it beats being integrated."

"Diego…" Sophie pictured the man. Twisted by nanobots. A vision of what might've happened to her.

"I had my doubts about him back on Mars. I feel guilty about that after everything he's done for us, I don't know how I could've doubted him."

"Or Ort."

"Agreed."

They sat in companionable silence for a while.

Being next to Emanuel really was like a dream. Maybe this was all some carefully orchestrated vision from the Organics. If it was, Sophie didn't care. This planet was beautiful and peaceful, and everything she had wanted since the Organics invaded Earth.

If this is a dream, I hope I never wake up.

The sky began to darken, and the first orange pangs of twilight shone along the horizon. TRAPPIST-1 was beginning to set, giving off its characteristic brilliant red hues.

Yes, this was everything Sophie could've hoped for. She was ready to slip off into sleep again, beside Emanuel. Her eyelids drifted, and she forced herself to stay awake. They watched the sunset, holding each other and soaking in the atmosphere. Finally, the sun disappeared beyond the tree-soaked landscape.

A sudden overhead roar crashed through the twilight, shattering their silence and threatening to throw them back into a nightmare. A bolt of adrenaline laced its icy fingers through Sophie's body, and she jumped to her feet, Emanuel close behind. Birds and other animals screeched and squawked, taking flight or sprinting away from the din.

"What the hell is that?" she yelled.

The sky seemed to tear into two pieces as an orange

streak blazed through the atmosphere.

Sophie looked across the river to see the children had long since returned to the colony. She and Emanuel took off at a sprint back through the woods toward the zoo ship.

"It's a spaceship," Emanuel said. "But who?"

Sophie held back her worst fear—that the Organics had found them.

They ran toward the zoo ship, where they would find shelter and weapons. While they were crossing the field toward it, she saw Diego and Bouma sprint inside, leading a group of humans and aliens. At least they would have their defenses ready to go should the worst happen.

As the ship approached, faster than Diego could set up any anti-air fire, Sophie noticed the sleek black shape of the vessel. A painful knot formed in her stomach. The ghostly pains of the nanobots within her returned. They'd since been eradicated, but her memories of what they'd done to her had not.

"It's an Organic ship," she said. Then she looked to the zoo ship. "Why isn't Diego firing at them?"

"Why aren't they firing at *us*?" Emanuel asked.

Was it the virus Sonya had reprogrammed coming to bite them in the ass?

They froze in their tracks. They would be dead running through an open field with no cover. They would never make it to the zoo ship in time.

But as the Organic ship lowered toward the ground, it still didn't fire. Nor did Diego shoot back. Were the Organics taking control of the zoo ship, just like they'd done to the Organic ships on Mars? Were they going to put every single alien and human on this planet back into an orb?

A ramp lowered from the Organic ship. Silhouetted against the bright white light exuding from the open hatch was a single humanoid shape. Then more.

They were too small to be Hybrids. Not crustacean enough either.

"Holy shit," Emanuel said.

"Holy shit," Sophie agreed. "People. Actual people!"

The humans began filing out of the ship and fanning over the field. One raised a rifle as Sophie and Emanuel approached. The human leading the group apparently saw they weren't using EVA suits or helmets, and took off his own helmet.

The knot in her gut loosened, and the cool sense of relief washed over her when she saw the bearded face she remembered from Earth.

"Captain Noble?" Emanuel asked, shock in his voice. "Is that really you?"

The man ran a hand over his shaved skull, his piercing eyes flitting from Emanuel to Sophie.

"God it's good to see you two," Noble said, his voice booming. "I never thought..." His eyes focused on the terrain over their shoulder. He walked toward them, holding his helmet under the clutch of his arm. An alien creature with squid-like arms moved behind him. Several other humans followed.

"This is Athena," Noble said, indicating a woman beside him. "She saved the rest of my crew and helped get our asses here."

"Athena, nice to meet you," Sophie said, reaching out.

They shook hands.

"I can't believe this is real," Athena said. "You really saved our asses back on Earth."

"How did you get here?" Emanuel asked.

Athena smiled. "An old friend helped us. You both remember Alexia, right?"

The name took Sophie's breath away. "Alexia? Our Alexia?"

"Yup," Noble said. "She hacked some of those Organic fighters, and when we found out you all had gotten the hell off Mars, she helped pirate this ship."

Sophie watched as children filed out of the Organic ship.

"This is Roots," Noble said. "Roots helped me escape on the Moon."

"Moon?" Emanuel asked.

Noble chuckled and shook his head. "It's a long story."

She'd thought the first new humans she would see would be grown out of vats. Now they had a handful more joining their side. More people to ensure the future of this colony. To protect the humans and aliens here alike.

Captain Noble whistled as he looked around the landscape. "It seems to me like you all might have a hell of a story to tell, too."

"We do," Sophie said. "Care to hear it?"

"If you've got the time."

Sophie looked up at the stars. This truly was a paradise. A brand-new planet with new and old allies, and endless possibilities for their future.

"We've got all the time in the world," she said. "Now come, follow me. I'll show you our new home."

—End of Book IV—

About the Authors

Nicholas Sansbury Smith is the USA Today bestselling author of the Hell Divers series, the Orbs series, the Trackers series, and the Extinction Cycle series. He worked for Iowa Homeland Security and Emergency Management in disaster mitigation before switching careers to focus on his one true passion—writing. When he isn't writing or daydreaming about the apocalypse, he enjoys running, biking, spending time with his family, and traveling the world. He is an Ironman triathlete and lives in Iowa with his wife, their dogs, and a house full of books.

Anthony J Melchiorri is a scientist with a PhD in bioengineering. Originally from the Midwest, he now lives in Texas. By day, he develops cellular therapies and 3D-printable artificial organs. By night, he writes apocalyptic, medical, and science-fiction thrillers that blend real-world research with other-worldly possibility. When he isn't in the lab or at the keyboard, he spends his time running, reading, hiking, and traveling in search of new story ideas.

Join Nicholas on social media:

Facebook Fan Club:
facebook.com/groups/NSSFanclub

Facebook Author Page:
facebook.com/pages/Nicholas-Sansbury-Smith/124009881117534

Twitter: @greatwaveink

Website: NicholasSansburySmith.com

Instagram: instagram.com/author_sansbury

Email: Greatwaveink@gmail.com

Sign up for Nicholas's spam-free newsletter and receive special offers and info on his latest new releases.

Join Anthony on social media:

Facebook: facebook.com/anthonyjmelchiorri

Email: ajm@anthonyjmelchiorri.com

Website: anthonyjmelchiorri.com

Did we mention Anthony also has a newsletter?
http://bit.ly/ajmlist

Made in the USA
Lexington, KY
10 April 2018